Ingram project margin

Doc Doc Zeus

by Thomas Keech

A NOVEL OF
WHITE COAT CRIME

ISBN 978-0-9983805-0-6   Hardback

Library of Congress Control Number
2017933787

Published by
Real Nice Books
11 Dutton Court

Publisher's note: This is a work of fiction. Names, characters, places, institutions, and incidents are entirely the product of the author's imagination or are used fictitiously, and any resemblance to actual persons, living or dead, or to events, incidents, institutions, or places is entirely coincidental.

Printed in the U.S.A.

Set in Sabon.
Cover art and design by Vanessa Snyder.

For Kate

ALSO BY THOMAS KEECH

The Crawlspace Conspiracy
Prey for Love
Hot Box in the Pizza District

Chapter 1

Diane

I know he's allowed to put his fingers inside, but I can't get used to being touched that way. My mother says everything I feel and think will of course be different now. And he has a medical word he calls me that means I'm not even a regular girl any more. I'm a *primipara*. The first time he called me that was after I asked why my medical examination went on for so long. He said everything inside me was different since I had the baby. I could believe that. I couldn't see what he was doing down there, but I had no choice but to feel it.

Dr. Zeus always scheduled my appointment last, when there were no other patients around. This turned out to be lucky for me – no nosey middle-aged moms to frown at the shameful slut who got herself pregnant at fourteen just because she fell in love and she and her boyfriend got so excited they screwed up the condom thing. But really, what I dreaded most was ladies in the waiting room talking to me and trying to be nice and then asking me the whole story of what happened. I'm not sorry, most of the time, that I refused to marry Carl, but maybe that's a sign of how cold I am because the next thing I did was give up my little baby girl to total strangers I never got to meet. It was the right thing to do, almost everybody said, but they never told me how much it would keep on hurting.

"Do you always schedule me as your last patient on purpose?" It was the first time I'd ever said a word while my feet were up in those stirrups. It just hit me that I ought to thank him for scheduling me after all the other patients were gone. You don't get to talk much to your doctor, so I guessed I had to say it right then, even while he was touching me where no one but

5

Carl had ever been allowed.

Then I was not being touched, and he came around so I could see him. His arms suddenly dropped to his sides. He must have already taken his gloves off. His face was red. He looked me right in the eyes while he put some instrument down on a metal tray and picked up a towel. He seemed upset. I felt stupid for upsetting him, so I guessed I should explain.

"I'm just saying thanks for making me your last appointment. It's so embarrassing to have to tell my life story to all the people in the waiting room."

His face stayed red and he didn't say anything for a minute. Then I got this surreal feeling like maybe I had no clue at all, maybe he had nothing to do with what time I came into the office. I opened my mouth to explain why I said that, but no words came out.

"You shouldn't be embarrassed, Diane. Everybody here has problems. All the patients have problems. I have problems myself. I'm sure the receptionist here, Mrs. Halley, has problems too, though she'd never admit it." He patted me on the shoulder. He was good looking, with dark hair and deep blue eyes.

It had been a year since I gave my baby away. I thought about her every day. I didn't even get to give her a name. Then I spent a year at the Academy School, which is just one part of the church I joined. I'm back in public school now, facing the same kids I stared down back then, daring them to laugh at me as my belly swelled up during the whole ninth grade school year. I wasn't sick at all when I was pregnant, and I think I pulled it off pretty well. My friend Kate told me once she thought some of the other girls were jealous.

It seemed like every time I tried to get back to a regular sixteen-year-old girl's life I got a message saying I had to go see the doctor again. Lately I'd been going almost, like, twice a month. Dr. Zeus didn't say there was anything wrong with me, but you had to wonder. The clinic where I saw Dr. Zeus was a special one set up by the church so pathetic pregnant girls like me could get checkups and have their babies and then come back for follow-up visits. My baby was long since born and long since given away, but he still wanted me to keep coming. He said I didn't have to tell my parents about the appointments. I hadn't told my mother about the last few. The less she had to think about my pregnancy, the happier she was. The clinic was just a couple of rooms built in a corner of the church's gymnasium building. The rooms didn't even have real ceilings.

My mother still finds a way to remind me every day how bad I screwed up. It's like there's this invisible wall of disapproval I have to jump over every time I want to talk to her, so I don't talk to her. I told Dad I was getting these messages to come back for check-ups, it was free, the church had arranged it and the church was paying for it. All he said was, "They should." Like he was blaming the church for getting me pregnant. I do still wonder how those church people tracked me down in the first place. Sue just showed up at my front door one day when I was about three months pregnant, beaming like it was a miracle she found me, and acting like I was going to give birth to the baby Jesus himself.

Dr. Zeus is a wonderful guy. He comes to the clinic once a week, and it's free to any girl they send there. The receptionist, Mrs. Halley, told me he also has a regular job at his main office and sometimes goes to Freeland Hospital, too. Dr. Zeus didn't say I had to have the baby and he didn't say I had to give it up. He always said he was there just for me, for whatever I wanted. I don't know if I'm smart enough to be a doctor or not, but some day I'd like to be the kind of person who helps people like Dr. Zeus does.

"You're a very strong young woman, Diane. You've been through a lot, and you've come through it all with courage and grace."

Thank you, thank you, thank you. But I didn't say that. Instead, I just started to cry. I don't know why. I pulled my feet out of the stirrups and swung my legs around so I was sitting on the table, facing him. I threw the paper sheet over my legs and blew my nose on a scrap of it. "Thanks. I didn't mean to cry."

It felt good to sit up straight. I have naturally good posture and I'm kind of tall. Sometimes that's all it takes to get a guy's attention, to get him to meet your eyes like he means it. When I was fourteen, Carl's eyes shone with so much adoration I fell in love with him right away. Maybe I'll never know that feeling again. He was sixteen then; he had a job and a car. He wanted to marry me in Florida where it would be legal and move there. I backed out, even though I really loved him. It seemed like a stupid plan. But once I gave up Carl, and the baby, I didn't have so much of a life left.

"Do you talk to anybody about your feelings?" Dr. Zeus asked. When I didn't say anything, he went on. "Do you have a boyfriend?"

"No. They all talked like I was a chosen person at the Academy church school. But none of the boys wanted to hang around with me."

"You have no boyfriend now?"

"I just started back at public school. But they all know me there too, from back in middle school. So it'll probably be the same thing. Only I won't be 'chosen' there. There, I'll just be 'used goods.'" This was so true I had to laugh.

He caught my eye, and I could see I'd made him smile. I couldn't believe I had the power to make this important guy drop his serious doctor expression, even for a minute. He wasn't a tall guy, maybe just a few inches taller than me. He had a chiseled face, soft eyes with wrinkles at the corners, dark hair with longer sideburns than most men. I guess he wasn't as old as my Dad, but he was old, maybe 40. I want to say that his face was growing wider, as men's faces do at that age, but I don't think it's fair to even think like that about your doctor who probably spent his whole youth studying just to learn to take care of people like me whose problems are mostly their own fault.

"You're a young, healthy girl."

"You said I'm a *primipara*."

"That's just a medical shorthand word for someone who's had one pregnancy. It doesn't define who you are. You seem to be a lovely young woman. Even your deacon says so."

"You talked about me with that guy?" My whole body tensed. "He's not really a deacon, you know. Is he trying to get me to come back?"

He touched me on the shoulder. "Diane, I'm your doctor. My only job here is to serve you, to take care of your needs. It would be unethical for me to try to influence you one way or another on a religious matter." I guess I still looked scared, so he went on. "I promise that's the last word you'll ever hear from me about that subject."

"Oh. Thanks. Really." I reached out and touched his shirt with just the tips of my fingers. He liked it, I could tell. But then I thought, *what am I doing,* and pulled my hand back. In truth I had felt lost ever since I left the Academy and gave up on fitting into the church. Everybody there said I shouldn't leave – except Sue. Sue was the one who had first tracked me down somehow and brought me into the church and the Academy, but she disappeared the moment my baby was taken away. I think that's all she cared about.

During the last few months of my pregnancy my path in life was set out right there in front of my face. I would have the baby and give it away. I would officially join the church and go to its Academy school. Once you were there, the church and the Academy figured out for everybody what the rest of the path was. After a while I figured out I didn't want to be on that path. But after I left there and came back to public school, my old friends didn't seem to like me as much as they used to, and I couldn't get into my schoolwork like before. Thank God for soccer. So I was hanging in there, but kind of a mess at the same time. I knew if I talked to Dr. Zeus about this stuff he'd give me some kind of pill. Isn't that what doctors do?

So it was embarrassing that I had reached out and touched Dr. Zeus's shirt. But maybe he had a six-year-old kid and was used to stuff like that. Maybe he'd seen a lot of weird women and decided just now I was one of them. It did feel really good when he said I was a lovely young woman. Mostly what I'd been told at home the last few years is how much trouble and expense I'd been. Finally I confronted Dad, got in his way in the kitchen one morning and told him yes, I turned out to be very expensive, and he was just going to have to live with that. Give him credit. He just laughed.

"You don't have a boyfriend," Dr. Zeus said now. "You're a healthy young woman. Do you have needs that you feel are not being satisfied?" He touched me on the back of my hand with two fingers.

"You mean … um … *sexual*?" The instant I said this I thought, God no, that's not what he means, you dirty-minded slut. I could feel my face get hot. I would have jumped up and ran out of the room except his fingers were still resting on my hand.

"I do mean that, Diane. It's perfectly normal to have sexual needs. Is that something you struggle with?"

"Um … uh…." The really dirty thing was I got excited right then – because he was touching me, but more because his office was a place where you could tell your secrets and nothing you could say would be too sinful or too pathetic. Everybody should have a place like this. But I could feel my face still hot, and then I started to feel warm all over. I could tell he saw that, and then I got even redder.

"That's not a mandatory question." He smiled and took his fingers off my hand and put them back on the edge of the examining table. He had the calmest, sweetest look in those eyes, like he knew me inside and out, all the good and all the bad, and still thought I was okay. He seemed happy I was there. Was this a great place, or what?

Carl had been so real, not like the fourteen-year-old guys I was around all day in school who hung around the hallways in packs and never seemed to want to look you right in the eye. Once when we were drinking out on my parents' back deck, me and Carl and Kate and her boyfriend Lucky, Kate made a joke that we were getting as dull as our parents. But I kept quiet because Carl and I would actually be doing parent stuff later that day. Carl really, really needed me, all the time, and that was the most exciting thing I'd ever felt.

Dr. Zeus was still looking at me. "Can we talk about something else?" I said.

He raised his eyebrows. "Certainly."

"Is it true you can't tell any of my secrets to anyone else?"

He made a motion with his hand like he was turning a key to lock his lips.

"Does it make you tired and cranky all the time, being a doctor?"

He slumped. "You want to talk about me? Is that how I seem, cranky? It's a lot of responsibility. But there are rewards, too."

"You have a house?"

He nodded.

"A vacation house at the shore?"

He sat back. "A condo."

"A boat?"

"A small one. I haven't gone to the condo in over a year. My wife got so tired of me being tied up at work she goes there by herself now."

"Do you have any children?"

"A girl. Younger than you. Much, much less mature than you."

"You might not want to leave her home alone at night with her boyfriend."

He grinned. "You have a real sense of humor, don't you? Not many of my patients have that. We're almost finished. You can get your clothes on now. Stop by at the desk and make an appointment for next week on your way out."

"Thank you, doctor."

He was already halfway out of the room, but he turned around. "It's a pleasure to treat such a mature and beautiful woman."

As I was getting dressed I was thinking I was getting a crush on my doctor and how stupid that was. I guess I do sort of jump into things. More courage than sense, my father says.

For months, my mother and father tiptoed around the house like they were afraid they'd wake up the baby inside me and it would pop out right then in front of their eyes – or in front of their friends. Mom was worse. Maybe she is a good person, but ever since it happened I feel like she just doesn't believe I'm in that same category of goodness that she's in. I guess I'm not.

One night my father came into my room but didn't talk about me at all. He just started telling me about some hilariously bad decisions he had made in his life. Then he sort of backed out of the room, awkward with his own daughter. I cried because I knew that was the most I was going to get. I kept trying, and for a while I thought Mom might not be frowning so much every time she saw me, but then Sue from the church started coming over every day and sort of took over my whole life. And Mom let her.

Sue told me over and over there was a higher purpose in being pregnant. There were no mistakes, just blessings, she said. She had never been pregnant. I asked her once if she'd ever been married, but she just started talking about Jesus's will. I did start to believe I was chosen for something special. My gross, balloon-shaped body was going to produce a miracle. She told me I was bearing the child for Jesus. That kind of creeped me out, but I thought I knew what she meant.

Sue was there for me every day, came to my house for hours and talked to me, exercised with me, read to me. I couldn't understand how anyone could put so much of their life into someone else's life. Of course she was paid by the church, but I knew she couldn't do all that for me without caring for me at least a little. She was only twenty-two, much shorter than me, and very chunky. She would tell me everything about Jesus's life but nothing about her own. She talked about the young deacon so much I started teasing her that she was in love with him, but Sue didn't like to be teased. He wasn't even a real deacon anyway. He was just a guy named Robert who wanted to go into training to be a deacon, but he used that title a lot.

Sue kept preaching to me what a blessing it was for me to have this baby. When I told my father this, he said he could have put off getting this blessing for another ten years. I told this to Sue but she didn't think it was funny. Sue didn't like jokes. She convinced me to take this blessing seriously. She said my life before I got pregnant was just a preparation for real life. I might have been doing fine in my middle-school work and had a lot of fun in soccer and laughed myself silly with my friends Kate and Lucky. I might have fallen in love with Carl. But she said these were all childish things. She showed me in the Bible where it said it was time to put away the things of childhood.

The thing I learned is, you have to choose. I'm not talking about having the baby. I never for more than a couple of minutes thought about getting rid of it. I don't think I made that decision for Jesus. I think it was just some animal part of me saying, Carl and I made this amazing little creature and I'm just going to watch it grow. Anyway, that wasn't the hard choice.

The thing is, if you think you're chosen, blessed by God in a way that some others are not, then you have to believe that you're better than those others. At least that's how it seemed to me. I tried to keep up my friendship with Lucky and Kate. They came over to my house a lot at first, but Sue was always there and it seemed we could never laugh, and I guess they got tired of it. Behind her back, Lucky always called Sue my "guard." I stopped talking about anything real with my parents. Sue and Robert, the pretend deacon, told me my parents could care for my earthly needs, but they couldn't help me get close to Jesus. They said I should feel sorry for my parents. My parents finally figured out what they were telling me and tried to kick Sue and Robert out, but it was too late. I wouldn't let them. Sue and Robert sort of controlled my mind until my baby was born and I gave her away. And I know my parents will never completely forgive me for that whole deal.

So after a holy birth and a baby girl I saw for maybe twenty seconds, then a year at the church's Academy school where all the kids thought I was so blessed they wouldn't touch me with a ten-foot pole, that feeling of being chosen wore off. So I went back to regular school. A tuition bill came from the Academy anyway, like they hadn't noticed I wasn't there any more. My father opened it and whooped and tore it up into tiny pieces and threw it all around the kitchen like it was confetti. But when I came back to public school, things weren't the same between my old friends Kate and Lucky and me. Maybe I shouldn't have been surprised. It had been a long time. We weren't fourteen any more. I had had a baby and had given her away. But at least I could still run. I made the soccer team. Things were okay. Regular life was a little bland, a little un-special after believing I was Jesus's holy vessel. People were nice, but there was no one who was really into me there. Maybe wanting someone to be into you is one of those childhood things that you just have to put away.

My mother doesn't know what to think of me now. My sister Lisa is fourteen, and my mother's trying as hard as she can to mold her mind before she gets knocked up like I did. Lisa has started coming into my room and flopping on my bed and rolling her eyes at how hard Mom is trying. She's even taller than me. Really long, skinny legs, nice dark hair the color of Dad's. My purple hair is the one thing I never changed. My hair would be light brown like my mother's if I let it go natural.

Lisa's never going to have the problems I have. She's always been my little sister, and so I kind of naturally made sure she would never think she was the hottest girl, or the funniest, or the one who deserved to be the center of attention – all ideas that can screw you up, I know now. Once you get some of those superior feelings, you can't ever get enough of them. But in truth I miss those feelings a little. I miss something. I miss my baby. I keep half expecting life will be the same great and funny adventure it once was, but now I really doubt it will.

By the time I came out of the examining room with my clothes on, Dr. Zeus's receptionist had left for the day, and he was sitting at the appointment desk himself. He turned and looked up at me with an easy smile as I came up toward him. He patted the wooden chair next to his desk.

"Oh," I said. "I could just call the receptionist tomorrow to make the next appointment, if you're busy."

His look made me feel like I was his favorite daughter or something. "Sit down. You don't have to be apologetic about taking up my time. You're the most interesting person I've talked to today."

"Oh. Do I still have to come every week?"

"You're an intelligent woman. Let me explain. Your body exhibits some … changes, due to the birthing process. I can't exactly call these changes an illness, and so the insurance company would not pay for the treatment. But I believe I could help you overcome these changes and function more normally. I could do this, but only if you're willing to come every week. The important question is one only you can decide –whether you feel these appointments are helping you. Are they helping you, Diane?"

"I guess so."

"You *guess so.*" His smile faded. "Well, if you don't think I'm helping you, I can put you on the schedule over at my regular practice to see one of the gynecologists there once every six months."

"Don't do that." The words came out faster than I'd meant them to. "I'd like to come back next week." I was surprised how sure I was.

His smile returned instantly. "I think that's a wise choice, Diane. There's no reason you shouldn't feel 100% right. We'll work on this thing together in the coming weeks. Besides ...."

"Besides what?"

"I thought our talks helped you a little bit," he said.

"They did," I said automatically. I seemed to be saying whatever he wanted. Had we really talked that much? Maybe so, for a doctor.

"You shouldn't be afraid to talk."

"I'm not. Nobody asks me anything, usually. They're all afraid I'm still acting all holier than thou."

"I haven't seen any signs that you're acting that way. We seem to be able to talk. Any time you want to talk, feel free to call me. Here, I'm going to give you my private number." He wrote his number on a little scrap of paper and put it on the desk near me. When I reached for it, he brushed my hand.

I was about to get up from the chair when I caught him staring at me.

"What?" I said, but I already knew.

That rush I felt lifted me out of the chair and almost floated me out of the office. I didn't know if it was because he thought

I was brave or because he thought I was beautiful, because he said both. I hadn't had a feeling like that in a long time. I had missed my old friends during the year I was away, and getting back with them wasn't as easy as I'd hoped. Maybe the bond between Kate and Lucky and me had been just an early teenage thing that never would have lasted for long anyway. Maybe there was something wrong with me that I couldn't get used to things changing like that. I could still feel a trace of Dr. Zeus's magic as I started my mother's car and drove home. Maybe things weren't working with Kate and Lucky because I was meant for something more.

I didn't talk about any of this to Lisa that night because I could not lay all this on a fourteen-year-old kid. I was trying to be a normal big sister to her. After my nine months of being the chosen one for the holy pregnancy and my year of being blessed at the Academy, I had decided to try to get rid of all those feelings of specialness. I wanted to be able to walk into school and just be a normal person and talk to people without anybody feeling higher than the other. But I knew that feeling, the feeling that God or Carl or anybody loves you more than anyone or anything else, is strong, and addictive like drugs.

Chapter 2

Hartwicke

He'd received the $10,000 letter a couple of years before. That's what they called the investigation letters from the medical board, because your own lawyer usually referred you to a very expensive specialist lawyer to prepare your response. In a panic, he'd paid the money. Now he was wondering if he'd been conned – but maybe the response did work, because he never heard anything more about the investigation. He wondered if he was due anything back from that $10,000 retainer. He thought he'd call his own lawyer about that, but then he remembered that every time his own lawyer picked up the phone, it cost him a minimum of a tenth of an hour, or $30, and if the guy had to go back and do a bit of research or make a call himself it could cost him thousands more. Better to let things lie.

Marcie denied the whole time she was the one who dropped the dime on him, but he had his suspicions. Throughout their long, on-again, off-again affair, she would take a special interest in ethics and morals every time his attention veered away from her. And, as a nurse, she would have known just where to file the cheapest complaint with the most impact. Maybe she had filed the complaint but dropped it by the time of their getaway ski weekend at the conference. Sign in, sign out, on the slopes by ten, cocktails and sex by two, sign in, sign out, black diamond slopes in the twilight, amphetamines and sex all night. But by the middle of the second day she acted like she had forgotten, once again, what she had ever seen in him. She left a day early because, she said, she had neglected to tell her boyfriend where the dog food was. He cherished her indifference. He helped her pack and leave his suite with the subdued eagerness of someone helping move out a previous tenant who had held over. She may have filed that complaint about him two years ago, but he knew now she no longer had the interest to follow through.

Hartwicke Zeus had finished a residency in internal medicine and had passed his boards on the second try. He was partner in New Town Physicians, a group practice in New Town, a spanking clean new residential and commercial development adjacent to the last subway stop. They had the entire third floor of a new brick office building. Dr. Zeus was not well-liked within the group. Two of the other physicians were females, and they seemed to be offended by every word he said. He ran through his patient appointments with startling quickness, and this was the cause of a more than a few patient complaints. It was not uncommon for his patients to ask for another doctor. Over time, he focused on taking on the new patients, and he was completely fearless in diagnosing their problems after a first, short visit. He missed most of the office's monthly case review meetings. He often parked in other people's spots. Most of all, however, his partners took a dim view of him because he had never paid the last two of the three installments he was supposed to pay in order to buy into the partnership.

Dr. Zeus sat back in his chair in the church clinic after Diane left. It had been a very long day. He started his office hours at 6:30 at New Town Physicians, and he had to endure the resentments of the other partners when he left at 4:30 one afternoon a week for his work at his second job at the church's clinic. He could not see their problem. He was one of two obstetrician-gynecologists at New Town's office, but he also handled a lot of internal medicine cases. In fact he handled more patients at New Town than any of the others, ordered more comprehensive lab work, and diagnosed and treated the diabetics and the hypertensives as well as anybody. In addition, he had developed an informal, self-taught specialty in treating patients with rheumatoid arthritis, patients that the other partners otherwise would have referred out. He was a big moneymaker for the practice. He resented his partners for still hounding him for his partnership payments. He was smarter and more ambitious and more energetic than any of them. But now it was after seven and he was tired. He was supposed to round on a patient in Freeland Hospital that night but decided to blow it off.

His wife Elena called him to let him know she was leaving for the condo at the shore.

"That's a three-hour drive. You won't be there until after ten."

"Kyra's spending the night with her friends. I told her to call you if she has any problems. I'm taking Sheila and Val. They'll keep me awake. You don't need to come."

He didn't understand his wife. She didn't fit into any category of woman he knew to exist. Standard pretty brunette, of course. She was smart, but she had that demoralizing ability to dull down the intensity of human emotion, which ability, he believed, was the essential characteristic of all human resources professionals. It had taken him only a year to realize she was not his cup of tea. But she was a dutiful wife, and she gave him his daughter Kyra. So they got along, even if she didn't seem to need anything from him other than his boatloads of money and an occasional weekend dinner together with Kyra. Elena was his wife, not his life. His passions were far too powerful to be satisfied by her body alone. And she could not possibly understand the strength of his emotions. He didn't even ask that of her.

He went back to the examining room and opened the supply cabinet. The work here was uninteresting, and the facility the church provided amounted to just three drafty, poorly-equipped rooms attached to the inside walls of a much larger building. Zeus once asked why the church didn't just send their patients to his regular office. He never did get a straight answer from the church people, but Mrs. Halley told him later the church didn't want its girls contaminated by contact with non-religious patients.

The work at the church's clinic was easy, if repetitive. The girls were young and generally very healthy and were simply growing babies the way nature intended them to. But he felt stressed that evening. He pulled a bottle of bourbon out of the bottom drawer of the supply cabinet and poured himself a shot. The church leaders would probably crap their pants if they saw that. He was sure Mrs. Halley would not approve.

He threw back the shot in two slow gulps. Oh, that burned just right! The warmth calmed his nerves and let him concentrate. Two separate things, he realized, were bothering him. There was that call from the lawyer, that special lawyer who dealt with those Board of Medicine things. He had no idea what it was about, but he decided not to call back right away. A worrisome call like that would easily be forgotten for the night after a few more shots.

More bothersome was this young girl, Diane. Today was the first time he had gone inside her without wearing gloves. He had wanted to do that from her first appointment, when he saw that young and pretty bitch opening up for him. Now he lifted his fingers to his nose, but he had wiped his hands too thoroughly, and too much time had passed. His erection gradually faded, though he could not get that girl out of his mind. But she was already suspicious of him, and the idea of her coming in for weekly appointments was so outlandish it wouldn't fool anybody for long. He reran in his mind the scenes that had just taken place – Diane pulling herself out of the stirrups unbidden, tearing off the examining table paper to cover herself up—and even to blow her nose! – and accepting his compliments like she knew she was worthy of them. He wondered if she was as bold as she appeared to be. And that body! He knew he could make it shiver with joy. He needed to do that. Feel that. He wanted her. He deserved her. He wasn't going to be able to dupe her like the stupid cunts he'd got off on before. But if he could slowly break her and train her to do what he wanted, it would be ten times the fun.

His eyes were caught by the plastic tray on top of the instrument cabinet. In one of the little compartments in the tray lay three cartridges of Diane's blood, drawn for repeat blood tests. The last batch had been analyzed two weeks before at PeakResults, the lab he owned. The tests altogether cost $898, ten percent of which would eventually work its way back into his pocket. The "Deacon," however, had squawked at the church paying for the blood tests last time. Dr. Zeus's plan had been to bold it out, never retreat, order the tests again and ask the deacon if he wanted the best care for Diane or not. The deacon was a young guy and seemed to be going out of his way for Diane. It was easy to see how that could happen. But this was no time to get the deacon worked up, no time to draw attention to his own unnecessary encounters with Diane on the examination table. The risk wasn't worth it, not for $89. He threw Diane's blood into the medical waste bin.

Chapter 3

David

Ms. Porter: Katherine, did you know Dr. Zeus before becoming his patient?
Ms. Bolt: Oh, no.
Q: You didn't know him at all before going to him for medical care?
A: Right.
Q: Okay. I just needed to clarify that there wasn't any prior relationship. He wasn't at any time a friend, a friend of the family, a relative …
A: God, no.
Q: Were you going to him for any specific gynecological problem?
A: No. We were done with all that. I came back to him because my knee hurt.
Q: Take as much time as you need to answer. I know it's hard to talk about these things. But these are just the easy questions.

"What are you reading, Dave?"

Dave resisted the urge to cover up the transcript. He knew that would just make him look more guilty. Frank had told him not to look in those old files. Frank, his boss, was inscrutable, and scary, not at all like the subdued professional who had interviewed him for the job as investigator for the Board of Medicine three months before. That subdued, professional Frank turned out to be a complete façade.

You wanted to stay on Frank's good side. Now Frank was frowning at him for looking at Michele Porter's interview in an old case. Frank had already told him he didn't want investigators looking over each other's shoulders, second-guessing each other's work. Dave had figured looking at this one file could be an exception since he was just trying to get up to speed and had no intention of criticizing anyone. But he already knew you couldn't tell how Frank would react.

"Um. A transcript from a witness interview … in a case I found in this drawer." Dave pointed to the bottom drawer of his desk which, he had been surprised to find out, was three quarters full with jumbled case files.

"Lemme see that." Frank reached across in front of Dave for the transcript, the powerful muscles in his arms trembling just a little. "Holy shit. This is the Zeus case. From two or three years ago. We didn't usually even do transcripts then. Whose case was it? Oh yeah, Michele's. Oh yeah, I remember this. She made me pay for a transcript on this one." He squinted as he flipped fast through the thick stack of pages pinned together down one side with gold-colored fasteners. "Michele sure took long enough getting down to business on this one."

"What happened?"

"Never went anywhere. He denied everything. Nothing in the medical records supported her story. Nothing but a *he said/she said* case."

"I just wanted to see how she did that kind of interview."

"Don't worry too much about that. We won't ever send a man alone to interview a victim in a sex case. A woman victim. They're always women. The first time you go, I'll send Pat or Michele with you. And you just watch."

"Thanks." Dave sensed it was time to screw up his courage. "You don't mind if I finish reading this, do you?"

Frank dropped the transcript back on his desk. "Knock yourself out."

> **Ms. Porter:** We're required by law to investigate these complaints. But you don't have to worry.

The investigation is confidential. Your name
would never be used in any way in public.
Ms. Bolt: Please. I can't do this. I can't live
it all over again. I just can't.
Q: We certainly can't force you to cooperate. The Board would never do that.
A: I would die. I would just die if my husband found out. I feel so guilty.
Q: Why should you feel guilty?
A: Because of the way it started ... and
ended.

"Ms. Porter, can I ask you something about one of your
old cases?" He was at her cubicle doorway. He wasn't even
sure if Michele knew his name. She'd been part of the group
interview he'd undergone before he was hired. She was pretty,
with an angular face, smooth brown skin, sleek black hair and
intelligent, piercing eyes. She was about 35, ten years too old
for him, and married anyway. He hadn't talked to her since his
employment interview, but it seemed like the other investigators were always recommending that he talk to her whenever
he came to them with questions about doing investigations.

"Dave! Come in. Sit down. Just call me Michele. How have
your first two weeks been going? Oh, just pick that pile of files
off that little chair. Put them on the edge of my desk here, and
sit down."

He glanced around. Besides the new stack of files he had
just placed on one corner of her huge desk, there was nothing
out of order. Her windowsills were clear. "Yours is one of the
neater offices."

"I try. What's up?"

"I was reading this interview you did a long time ago, in
the Zeus case ...."

"Oh, that one's so sad. I know what your question is and
I'll answer it. Yes, I believed every word she said."

"But nothing could be done?"

"Welcome to the real world, New Guy." He must have changed his expression, because she went on quickly. "Don't be offended, David. You seem very dedicated. I just meant you're young. I'd give anything to be your age again. What are you? Twenty-five?"

"Exactly."

"Single? Married? Girlfriend? We can't ask any of this good stuff in the interviews any more."

"Single. Girlfriend."

"Nice."

"She's in law school. In North Carolina."

"So you disappear from this town every weekend?"

"Pretty much."

"Did Frank show you around?"

"Yeah. Yeah, he did, but ..."

"More confused than ever?"

His laughter came from relief. "I thought I was pretty good at distinguishing the wheat from the chaff, but ..."

"... there's a lot of other shit flying around here?"

He liked this woman, even if she didn't let him finish his sentences.

"I gotta admit, I'm a little confused by Frank." She raised one eyebrow at the word confused, but she let this one go. He knew that she knew that he meant afraid. "I mean, he, like, *barks* at me, then he slaps me on the back and says I'm doing a great job."

She raised both eyebrows this time. Her voice was soft and lilting but her words were matter-of-fact. "It might make you feel better to know that he's been here twenty years and he's never fired anybody, never suspended anybody, never even reprimanded anybody. He just doesn't do that. Too many personnel rules to follow."

"That's good to know."

"Except one thing. Never complain about him to the Board. Even as a joke."

••• •••

His girlfriend Sarah was supposed to call him at two-thirty, when she got out of class, or maybe a little after. When she didn't, the automatic backup plan was for him to call her after dinner. He didn't mind calling after dinner because he now had a few uninterrupted hours to try to make some sense of the cases Frank had put on his desk this week. He shoved the *Zeus* transcript back into the file and tried to focus on some of the things Frank wanted him to do right now. But Frank stuck his head in his cubicle and interrupted him with a new task.

"I'm going out on surveillance early tomorrow morning. I can't make the Board's settlement conference in the Agazzi case. You'll have to do it for me."

"You know I've never been to a settlement conference, right?"

Frank's grimace was exaggerated by the loose, doughy skin of his face. Dave thought he looked more like an ex-fighter than the ex-cop he really was. "All right. I'll have Michele sit with you. But you'll have to do the talking. You might as well get your feet wet."

"The talking?"

"Yeah, we have to explain the settlement to the Board's committee. Don't look at me like that. It's not that big a deal. The prosecutor's there, the defense lawyer's there. Sometimes the committee doesn't trust either of them, so we have to explain the whole thing first, then get the committee to approve it."

"Explain the whole thing?"

"Don't give me that dumb rookie look, Mr. Summa Cum Laude. You have the rest of the afternoon to look over the file, get up to speed. After that, come to me if you have any questions."

The case actually was pretty simple, at least for Dave, who was a fast internet researcher. There was a complaint against Dr. Agazzi filed by an insurance company for overbilling in the cases of seventeen patients. But apparently the prosecuting lawyer assigned to the Board, Nancy Hunt, hadn't been willing to litigate all of these cases, and so she had dropped eleven and had charged Dr. Agazzi in only six. And that made it much easier for Dave too, since he only had to look at six cases in the short time he had to come up to speed.

The file was pretty much a scramble of medical records and bills. Another investigator had originally been assigned the case and had convinced Frank that there was overbilling, but no one had written anything down about that. Dave opened the search engine on his computer and typed in "medical billing." Within an hour he knew more about medical billing than he could tell from the Board of Medicine's file. He found out that almost all doctors had contracts with insurance companies, and in those contracts the insurance companies would pay only so much for each procedure. Those procedures were precisely defined in a compilation called the CPT Code Handbook. Doctors billed by the code, and they were paid by the code.

But Dave also found out there were over 10,000 codes, and that most of them overlapped with others. Also, a doctor could sometimes use different codes, depending on the severity of the patient's illness. And the codes could change depending on the degree of specialization of the doctor. Dave immediately understood how hard it would be to prove that anybody was using the wrong code, much less doing it on purpose.

Fortunately, Dr. Agazzi had made it easy for everyone. He used only one code, Code 99215. Code 99215 was supposed to be used to bill for a comprehensive examination. The amount paid to the doctor for a "comprehensive" examination was the highest that could be paid for an office visit. Dr. Agazzi billed $247 for each visit of these six patients, billing each time for a "comprehensive" visit.

The code book had an elaborate description of what a comprehensive visit should include. Dave did not understand every detail. He did understand, however, two specific requirements: first, that a comprehensive examination should be done no more than once a year; and second, that the examination should include at least forty minutes of face-to-face time with the patient. But Dr. Agazzi had billed for five comprehensive examinations of one patient within a two-month period, and on one day he had billed for five comprehensive patient visits within a half-hour time span. Dave had not been a math major in college, and he was new to the medical world, but even he, as he closed the file and headed for Frank's office, found himself thinking that he could understand this case.

But Frank was quick to tell him he was wrong.

"Listen, Newbie." Dave could tell that Frank was one of those people who habitually made up his own nicknames for people. Frank was sitting at his own desk, his back and arms held in a rigid posture as if he were anxious to leave. "These cases are complicated. The doc can write down anything he wants in the medical record, and who can say it didn't happen? Agazzi's got Grunk. We deal with that scumbag lawyer all the time. He'll spend whatever it takes to get an expert to testify that Agazzi's coding was acceptable."

"But how can he say it's acceptable to bill for six forty-minute exams in a half hour?"

"Oh. Agazzi did that?"

"Yes. And a comprehensive exam is supposed to be done only once a year, but Agazzi was billing for doing them once a week."

"Oh." Frank obviously knew very little about the case, but this didn't seem to bother him. "Well, there must be something wrong with the case, or Nancy Hunt wouldn't be so hot to settle it."

"That's how this works?"

"Yeah, just like Law and Order. The prosecutor and defense agree on some kind of plea, just like in criminal court, and the Board committee is like the judge who decides whether to accept the deal or not."

"So my job is to make this deal sound, um, *right*, to the Board committee? Even if it stinks?"

"You got it, Newbie. They didn't teach you that at Rutgers, I guess."

Frank then went on to give him a short, gruff lecture about the ways of the world. Then, before Dave could respond, Frank dropped the file he was holding onto his own desk, picked up his keys out of a side drawer and left for home. Back at his desk, Dave was trying to appreciate that his task tomorrow would be fairly simple: convince the Board committee to go along with the proposed settlement of the Agazzi case. The settlement made no sense to him, but he had been at this job long enough to realize that he really was just the new guy – and also that nobody cared what he thought.

He sat for a minute wondering what Sarah was doing at that moment. He met her in college while on a road trip to Princeton with his roommate two years ago. She loved Princeton, and the school seemed to love her, graduating her with honors and high praise for her thesis on the European reaction to the Iraq war. But now she was in law school and seemed to think it was a grind. He wondered if that grind could be any worse than sitting in a cubicle at the Board, waiting every day for some complicated case to be dumped on his desk that somebody else had started but hadn't had time to finish.

Dave still had faith that behind all this paperwork and tedium and general disorganization, the Board was doing some good for the people of his state. He had majored in public policy in college, aced it. He'd imagined himself one day as a speechwriter and advisor to the political stars. There was still a plan for that. But when he graduated he had needed a job right away. His present job didn't involve speeches or theory or policy at all. He told himself he was content with that, for the moment. Sarah said she understood that too.

"It's real life," she always encouraged him. "You're dealing with real life."

Michele, on her way out, stopped outside his cubicle to arrange her pocketbook strap on her shoulder. "Did you talk to Frank?"

"Yeah. I know what to do, about selling the settlement, I mean. Not that it makes any sense to me."

Michele screwed up her face. "Sense." She suddenly lowered her voice. "Frank will bury a doctor who's shooting up in his office or selling narcotics on the side, but if a case is going to take a whole lot of an investigator's time ... or if it involves higher mathematics, like adding or subtracting, he won't let us touch it."

"It's not a problem understanding math. It's that ... oh well, you're on your way home. And thanks for talking to me today about that Zeus case."

"Yeah. That was really sad. I tried my best on that. Oh well, we can't win them all. I got two little girls in day care I have to pick up." Michele turned without another word and disappeared down the passageway between the cubicles.

Dave had nothing to do until dinner, which he would probably order later from Humongous Pizza and eat in front of the TV with a file in his hand. He stared at the fabric wall of his office, which was blank except for a blow-up of a picture of Sarah he had taken with his cell phone. He thought about her career path versus his. His career path had taken a few unexpected turns, primarily due to his student loans, while Sarah's path seemed clear and assured. At that moment, she was taking a long weekend break from law school, flying to Madrid with her father. Dave had never been out of the country.

He was a graduate of the Honors College at Rutgers, but he still felt like a rube around her. She didn't seem to notice the difference in their status. She said she was jealous that he was dealing with human beings, maybe helping some of them. Her greenish-brown eyes still went wide when he described his cases.

> **Ms. Porter**: Maybe testifying against him will help in your own recovery.
> **Ms. Bolt**: God, no. I can't see how. It's so humiliating.
> **Q**: Can I tell you a story? We had a case of a doctor. I'll call him Dr. X. A woman complained that he took inappropriate sexual liberties with her. I won't describe them, but they were really gross. But she didn't file a complaint for ten years. When we asked why she waited so long, she said she thought, what's the harm in letting it be forgotten?
> **A**: That's how I feel. Let's everyone just forget it.
> **Q**: She only changed her mind ten years later, when her daughter became a teen-ager and made an appointment with Dr. X. She realized he might be still doing it to other women. But all those years, she hadn't thought of all those other women, all those other daughters.

Chapter 4

Diane

I got back from Dr. Zeus's office still floating on some kind of dreamy cloud – until Dad started in on me at dinner.

"I met your friend Robert for lunch today." Before I could even pop my eyeballs back into my head, he went on, right at the table, right in front of my family. "He says he's an assistant deacon now in the church."

I couldn't believe he'd do this to me in front of everybody. Was I supposed to say something now? About Robert?

"So, Dad, you're thinking of joining the church?"

The best defense is a good offense. He smiled. He taught me that. He's a lawyer. He does trials and all.

"No. I'm sure we all remember Robert from when Diane was … in her condition." Dad still can't say the word *pregnant* when it's about me. "Robert's not trying to convert me. He made an appointment to see me. He's trying to figure out what he wants to do with his life, career-wise."

"I thought you said he was a deacon." Lisa turned to me. Was she coming out of her two-year sulk just for the chance to embarrass me?

"He's some kind of assistant deacon," Dad explained. "That's not a full-time, paying job. At least not in that church."

So then he looked at me like I was supposed to explain something. I looked down at my plate. Lisa was looking at me too, but I stared her off. Then I stared him off.

"He just wanted to ask me about my job, what it's like to be a lawyer. He's making the rounds, looking at different career paths. He seems like a nice kid." Dad stopped talking, but it was too much to hope that it was over. "He asked about you,

Diane. What's the matter? Don't you like him?'"

I looked down at my plate. "Sure. He's okay."

"That's not a very enthusiastic answer. Robert told me he tried to start up a romance with you."

"Dad, stop it! I can't believe you …." I stood up, almost knocking my chair down. Robert was the one I was really more pissed at, that he'd talk to my father like that.

Lisa was grinning. She was just getting over her mopey ways. She had those dark eyes she got from my mother. She looked like she was busy thinking, probably imagining the worst things ever between me and Robert. As if her pathetically infantile experience with boys could give her any idea.

"Honey. Let's talk about something else." Mom came to my rescue for once. "Diane, come on, sit down."

Dad put both hands up like he had touched something hot. "Oh! Oh, okay." He always likes to pretend he's, like, all not knowing what to say because he lives in a house that's all women. But he still looked at me then with a tiny smile because he had managed to embarrass me, something he used to do on purpose all the time before I got myself pregnant.

Lisa was in my room the second dinner was over. She's two years younger but two inches taller than me, and skinny as a scarecrow. At school, they're trying to get her onto the basketball team. She has dark hair, thick and pretty. Cut too short, I tell her once in a while. She has to try not to cringe every time I trash her. I shouldn't do that. She hasn't come into my room for a while. We were better friends when we were little.

"Nobody tells me anything."

"Deacon's that guy, Robert, who came over with Sue sometimes when I was pregnant." Lisa acted so shy back then. She always left the room when they came over.

"The guy who always wore those black pants? What a dork." So now she was sitting at my desk, looking in my make-up mirror, posing with those large eyes which I always tell her look poppy like a frog's.

"Lisa, you're really pretty."

"My pediatrician told me that too. Can you believe that?"

"What?"

"It was part of his good-bye speech. He says he refuses to treat anybody who's taller than him. I have to find a new doctor."

"Don't go to any church doctor," I said. "And keep away from Robert."

··· ···

He had started calling himself Deacon after what happened on the softball field and in Fellowship Hall.

You would've thought Robert could catch it, just a soft throw right to his glove side – but he screwed it up and the softball hit him right in the face. He let out a little "oh" and bent over with his hands over his eyes. I dropped the bat and ran to him. The coach had put him on first base because he thought he could at least catch something like that. I followed him over to the bench and sat down next to him, feeling guilty for getting him on the church softball team in the first place. When he took his hands down, his face was red, but his eye wasn't hurt.

"I'm all right. I'm all right. Get back in the game, Diane. You're really good at softball."

But it was just practice, and the coach sent us home for the day.

"Your face is all funky from rubbing it." You would think a nineteen-year-old guy could take a little hit like that without so much drama.

We went to Fellowship Hall, a big room right off the main church, mostly empty except for some folding tables and a few leftover church benches around the edges. There was a counter with a sink. There was no mirror, so I wiped his face off, and he dried it on some paper towels. His hands were shaking.

"Would you sit with me for a minute?"

I said sure. He was literally the only guy in the whole Academy who didn't seem afraid to talk to Jesus's holy vessel or whatever the hell else they thought I was. And the choice was to stay with him or go to late afternoon religious instruction.

"You're a very kind person," he said. "I didn't see that in you before. Sue always talked about you when you were pregnant like you were sort of a, I don't know, *project*."

"I don't want to think about Sue."

"She was just trying to do Jesus's will."

"Hmm."

He got the message I didn't want to talk like that.

"Hey, you're really good at softball, Diane. Have you been playing, like, for years?"

"I never played before. I'm into soccer, but the Academy doesn't have a soccer team."

"Maybe I can talk to Pastor, get him to start up a team next year."

I didn't realize until then what a drag it was to think about being there another year. I wondered what Robert thought about the whole Academy thing.

"Diane, I don't think I could have been as strong, as tough as you during … all your tribulations."

"I guess we each have our own crosses to bear."

Oh God, don't tell me that's *me* talking like that! That was the way everybody talked at the Academy. At the Academy good things were blessings and bad things were crosses, and all things just sort of blended together into a kind of holy mush. And I couldn't believe I had called a baby – *my* baby – a cross. That's when it first hit me how bad they were messing up my mind at the Academy.

He slid a little closer to me on the bench. He might not have been bad looking except for his dorky haircut. But there was a look in those brown eyes like a scared baby that would have made Carl look like Vin Diesel by comparison. And he wore those same black pants everywhere, even to the softball game.

"I sometimes pray that I can be as strong and straightforward as you."

"Robert, the whole pregnancy thing was all kind of an accident."

He leaned toward me. He didn't say anything, and it was getting weird. I only went to Fellowship Hall with him because I thought he liked me and I felt a little sorry for him. I knew he wasn't as bold a guy as Carl or as Kate's boyfriend Lucky. But it seemed like regular guys like them never talked to me any more. Robert knew all about my baby, the biggest thing about me there was to know. I didn't know anything at all about him. He was too old to be still hanging around the Academy school. He was always talking to the pastor a lot. I asked him what he did all day.

"Right now I have a job as a clerk in a Walmart pharmacy. I'm trying to figure out what to do. I need a career. Pastor Bill invited me to be a sub-deacon on my next birthday. That path could lead into a full-time ministry."

"Are you doing that?"

The look in his eyes was a little more solid. "Yeah, I will. I think I would be a good deacon."

If being a good deacon meant boring everybody to death, I guessed he'd be a good one.

"I finally have the courage to make the choice." He put his arm on the bench behind me without touching me. "Whatever courage I have, it comes from you."

"What?"

"I've watched you in services, on the athletic fields, reading to the little girls. Every move you make is perfect. One day while I was praying it was revealed to me: Jesus sent you into my life to show me how to live."

Oh no.

"I'm in love with you."

He grabbed my hand, and I let him. He was almost like a man. I liked that at least he was real, he wasn't bullshitting me. He wasn't like those zombie boys in the Academy shying away from my glance or those guys in my neighborhood just talking trash. He really did know me. He had seen me bloated up like a cow and then crying my eyes out afterwards, and he still wanted me. Maybe the adult world was calling me now. The real world. But ....

"Uh ... thank you."

He put his other hand on my shoulder and I jumped. He didn't notice, he was so into his own head or whatever. "I have this feeling that we can do miraculous things together. I'm sure you'll feel that way one day too."

I didn't think so. But he put his one hand up and stroked my hair, and that felt so good. It had been a really, really long time since anybody had touched me. I was breathing faster. But I knew I could never be really into him, with his pale face and thin hair and the way he held his back and neck stiff even when he was leaning closer to kiss me. I let him kiss me, and just like I imagined, his lips were cold, pressing too hard. His breath wasn't super-great either. But maybe this is what romance is like when you're old.

I finally pulled back. I had to turn my head to stop him. The whole place was dead quiet.

"Sorry," I said. "You're a good person, Robert."

"This is the right path," he said. "I know."

"Maybe not for me."

"Maybe you'll see the right path more clearly one day."

He slid back from me a little and rubbed his hand across the smooth wood of the church bench. He sat up straighter. He was looking kind of past me then. I could hear him swallow. His face went from sad, to blank, to fake-happy.

"I'm going to go for it," he suddenly said. "Sub-deacon. I'll still have a regular job, but I can do both, with your inspiration, and Jesus's help."

"I bet you can." All I cared about was getting out of there.

"Pray with me now." His voice had changed. It was deeper, reminding me of Pastor Bill on Sundays. I could tell he wasn't going to try to touch me again right then, and I was so grateful for that I promised him I'd still be a member of the church even if I left the Academy school.

Chapter 5

Hartwicke

Arriving at Freeland Hospital where both he and Marcie worked, Dr. Zeus drove carefully past his reserved parking spot and crept slowly, furiously, through each aisle of the general staff parking lot, looking for his Jaguar. Marcie had stolen it when she arrived back at the airport from their assignation at the conference in Denver months ago. She had taken his keys from the bureau in his hotel room when she left. And she didn't even warn him. Arriving back in town himself two days later, he had searched the various airport parking lots for an hour before pulling his phone out to call the police – until he thought better of that. He called her instead.

She was unrepentant. "How was I supposed to get home?"

"Bring it back. Pick me up."

"We're through, Mr. 'Let's-take-a-selfie-while-you're-naked.'"

"I haven't sent it to anyone."

"I know. But *I* might."

She stopped talking then, making him suffer through the silence while he tried to figure out what she had in mind. She had taken the same picture on her own phone. It was during their first night at the conference, after a bit of cocaine and a lot of other guilty pleasures. He had put most of his own clothes back on so the picture would document who was the master and who was the naked little pet. She had laughed and laughed. But now she was reminding him she had a picture which could blow up his marriage. As he stood there in the airport parking lot two nights later, he wondered if she had had this in mind the whole time.

"Bring me my damn car!"

"I don't think so. My own car's not running too well. I'm going to keep yours for a while."

She kept the Jaguar and, when he didn't come get it – he couldn't call the police, and he didn't have an extra key – she started driving it to the hospital right in front of his face. It was a case of half-accidental, passive-aggressive blackmail, just what he should have expected from his brazen sometime lover. She'd rather have him angry than have him forget her. Their on-again, off-again affair had stretched over seven years. The sight of any woman with red hair and a tight skirt brought back erotic memories of her he could not always subdue. Her husband had left her a year ago. He had said he would never leave their two young daughters, but it seemed Marcie was too much for him, too.

She'd had his Jaguar for three months now. Every way to get it back was too risky. He had no idea what he would do if he saw it in the parking lot then; he just wanted to see it. He made a second, even slower tour of all the aisles in staff parking before aiming his rented Kia, the same car he'd rented that night at the airport just to get home, into his slot in the Physician's Reserved Parking Lot. Now he was late.

Being late seeing a patient didn't matter. They were in the hospital, after all. They weren't going anywhere. But he had a meeting with Jack Billings, the CEO of Freeland Hospital. Zeus was trying to get the hospital to use the laboratory he owned, PeakResults, for some of their blood work. PeakResults was not doing so well financially, probably because they could handle only a limited number of kinds of tests. People didn't want to have to stop and think which lab handled which kind of tests. They wanted to use a lab that could do almost anything, like the giant All-Point Labs. So Zeus had gotten together with his business partner and their lawyer, and after a year of negotiations and thousands of dollars of attorneys' fees, they reached a tentative arrangement with All-Point Labs.

Under the arrangement, PeakResults would send anything it couldn't handle to All-Point, which would do the work and send the results to PeakResults, which would mark up the price 40%. The problem was the deal wouldn't actually start until PeakResults started sending a certain minimum number of tests to All-Point. PeakResults hadn't yet sent the minimum numbers to All-Point, and in fact its numbers were going down. Dr. Zeus knew his practice partners at New Town were the cause of that. They were jealous of him and they were slowing down their referrals to his lab.

••• •••

"How could I justify sending out our testing to PeakResults when we can do almost all of the work in-house?" Jack Billings, the hospital CEO, asked, his words slowly gurgling out between bites of his sandwich. "Besides, now that you're a nominee for the Board of Trustees of the hospital, it might be a conflict of interest. Tell you what. Why don't you let me ask the hospital counsel if it would be legal before we go any further."

Zeus understood what was happening. Billings was threatening to turn over the issue to the hospital's lawyer, and the lawyer might very well declare Dr. Zeus's scheme to be illegal. At the minimum, turning it over to the lawyer would slow down the process for months. Zeus was quietly fuming, but he didn't want to let Billings see how desperately he wanted this deal to go through. He had already offered Billings a one-half percent cut of any lab work Freeland Hospital sent to PeakResults. Zeus could see now that something more than money was needed. But he had an idea what would do the trick. It had worked once before.

He finished his rounds on the patients in the hospital. He had no babies to deliver that day. All of his patients there that day were actually sick. Three pneumonias, one skin infection, one meningitis. Two of the pneumonias were getting better and the other wasn't getting worse. The skin infection could probably be discharged the next day. Everything was fine except for the nurse's attitude toward the meningitis patient. Zeus used to enjoy sliding around behind the nurses in the tiny hospital rooms, but by now most had learned to avoid him. Only the really new ones let him get close.

"Did you see the *petechiae*?"

He hadn't, but he was sure he would have. He resented her sticking her nose into his patient's case. He ignored her.

"We tried to page you. The *petechiae* is on the chart."

He looked at the screen, shook his head no – very slightly, so as to contradict her without really acknowledging her presence.

"The *nurse's* notes," she added.

He rolled his eyes.

She stepped up to the patient, pushed back the sheet covering his arm, and exposed the skin covered with tiny red-pepper-like dots. It was a sign of septic meningitis, blood poisoning, they both knew.

He ignored her and typed in the chart an order for massive antibiotics and walked past her out the door. The nurse was pretty, and five years ago he would have found some reason to squeeze past her. Her sarcastic attitude would have made the encounter all the more spicy. But the forces of political correctness were relentlessly closing down his options.

His daughter Kyra was the one female who had never once tried to use her female wiles to take advantage of him. Of course, she didn't need to. As her father, he had given her every single thing she ever wanted. Kyra was twelve. She didn't talk to him much any more. Her raging estrogen storms threw up a barrier no father could pass through. Because she was descended from him, he knew she would come out all right. She would make space for herself. She would be a fascinating woman, one that men would vie for, cry for, die for. He looked forward to being her father then. He was ready to teach her to use what she had.

His phone chirped, and he read a text message from his wife asking him to call her about the car. It was not a good sign that the Jaguar was missing from the staff parking lot that morning. Marcie had not only stolen his car but had been taking it in to the dealer to get it fixed on his credit card.

Which, he figured out weeks later, she had taken from the hotel bureau along with his keys. He didn't find any of this out until Elena saw the charges on the credit card statement. Elena had bought his original story about the Jaguar breaking down and being towed from the airport. She didn't even look skeptical when he told her the dealer was having trouble finding the parts. But it had been three months now with no Jaguar, and he didn't know how much longer Elena would buy the story.

He never flinched from taking Elena's calls. He knew she tried to handle him the way a human resources professional would handle a difficult employee, even though he'd made it clear long ago that he was who he was, and she'd just have to deal with it.

"I just looked at our credit card statement, and we got charged *another* bill from the dealer about that car." Just what he'd feared.

"Damn! They're always finding more things wrong."

It wasn't the money he was worried about. He could have canceled the credit card. But the fact remained he didn't have the car, and sooner or later Elena would be calling around at the dealership and would find out that Marcie had been driving the car and signing the credit card bills all along. Zeus wasn't sure his marriage would last, but if it ended, he wanted to be the one who decided when.

"I looked into the charge," Elena went on, to his dismay. "It's for a headlight. They never mentioned a headlight before. Was there a headlight broken out when you drove it in there?"

He was used to thinking on his feet. "I don't know. I had it towed in. Could have been the tow truck." Vagueness was one of the best defenses.

"They've had the car so long, and they didn't notice the headlight before? I think they're soaking you because you're a doctor. $1,343 for a headlight, for God's sake. I'm calling down there."

"I'll do it. You know they won't talk to a woman."

Now he'd have time to think up an excuse for the $1,343 bill. It was hard to believe it was for just a headlight, but he was glad she'd heard that figure. Now she'd believe, as most people seemed to realize, that the cost of maintaining those old Jags was astronomical. Eventually, he knew, she'd shrug and write it off as just another cost of being married to him. But he could tell she was adding up those costs. The only thing holding them together now was Kyra. He always reminded his wife that it was he who paid for the private school, the fancy summer camps, the school trips, the music lessons, the braces, the clothing. Sometimes he told Kyra this too. Kyra acted embarrassed when he mentioned it, but he thought she needed to know. He made sure they both knew who was paying for everything.

But he didn't have any control over Kyra right now. When he had time to see her, she would talk to him or not, depending on the mixture of her hormones at that instant. She wasn't showing him any appreciation for all he had done for her. He was sure Elena could take her away from him completely if there was a divorce. The women always got the kids, and they got your money too. And Kyra was too young. She wouldn't understand. Probably cling to a new dad who'd later get his rocks off dreaming of his teenage stepdaughter in the next room.

Bitches all, always slaves to hormones, never know what they want. Underneath, the chronic need to be controlled by the right man. That instinct was a throwback to pre-history, pre-civilization, the strongest stallion taking all the mares for himself, the lord of the manor doling out the women after he had tried them all out first. Zeus was sometimes frustrated with the small life afforded him by civilization, which to him represented the collective consciousness of the weak. He hated having to duck and dodge his wife's questions long after the time when she had anything to offer him. At the same time, he could still be smitten by a thick mane of glossy hair, a pair of trusting blue eyes, young breasts wobbling toward his touch. He felt weak in the knees when he remembered his young patient Diane tearing off the paper from the examining table and shaking out her purple hair, looking up at him with the awe that he knew in his heart he deserved but so seldom received. Only one more week until their next appointment.

Chapter 6

David

They told him that Michele would hold his hand. He had never presented a case at the Board of Medicine's Settlement Committee before. He had never even seen a settlement committee meeting. He didn't even know Michele that well. She was certainly the most striking person in the room. The doctors on the committee – five middle-aged males looking uncomfortable in their bland suits, two middle-aged females looking slightly more at home in their bright ones – were no match for her. And Michele seemed completely comfortable with what they had to do before the committee that morning. In most ways.

"You know it's a crock, don't you?" She whispered to him as they sat in the row of chairs at the back of the room, awaiting their turn.

"What do you mean?"

"You read the file, right?'

That's what he had done at home all last evening, all the while keeping one eye out for any text message from Sarah. What was supposed to happen at the settlement conference didn't make sense to him then. But he had learned, in the bungle of white collar jobs he had had since graduating from college, that his opinion didn't usually matter and – more alarmingly – it wasn't always right.

"You mean, the punishment doesn't match what he did?"

"We don't call it *punishment*, we call it a *disposition*," she whispered. "No doctor wants to admit to upcoding because that falls under the category of 'making a false record in the practice of medicine.' That sounds so bad, like the doctor actually did something wrong."

"But he did."

"Frank told me to get this over with."

She said that last thing a little too loud, evoking a quizzical look from a board member sitting near the end of the table at which the committee members sat. But Michele's *faux pas* was immediately drowned out in the flurry of chair scraping, briefcase snapping, pocketbook closing and paper shuffling that signaled the end of the previous case. They moved up to the presentation table, where he and Michele sat together between the two opposing parties, all of them facing the committee. They were squeezed in so tight she practically *was* holding his hand. David had declined Michele's offer to take the lead, so it was his job to summarize the case for the committee.

"Why us?" he whispered to Michele at the last minute. "Why do we present the case when the prosecutor and the defense lawyer are going to do the same thing?"

"Because the Board trusts its staff more than the lawyers."

He spoke up clearly, trying to present the facts objectively. Dr. Agazzi had been charged with creating false medical records by upcoding bills, to the point where he could not possibly have done all the things he had billed for. Dr. Agazzi had upcoded bills for each of the six patients. He explained that legally, the Board could do nothing to recover any money Dr. Agazzi had stolen. It was up to the patient or the insurance company to get back any money the doctor scammed. The Board could only decide if the doctor had "submitted a false record in the practice of medicine" by submitting the false bills. If Dr. Agazzi was found guilty of submitting a false record by submitting bills for false CPT codes, the Board could take away his license, suspend him, fine him, put him on probation or give him a reprimand.

"Now that I've given you a brief overview of what the investigation found and what the charges are, I'll turn it over to the prosecutor and the defense attorney, who will explain to you what they are proposing as a settlement of the case." Dave glanced over to Michele to make sure he got it right. She gave him a slight nod. "It's like a plea bargain, right," he whispered. She nodded again and smiled, as did the two committee members who were sitting closest to them.

The prosecutor went first. Nancy Hunt was thin and pretty, but today she had a severe look etched on her face like she had to hold herself back from personally administering justice to Dr. Agazzi right there in the room. She explained, in a flat yet accusatory voice, and in more detail than anyone wanted to know, how the case came about, the multitude of false CPT codes Dr. Agazzi had billed for, the impossibility of his completing five forty-minute comprehensive examinations within a half hour, the total of $4,565 in overbilling that had been discovered in the cases of just six patients.

Then she went on to her main point. "The Office of the Prosecutor has discussed this case with defense attorney Grunk, several times. We have reached a proposed settlement of this case, which will become final as soon as the Settlement Committee agrees. Under this agreement, the charges of making a 'false record in the practice of medicine' will be dropped. The charges of 'unprofessional conduct' will be dropped. Instead, Dr. Agazzsi will be charged with 'failing to maintain adequate medical records.' Dr. Agazzi will admit to failing to maintain adequate medical records, the Board will reprimand him, and he will have to take a CPT coding course. Now, if I can now turn the floor over to Defense Attorney Grunk ...."

"Just a minute."

A committee member had spoken. Michele and Prosecutor Hunt and defense attorney Grunk all sat up straighter and glanced at each other out of the corners of their eyes. It was not a good sign that a committee member wanted to speak.

"Just a minute." It was a kindly-looking old gentleman with sharp eyes who, Dave later learned, had only been on the board about three months. "I've looked at Dr. Agazzi's medical records and billing records for these patients. There's nothing inadequate about them at all. They're just false. Why should we drop the false records charge and replace it with an inadequate records charge? I don't see any logic to that at all."

It was a really good question, Dave knew. He couldn't wait to hear the explanation. But in response, Prosecutor Hunt simply stated, in a flat voice, "This is the agreement reached by the prosecutor's office with the defense attorney." Then she folded her hands on the table in front of her and sat mute.

Dave looked at Michele for a clue. Michele must have noticed he was confused, because she broke protocol and leaned over and cupped her hand to his ear and whispered very quietly. "What she's saying is *fuck you*, I have the votes to get this settlement through this committee without answering your question."

Dave was still letting that thought sink in when Eli Grunk, Dr. Agazzi's defense attorney, began to speak. "We do want to apologize to the Board," he started, pushing his long but obviously receding grey-blonde hair back and smiling with the air of a man who at forty-eight still thought he could charm everyone in the room with his dashing looks.

"It's true that errors were made. Serious errors, which horribly inflated these bills. But Dr. Agazzi had nothing to do with those errors. And he has now corrected the system that created those errors." As he spoke, Attorney Grunk held his hands out in front of himself, palms upward, as if bearing intangible gifts of honesty and insight. "As much as I hate to point the finger of blame, it has to be done in this case.

"Dr. Agazzi left the billing to his office administrator, Mary Connelly. We're not saying that Ms. Connelly had any criminal or fraudulent purpose in creating these errors, but she apparently did not know as much about medical billing as she had claimed when she was hired." He paused to let the committee appreciate his diplomatic, non-accusatory language. "Ms. Connelly no longer works for Dr. Agazzi. Dr. Agazzi was appalled at her mistakes – and I've known him well for years, not only professionally but as a friend – and I can tell you he is heartsick, just heartsick, over these errors. And *I'm* heartsick, frankly and truly, that a mistake like this could lead to public charges against this honorable man, and this good, good doctor."

Nancy Hunt, the prosecutor, responded in the same flat tone she had used throughout the meeting. "We subpoenaed Dr. Agazzi's office's payroll records. We subpoenaed Dr. Agazzi's personnel records. We also obtained an affidavit from Mary Connelly. Ms. Connelly was out on unpaid maternity leave during the entire two months these false bills were submitted. And all of these bills were personally prepared by Dr. Agazzi, in his own hand."

"You just said that Dr. Agazzi created those false billings with his own hand. Doesn't this mean that your proposed settlement is wrong? Yet you want the Board to drop the charge of false billing?" It was the new Board member again.

Michele touched a pen to Dave's arm to signal him to keep quiet.

"This is the agreement reached by the prosecutor's office with the defense attorney." Prosecutor Nancy Hunt repeated robotically.

No one said anything else, and the committee didn't ask any more questions. Without discussion, the committee quickly voted 6-1 to approve the settlement. After another round of snapping briefcases and shuffling papers, Michele and Dave went out into the hallway with the attorneys and their helpers. Then Michele quickly pulled Dave into a little waiting room off of the committee meeting room where the staff often went to figure out what had to be done next. She closed the door.

"You look a little stunned." She was obviously trying not

to smile.

"*What* exactly happened in there?"

Her smile broke through. "Don't think about it logically. Think about what everybody wants, and what they got out of this. Frank got rid of a case he was scared to deal with. Dr. Agazzi got to hide from the public what he actually did. The Board got to put a little ding on this scoundrel's record without having to do any of that hard addition and subtraction work. Nancy Hunt got to chalk up a partial win and go on to some other case that she probably thinks is more important. And Grunk got paid thousands of dollars and now gets to brag that he got *even this guy* off."

··· ···

"How's your job going?" Sarah asked him when she finally called from the airport on her way back from Spain.

"Well, it's not boring. I can definitely say that." He told her about the Agazzi settlement.

"Wow. That doesn't make any sense. Real life. Versus what I study day and night in law school."

He knew she was trying to make him feel good. The day she was accepted into Duke Law she stepped onto a higher career track than any he would ever be on. Because he had graduated with a huge student loan debt, and because there weren't many jobs of any kind around, he took the first job he could get after he graduated. He had applied to be a governmental relations specialist for the state environmental agency, but instead he was offered the job of eligibility technician for the welfare department. He took that job because he needed one right away, but he came home every day depressed from dealing with the endless stream of people who came into his office with no jobs, no money, no hopes and no clue – and the endless tangle of red tape he had to work through with each of them. This job at the medical board was thrilling compared to that one. But it still wasn't anything to brag about.

"You're headed for the top," he told Sarah now. "Back here, we seem to be down at the bottom, fighting in the ditches, and with one hand tied behind our backs."

He tried not to let the real worry creep into his voice. She was rubbing shoulders every day with the super-smart kids, the overachievers, the kids whose parents had connections, while he spent his days expediting seedy little compromises with seedy little doctors.

"Oh, don't talk like that," she said immediately. "You're trying to hold doctors accountable. All I'm doing is studying legal theory night and day." Then her voice dropped. "I miss you. Will you leave right after work Friday so we can have dinner down here? And you can tell me all about that School for Scoundrels you work at."

She could always cheer him up. But he wondered how long that would last. He had a sudden insight that once Sarah graduated from Duke Law School, she would never in her life be in a situation where her opinion didn't matter. Meanwhile, his opinion didn't matter at all at the Board. He worried that the day would come when his opinion wouldn't matter to her either.

> **Ms. Porter**: What were you going to Dr. Zeus for?
> **Ms. Bolt**: I had a problem with my knee. At first he just felt around my hip. He said he couldn't feel any abnormality. He just told me to use aspirin or ibuprofen.
> **Q**: Did you feel there was anything unusual about the way he touched you on those first visits?
> **A**: Unusual? No. The only thing unusual

was his attitude. He was a little gruff, like I was wasting his time complaining about my little problem.

Q: Did his attitude change?

A: Not really. I came back because my knee still hurt. Then he prescribed Celebrex.

Q: Did that solve the problem?

A: Not really. So I kept coming back because it still hurt. Not all the time, but sometimes. He had an x-ray taken in his office, but he said it didn't show anything. He sent out for a lot of blood tests. He said all the tests came back normal. He sent for the same tests all over again. He said I didn't have any indicators of rheumatoid arthritis.

Q: Was there a change in his attitude at that point?

A: He was still very quick, very gruff. It actually seemed like he was disappointed I didn't have rheumatoid arthritis.

Q: But didn't you tell your therapist that he molested you?

A: Yeah. But that was, like, after he changed the treatment plan.

Chapter 7

Diane

About two weeks after the appointment where he told me about his daughter and his boat, I got a text from Dr. Zeus that the test results had come back and he would like to explain them to me in person. I thought it couldn't be anything that heavy, or his office would have called my mother. I liked that he texted me instead of having his office call her. It made me feel like a free person on her own, and one who deserved the personal touch.

He talked to me nicely as soon as he came in the room, but then I started thinking about how I would be lying back on that examining table soon with my feet in those stirrups. I wished we could have gotten that part over with first. But he said he wanted to talk to me first, and so that made me feel like I was not just your average kid patient. But then I was thinking maybe he was going to tell me there was something really wrong inside me.

"It's good to see you, Diane. How did you get here today?"

"Borrowed my mother's car. After I got back from school."

"You drove by yourself?"

"Was I supposed to bring somebody?"

"No, no. This is fine. You're a remarkably independent person, aren't you?"

I didn't know what he meant. "My parents let me do a lot on my own. I guess they figure the worst has already happened." Dr. Zeus jerked his eyes toward mine. "That was a joke," I said real quick. I hoped he didn't think I was an idiot.

He smiled. "But having a baby is not the worst thing. Not at all. You've had a profound experience, Diane. You were given a miraculous gift, a human child, and you gave it back to the world. That shows a generosity and maturity that's amazing. Your ordinary teenage friends couldn't possibly understand that. That's their problem, not yours. You are an exceptional woman, Diane."

So I had this flash fantasy of him coming to my school and telling everybody how great I was. Nobody talked to me at all at public school at that point. Even Kate and Lucky weren't so hot on getting together like they used to be. And I guessed most dudes figured I'd slap them silly if they ever tried to touch me. Not one boy there had even started a conversation with me. And I know I look pretty good, so that's not it. Dr. Zeus said it didn't matter.

"Don't try to be somebody you're not, just to fit in," he said now. "You are way beyond these other kids in many ways."

"Oh." But the truth was, I only felt this good right when he was actually saying it. So I wanted him to keep saying it. His sharp blue eyes studied me up and down, and I could tell he wasn't disgusted by what he saw. Then his eyes caught mine. A kind of soft, warm wave washed over me, so gently. I hadn't felt so calm in ages. It seemed like things could be okay if he would keep on believing in me.

Then, the stirrups. I held my breath. He kept saying relax, relax, but I couldn't. It seemed like it went on for a long time. Then he practically threw his instruments down, turned away and rushed out of the room. He didn't say anything as he left, and he didn't come back. Thank God I had my clothes on by the time his receptionist came in. She told me to go back to his office to talk to him.

"You were nervous in there," he started. It was true, but I didn't feel nervous then, in that chair, with my clothes on. Actually, Dr. Zeus seemed a little flustered.

"I tried to hold still. I'm really sorry. Did I screw something up?"

"Not at all. I didn't find anything abnormal upon examination." He stopped for a second before he went on. "Tell me, Diane, are you nervous now?"

"No."

"Nothing bothering you?"

"No. Should it?" I could tell then he was definitely nervous. That made a tiny little thrill run through me. I'd seen teenage boys get nervous, but Dr. Zeus was a real man and he wasn't going to snicker to his friends or say something gross or go right out and chug enough alcohol until he barfed like most boys would. But why would Dr. Zeus be nervous?

"Diane, are you okay?"

What *was* I doing? I had been sitting there thinking this weird stuff while my doctor was trying to talk to me. I was mortified that he called me out on it.

"Yeah. I'm okay," I answered without meeting his eyes. "Should I come back, or what?"

I looked up and saw he was looking right at me, and I heard him sigh like he was brushing off his nervousness or whatever it was. It was like the doctor in him had come back on board and chased the teenage boy away, leaving me as just the idiot teenage girl, stammering the most obvious patient question you could think of.

"It's really up to you," he said very gently. "Do you feel our counseling, our little talks, are doing you any good?"

It didn't seem like counseling. "I like talking to you, person to person, not like a doctor, if that's what you mean." My heart started beating faster when I said that.

"You can come back and visit me whenever you want. We could just talk, if that's what you want."

"Is that, like, what people normally do?"

"No," he said. "Nobody talks to me much. Not as honestly as you do."

"Oh."

"Diane, I feel very comfortable talking with you. So I'd like to keep this talking going, if it's helping you, and if that's what you want also."

"*You* want to?"

"I do. You remind me what it was like to be so young and open to life. That's a feeling I haven't had in a long time." He stopped for a second and smiled at me. Maybe telling their own feelings is what real men do when you open up to them. "But I have an idea," he went on. "Let's not tell anybody what we talk about." He looked sheepish when he said that, almost like a shy teenage boy. I had a flashback to Carl, his humble little smile every time I found him out. It made sense, when you thought about it. Men were just teenage boys who had had more birthdays.

And so, like a week later, I was on his boat. Going for more test results, as far as my Mom was concerned.

··· ···

I almost didn't make it to the boat, so much craziness happened that week. First, I almost fell over in school one day when I saw Rat from my old days at middle school walking down the hallway as I came out of my European History class. Kate had told me he didn't want to be called Rat any more. She didn't tell me what he wanted to be called. And I hadn't expected to see him in our high school.

"So, hi, hey." I ran to catch up to him. "I know it's not Rat. You use your real name now? *Ellwood*?"

Nobody who was there would forget the day Ms. Nesbitt called him out in front of the whole class when we were in middle school. Rat had spent that whole year hanging around in the woods behind the school, supplying us with pot and alcohol, shooting off his rifle, pretending to be tough. He had been sitting by the side of the trail that morning with a group of friends, passing around a bottle of whiskey, when Ms. Nesbitt brought her whole class past him. She didn't mean anything, but when she called him by his real name it sort of broke the spell. I mean, *Ellwood*? He lost his reputation right then, right in front of all of us. I had always known he was just playing tough because he was always nice to me and Kate, and Lucky was never afraid of him. But he never scared anybody at all after Ms. Nesbitt called him by his real name.

"Hi, Diane. I go by *Woody*." He seemed quieter now.

"You go to school here now?"

"I take classes." He had to lean his head down a little just to speak to me. His blonde hair was still in a buzz cut. He was still tall and lean but didn't look as awkward as he did two years ago. I remembered him skateboarding like a clumsy maniac down the trail, sitting like a master of ceremonies in his special spot in the woods, watching us get drunk on his wine coolers. He still had his ball-point-pen ink tattoos on his arms, but when I tried to see if I could still read the most obscene ones, he twisted his arm away. We both had classes to get to, but he turned around again as he left, and I don't know why but I said, "Let's talk some time. Catch you later."

Then there was a very good reason to catch him later. Robert was trying to get me back into the church, and I had promised I'd go to a two-day praise weekend he was running for the church youth group starting that Saturday. Robert wanted everybody to call him Deacon even though everybody knew he was just in training to maybe be a sub-deacon one day. But it worked; everybody called him that. Must have been those long black pants. I had promised I'd go to the praise weekend on that day he gave me that awful kiss in Fellowship Hall. Really, I had just been trying to change the subject, but he didn't let me forget I'd said that. He came over to my house and talked to my mother about it when I wasn't even there. My mother said it would be rude to back out. Deacon was so sincere, she said. The people at the church had helped me so much, she said, and they had only my best interest at heart. I guess that's why Dad also said I should go this one last time. And besides, there was no one else to teach soccer to the little girls.

I tracked down Rat in the halls the day before. I told him my story. I told him I'd promised to go. "But nobody said I couldn't do it stoned. Please, give me something so I can get through this."

"I'm not doing that any more."

"Please. Just this one time."

He took me to the place where he lived, which was just a garage behind somebody's house. It was just a small garage, but he had put in a big window at the far end for light. He didn't charge me anything for the pot. He said he wouldn't do it again. I thanked him and thanked him and said I couldn't get through the retreat without it, but he just kind of grunted like I was just another weirdo he knew from his past.

It was weird that I had to beg Rat for weed. In the old days, when I was hanging with Kate, I used to think I was doing Rat such a favor just by letting him talk me into drinking one of his wine coolers or smoking one of his joints. Now he didn't want to be called Rat, and he didn't really want to give me anything.

The praise weekend was awful. Pastor Bill had always been kind, but he was getting old, and this time he let Robert practically run the whole show. I couldn't stand the way he looked at me, and he looked at me a lot. The kids my age were polite, but they never looked in my eyes when we talked. The girls acted like they'd get pregnant themselves if they looked at me. The boys were curious at first, like they thought they might see a scarlet *p* for *primipara* burned into my forehead if they looked close enough. Mostly, their eyes darted away when I said hi, which I started doing a lot. I could clear my way across the activity room with a couple of stares and one or two bright-eyed *hello*s.

It actually could have been a little bit of crazy, stoned fun except for Robert. He was always trying to catch my eye when he was supposed to be talking to a whole group. During the prayers where everybody holds hands he was always next to me. I started giggling at what an obvious dork he was, and he got mad. That was fine with me. I kept giggling at everything he said, and a couple of the younger kids started giggling too. Kids were staring. He said he needed to talk to me alone.

"I'm not going anywhere alone with you." I wasn't afraid of him, but everybody heard us, and then the little kids were kind of looking at me like they were scared. Much as I thought the whole thing was bullshit, I couldn't bring myself to break the spell of the little kids' happy fairy tale retreat. And then I saw he had started all this tension on purpose. Even though he was a dull-as-dishwater, plodding kind of guy, he had that same sixth sense to take advantage of any discomfort in the room that I'd seen in Pastor Bill sometimes. Some of the older kids might have thought there was something going on between Robert and me if we went into a room alone. After all, a Jezebel like me might just do anything, even to a holy sub-deacon-in-training. I just had to choose, so I finally gave in and went off alone with him into a little side room.

He came in after me and shut the door. It was a tiny room. It did have a window, but no curtains, no rug, no table, just a tile floor and six of those folding metal chairs.

"The church is still doing so much for you, even now," he started, his voice echoing off the tiles.

I guess he meant that gloomy little clinic where I saw Dr. Zeus. It had walls and doors but not really a ceiling, and so when you were lying on your back you could see some of the metal wires and rafters over the basketball court and sometimes feel cold air come down over you when your clothes were off. It was like you were in some kind of factory and you were one of the things being worked on.

"The clinic. Yeah, that's good. I am grateful for that," I said.
He just stared at me.

"Okay," I agreed. "I won't laugh at you any more out there. Just let me go off to my room. And don't call me back until it's time for the bus to take us home."

"You're not being disruptive." He bowed his head. "Your personality, your spirit, that's what's giving life to this whole weekend."

"You mean how I kicked your ass in the soccer game?"

"Yes." He looked up for a second, then cast his eyes down again. "And in softball. And you got everyone to play. The little girls want to do whatever you do. I've never seen any other person so lovely – I mean lively – so blessed in spirit."

"Look, most of the older kids out there think I'm Mary Magdalene or something."

"Whom Jesus loved." His eyes were on me. We were both standing up, me with my back to the window. He started walking toward me. "Jesus loved Mary Magdalene."

He put out his hand. "Hold my hand again, please, Diane."

The idea made my skin crawl. I wouldn't do it.

"You are blessed, Diane. I was a stumbling blind man before you came along." His voice was shaking. "Jesus has opened my eyes to you." He was closer, almost leaning over me now. His arms were trembling.

"Leave me alone!" I balled my hand into a fist behind my back.

"You kissed me before," he complained.

"I was just trying to be nice."

He stood real close to me, breathing slow and heavy like he was meditating or something. But he didn't try to touch me. "I watched you everywhere you went this weekend. You were wonderful. You were just glowing with love and spirit. I'm so lucky I was here to see it. It felt like Jesus was letting me see your soul, so beautiful and pure."

"You must have been smoking pot, too."

He stepped back. "I know you will one day hear the word of Jesus and be moved to praise Him by following His will. I pray I will be there when it happens." Then he let me go.

On the last day, Pastor let him preach a practice sermon. He actually said Jesus had sent him a special earthly love that was a mirror image of Jesus's love for us. I thought I would kill him. Luckily, nobody thought I was worthy of Robert's holy love, and so nobody suspected it was me. Also, nobody seemed to give a crap about who he had the hots for.

The Monday after the church retreat I brought the rest of the pot back to school and handed it back to Rat.

"You didn't use it all?"

"No. A couple hits was all I had time for. You had to be in some group the whole time."

"I don't want it back. Keep it." He turned away.

"Why are you acting so pissed at me?" I followed him down the hall. He turned a corner and I still followed him. "Come on, Rat. What's the deal?"

He stopped. "*Woody.*" That was all he said. Then he turned away again.

"OK. Woody. Come on. Stop acting like I'm a freak or something."

He stopped again. "Just don't ask me for drugs."

"Are you, like, going to be a cop now, or something?"

We stepped over to the side of the hall to let the others pass, each of us then standing there, leaning against the wall. He was taller than almost all of the boys in the school, but still as skinny as he used to be. Carl had been taller than me too, but not by much. I was the love of Carl's life, I knew. He would have spent his whole life trying to make me happy. It wasn't good enough for me. Now I was stalking down the hall a guy I used to think of as such a loser, practically begging him to talk to me.

63

"No. Not a cop."

"But you're back in school? For real? I am too. I was in Christian school for a whole year. You know, after I had the baby and all."

"Yeah. I heard about your baby. I'm sorry. Is that what I'm supposed to say?" He dipped his head, his eyes still on me. "I don't know the right thing to say, Diane."

So maybe this is why nobody talks to me, I was thinking.

"I always knew," he said then, "if anybody could pull that off, it would be you."

Now *that* was the right thing to say.

"Thanks. I'm glad you're here, and have a job and all. Things are so different now."

"Tell me about it. I had to work my way back in. I had a job first, then I got it changed into an internship, now I'm in regular high school classes too, part time." He kept looking at me. "But you seem the same."

"Look, I know I'm not as hot as I used to think I was."

"Nobody could ever be that hot." He smiled, and I laughed, the first time I had laughed in a long time.

Chapter 8

Diane

I had a major urge to tell Woody I was going with Dr. Zeus on his boat the next day – maybe so he would know at least somebody thought I was hot – but I didn't. I wore a sleeveless blouse and long white pants and sandals with two-inch heels that made me almost as tall as Dr. Zeus. I thought I looked good, but I didn't have anybody to check with, so I didn't know if this was what you were supposed to wear on a boat. I certainly wasn't going to wear a bathing suit, though it was hot enough for one.

I had been out on a boat only once before, when I went out on a lake with my uncle and cousins on a dorky vacation our two families once took in the mountains. My father didn't like boats.

Zeus had to drive more than half an hour out of town before we got to his boat. The drive was smooth and fast, and I asked him if the car was expensive.

"Not exactly. It's a Kia. I'm renting it while my Jaguar gets fixed."

"I knew you'd own a fancy car."

He shrugged. "There are compensations."

I didn't know what he meant exactly, but I didn't feel like I had to understand everything. This was a free day, my free day. Dr. Zeus drove really fast, zooming us right out of the ordinary world. He played classical music on the radio. He really was cool and smooth. I wondered if it had just been my imagination that he was lonely.

We drove for maybe forty minutes, off the flat main highways and onto smaller roads that twisted and turned down and down under tall leafy trees until we came to a marina on the water. It was a river, he told me, but it looked about two miles wide and I couldn't even tell which way it was flowing.

"Who else is coming?"

"It's just you and me."

The people at the marina had his boat ready to go at the end of the pier, but there was a big guy in a sweaty grey T-shirt and jeans standing next to it like he wasn't going to let us pass. "Your bill is three months overdue," he said, staring at Dr. Zeus but then glancing past him and at me for a second. "I left a message on your voice mail, but I guess you didn't get it."

"I called this morning and they said it would be ready."

"Yeah. They didn't know about the bill. That's the only reason it's ready. Half ready. It's safe to take it out now, but it's not pretty, and it's not going out of here again until the bill's paid."

Zeus held out his hand to help me up. I knew I'd have to take off my two-inch heels to keep my balance once it started moving. The boat moved around a little even in the calm water. It was long and white and very clean on the outside.

"Look around," he said. "Go look up front if you want. You might want to do that now, because when we get going there might be some spray, and you could get your clothes soaked."

"Where's the motor?"

"Inboard motor," he smiled. "Like a car. Three hundred and twenty horsepower. You just turn the key."

"So, are you going to let me drive it?"

He had to go back to the marina office, I guess to pay his bill. He left me sitting there in the back on some plastic cushions that fit together on a bench behind the steering wheel. I could feel the boat waddle under me in the tiny waves coming from the river and I could hear a kind of *yuk-yuk-yuk* sound like the water was sucking at the boat from underneath. The sun was so hot I almost wished I had worn a bathing suit. I got out my big straw hat from my bag. Another marina guy, this one a tiny Hispanic man, came out with a clipboard and walked onto the boat, looking around and writing things down. He looked like he was shy, or maybe he didn't understand English. He was so sweaty and serious I felt stupid and useless by comparison, just a human decoration sitting on that cushion in my white pants and straw hat. Anyway, he didn't say anything to me before he turned around and went back to the office. It was another few minutes before Dr. Zeus came back.

That September afternoon was really hot and bright. He turned the boat on with his key. The motor growled slowly and sent streams of bubbles out the back. We slipped our way easily out into the middle of the river, where he turned up the engine. Then the front of the boat rose out of the water and we were racing through a loud rush of noise and foam. I stood up next to him to see where we were going. He weaved us through a line of slower boats. We could see them bouncing in our wake. When we were alone he slowed down going toward the open water ahead. Then the river completely opened up into the bay, and it was all water as far as we could see in three directions. I liked the feeling of being totally free of the land. The water was bright, pale blue and calm on one side of the boat and cobwebbed with moving strands of sunlight on the other. He slowed down almost to a stop.

"Climb up front. It's a lot cooler there."

I climbed up, sat down, and lay back against the windshield on the passenger side. The glass was so hot I had to put a towel down first. It was quiet enough that we could talk over the top of the windshield to each other. The sky was an epic blue. The trail of the sun on the surface of the water was so bright it hurt your eyes. Sailboats were all around. In the distance there was a huge grey shape that gradually turned into a freighter. We inched towards its path.

"Let's get closer. I want to see that."

"We don't want to get too close. Those things can't stop."

We got close enough that we could have seen the faces of crew members on deck – if there had been any. But there weren't any. It looked like a robot ship. Up close it was like a giant grey wall going past much faster than it first looked. The little boats just had to get out of its way. That seemed only fair, since we were doing nothing but playing.

"This is great." We were rocking in the long, slow wake of the big ship, the shore on all sides dipping in and out of view. The sea breeze played with the sun's heat on my skin. I lay back with my hat over my face, probably not the sophisticated companion I had hoped to be, but comfortable at least.

"My wife," he said, "takes antidepressants. I keep telling her getting out on the water on a day like this is all she really needs."

I was kind of shocked he talked to me about his wife's problems.

"She doesn't like the boat?"

"She doesn't like me."

I didn't know what I was supposed to say to that. Was he just kidding? Maybe he wasn't kidding and it just slipped out. I pretended I didn't hear.

We stayed out there until the heat started bothering us. Also, I started to need to pee. I didn't know what you were supposed to do when that happened on a boat, and I wasn't going to ask. If I asked him right after he told me that really personal stuff about his wife, it would sound like such a stupid kid question. So I had been waiting and kind of hoping he'd have to go first. We finally turned around and weaved our way back through the river traffic, slower this time. The moving air felt cool. He didn't say too much. Maybe he was embarrassed about what he had already said. I had no clue. He wore a men's straw hat, a black bathing suit and a bright blue polo shirt that matched his eyes. Finally we stopped in a little cove on the other side of the river from the marina. He showed me how to throw the anchor out.

I finally got up the courage to ask him if there was a bathroom on board. He slid open this wooden door, and there were steps down into this little room with cushions on both sides and this tiny table in the middle. It didn't smell very fresh in there, and when I opened the door to the tiny bathroom at the other end of that room, I almost gagged. I stopped there, breathing only out of my mouth, listening to the creepy sound of the water sucking at the bottom of the hull, the sound now echoing inside this hollow room. But I had no choice. I held my nose and went in.

"You're a brave soul," he smiled when I climbed out.

"It's really gross down there."

"That was supposed to be taken care of. There was some kind of misunderstanding with the marina."

"You didn't pay, right?"

"Okay, I didn't pay." He laughed. "Diane, I promise you, next time, this boat will be spotless."

There would be a next time. Next time, he would fix it up. For me.

"Why does your wife take pills?"

"She's not happy. I can't make her happy. So I prescribe them for her. It's the least I can do."

I didn't know people stayed married when they weren't happy. Kate's and Lucky's parents all split up when they weren't happy. I didn't know what Dr. Zeus wanted me to say, so I didn't say anything. But I felt like I was supposed to say something. It was like he had asked me a question and I was ignoring it. I guessed the next question would be: how could he be happy if she wasn't? Was I supposed to ask that?

He set up this canopy to keep the sun off of us. When he took his hat off I could see the blue sparkle of his eyes again. His legs were maybe a little skinnier than I would have guessed.

He brought out the lunch he had picked up in a restaurant on the way down. And he pulled a bottle of wine from a little cooler. He said I couldn't have any wine, though. I guess I looked pissed, so then he put it away.

"Why'd you bring it if you're not going to drink it?"

He looked so graceful and strong, now lying on his side across the cushions on the other side of the cockpit. Looking at me.

"You know, you catch me up every time," he said all of a sudden.

"What do you mean?"

"I did bring the wine for you."

"What?"

"I admit, I wasn't thinking about this trip as your doctor. I was thinking of it as a man. I was thinking about this day as almost like a date, stolen time with a beautiful woman."

I took a breath.

"I shouldn't complicate our friendship," he murmured. He didn't look right at me. He was looking out over the water, where the smooth surface of the river reflected exactly the gold clouds in the sky. "Forgive me."

Out there on the water, in that little cove, in the shade from the high green trees on the hills that crept all the way down to the shoreline, looking up at the open sky and across that wide river, I felt like this was a different world, the one I belonged in. Dr. Zeus rummaged in his cooler and came out with a beer for himself and some sodas and water for me. He waved for me to come and sit next to him. The cushion was hot from the sun. He seemed relaxed, not like a busy doctor at all, and I was glad for him. I didn't know if I'd ever be able to work so hard and for so long like he worked to become a doctor. Not that I'm smart enough anyway. He sipped his beer without saying anything else. He was so gorgeous! I wondered if he had ever made love to anybody on this boat. Just the idea stirred me up every way you could think of.

He leaned back and hung his beer hand over the edge of the boat. Most of the trip he had held himself stiff, almost like he was posing, but now he stretched his legs out and up over the steering wheel console. I'd never been out on a boat alone with anybody. I knew he was thinking it was kind of like a date, and so I didn't know what to do. He looked over at me and smiled with those blue eyes, but then he closed them like he was so comfortable, and it looked like he was dozing off. I got the idea. You don't have to do anything. That's the idea of a boat. I lay back on the cushions, letting the boat rock me, looking up at the sky. I couldn't sleep but I could sure daydream. It wasn't about him. The great thing about being with him was I could be my same old self, still think about the same old things – not like with a boyfriend where you're always wondering what is he thinking and what am I going to do if he's thinking that. I knew Dr. Zeus liked me just the way I was, and I knew he wouldn't push me into anything. I let my head relax into the cushion and fell asleep.

When I woke up he was sitting up, watching his empty beer bottle like he was afraid it was going to fall off the boat. It was on the very back edge of the boat, which was tilting as we rocked in the ripples. I reached out to get it, but he waved my hand away. He was holding his own hand out real close to the bottle at first, but then he moved his hand away, very slowly, still watching it, smiling like he was in a trance, waiting for it to start to tip over. He looked at me just then with those smiling eyes, like he was proud of doing something so stupid, and as he was looking at me the bottle finally did fall over, slipped out of his reach, clanked on the swimming platform that was attached to the back of the boat and fell into the water.

"I saw my ten-year-old cousin do that on a boat once." I blurted this out before I could think.

"You make me feel like a kid," he smiled.

"How old are you?"

"Forty-three. Old enough to be your father. But there's no reason we can't be friends."

I'd never been friends with a man. I had an uncle, my mother's older brother. He was maybe about Dr. Zeus's age. He was a complete nerd, but we got along all right.

"Why didn't you bring a bathing suit?"

"I don't know. I was shy about that, I guess."

"I didn't really have you pegged as a shy person, Diane."

"That must seem so silly to you, considering .... Sorry. I don't really know how to act with a guy who's so much, you know, older. Oh. Sorry. I didn't mean you were old."

"I feel like I'm talking to an adult, a woman who's been through more than a lot of other adult women, but who still has a young heart."

"Oh." A ripple from the middle of the river rocked us side to side until we were touching shoulders. Those sketchy thoughts came back. Stop it, Diane.

"I don't want to pressure you. We don't have to be friends."

"No, I want to."

Who else was I going to tell about scoring pot from an old dealer friend so I could make it through a church weekend? I told him the story.

"Let me get this straight. You used pot because the church causes you anxiety?" he asked. "Does the church always make you feel like that?"

Until then, I'd felt too guilty to say it. "Yeah. The people in church usually make me feel like there's something wrong with me."

"Really? Why?"

"Everyone there is so blessed. They talk about it all the time, and I know they can feel it, feel that they are blessed. Even Robert, weird as he is. But I can't."

"I wonder why?"

"It's pretty obvious, isn't it? I'm the only girl there who got pregnant at fourteen."

"That doesn't mean you can't be blessed."

"That's what they say. That's what they tell me. But they don't mean it. I mean, all those church people have to, like, take an extra breath before they talk to me."

"They're uncomfortable around you?"

"I guess."

Then Dr. Zeus took my hand in his. "You're very beautiful, Diane." It was like he knew my heart would start pounding, so he waited. The cushion we sat on swayed sideways and down, sideways and down as the boat pulled on the anchor. The river reflected the pinkish sky like the whole world was blushing.

"I'm not talking to you as your doctor now," he said, "but as your friend." His fingers were long and his skin felt cool. "Most people go to church because they feel the opposite way. They go because it makes them feel like they belong. It seems like attending this church hasn't been good for you."

"My Dad says that too." That felt really weird saying that just when Dr. Zeus was holding my hand. But who says I can't have a friend as old as my Dad? "But do you think, really, honestly, that it's okay to turn my back on these people? They helped me so much."

He let go of my hand and turned to me. His eyes looked troubled, I guess for me. "What you're saying about these people is: they don't believe in you."

"They were good to me."

"I think they're looking at you as a child gone wrong, not as an adult. But nobody can be good for you, in the long run, if they don't believe in the real you."

It seemed so simple when he said it like that. I wanted to take his hand again, but I thought that would be wrong. I said thank you. I also leaned back a little so our shoulders were touching. I knew I shouldn't do that, but I made it seem like an accident. And it felt so good. For a long time, nobody said anything. The boat was rocking me against him. The river was like a mirror of the sky, only with ripples.

"The church even pays for you to be my doctor."

"They don't pay me. They just set up that clinic. I get paid by your insurance company."

"Oh. They made it sound like they paid." I started to feel like a dumb kid, and I leaned away from his touch. "Do you really think it would be right if I totally stopped going to that church?"

"The church is supposed to be for you. If it's making you unhappy, maybe you should stop going."

"That's not what they say. They say the church is for doing Jesus's will. Praising him. That's the only way you can do yourself any good."

He looked out over the river, his eyes not really focused on anything, like he was thinking hard about my problem. "Then I guess it's a matter of whether you believe that," he said.

He opened a bottle of water for himself. He opened a soda for me but I didn't want to drink anything else. I was hoping we would talk some more. *We*! I was already thinking like we were a couple. But he helped me get that idea out of my head by talking like a doctor again.

"You don't have to smoke pot for anxiety. There are plenty of medications that are more effective at relieving anxiety."

"It was mostly just the church."

"I can prescribe something if you need it. Just let me know. You don't have to go through life feeling bad."

He stood up at the steering wheel. He showed me step by step how to start the motor. He showed me how to steer it and told me I could drive it back to the marina when we left. And I could take it out for another spin around the river first, if I wanted to. I didn't want to go anywhere right away. The wide river was like a church-free, school-free, parents-free zone where you could say what you really thought, and where somebody would listen to what you said.

The only thing was, I was still hot, wearing those long pants. You could swim off the back of the boat and get back on by climbing onto the platform that hung out behind; but I had been too chicken to bring a bathing suit. And I had gulped down so many of his sodas while we were talking I had to pee again. That was so embarrassing, because I wasn't going down to that gross boat toilet again, and I wasn't telling him either. We were sitting next to each other again, like friends. I felt really sad that I had to ask him to go back.

When we got back to the marina I jumped off and ran up the pier and barely made it to their old, creaky, smelly wooden bathroom before they closed it for the day. Dr. Zeus was arguing with the marina guys when I got back. I hoped he was telling them to fix the stupid bathroom on that boat.

He drove his car really fast on the way home. "We need to get you back in time so you won't be missed."

"Why?" I was playing with him, I knew. I guessed you could play with a friend.

"It would be frowned on, you know, you skipping a half day of school and soccer practice and going on a boat trip with your doctor instead."

"Do you think it was wrong?"

He took one hand off the wheel and reached over and touched my knee. "Of course not. We're getting to know each other. That's what friends do. It's a wonderful thing."

"So I should tell everybody?"

He took his eyes completely off the road and looked at me, and I could tell from the look on his face that my teasing had gone too far. It was scary to think that even the fabulous Dr. Zeus was worried. And it was so unfair that he should have to be worried. Just for the day, just for me, he had given up his glamorous doctor life and come down to earth as a regular man. A regular human guy. A guy who could get in trouble. Just for me.

"Can't you tell I'm teasing you?" I said. "I would never tell anyone about this day."

"Diane," he said when he let me out, "this was way, way more fun than I ever expected it to be."

······ ······

Lisa came into my room that night.

"I came to watch you at soccer practice today."

"Close the door."

Lisa closed the door, and so I knew she wouldn't rat on me. Unless there was something in it for her.

"Why did you come to see me at soccer practice?"

"You're supposed to be so good."

Her arms and legs are so long and skinny, Lisa doesn't fit in with regular-sized furniture. She sat down on my bed and put her feet up and put her palms on her hips with her elbows sticking out. She reminded me of a praying mantis folding in its backwards-hinged arms, but I didn't say those kinds of things to her any more. The truth is, I know I look good, and Lisa grew up so tall and skinny she could be kind of funny looking from certain angles. But now I could tell her body was catching up to her bones, and her eyes were gorgeous, and she was already starting to look as good as any model on a runway ever looked. I didn't say that to her either.

"I took off with someone."

"I saw you talking to that guy Woody at school last week."

"How do you know him?"

"Everybody knows him. He's, like, older, and he has a job and all."

"It wasn't him."

"Who was it, then?"

I couldn't tell her. She was pissed, and she left my room. It didn't seem right that I couldn't tell her. We'd always trusted each other. Maybe I scared her off two years ago with my big pregnant belly – then ignored her during all the time I was holier than thou. I wanted to be her friend again, but now I didn't see how she would fit in with me and Dr. Zeus.

Chapter 9

David

> **Ms. Porter**: Katherine, can you tell me
> what happened with Dr. Zeus on that day
> when the tests came back?
> **Ms. Bolt**: He said I didn't have rheuma-
> toid arthritis. I said my knee still hurt. He
> stared at me for a second like I was really
> annoying him. Then he said okay, it's time
> to move to Plan 2. That's what he called it,
> Plan 2.
> **Q**: What was Plan 2?
> **A**: Stronger painkillers, and massage. He
> gave me a prescription for oxycodone. He
> told me to get it filled right away and take
> the first dose and come back to him at the
> end of the day.

As he read the transcript, Dave twisted in his chair. No matter what had happened to Katherine, her case was over, and he wouldn't be able to do anything about it. He wasn't sure he could do much of anything about any of the Zeuses or Agazzis of the world. He blamed himself for getting into such a powerless position. He'd spent a lifetime fighting off persistent thoughts that he was a loser. Graduating *summa cum laude* hadn't helped. The proof of his loser status was his current job. He was barely making enough to pay his rent and his student loan payments. And he was basically impotent at the Board. Every day, he saw scoundrels who happened to have a medical license fight the Board to a standstill because they could make disciplining them more trouble than it was worth. And there was apparently nothing he could do about it.

One good thing about being at the bottom of the totem pole was that nobody was shooting for your job. It was a small consolation, Dave realized, and he felt small for taking comfort in that fact. He stared at the picture of Sarah thumbtacked to his cubicle wall. Sarah wasn't small in any way. She was five-feet-ten and blonde, a volleyball player in college. She walked straight and she talked straight. She had turned down a job at the State Department because she thought working for that bureaucracy might not leave her with enough options. Now she sometimes complained about still being in school, and how dull law was, but Dave had no doubt she would excel there. She was just as engaged and competitive as he was. Her family was rich, and Dave never ceased to wonder at her seemingly unbalanced life experience. She had explored Machu Picchu and snorkeled off the Great Barrier Reef, but before she came to college she had never shopped at a TJ Maxx, brought her own clothes to the dry cleaners, taken a vacation by car.

He was glad now for an excuse to go stand in Michele's cubicle doorway.

"Michele, can I close the Agazzi case now? Are we done with it?"

Michele screwed up her mouth.

"Actually, what Frank would love," she said, "would be for you to hand him the case completely finished, so he can just close the file."

"So, what'll I do?"

"As soon as the Board approves it, post the reprimand on the Board's website. Then, we're done, in theory. In theory, Dr. Agazzi has to find the coding course himself and submit it to us for approval. In reality, we'll probably have to find the course for him."

"How do we do that?"

"Wait. I think I have a pamphlet for one of these courses here." She opened a file drawer and quickly found it and handed it to him. Dave read the course title on the first page.

"Michele! We're really going to send him to a course called MAXIMIZE YOUR PROFITS USING CPT CODES?"

"That's the only kind of CPT courses there are," she shrugged. Then she laughed when she saw the look on Dave's face. "Don't get upset. Dr. Agazzi won't understand any of it."

··· ···

> **Ms. Porter**: Did you take his advice and fill the prescription?
> **Ms. Bolt**: Yeah. I took it like he said, two pills the first time. And I came back to his office later.
> **Q**: Were there any other people there then?
> **A**: There were a couple of receptionists there, but they, you know, had their pocketbooks on their desks and were getting ready to go just as I walked in.
> **Q**: What happened next?
> **A**: Right after they left, he opened the door to that examination room. He looked at me and didn't say a word.

Dave tromped back to Michele's office. "Frank would get the Board to charge Dr. Zeus for what he did to this woman if he could prove it, right?"

"Frank loves sex cases. If they're easy to prove."

"You couldn't find anything to corroborate her story?"

"I subpoenaed her medical records and the prescription records from her pharmacy. He prescribed Celebrex, then massive doses of oxycodone, like she said. Wellbutrin. There were a lot of blood tests in her medical records. There were bills for two comprehensive examinations and six follow-ups. Dr. Zeus's own notes basically corroborated what she said, except of course there was no mention of sex. There were a couple of appointments at the end where there was no record of any examination and no tests were ordered. They were billed as counseling sessions. And so there were medical bills for counseling."

"He's just a regular doctor. He can charge for counseling?"

"He diagnosed her with depression in her medical records. He prescribed Wellbutrin at one point. Nobody can say he didn't counsel her."

"Did he counsel any other patients?"

"No."

"Michele, you know that counseling crap is bullshit."

"We all do, but it's her word against his. And she's got a diagnosed emotional problem."

"Diagnosed by Dr. Zeus."

Michele's usual cheery smile faded, and she lowered her voice. "If it was up to me, I would have asked the Board to charge him. But Frank wouldn't allow it. He says the Board just won't buy a *he-said/she-said* case. He always says there are plenty of other bad guys to go after who don't even bother to cover their tracks."

"But seeing Dr. Zeus get away with it – how can you stand it?"

"Dave," she put down the file she had been holding the whole time. Her look made him feel naive. "Maybe you shouldn't take it to heart. There are always going to be bad guys around. In any profession. We do what we can."

But he did take it to heart. Never prosecuting a *he-said/she-said* case had the same effect as assuming the women were always lying – unless there was some extraordinary circumstance that conclusively proved that the allegation was true. Usually the extraordinary circumstance was two or three other women making the same allegation. The functional result was that it took two or three women's testimony to equal the testimony of one doctor. The system seemed rigged.

… …

When he first met Sarah, he expected her to act like she was superior. She had the money, and all the looks and brains and self-confidence you'd need to become some kind of upper-class icon; but she refused to accept that role. She had traveled the world on her parents' dime but didn't act like that meant she was anything special. She didn't really feel entitled, but people expected her to feel that way. The conflict came out in a quirkiness to her character that set her a little apart, into a one-person social class of her own. Dave first met her in front of her eating club at Princeton. His roommate was in a band, playing a gig on the lawn on a warm September day. Dave beat her in a game of speed chess, and she followed him across the lawn, demanding a rematch. He loved seeing this big, beautiful, smart girl not quite holding herself together. He didn't know then that it was a permanent condition. He didn't even dream then that he could be the cure.

When he had arrived in Durham to meet her two weeks before, she had kissed him wildly, pushing him so hard against the retaining wall in the parking lot she almost knocked him down. "Mr. Smartypants, Mr. Public Policy Genius, I hope you get cursed one day and have to go to law school too," she greeted him.

"I love you too."

The first year was supposed to be the toughest, she told him. After that, there were clinics where you could help real people with actual problems. There were international institutes in Hong Kong and Geneva. She had a couple of teachers who themselves were famous national political figures. She was impressed that one of them had defended President Clinton. "But I'm trying to keep this all in perspective," she rolled her eyes. "I haven't done anything myself. I'm just a student. And I'm starting to think anybody who has a big bank account and an exceptional tolerance for boredom could be a successful student here."

Seeing the real Sarah, as opposed to his idea of Sarah, always calmed him down. She loved him. She said she was jealous. "You can go into the secret world of doctors and patients and diseases," she said, "and look for hidden evil."

"You do make it sound good," he laughed, when she finally loosened her fierce embrace. "It's really not quite that dramatic."

As the weekend wore on, however, he started to think he was seeing the handwriting on the wall. One of her new friends was the daughter of a U.S. Senator. They all talked about internships in Congress like it was charity work. He stopped talking about his own world because it suddenly seemed so small. Maybe if there had been some political science majors among them he could have discussed the way the Board actually operated as an interesting political case study. But the only cases her friends seemed interested in were legal cases. He struggled to hold himself together until he left on Sunday afternoon. Even their farewell didn't seem right. They had always promised to be honest with each other, but the joy and optimism he expressed to her that afternoon as they kissed goodbye was definitely fake. She had everything. Her father was wealthy, and she was an only child. She had loved her mother, who had died just two years before. Dave asked her once if she thought her father was doting on her so much to make up for losing his wife. She looked at him like he was crazy. "No way. He's always been like this. I mean, he's a dad, right?"

· · · · · ·

Ms. Bolt: I had never experienced a drug
that could make you feel so good. When
he opened that door I almost floated in.

Ms. Porter: You were under the influence of oxycodone at that time?

A: Oh, yes. I'd never felt anything like it. He told me to take my clothes off and put on one of those paper gowns while I was behind this little partition. While I was putting the paper gown on, he called over the partition that it would not be necessary to tie it. That sent some kind of shock through me.

Q: What happened next?

A: I came out and he had me lie down on my side so he could massage my back.

Q: Where was the paper gown at this time?

A: He was standing behind me. He pushed it like up and away. Then some of it was like around my head so I couldn't really see much of anything, and the rest of it was hanging down off the side of the examining table in front of me.

Q: And were you otherwise totally nude?

A: Oh, no. I still had my panties on at that point.

•• •••

"Social life?" Sarah had scoffed. "Are you kidding, Dave? You being here – that's about it. I spend all my time at night reading cases."

"Really? What are all these cases about?"

"It's not like what you'd expect, you know, *Brown v. School Board of Kansas* or *Miranda v. Arizona*. It's mostly things like wills and property disputes that happened in the eighteenth century. It's pretty boring. But, I have to admit, it's the same thought process the Supreme Court still goes through now." He could tell she was overwhelmed by the reams of detail she had to memorize, but he could also tell that she would nevertheless plough right through it. She was as tough as she was tall, and he never beat her again in a chess game. He found himself wishing he could do something really dramatic at work that she would be able to brag about to her fellow law students. It didn't seem like that was going to happen. Pay off your student loans, then look around for a job worthy of your talents. That was the smart thing to do.

Frank still had him picking up scraps of cases that other investigators hadn't finished. In most of them, the previous investigator hadn't done anything in a long time. He was supposed to pick up the trail where they had left off. Sometimes he could talk to the old investigator and get an idea why the case had been put on hold. But there was also a high turnover of investigators, so in a lot of cases the previous investigator was "no longer with the Board." Those were the exact words he had to tell to prospective witnesses when they asked why the case had been delayed for so long. Few seemed satisfied with this answer. He was put in the position of constantly apologizing to people he had never met for the negligence of other people he had never met either.

None of these cases seemed as important as Katherine's case anyway. He couldn't resist putting these other cases aside during his breaks to peek at the transcript of her interview. There was no one to talk to about this case now. The last time he tried to talk to Michele about Katherine's case, her eyes kept wandering down to her own paperwork on her desk. He was beginning to have this fantasy that he could reopen the case himself, find the smoking gun and rip Dr. Zeus's defense to shreds. He wanted to describe his frustration to Sarah. He wondered if Sarah would encourage him – or stare at him quietly with those intelligent hazel eyes and tell him flatly to just let it go.

··· ···

During his junior year of college, Dave had planned to walk the New Hampshire part of the Appalachian Trail on spring break with his roommate. They would camp out, hike fifteen miles a day, hitchhike to visit the bars and liquor stores off the trail which they located on the internet. They would plant a car at each end, split the food and gas costs, see the mountains up close, drink as much as they dared, and have stories to tell when they got back. It seemed like a perfect guy vacation until he met Sarah. Then he didn't want it to be just a guy thing.

His roommate consented to his inviting her along, but she told him she was spending the break with her father at a hotel in the south of France. She claimed she would rather go hiking with him instead.

He didn't really believe her. He Googled the hotel, the beach at Nice, trying not to linger too long over the pictures of the topless sunbathers. He wondered what it would be like if she asked him to go – but then he realized it wouldn't work. His entire vacation wad wouldn't be enough to pay for a single lunch at that hotel.

"Your vacation sounds like a real adventure," she insisted. "I don't like just lying around on the beach." She said she was jealous. "Text me every day," she pleaded, "with the exact coordinates. I'm going to Google Earth your exact path every night."

The trip was harder than they expected. Their feet hurt so much after the first day they had to take a day off just to rest. His shoulders ached from the weight of his backpack. The bars were further from the trail than they expected, and they weren't very successful hitchhiking. That might have been because they were filthy. But the skies were clear and the views were stunning. The early spring buds on the trees barely covered the shapes of the mountains with a veil of the palest see-through green. Sarah sent a picture to him every night, of her in the hotel, in a restaurant, on a boat, at the beach (not topless). His roommate saw her pictures, and the selfies Dave was sending back to her of the mountains, and of their tiny tent pitched in the dirt.

"Get real, man. This girl is from another planet. Maybe you should stick to your own kind."

Then there were no messages from her for three days. Dave faithfully texted her, but he began to think his roommate was right. Sarah was from another planet. Over those three days, as they got more used to the routine, and his body hardened, and the stark beauty of the mountains was just there, always there, to the point where he could take it for granted because that beauty was permanently impressed on his brain, he tried to convince himself that his world was just as good as Sarah's. He still couldn't really believe that was true until one evening when they finished a tough climb across a windy ridge and descended to a high, isolated meadow where, in the last rays of the setting sun, they could see a moose and her calf grazing in the distance, a spectacular sea of purple wildflowers rippling in the breeze, and Sarah sitting alone on a rock, hands on hips, waiting for him.

··· ···

> **Ms. Porter**: Did he use his bare hands to massage your back?
> **Ms. Bolt**: Well, yeah. But I couldn't see how it was going to work because I was lying on my side. I'd been to a masseuse before. I remember thinking he wasn't very good at this.
> **Q**: Did you question him about the way he was doing it?
> **A**: No. To tell you the truth, it all seemed funny to me at first. I'm sure it was the

drugs. I had forgotten about my pain
twenty minutes after I took those pills,
before I even went back to his office.

He put down the transcript and went back to his task of
apologizing to a witness who hadn't been contacted in four
months. He didn't take the transcript to his apartment that
night. He broiled a small steak and boiled some broccoli for
dinner. As he was eating it, cutting up one small triangle of
meat after another on his big white plate, he realized he never
ordered steak when he went out. He loved to eat more complicated and exotic dishes, but he'd never spent the time to learn
to make them himself. He'd always told himself there were
more important things to do. But maybe that wasn't really
true. Maybe the glorious career role he'd planned for himself
was just a dream. Maybe he would end up being Sarah's house
husband and chef. But just the idea made him squeamish.

The next morning, he put aside his list of apologetic phone
calls he had to make and peeked at the transcript again.

> **Ms. Bolt**: I didn't even realize it at the time,
> but I was probably laughing at the way he
> was doing the massage. Then his attitude
> changed like, really suddenly.
> **Ms. Porter**: In what way?
> **A**: Suddenly he was real short, quick and
> grumpy. Like he had been on my last visit.
> **Q**: Did he continue to massage you?
> **A**: He turned me onto my stomach. I
> remember saying something like "Now,
> that's more like it." I still thought it was
> funny. He grumbled something, and I
> should have realized …. Then he pulled
> me back to the edge of the table and
> pulled my panties all the way off.
> **Q**: Did you resist at that point?

A: He was so fast, it just happened in a
second.
Q: What happened?
A: He raped me.

Chapter 10

Hartwicke

18. Since your last renewal of privileges at this hospital, have you been the subject of an investigation by any law enforcement agency of the federal, state or local government for any action that may cause this institution to reasonably question your continuing qualifications to perform your functions for this institution? If yes, explain in sufficient detail on the "Additional information" section of this form.

"What does that mean?" Dr. Zeus knew he had to renew his privileges at Freeland Hospital every year. But each year, the application seemed to get longer. He immediately got on the phone to Bill Ferris, his regular attorney. "How should I answer that question? I mean, is the medical board 'a law enforcement agency?'"

"That's a good question," Ferris replied.

Zeus quietly fumed over Ferris's non-answer. "And what about *investigation*? Is the Board still investigating me?"

"As I recall, Eli Grunk was handling that Board matter for you, right?"

"Yeah." Zeus didn't say this, but he had been hoping to avoid calling Grunk, at $450 an hour, when he might get a quick answer out of his regular attorney for free. "But I thought you might be able to answer this question right off the bat."

"I can't say. I don't even know what happened at the Board. Did you ever get any kind of a close-out letter from them or anything?"

"No. I don't think so. I guess I'll have to call Grunk."

"I think that would be the wise thing to do."

Zeus called Grunk and repeated the same question.

"The short answer is yes, the Board is a law enforcement agency, and you do have to tell the hospital you are under investigation."

"But the Board's not actually investigating me any more, is it?"

"Not as far as I can tell. I mean they're not actually doing anything. But if you remember that letter we first got from the Board, their investigation officially stays open unless and until we get a close-out letter."

"That doesn't seem fair."

"Yeah, it sucks. One thing I can do. I can call them and complain. They aren't doing anything, so I could call them and argue that the case should be closed."

"Yeah, why not?"

"Okay, there's one drawback to that approach. Sometimes, if I complain like that about an old case, they just go ahead and close the case. But sometimes it has the opposite effect. Sometimes it stirs them up, and then they really heat up the investigation. Depends on what you feel more comfortable with."

"Never mind. Don't call them."

"I see." From the shift in Grunk's tone of voice, Zeus could sense that he had just been put into a different category of client, the category of clients who were guilty.

Later that day, Zeus brought up his application for hospital privileges at Freeland Hospital again on his computer. The question about whether he was currently being investigated had to be answered by checking either the "yes" or the "no" box. Grunk had told him the hospital didn't have its own investigators and was not likely to dig any deeper. Zeus checked the "no" box.

··· ···

When he dropped Diane off back at her high school after the boat ride, and just as she got out of the car, Zeus told her he was cancelling her next appointment. There was just no medical excuse for seeing her every week, or even every two weeks. That would be too dangerous; it would eventually draw someone's attention. He said he needed to see her only every six weeks. He told her she could call him on his cell phone or drop in either of his offices any time she wanted. He gave her his office schedule.

Zeus had flattered this artless young girl shamelessly during the boat ride, and it seemed to be working. But she was so emotionally poised and physically delectable he was now having daydreams about her. He was tired of his wife. He was tired of those pathetic bored housewives who whined their way into his office with their vague pains. He was tired of that hellcat Marcie. He wanted Diane, but he couldn't do her without committing a felony.

He had always dated for the sole purpose of getting the bitches into bed: girls when he was young, then women, flattering some, wheedling others, drugging some. He believed it was unfair that women held the keys to satisfying his primal needs. Their manipulative traits, and the fact that they didn't really need sex like he did, gave them all the natural advantages. On top of that, all of the rules of society were skewed in women's favor. So, for all of his life, Zeus had done everything in his power to level that playing field. His approach had grown immeasurably more sophisticated over the years, but he had been playing basically the same game since high school.

High school studies had been easy for him. He took no part in the nervous speculation about tests or projects or the SAT that the other students in the advanced classes constantly droned on about. He knew he was smarter. He was of medium height and had always been good looking, though the popular girls mostly ignored him in favor of the Neanderthal jocks. That didn't bother him, at least at first. His father was very successful and was often away on business. His mother did nothing, as far as he could see. He started driving his father's new Jaguar whenever he was out of town. He didn't ask permission, and his mother was afraid to stop him. Instead of getting a job, he got his father to pay him for getting As. He multiplied the money by dealing pot. He never had to approach people to sell because the car was magnet enough.

Kirsten was smart and skinny and flat chested, and he had guessed correctly that with the right kind of encouragement she would part her long legs to give him access to her hot little slot. She was a loner. He never saw her talking to any other girls at school. She didn't try to fawn all over him at school. She took him to her bedroom one day after school, then again on the same day the next week. Like a trained dog, he salivated in anticipation the third week, but she said she had something else to do. He was furious. It wasn't enough for him that they did it the following week. He couldn't stand being under her control. Kirsten didn't act impressed with his car, his looks, his brains or his clothes. It seemed like she was just using him to satisfy herself whenever she was in rut. So he slipped her a roofie on a study date one night. She woke on her basement sofa in the middle of the night without any idea what had happened. So he did it again the next time he saw her.

Kirsten wasn't so stupid as to let it happen a third time. Her chemistry grades were even higher than his. She never let him near one of her drinks again. He tried to ply her with pot to persuade her to do it on an off-night, but she just narrowed her eyes like she was gauging if he was worth the trouble. Apparently, he wasn't. He was willing to double down to get what he wanted from her. He let his connection use his father's car for a night in exchange for half a gram of cocaine. It hit her just like it was supposed to, and she asked him in, begged for more. He thought it was a fair trade, but after they did it once or twice more she disappeared from school and he never saw her again.

That old teenage affair seemed colorless in retrospect. He remembered her narrow, pale face with that snippy little mouth and the way she would occasionally raise a single thick, truncated eyebrow to question something he was saying, but he couldn't hear her voice or remember a single thing she's ever said. He didn't have any curiosity about where she was now. He just remembered the sweet deal they had once she was under his control. When his father died, he kept the car, never bothering to get it registered in his name until he was stopped for a speeding ticket in college, when the police wanted to know how it could belong to a man who'd been dead three years.

By the time he got back to his office from the boat ride he was overwhelmed with fantasies of fucking Diane. The fact that it would be the most dangerous seduction he had ever tried made the fantasy irresistible. She would be pure jailbait on his boat, or in his condo, or even on the sofa in the basement of his house, so he focused on the only way he could legally touch her. It wouldn't be the same, of course, but maybe it would ease his urgency for the time being. And maybe that would be a good way to break her in.

When he walked back into his regular office, everyone, including the receptionist, was a little more friendly than usual. Apparently, his $75,000 payment to his practice partners had bought a lot of cheer. That was the amount his lawyer Ferris had told him was the minimum amount that would keep them from suing him right now.

Chapter 11

Diane

Woody didn't tell me at first whose garage he lived in. I went over there to ask another favor of him, but then I got really curious about his situation.

"Ms. Nesbitt! You mean our teacher from middle school? That's her house? You live in her garage?"

He got a look on his face like he was used to being laughed at. I felt bad for making such a big deal of it.

"Yeah. I'm eighteen. I can live where I want. I can't afford a real place to live."

If you had to live in a garage, I guess it wasn't so bad. He had a fancy, half worn out oriental carpet on the floor, a real bed and a desk. You came in through a door on the side. On the back of the garage there was a window that he put in. It lightened up the room a lot. "You won't believe this, Woody. I was so dumb when I was fourteen, I used to think you lived in the woods." He didn't say anything about how dumb I used to be, so I went on. "What about your parents?"

"My mother's dead. My father split."

"Oh. I'm sorry. What do you do for a bathroom? And what about food?"

"She lets me use her bathroom. And refrigerator. I cook mostly on the grill outside."

"You cook your own food?"

"Yeah, and sometimes for her too. I know how to cook. I've been cooking since I was ten."

I guess I should have known that the guy who got a whole crowd of middle school kids to sneak out of their houses after midnight and skateboard down the trail by flashlight, drink whiskey and cook hot dogs at illegal bonfires in the woods, and smoke pot, would know how to take care of himself. I knew he was the right guy to answer my question without making a big deal about it.

"Woody, what are these pills?" I reached into my jeans pocket. I pulled out a couple of them and held them in my palm up toward his face. They were little round white pills with something that looked like the outline of a breast cancer ribbon cut into one side.

"Where'd you get them?"

"From a doctor."

"Why don't you just look on the label?"

"There's no label. He just gave me a bunch and told me to take one when I feel bad."

I was pretty sure Woody knew a lot about drugs. And he wouldn't hound me about the whole thing. That was one reason I liked him.

"Let me see." I poured them into his hand. He stared at the markings on the pills like he was studying sacred writings. "Xanax," he said finally.

"What do they do?"

"Supposed to mellow you out. Your doctor didn't tell you what they're for?"

"He said to make me happy."

I'd never seen Woody frown before. "That sounds like something I used to say. This guy's a drug dealer?"

"No, of course not. But ...." He kept staring at me like he knew there was more to it. And there was. I felt I could tell him then. "I might be falling in love with him."

His grey eyes widened. He had been sitting on the edge of his bed, but then he lay back and propped himself up on an elbow, his eyes still focused on me. He didn't say anything.

"It's kind of weird, I know," I said to fill the silence. He still didn't say anything. I sighed, tried to smile. "I guess there's no use in me trying to get interested in normal guys."

He sat back up, his hands down on the bed on either side of him. He was quietly rocking back and forth, like he was thinking hard.

"I wouldn't know about normal," he said then. More slow rocking. "We can't take these pills here, though. Ms. Nesbitt made me promise there would be no drugs in here – except pot. I think she might smoke that herself. That is one good lady. I just can't lie to her."

I hadn't come there to take the pills with him. But I didn't say that. I decided right then I would take one with him if he wanted, as long as they weren't some kind of heavy-duty narcotics, which he said they weren't.

As soon as you tell someone a secret it seems like half the effort in your social life is trying to manage things so it doesn't get out. I didn't want even Kate to know about me and Dr. Zeus, but at the same time I really wanted her to get to know what Woody was like now. When I told Kate I wanted her to meet him, she asked what did I mean, she already knew him. I said, "You know Rat, but you don't know Woody. Did you know he worked with your mother for a while, in that company Anton owns?"

"No! Is that true?" Kate used to be a little short but she'd grown taller in the last two years. Her thick blonde hair was cut shorter now, bobbed straight and turned under at her jawline. I had forgotten how much I missed being with her, laughing along with those smiling green eyes. I was afraid the fun we used to have had just been a kid thing, a young childhood thing – and once I had a child of my own I had to put away the things of childhood. But now we were laughing again.

I guess I don't have the right to say that Kate was lucky. My parents were both still there and pretty nice to me. Kate's mother left her father when Kate was fourteen, and she didn't even try to take Kate with her. And to make the whole thing even more embarrassing, she left to live with Anton, a loud and really tacky local real estate guy who even the kids know is a total asshole. But I still do think Kate was lucky. She met Lucky, this really solid and great looking guy who knows everybody, and everything that's going on, and is funny as shit. Kate and Lucky got together back then, and they were still with each other two years later. I knew it was going to be one of those things where boy and girl fall in love at fourteen and it lasts for the rest of their lives. I was already disqualified from that ever happening to me.

Woody is maybe not the guy you'd pick to help repair yourself socially, but I arranged for Kate and Lucky and me to get together with him in his garage one afternoon. Woody and Lucky had been both friends and rivals for king of the woods in the old days, but I wanted them to see the new Woody. Everyone was nervous until we smoked a little pot. Woody told them about his first job, which was working in Anton's real estate office.

"I was the runner. I was the guy they sent to go find stuff, or pick up anybody that needed picking up. I was trying to figure out how the whole business worked, but they had me outside picking up packages for Anton all the time. Anyway, after about six weeks he asked me to score some cocaine for him."

"Did you do it?"

"Hell no. I felt like: *is this shit never going to end?* You know what I mean? I quit right then. When I told her what happened, Ms. Nesbitt convinced me to go back. She said tell Anton I would be applying for other jobs and I wanted a *super-excellent* reference from him. You should have seen his face. He typed it up and gave it to me before I even left."

"Did you talk to my Mom much when you were there?" Kate asked.

"Not really. What was I going to say: 'Hey, I used to give your daughter wine coolers in the woods?'"

Like I asked him to, Woody kept secret what I had told him about Dr. Zeus.

••• •••

I went out on the boat again with Dr. Zeus. It didn't start all smoothly like the last time. He called my cell about two weeks after the first boat ride and asked me to come into his office at the church. I asked him why, and he really didn't answer. Instead he asked me if I had taken any of those pills he had given me.

"The Xanax? Yeah." I didn't mention that I had taken only one.

He told me if I was anxious about the appointment I should take one or two before I came in. When I got to his office, I went through the regular routine where you go in the room and somebody comes in and tells you to take your clothes off. So I was sitting there in my underwear with that paper gown on when he came in kind of out of breath and wanted to put my feet in the stirrups right away. I said no. My heart was beating fast but I just felt like: *no.*

"Didn't you take those pills?" he said right away. "I thought that would calm you down. I know this isn't your favorite part of our visits."

I told him I had, but that was a lie. I sat there and didn't move. We kind of stared each other down. It went on for a long time. He stepped back, looking a little freaked out.

"Okay," he said finally, his voice almost cracking. "Okay. I can see you're nervous about the exam. Those pills don't work the same for everyone. We can skip the exam. Should we just talk?"

Even though he was my doctor and knew everything about me, inside and out, I didn't tell him about Woody. I told him my sister was suspicious about where I was that time we went out on the boat. I told him I had kissed Robert once and how that turned into him having some kind of bizarro crush on me. He asked me if I secretly, deep down, liked Robert having a crush on me.

"You got to be kidding. He makes me want to puke."

He laughed. The happy look was back in his eyes. Then he asked, in a kind of a humble way, in a voice so low I could hardly hear, if I "might" want to go out on his boat again the next day. "The toilet has been completely cleaned up since the last time."

I said I would go. He asked me what kind of wine I liked. I said I don't know, how about wine coolers? I thought maybe that was a juvenile drink, but I wasn't going to start pretending I was all sophisticated. I didn't have to pretend. He kept telling me all the time he liked me the way I was. I was a little afraid of what drinking might lead to, but I wanted to find out.

The marina people greeted him so nicely I knew he had paid his bill. They all kind of looked down at their feet each time I came by like they'd never seen a tall, purple-haired sixteen-year-old girl before. I could tell they knew I wasn't his daughter. He wore a blue bathing suit and a black polo shirt this time. I wore the same white pants, over my bathing suit this time. He let me drive the boat all the way out of the marina and down the river to the bay. I liked having control of the thing. I drove a lot slower than he did. You could see the people in the other boats better that way. I waved to them all.

He showed me buoys and how they worked.

"What? No GPS?"

"That's on that screen there. It's not working. Just look at the buoys. *Red-right-return.* That's all you really need to know for today. Stay on the correct side of the buoys."

"What happens if you don't?"

"You crash. The hull is crushed. The boat sinks. You drown if you don't have a life jacket strapped on."

"Do we have life jackets on this boat?"

"They're in a cabinet down below. I never bother with them."

"We're not going to crash."

It was pretty much the same route as the last time, except we went farther across the bay because there weren't any big ships in the channel. I wanted to go up front, so he took the wheel. The water was so calm and he was going so slow I could stand up, at least with my feet spread apart. I took off my blouse and pants and dropped them on the deck. My bathing suit was a teal bikini, pretty small. You never know for sure if you look like just a bunch of bones or like somebody's fantasy sex dream, but when I turned around and caught him looking I wasn't worried.

I laid the towel at the base of the windshield and sat on it cross-legged, holding my arms up into the wind like I was on a roller coaster. We shouted a conversation over the top of the windshield. He seemed to be staring at me. I was glancing to see how long he kept looking. At the same time, I was thinking: what the hell am I doing? When he turned away to look at the shore, I put the towel on the windshield and lay back on it.

Later I stood behind the wheel and steered the boat back. He sat on the cushions behind me, and I heard the fizz as he opened a beer. I was going a little faster and the boat was leaning from side to side as I weaved in and out of the other boats, but then he told me that was illegal because our wake could screw up the smaller boats. I didn't mention he had been going twice that fast the first time we were out there. Almost everybody I waved to waved back. There were a lot of other women who looked great in their bikinis. I wondered how many of them were wives, or if this was just where you took your secret girlfriends. The white boat made a path of foam through the smooth blue-green surface of the water. The breeze felt great on my bare skin. There was this awesome feeling of not knowing what would happen next.

"Let's go back to that cove across the river from the marina, where we stopped last time," he said.

"Okay." I steered there. "Can you get the anchor and throw it out?"

He obeyed automatically, and that brought on a little rush all by itself. The boat slowly swung around in a half circle at the end of the anchor line. He was looking at me. He patted the seat for me to sit down next to him. I did, but without touching him. He looked gorgeous, and I wanted to run my fingers through his dark hair with its little touch of grey at the sideburns. Just stop it, I told myself.

"What's your wife like?" I said.

"I am married," he said. "Legally married. My wife and I haven't touched in four years." I stared at him, my mouth open. Who could be married to this guy and not want to touch him? Did this really happen in marriages? He went on. "You have to imagine what it's like to live with someone who doesn't want to have sex with you, doesn't want to talk to you, doesn't really even see you."

"But I can't believe any woman wouldn't want to …. You're so cool. And so nice."

He looked at me close, met my eyes. "Thank you. You're very kind." He looked away over the river. "It doesn't do any good to have all the money and success in the world if you can't open up and share yourself with someone."

I was thinking he could share with me if he wanted to. Is that what he meant? I didn't say anything, and after a minute he went on.

"Forgive me if I've been acting too forward. You've brought me the happiness that's been missing for so long in my life. I have to go for that happiness, Diane."

A little shiver went through me because I thought I knew what he was talking about. I didn't say anything.

"I've been very lonely for a long time," he sighed. "I didn't want to admit it, even to myself. You inspired me to admit it. Then you cured it. I can't thank you enough."

So, he put his hand on top of my hand, which was resting on my leg. I was too stirred up to think. I had to be careful what I said because everything I said mattered to him. I didn't want to hurt him. I wanted to make him feel better. And I wanted to feel better too. His touch was making my body jump inside, making it itch for more.

The boat swayed up and down in a passing wake. I knew most people would think I was a jerk if I made love to him. But most people already thought I was a jerk anyway. When you're sixteen and you've already had a baby and you've given it away to God knows who, you're in another universe. Every step forward is onto a strange planet.

I turned to let him kiss me. He was so gentle at first I almost melted inside. I let him strip me, and we put the boat cushions on the floor. He whispered my name every time he came up for air. He knew just where I wanted to be touched. I was losing control, making noises, but I managed to stop and ask if he had a condom. That was the only downside. For an instant he got a pained look on his face like he was making love to an ice queen, one who gave up her baby, one who sent her baby's father away. But I said he had to, and he put one on.

Chapter 12

Hartwicke

He took her in the cockpit of the boat, her long white limbs splayed out over the bed of cushions he had made on the floor, her breath hot in his ear just as a cool breeze off the river tickled his ass. He wasn't used to working this hard for a piece of pussy. But there was something extraordinary about this teenager. Even as she molded herself to his body he knew that he was not entirely in control. The intimate, sliding touch of the condom with each move reminded him that she was calling the shots. They both knew she was jailbait. But it wasn't just that. Pliant as her body was, there was a steely will deep inside that withheld from Zeus the total female surrender that he had always thought of as his due.

He was quiet afterwards, and she didn't try to engage him in conversation. She just arranged herself comfortably around his body and let him put his hands wherever he wanted. She didn't put her bathing suit back on until it was time for her to drive back across the river to the marina. Even there, she walked boldly through the marina workers wearing just that little thing, almost daring them to stare. None did. She carried her clothes to the marina bathroom and put them on there.

"So, what are you thinking?" she suddenly asked. She'd drunk only one tiny paper cup of the bottle of Merlot he'd brought along. He'd finished the bottle by the time he pulled his rented Kia out of the marina. This was the dangerous time with women. When the tenderness they wanted after sex didn't come, when the male arm didn't stay curved protectively around them as their hormones of helplessness flowed, they could lash out with a viciousness proportional to their previous passion. Diane was especially dangerous because what he did was actually illegal, a felony. He'd made sure to tell her she was extraordinarily beautiful and passionate, and that he'd never met a woman with such spirit. It was hardly a lie. But she'd been eerily quiet on the way back.

"You're thinking … what?" she went on. "That I'm okay – for a teenager?"

He mumbled something.

"What?"

"*Goddess*. I was thinking: *goddess*."

She didn't say "thank you" like he expected, nor did she smile a little simpering smile like he feared. He loved her for that. She wasn't surprised. And why should a goddess be surprised?

"I'd like to give you something, as a present," he said as they wound their way up the steep, narrow, tree-lined road toward the main highway.

"Please don't say money."

"God, I didn't mean that! I mean I'd like to give you a real present, something beautiful you could look at sometimes and maybe think about me. Jewelry or something."

"I'm not really big into jewelry."

"I'd like to take you on another trip sometime, one where we could be together all day, maybe all night."

"Yeah, that would be great. I don't know how I'd ever get away with that, though."

Zeus instantly recognized the dilemma he'd gotten himself into. The same tender youth that made her so fresh and pliable also trapped her into a supervised routine that even a physician could hardly penetrate. The laws violated the whole concept of evolution by keeping the most desirable males like him from copulating with the most desirable females at the peak of their ripeness. The more desirable they were, the less access was granted. He could work his way out of that trap only if she too was extraordinarily willing and resourceful. But he suddenly felt crazily optimistic. He was starting to believe she would keep surprising him.

· · · · · · ·

He was in such a mellow mood after fucking Diane he didn't think anything his wife said could bother him, but then Elena started nagging him about the car. The dealer had charged their credit card $275 for an oil change for the Jaguar. She couldn't believe it needed an oil change since it had been supposedly sitting at the dealership and hadn't been driven for three months. It was one of those rare nights when they ate dinner together. Elena didn't deign to cook for him any more, but she had created a list of restaurants that delivered really excellent, high-end food. The minute Kyra left the table to do her homework, Elena started hounding him.

"You said you would pick up that car. If you don't have a single spare hour to go over there and get it, I will."

"All right! All right." The words came out loud and flat, with a hint of resignation. Almost everything she said annoyed him now. She had seemed to be such a sweet little bunny when he first met her in the hospital, her dark hair always short and pert, her brown eyes bold, her speech curt and candid. She worked in personnel at his hospital at the time, and she had been assigned to investigate some trivial complaint some nurse had filed against him. Elena declined his invitation to discuss the allegations over dinner at a restaurant of her choice. He had been impressed by the fact that he couldn't throw her investigation off course. It was a matter of ethics, she claimed. Her investigation had resulted in a private letter of reprimand from the hospital. The letter had no effect whatsoever on his career, and in fact he'd been able to have it removed from his personnel file three years later. But he'd pursued her after the investigation was closed. Her father was then CEO of another hospital. Not a bad connection to make. Zeus had wanted to see if he could get her interested in him once her ethics were put to the side.

He had suspected this woman couldn't uphold in her own life those impersonal professional standards she adhered to so strictly on the job. He had been right. It was just a role she played on the job. In her personal life she had the same needs and weaknesses as any other woman. She surrendered to the alpha male in him. She fell in love with his looks and his charisma and his power and his money. After Kyra was born, however, those impersonal standards started to creep back into their marriage. There was now a measure to things, and he was not measuring up. A night out at a fancy restaurant no longer did it. The condo at the beach did it only for a while. The boat didn't help at all.

"Don't yell, Hardy. Just get the car. We can't afford to let Avis keep running up the bill for that rented Kia when your Jaguar is just sitting there at the dealership. I'm taking a half day off Wednesday. If you don't get that car back by then I'll go get it myself."

There was no room for error in her straight fucking logic. She'd gotten pretty far in the field of human resources by stepping up to the plate fearlessly time and time again. She could hit any fastball thrown at her. But he knew she'd never make it in the big leagues because she didn't really understand power. She wouldn't bend. She could never hit a curve.

He had drunk almost the whole bottle of Merlot in the boat and the car, followed by three gin and tonics at dinner. Visions of Diane's naked body, and echoes of her helpless whimpers, floated around in his mind, making it hard to concentrate on Elena's demands. He held himself together enough to avoid a lecture from her about his drinking. He did need to get the damn car back. He told her he'd do it Wednesday.

"On Wednesday we have to go to the interview for Concord Mews."

"Jesus Christ! Don't they know who we are? Didn't you tell them who we are? We already applied. We already paid the deposit. Kyra's got the grades to get in. Why do we have to go there and beg, too? And why Wednesday?"

Sometimes she just doubled down. There it was, that molded haircut with nothing out of place, the stylish but modest glasses pushed back so as not to distract from the importance of the lecture she was about to give, the neutral facial expression not quite hiding the condescension underneath, the hands folded on the table. Next would come the human resources voice. He couldn't stand that patronizing human resources voice. He was glad she didn't work at his hospital any more.

But Elena was more blatantly accusatory than usual. "Because, Hardy, Concord Mews, the school *you* insisted on for Kyra, absolutely requires a parent interview. And because we've known that for six months. And because at your request I've already put it off until the last possible date."

"Well, then I better go get that goddam car tonight." He gulped down the rest of his drink and stood up and powered away from the table without another word, slamming the door on his way out.

••• •••

Jesus Christ, she parked in his spot! He screeched his Kia to a stop right behind the Jaguar now parked so brazenly in the hospital parking lot right under the brown wooden sign with the letters "Reserved for Dr. Zeus" etched in silver paint. At least this meant she was there now, on shift in the hospital. He'd find her and take those keys from her if he had to wrench her arm off. He gunned the engine to drive toward the general employee parking lot, but then screeched to a stop again before he got twenty feet. He wasn't going to waste even that much time. He ditched the Kia in the middle of the driveway and got out of the car to run to the hospital entrance.

He was just inside the employee entrance, just about to show his credentials to the security guard who was eyeing him oddly, when he heard the roar of the Jaguar's engine outside. He banged back outside through the door just in time to see it jounce over the speedbumps in the parking lot so fast both ends sparked on the ground. Marcie must have been sitting in the Jaguar when he pulled up behind it. She must have hidden down low in the seat and waited for him to pull the Kia away. If only he had known he had her trapped! Now he could only watch as she pulled out onto the street. He ran back to the Kia, which was standing in the middle of the driveway with the driver's side door still open. There was a security guard approaching it just as Zeus jumped in and slammed the door.

She lived on a street of tiny brick, one-story houses, two-bed-room mostly, though in some cases a third had been added. She had a little yard that didn't have much grass, probably due to the high canopy of shade trees. She'd lived there since before she had kids, before she was married. She seemed rooted in that neighborhood. She had always had the self-assurance of someone who knew where she came from, together with a catlike strength that seemed to grow from those roots. He didn't understand her at all. He pulled to the side of the road a few feet from her driveway and waited with his lights off. The street lighting was spotty, and there were no lampposts right in front of her house.

Finally she arrived and turned in the driveway, her head-lights flashing across his Kia as she turned. He had a moment of panic when he saw her drive all the way down the driveway toward her little wooden one-car garage, but then he realized she'd never take the trouble to lock *his* car in a garage. And, knowing Marcie, the garage would be full of junk anyway.

He pulled into the driveway behind her, thinking he would

easily block her, but she suddenly backed up so fast he had to slam on his brakes. Then she turned the wheel and curved the Jag onto her front lawn. He turned too and they played a game of chicken on the front lawn as he tried to keep her from crossing onto the road. Alcohol and adrenaline surging through his body, Zeus blocked her again and again. Finally she put the Jag in first and stepped on the gas, sending up a shower of dirt and torn-up grass onto Zeus's windshield as she raced back to the driveway. He beat her to the end of the driveway, but she tried to squeeze past him until there was a very expensive-sounding crunching noise and both cars stopped. The Jag was pinned between his Kia and a high, thick hedge.

He found himself standing behind the cars. It was dark, both engines were off, and the silence was scary. He counted to thirty, but her door didn't open and no sound at all came from her car. He checked his face and chest with his fingers, trying to tell by the sense of touch whether he was bleeding. He knew people sometimes didn't feel their injuries at first. He couldn't feel any blood with his fingers. He checked that his arms and his legs and all his fingers worked. Still no sound from the Jag. The Kia had hit it on the passenger side, near the headlight. The driver's side was wedged against the hedge. He felt his way carefully around the Jag in the darkness. He was sure Marcie never wore a seatbelt. The accident hadn't happened on a public road, so he figured he wouldn't have to report it if she wasn't injured.

He edged his way between the hedge and the car toward the driver's-side door. He jumped when he saw the window silently coming down, seemingly on its own. He could see nothing but blackness inside. The old Jag didn't have power windows, so she had to be alive enough to roll it down.

"Marcie, are you okay?"

"You fucker!"

"Are you bleeding? You got to get out of there. You could

be in shock and not realize it."

"Don't be such a wuss. Move that car, and I'll get out and give you the keys."

"I can't trust you on that, Marcie."

He stood there until she finally squeezed herself out of the window, forcing him to edge his way back out. Then she stood behind the car. He noticed she was not hyperventilating, and he tried to follow her lead on that. His eyes were getting used to the dim light. He could see that her hair was cut short now. She always wore tight clothes to emphasize her shapely but wiry body, and those generous plastic breasts.

"We need to go inside, in the light."

She punched him in the face.

Eventually he got her pinned against the car so she couldn't knee him. He dragged her toward the house, the two of them wrestling together in a kind of punch-drunk waltz. He knew she was calming down by then because she didn't try to bite him.

"My keys," she said. He let her get her house keys out to open her front door, but as she stepped inside he put his foot in the door and grabbed them back, staring at the key ring after she turned on the lights. He frantically pulled the Jag key off. Then he looked at her.

"Check your pulse and blood pressure, Marcie."

"Oh, I bet you'd *love* to do that." She took his hand and put it on her chest, under her breast, and held it there. She was breathing hard. Her pulse was strong and definitely elevated. What was that look on her face? Surly? Her mouth was slightly open, her flame-red hair framing those ever-defiant eyes. Then she shocked him by checking his own pulse, but with her hand in a different place, a very unusual place to check for a pulse. He knew she would find a strong one there. That's what she liked. The woman was every bit as uncivilized as he was. They felt their heat rise together. She opened her mouth, and his opened as if on command.

Chapter 13

Diane

I guess I wasn't meant to live a normal life. The next day, before I could even find my old friends Kate and Lucky and my new friend Woody in school, I got called to the principal's office. I knew I'd done some things with Dr. Zeus that weren't supposed to be right, but I would be an adult in a year and a half and couldn't see the harm in jumping ahead a little. I was afraid the school might notice that I cut another half day of school and soccer practice. Dr. Zeus wrote me a note for that. That would work for the school, but I couldn't show it to my parents, or make it sound right to Lisa.

"Oh, yes. You're Diane, right?" the school secretary said. "Go right in the office back there." Then, just as I was going in, she called after me, "There's someone from your church in there. He says he's a deacon."

"Jesus Christ!" I said to Robert as soon as the door closed behind me. "A black shirt now, too? You're pretending to be Pastor now?"

"I am sort of your pastor now." When he said that, there was a weight to his voice that scared me. There was a desk in that tiny room with a chair behind it and a couple other chairs facing it. He was sitting on the edge of the desk with his knees sticking out so wherever I stood I was practically touching him.

"The pastor of your soul," he went on slowly, taking his time. I got the idea he was enjoying how uncomfortable I was in that little room. His face had that blessed look he used in church after he'd succeeded in making people uncomfortable, to show them he was the only calm one who would be able to give them the cure.

"Move your legs over so I can sit down," I said. He got off the desk and sat in the little chair behind it, moving quick like a scared little boy. "Okay, why are you here?"

"Pastor Bill had a stroke. Just a small one, but I handle a lot of the church stuff for him now."

"Oh. I'm sorry."

He didn't say anything.

"Well, thanks for telling me." I got up to go.

"That's not why I'm here. Please, please, sit down." I did. "I promise you, Diane. I'm not trying to engage in any physical contact with you."

"Okay. What is it, then?"

"I love you, Diane." I guess he heard me sigh because he went on real quickly. "I can't stop thinking about you, day and night. You are with me every second of every day."

It made me queasy to think I was in his head that much. My heart was racing. I counted the steps to the door. Then I thought, no, that's not fair. I knew what he was feeling. "I'm sorry. I don't love you, Robert."

"I didn't understand it before. I didn't understand why Jesus would allow me to suffer so much yearning, so much pain. But now I understand why. Jesus has forced me to understand you, to focus my whole life on you. Now I understand God's plan."

"Good for you." I stood up and stepped toward the door without looking back.

"I know you've been seeing Doctor Zeus."

My hand was already on the doorknob, but his words froze me right there. When I'm attacked, I automatically think about what my Dad would do. So, even though my knees were shaking and my armpits started dripping sweat, I took a quick breath and turned around.

"My doctor's appointments are none of your business." I could feel my face getting red, but I forced myself to meet his eyes.

"They are the church's business," he said, now suddenly in his bland, blessed tone. "I have access to all of the church's financial records. The church is paying the copays for your doctor's visits. Jesus has moved me to search out everything about you. You've seen Dr. Zeus five times in the last two months."

So he was stalking me. I had already suspected that. But then it dawned on me that maybe that was all he knew – that I saw Dr. Zeus five times.

"He's my doctor, you idiot." I knew I was channeling Dad.

"He's the church's doctor *for pregnant girls.*"

"I'm not pregnant."

"You have fornicated again. Diane, I don't blame you for giving in, for defiling yourself again. You must have so many temptations, so many men on their knees."

"I haven't seen any men on their knees."

But then I saw my first one.

"Jesus has chosen me to save your new child from the abomination of abortion. Please. Let this precious child be born, and I will be the father like Joseph acted the father unto Jesus."

"You are out of your fucking mind." I had to hold myself back from smacking that pompous nineteen-year-old face. "Leave me alone or I'll get my Dad to call Pastor."

"Ha!" He suddenly stood up. His face was almost touching mine. I stared him back a step. He started jiggling like he couldn't stand still. "Your Dad thinks I'm a nice kid! Your Mom treats me like I'm her adopted son!"

"So what?"

"Pastor's so sick I'm practically running the church anyway. Who do you think writes his sermons? Who do you think tells him what papers to sign and what not to sign? Who shops for him, who cleans his house? Who cuts his fingernails?"

... ...

Soccer is a different world. I mean, people were made to run, right? And twist, and pivot, and dance with a ball that's alive and obedient and wild all at once. And pass it to someone else who dances with it in her own way and passes it back, and you pass it back again and the two or three or four of you create a whole living choreography that's beautiful but different every time. The other girls were a little pissed at first that I took the place of one of their friends on the first team, but they started to think I was okay after a while. The coach pretended not to like it that we laughed so much, but it was really fun to laugh again.

I asked Woody to wait for me after the next practice because I was afraid Robert was stalking me. When practice was over I saw Woody sitting way at the top of the stands. There were only two or three other people there. Robert wasn't there.

"I forgot you were supposed to work after school today," I was climbing up into to the stands to see him, my spikes clanging on the aluminum steps. "I never would have asked you. I could have gotten somebody else. I'm sorry."

"I could tell you were scared."

Fifteen minutes later we were in his tiny garage house. He sat on his bed so I could have the only chair. I reached into my pocket. "I don't know what these are." I showed him the pills Dr. Zeus gave me the day before.

"Holy shit! Oxycodone. You don't want to take these. I didn't know doctors could hand these out."

"It's his own stash. I mean *prescription*." I started laughing. I was thinking of the way Dr. Zeus had poured out the pills from a prescription bottle onto a white piece of paper on the console of his car, then divided some off for me with a plastic knife left over from our picnic on the boat. His hands were shaking then, which was so the opposite of the way he usually was. He didn't even seem like a doctor then, which is why I accidentally called it his stash.

Woody breathed out real slowly, not meeting my eyes. "Diane, I know a lot about those pills. You seriously don't want to take them."

"Come on. He's a doctor ...." Then I stopped. There was a new feeling that had been sort of creeping up on me. I needed Woody to know I took him seriously. I looked at him "Really?"

He had a faraway look in his eyes. "Don't take them," was all he said. Maybe taking him seriously meant I shouldn't demand that he prove everything he said. I wanted to show I believed him, so I walked outside and threw all the pills in Ms. Nesbitt's garbage can.

I told him I was still dating Dr. Zeus. Woody wasn't the kind of person who would criticize. He gave the impression he'd been where you'd been and he understood. But I might have been just imagining he was okay with me dating Zeus. He didn't really say very much.

"Does he say he's in love with you or something?" Woody finally mumbled.

"Not exactly. But he did call me a goddess."

His laughter made him cough. He put down the joint he had just started, wiped his eyes.

"I'm glad you think it's so funny."

"I got no clue about this kind of thing," he said after a minute. "It sounds like he likes you. But I don't know. You're flying in a totally different world than I am."

"Don't you think it's all the same world?"

Woody reached all the way over to put his joint in an ashtray on the desk across from the bed. His sleeves were rolled up and his crude tattoo was showing. "Diane, I'm not anyway near in the same world as you."

Chapter 14

David

"I can't tell you my name, sir."

Dave sighed. He tried to keep his voice calm while resisting the urge to scrunch up the blank intake form with his free hand. This was his first Intake Day. People were supposed to file their complaints online or in writing. But the Board still had a phone line, so somebody had to answer it. The guy on the line wouldn't say who he was.

"Can you at least tell me if you are the girl's father?"

"No, but I'm sure the doctor is getting ready to perform an abortion on her."

"How do you know? Have you seen any of the medical records?"

"No, but I have financial records that show she has seen this doctor six times in the past two months."

This had been going on for ten minutes. Dave wanted to hang up and get some advice from Michele and call back, but the caller wouldn't even give his number. Dave finally just put him on hold. That meant he had to barge in on Michele while she was having a conversation with another investigator, a middle-aged blonde woman with a distraught look on her face.

Michele waved him in. "You look a little frantic."

"My first Intake Day. Sorry. Can I talk to you just for a second, Michele? I have this guy on the phone." He looked pleadingly at the blonde investigator, who sighed, then slowly got up out of the chair and left. "Sorry to interrupt your conversation," he said to Michele as respectfully as he could. "The guy's on hold."

"David," she began very formally, "you have just interrupted a 20-minute *introduction* to a conversation about Kendall's cat, Fluffy. Fluffy apparently has some type of digestive problem. I was looking forward to getting into the details of her illness when you cut in. Now, what is the silly little medical board problem you want to talk about?"

He was going to like working with Michele.

"I'm on intake and I have this guy on hold. He won't tell me his name. He says there's this doctor who has seen this teenage patient six times in the past two months and is getting ready to perform an abortion on her without her parents' knowledge. I'm totally lost here. I mean, I don't even know if the doctor has to tell the parents or not. Aren't they always changing the law on that?"

"They are, but you don't have to worry about that. This isn't an abortion."

"What?"

"Nobody goes to a doctor six times for an abortion. They're done as quickly as possible, usually on the first visit. Never later than the second visit. This girl is going to the doctor for something else."

"So, what should I tell this guy? That he's a complete igno-ramus about these things – like me?"

"Tell him thousands of girls go to doctors every day for different reasons, and we can't open a case based on his suspi-cions without a lot more specific information. You do have to wonder why a guy with no specific information is so interested in a teenage girl's gynecological problems – but don't say that to him."

Back at his desk, Dave looked at the still-blank intake form before he picked up the phone again. The caller had sounded so earnest, and he had jumped into the story so quickly, that Dave hadn't been able to fill out any information at all on the form before running to Michele for advice. Michele had told him making a record of the call would protect him if the caller later complained about how Dave treated him. Dave was determined now to get at least some basic information on the form before ending the call.

But the caller again talked around and around Dave's questions, and Dave could not get him to give his name or provide any real facts. Dave scrunched up the form without having made a single mark on it.

"I'm sorry, sir," Dave finally gave up. "But you haven't provided us with enough information to open any kind of case."

"So the medical board does not even care what Dr. Zeus is doing to that girl?"

… …

Ms. Porter: Did you agree to have sex with him at that time, Katherine?
Ms. Bolt: No.
Q: Did you tell him to stop?
A: When I realized what was happening, yes.
Q: Did you scream or call out?
A: No. I was too shocked. It happened real quick.
Q: How long would you say it took?
A: Real short. He was real fast. But the look in his eyes afterward – it was awful.
Q: And you didn't call the police?
A: No.
Q: Why not?
A: I was so ashamed.
Q: Why should you be ashamed? You were drugged, then attacked.
A: I didn't want my husband to know. I didn't want the police, you know, examining me. I wanted to pretend it never happened.
Q: And was that the last time you saw Dr. Zeus?

A: Do I have to answer that?

....

Frank refused to open an investigation, even after Dave had finally pried the patient's name out of the anonymous caller. "One anonymous caller thinks one adolescent girl is getting an abortion without her parents' permission, but we know for a fact he's totally wrong," Frank scoffed. "That's not a case. That's not even the beginning of a case."

"But it's Dr. Zeus. He saw this girl six times."

"That's what doctors do. They see sick people. A number of times. Forget it, Newbie. We'd be shooting in the dark. And Zeus will claim we're harassing him."

Without an investigation being opened, Dave could not issue a subpoena. In fact, he couldn't do anything more with the case. He did file a fresh intake sheet, one that now had the names of Dr. Zeus and his patient, Diane Morrell, written on it, in the non-public correspondence files of the Board. Michele told him not to do anything else on the case.

"But it's Dr. Zeus! He might be doing again what he did to Katherine Bolt. We're going to just let this go?"

"Yes, we are, Dave. We are a professional board. We only act when there is enough evidence." Michele's eyes flashed with irritation, and Dave was taken aback. She had become his unofficial mentor, and his only friend, among the staff. He swallowed hard at the aggravation in her voice. A few weeks earlier she might have explained very gently to him the ways of the world, but now she expected more of him. Worried that maybe he didn't have tough enough skin for this job, he lowered his head and went back to his cubicle.

He stared at the far wall of his cubicle where he had now pinned a calendar next to the picture of Sarah. The two items were related. Time was ticking away in his life while Sarah was building a real career. He wished he could at least do some good in this piddly little job. The Zeus case seemed like his only chance to make a difference. The Board had tied its own hands behind its back with its strict standards requiring so much evidence to even open a case, while Dr. Zeus ignored all rules and common decency itself and preyed on women without restraint. He decided to look deeper into the records in Katherine's case, scouring even the billing records.

Dave fumed about what he found. He couldn't sit down. He did a walking tour of the building for a half hour, paced back and forth from his cubicle to the water fountain seven or eight times. He couldn't concentrate on any of the old cases he was supposed to be reviving. He barged into Michele's cubicle. She was on the phone but he sat down anyway and stared at her until the call was over.

"Zeus charged for an intermediate office visit, Code 99214, each time he raped Katherine."

"Yes?" Michele's look was wary.

"So we're going to accept that? He was paid for each rape?"

"You need to calm down, Dave."

"No I don't." Dave left her cubicle, made a phone call, then told Frank he had a student loan snafu he had to clear up in person at the bank.

He drove right to her school and showed his Board of Medicine investigator card to the receptionist, making it clear that this was an utterly confidential matter. He asked if there was any place private where he could talk to a student named Diane Morrell, and they showed him a tiny little office with a desk and three chairs. She showed up, standing tall in the doorway with purple hair and a jaw set like she was expecting trouble. She refused to come in. But at least she refused quietly. She agreed to talk in the reception area, where she stood on the other side of the counter from him. At first she would only whisper the answers to his questions.

Dave didn't know much about interviewing, much less interviewing a teenage girl patient. So far, his entire interview training had been Frank's one warning – never interview a woman alone in a sex case. So much for protocol.

"Sometimes the Board does random quality checks on physicians, and we ask the patients' help," he lied. "We're interested in a Dr. Hartwicke Zeus. I understand that you may know him."

"Yeah." Her eyes shifted down, then shot straight up to his. "He's been taking care of me ever since before I had my baby."

"Baby …. Oh." Caught off guard, he tried to recover. "And when did this happen?"

She squinted at him like he was crazy. "A little more than a year ago. Why?"

"This is just a general survey we do once in a while. There's really only one important question. Were you satisfied with the treatment you received from Dr. Zeus?"

"Sure. I had the baby, and I gave it away. Maybe that wasn't the best thing I ever did, but it wasn't Dr. Zeus's fault. I still see Dr. Zeus for the aftereffects and stuff."

Aftereffects? But he definitely couldn't ask about that. There was no way he was going to ask a sixteen-year-old girl about her gynecological problems. He wished Michele were with him. This wasn't the way he had hoped the interview would go. He was supposed to be digging for dirt on Zeus. He told himself he had to say something to break the ice so this straight shooting girl would feel free to spill the beans on Zeus.

"Um …. Giving away your baby – that must have been tough."

Her voice broke. "It was."

"I'm sorry. I don't mean to make you talk about a sensitive subject."

Maybe she wasn't quite as tough as she seemed. But she stood with her head held high, her jaw clenched, looking straight at him, as if to say: *next question*? He found himself backing away from her. "Well, the Board just wants you to know that we're here for you. If you ever experience any problems with your physicians, Dr. Zeus or anybody else – problems of *any* kind – remember that the Board is here to help you. The State Board of Medicine. We're on the net." It wasn't an accident that he didn't leave his card.

On the way home Dave felt strangely exhilarated. He didn't think the purple-haired girl was the type Dr. Zeus could take advantage of. And she was a breath of fresh air compared to the sad-sack Katherine he knew from the transcript. He was glad his job put him in a position to meet people like this teenager, and like Michele, whom he never would have run into if he had gone directly into the public policy realm as he had planned. Maybe this job did beat spending your mid-twenties with your nose buried in law books.

Chapter 15

Diane

Dr. Zeus bought me a Tracfone so nobody could keep tabs on us when we called each other. It wasn't exactly the latest model, and I had to hide it in the bottom of my backpack anyway. He called me every night after 11:00 so we could talk while my parents were busy watching the news and Lisa was asleep. He always wanted to talk about plans for meeting again, but sometimes I made him first listen to me talk about school and soccer and Lucky and Kate and whatever else was on my mind. I liked that he would listen, but I felt guilty because I knew he was such a busy man.

He took me to his condo at the beach one night, speeding down the beach highway 100 miles an hour in his old Jaguar with a big dent in the passenger's side door – and without telling me first where we were going. We sat out on his tenth-floor balcony watching the ocean in the moonlight. That's all we did that night.

I mean we didn't make love. I had been lying to him about taking the oxy pills that he gave me from his own stash. Woody told me not to mess with those, and I figured Woody knew what he was talking about. We were watching the lines of waves breaking into soft white curls under the moon when he suddenly put his hand out to me with a pill in it. It was one of those same pills. Just then he popped one in his own mouth with his other hand.

I couldn't think of an excuse not to take it, and I felt bad for lying to him all along about taking the pills he gave me to take home, and so I took one from his hand and swallowed it. After it kicked in all I could think was: *why would Woody want to deny me this pleasure?* My body was just vibrating with happiness. The breeze on the balcony felt like the softest caress. The moon was unbelievably bright and beautiful. Tiny clouds scooted across in front of it like they were playing in its light. I had enough sense not to touch him then. He asked me to stop calling him doctor. I asked him his first name, but then he said Hartwicke and I laughed so hard I decided to just call him Zeus. Anyway, I knew making love with him right then would be fantastic; but deep down inside, deeper than the joy of the oxy, I was super mad at him for taking me there without asking and then practically forcing me take that pill. But we still had a delirious couple of hours watching the tide, high.

After that I started taking the oxy from his hand. He offered me one right away the next time we met. We were in his clinic in the church gymnasium building.

"You deserve to feel good," he told me then. The clinic had closed and no one else was there.

"Do I have to be examined today?" I thought I'd ask this before the drugs kicked in. I was sitting on the examining table, but with all my clothes on.

"No. That text I sent …. I was just lonely. I needed to see you again."

"I like talking to you."

He took my hand. "It looks like we both found something we really need."

That was so true. "Yes." I wished I could shut my mouth, and shut down my mind, right then, but I couldn't. So I said what I was thinking. "But you're married."

"Legally, yes. But not really. All I think about when I'm home is when can I see you again."

"We could maybe just talk."

He nodded, but the look in those blue eyes was so disappointed. He seemed like he was really trying to hold himself back. "Yeah, we can just talk," he said. He let go of my hand

and walked across the office and came back with a bottle of whiskey in his hand.

"No. Don't." I pleaded. "You already took that oxy. You're going to get really messed up."

"I want to be messed up."

"Don't say that. I don't want to make you feel that way."

He came closer and called me an angel, and then I let him kiss me. I wanted to kiss him just once but we couldn't stop.

I dreamed about him every night. We went out on the boat again. Just when I thought I knew everything that was going to happen, he asked me to do something I'd never done before. A sex thing. I was really nervous but sort of okay with that. He said he'd never been with a woman who could excite him like I could.

He told me on the phone every night he couldn't wait for our next meeting. It was fun to have sex with him, but the way he talked to me as his friend was even better. And, to tell the truth, the oxy high was a little weaker every time. I could still remember how good that drug felt that first night at his condo, and when one pill didn't do it for me any more I once asked him for a double; but at the same time I kept hearing Woody's voice saying keep away from that stuff. I didn't like what was happening to me with the drugs, but Zeus said they wouldn't hurt me. I was so much under his power I would usually do anything he said; but one night just out of meanness I made him call me 17 times before I picked up.

··· ···

Woody was just standing up from his desk with his keys in his hand when I opened the door to his garage.

"How many of those pills are you taking?" was all he said.

How did he know?

"I'm trying not to take any. You saw me throw away that

handful he gave me, and I tore up that prescription. But every time I go there he takes one himself first. He says a little bit is good for us."

"My mother was addicted to those pills." Woody had never said much about his mother. "She sold everything in the house to buy 'em. Then we lost the house. Then she died anyway." His sudden bitterness scared me. I didn't know him that well. I had just assumed his wild days were over and he was living a normal life now. But I guess people who have never been damaged don't generally live in garages.

"That must have been awful."

"I'm not asking for pity," he snapped.

"Sorry." He looked at me, then glanced away. I could tell it was still my turn to talk. "Okay. I won't take any more."

He sat back down at his desk, so I sat on the bed. The evening sun coming through that extra window he'd installed in the back lit up his buzz cut, showed all the dust floating in his little garage house. He had to work that night and he wasn't doing any pot.

"Would you still be his girlfriend if he didn't give you any drugs?"

"Of course. He's the only person who understands about me giving up my baby."

"That was really hard?"

I looked at him. Are all males mentally challenged? "I don't want to talk about it." But I wanted to talk about Zeus. "He's wonderful to me. I'm happy all the time."

"That's good," Woody said; but he didn't look like he really believed me.

"Maybe not *all* the time," I confessed. "Can I tell you something weird? Sometimes I tease him just a little. I don't know why. I don't want to be a mean person."

Woody leaned forward and started doing some trick with his pen, making it roll over his outstretched fingers and appear and disappear again. In the old days he was always fiddling with his hands, carving pieces of wood with his knife, poking on his ballpoint-pen tattoos or making new ones. It was just his way of keeping people from trying to get to know him. I couldn't see why he was ever afraid of that.

"Diane, you are not mean."

"Sometimes I don't pick up right away when he calls. He has so much power over me. I like to think I have a little power too. That's kind of pathetic – not picking up the phone right away – don't you think?"

"No. Weird, maybe, like you said."

"At least I don't live in a garage."

He stood up to leave, his keys now clicking and appearing and disappearing through his moving fingers. I jumped up and grabbed his hand to make it stop. While I was at it I grabbed his arm and stared at his biggest tattoo.

"What are you doing?" He was miffed.

"Trying to figure out if there's any way you could make this tattoo less harsh."

"What? You don't like *F-U-C-K Y-O-U?* You think it's weird?" He pulled his arm away roughly and turned toward the door.

"It's none of my business," I called after him. "If it's how you feel, it's how you feel."

"Whatever," he grumbled as he went out the door. He did leave the door unlocked so I could stay as long as I wanted.

I lay on his bed in that garage behind Ms. Nesbitt's house, wondering where his head was at. I could have smoked one of his joints. I knew he wasn't really that angry with me or he wouldn't have let me stay in there after he left. I knew a lot about him, though I didn't even know his full name or where he worked. I had a European History paper due the next day that wasn't half finished, but I wanted to stay a while.

Staying there was cool at first, but then I fell asleep, and when I woke up it was dark inside the garage. I knew Woody had lights, but I couldn't find them. I felt my way to the door and outside, hoping Ms. Nesbitt wouldn't catch me creeping across her lawn in the dark. Her driveway ran under a dark tunnel of overgrown bushes right as you almost reached the sidewalk. I was safe there from being seen from the house, but then I worried about her suddenly turning into the driveway and nailing me with her high beams. I was trying to hurry and get out of that extra-dark spot when I saw a faint white blotch floating in the darkness somewhere in front of me. My heart jumped, and I tried to swerve away from it, but it moved too. Then I froze. But it kept on moving. Then it came right up in front of me, and I panicked. Then I saw the white blotch was a human face.

"You must not destroy that holy child within you!"

I screamed. It was Robert, all in black. The white blob that was his face moved back a step. I tried to catch my breath. He didn't say anything else. I put my arms up to fight him off. I knew I should say something.

"Robert, you're demented." I was too scared to be nice. "There's no child. Other than the one I already gave away. Why are you always reminding me of my baby girl over and over?"

"Jesus Himself has chosen me to save you. It is God's plan." I could see his features now. Not much better than the white blob.

"You need to see a shrink."

His voice sank lower. "Diane, my life is meaningless if I can't save you."

"Get out of my way. I don't want to be saved."

He moved to block me, but I darted right past him before he could react. I'd almost forgotten what a clumsy dork he was. There was no reason to be afraid of him outdoors. But he was definitely an indoor threat. He had been talking to my mother again, I knew. She always commented on what a nice boy he was, as if she was thinking of him as a possible boyfriend for me. He was supposedly trying to talk her into bringing Lisa into the church, but my mother said the conversation always turned out to be about me. She thought he had a crush on me. She thought it was cute.

••• •••

I told Zeus not to call me that night. I had to talk to Lisa. Like I said, we're not exactly BFFs, but I know some things she needs to know. She rolls her eyes a little when I get in that mood, but not as much as when Mom tries to talk to her.

"That guy Robert is talking to Mom about you," I started. "He's hanging around Dad, too. He came to my school. He's stalking me. You got to be careful of that guy."

She put down the book she was reading and rested her face on one hand. She was pretending to be bored, emphasizing that pose with her dramatic eyes.

"Who?"

"Robert. The guy with the black pants who calls himself Deacon. He's not even a real deacon, you know."

"He's talking to Mom about me? Why?"

"To get you to join the church, he says. Who knows, really? I let him kiss me once, and now he's stalking me. I mean it. He's a stalker. Keep away from him."

Her smartass look faded. She had no reason to listen to me or to follow my example in life, but I hoped she'd keep away from Robert anyway.

But she was thinking about me. "Is there any guy in the world who is not after you?"

"What do you mean? You think it's a good thing to be stalked?"

"I mean, you've never been alone. When you were my age you and Carl were so in love."

"And how'd that work out?" I couldn't believe I'd said that. I'd never talked about Carl like that before. Was Carl soon going to be just a throw-away joke to me? Would I talk that way about my baby some day?

"It wasn't a good thing, Lisa. It was so sad in the end. But I'm sorry you didn't get to see her – the baby, I mean."

Chapter 16

Hartwicke

"The hospital lawyer didn't say anything specific," Billings began, pushing his black-framed glasses back up his nose and shifting his great bulk to the other side of his oversized executive chair. "He said 'it might be problematic' under some federal law if we send our lab tests out to a lab owned by one of our physicians."

Billings was stalling. Zeus knew from experience how stubborn the hospital CEO could be. Once before, Billings had required an extraordinary favor from Zeus before he would allow his name even to be placed on the list of nominees to the Board of Trustees. Then the nomination process had been delayed, and Zeus hadn't yet been made a trustee. And now Billings wasn't moving on the PeakResults plan either.

The plan was to run the hospital's lab tests through PeakResults, Zeus's company. The hospital's business would transform PeakResults from a struggling start-up into a cash cow for Zeus. Billings, for his services in getting the hospital to agree, was already penciled in for one-half percent of the gross.

"Just get me on the Board of Trustees now, and you and I can push this PeakResults thing through together."

"But the lawyers ...."

Zeus raised his voice, something he had found was often useful with cowards like Billings. "Don't give me that lawyer crap. If we want to do something, we do it. Your high-paid lawyers will figure out later a way to pronounce it legal."

But Billings was not intimidated. "Hartwicke, give me a break. This is a major change you're talking about. Hundreds of thousands of dollars of our lab work suddenly being sent to

PeakResults. Everyone, the accountants, the Board of Trustees, *everybody* is going to look it over carefully." Zeus recognized from Billings's tone that the man wasn't going to budge.

"John," Zeus continued the first-name talk, "you're a smart administrator. I know you're the kind of man who's attuned to the business side of things." Zeus thought Billings would understand that "business" meant "money," and "attuned" meant he was willing to offer Billings a bigger piece of the action.

The answer surprised him. "Hartwicke, I don't even know how to pay my own gas and electric bill. All I know is my wife gives me an allowance every month, and if I spend more than that I have hell to pay."

"So you don't wear the pants in your family."

"Maybe not. But I don't care. I'm not into money. You know what I want, Hartwicke."

··· ···

He hadn't been using the driveway at home; instead, he parked the Jag on the other side of the street so the crumpled fender on the passenger side wouldn't be visible to Elena. He dreaded taking the car in to the dealer to get it fixed. Elena was already harping about the bill from the rental company for the damage to the Kia.

"Our credit card company will pay for the damage you did to the rented Kia. But we have to file a claim," she explained to him again, as if he were a little child. She got him to sit down in front of her computer so he could fill out the online claim form, but there were a lot of embarrassing questions such as what other car was involved, who was driving it, where and when did the accident happen, and so on. And Elena was looking over his shoulder the whole time, afraid that he'd get frustrated with the awkward software and give up.

He pretended he was frustrated. "Just get me a paper claim

form and I'll have my secretary fill it out when I go in to work."

"Really? You can't handle this right now? Do you want me to do it? Why don't you just give me the information and ...."

"No!"

There had been times earlier in their marriage, when his temper flared and her indignation rose at the same time, when they would end up in the bedroom, their sharp, wordless need for each other suddenly rising up. For an instant he thought that was happening again. She shuddered with indignation.

"You are such an irritating man." She put her hands up like she was going to grab him and shake him. That was how it sometimes started. But then she turned away. Then she turned back for one last patronizing harangue. "The bill's $2,249 for the damage you did to the Kia. Because we rented it on a credit card, the credit card company will cover the damages. But you have to file the damn claim soon, Hardy."

••• •••

Diane wanted him to come watch one of her soccer games. Of course she did. She was a healthy, active young girl. But he had never gone to even one of his own daughter's school concerts. He was not used to being just one of a crowd of spectators. He was used to being the center of attention, the god-like figure at the very nerve center of the medical system, around whom all patients and nurses and hospitals and pharmacies and laboratories gathered, eagerly awaiting his word. A god shouldn't have to sit in the stands for hours and watch a girls' high-school soccer game. So he put her off. But the next night she ignored over 20 of his texts before she picked up.

"I'm pretty good at soccer. Won't you come watch me?" she asked again.

"What would I say about why I'm there?"

"Oh. You don't have to talk to anybody. I'd just like to see you in the stands. We could talk about the game, you know, later sometime."

He put her off again. After that, all of her practices suddenly seemed to become very important to her. She wouldn't skip another one, not for a ride on his boat or for anything else. The ironic thing was, he really would have liked to see if she was as quick and graceful as he imagined her to be. Diane was every bit as feisty as Marcie, but she also had an underlying sweetness and naiveté that made breaking her the most satisfying erotic challenge of his life. She even distracted him for a time from noticing just how much his own daughter Kyra had grown.

He still had high hopes for Kyra. He had not spared any expense on developing her: special pre-school, private kindergarten, elementary and middle schools, ballet lessons, piano lessons, cello lessons, French tutors, summer adventure camps, summer arts camps, two trips to Europe with her parents and one to South America complete with helicopter rides over Sugar Loaf and Corcovado. There was every reason to hope she was growing into the type of sophisticated woman he could be proud of. Recently, Elena had surprised him by telling him Kyra had grown three inches since her twelfth birthday.

··· ···

"Why are we here?" Zeus began. He was glad Concord Mews at least provided comfortable, swiveling leather chairs for those parents undergoing the degradation of being interviewed to see if they were good enough to send their daughters to this so-called Little Ivy League prep school. The chair was so big and soft he sunk almost below the surface of the leather as he swiveled slowly back and forth. Elena, meanwhile, sat on the very edge of her chair, alert, with documents and paper and pen in hand.

"You know who we are," Zeus went on. "I'm a physician, a partner in New Town Partners. I'm on call at the Freeland Hospital five nights a week. I volunteer one afternoon a week at the clinic run by the Church of the Academy. My wife used to work at Freeland Hospital too, and now she's the Director of Human Resources at Garden City Hospital. She works sixty hours a week. What more do you need to know that's important enough to drag us in here when we all know Kyra meets all of your academic standards, and we're fully capable of paying the bill?"

In the silence that followed, Kiley Fontaine, the Dean of Admissions – they actually called him a dean – said nothing at all. He was a young guy with close-cut, dark hair, glasses, not wonderfully good looking, dressed in an expensive sport coat with the stereotypical leather patches on the elbows. He was a slight man with a subtly insolent manner who might do well counseling students in a high school but who would be eaten alive in the worlds of medicine or business. Without responding to anything Zeus had said, Fontaine simply shifted his gaze toward Elena.

"I think what Hartwicke is trying to say," Elena began humbly, as if she knew she couldn't repair the damage from her husband's outburst in a sentence or two. Her quiet tone signaled that she was just launching into a long, reparative presentation. "What we're trying to say is we have provided a lot of information already in the application packet. We'd like to be sure that you've got it, first."

"I've read the application packet, Ms. Zeus."

"And so, then …. We're here now, and we're happy to give you any more information that you need. Information about us, or about Kyra, or anything. I know I'm prejudiced because I'm her mother, but I think you'll find Kyra is a wonderful child. She works hard, gets good grades, has a lot of friends and is interested in everything. We're sure she would make a positive contribution to your school."

"Of course, we have interviewed Kyra already. I agree that she's a delightful child, maybe a little shy, but with a sly sense of humor. Her grades are fine. However, we did notice one thing. When we asked where you worked, Dr. Zeus, Kyra didn't know."

"She knows I'm a doctor."

Fontaine sniffed as if he detected a slightly foul odor in the room. "Of course. But she didn't know what kind of a doctor you were, or where you worked, except at 'some hospital.'"

"I work at different places. What's that got to do with anything?"

"She talked about maybe going to medical school one day. But it seemed curious that she'd never gone in to work with you."

The little shit was needling him.

"Oh, you mean Take Your Daughter to Work Day? I guess you can do that in a place like this, sit in an office or correct papers or watch a class or talk on the phone with other Ivy League graduates about how superior you are or something. My job is life and death, real people with real diseases, real pain. Not something you can bring a little kid to participate in – even if it wouldn't violate federal privacy laws."

Zeus thought he had made his point well. Fontaine tilted back, dwarfed in his own chair, which was even larger than the visitors' chairs. "We find that those kids who have a lot of parental involvement tend to do better at Concord Mews. We have a lot of parent-child joint activities. And a lot of groups made up only of parents .... "

"I can assure you that we will be involved in the school and in Kyra's education as much as humanly possible," Elena cut in. "Kyra is our only child, and we are devoted to what's best for her. We both have jobs, but we can make whatever arrangements are necessary to .... "

"We do a lot of fundraising through the parent groups," Fontaine cut her off. His tone was testy now. "If your time is short, there may be other ways you two as a couple can contribute."

"Do you mean ... money?" Elena sounded defeated. "In addition to the tuition?" Fontaine sniffed a yes. As much as Zeus sometimes hated Elena, he couldn't stand seeing his wife being bested by this haughty-ass sniveler.

"Quit wasting our time," Zeus jerked forward in his tippy chair. "He means money, Elena. Come on, Fontaine. How much extra do we have to pay to get Kyra in here?"

Elena was furious on the way home. "You cost us $15,000 a year extra for four years just because of your nasty attitude."

"We had to pay. That's what they brought us in to tell us. We could have maybe cut it down to ten thou or twelve-fifty by making nicey-nice noises with that snotty fart for the next four years. It's better this way. The cards are on the table."

When he came home later that night Kyra was waiting for him. That was a first.

"Mom told me what you did. She made it sound like you bribed them."

He put his hands out, palms up, and shrugged. "That's what it was. That's the way the world works. Every parent has to pay extra. We just wanted to know the price up front."

"I was in the top 25% of all the kids who applied," Kyra complained.

"I know. That's great. But we still have to pay. Think of it this way, honey. They know we're on top, financially speaking. When they beg for it like that, we have to throw them a few crumbs."

"Oh. I guess that's what they were really doing, begging. Right?" She smiled, and he could see right then that she did get it. Kyra was smart and tough. She was not afraid of him and therefore would not be afraid of any man. She knew how to use those eyes, and that quick grin. Her shyness was a kid thing that was wearing off fast. She was getting taller and prettier every day. He could tell she would learn to take advantage of her looks. "I hardly ever see you, but I am glad you are my Dad."

"You're going to kick ass, kid. I know it."

Chapter 17

David

He was a cooped up in a tiny studio apartment hundreds of miles away from his girlfriend; and while he'd been down to North Carolina to see her several times, Sarah hadn't come up since he had moved there four months before. Because she was finally coming now, he cleaned up the place, but that made him realize how sterile it looked. He didn't have a rug or tablecloths or curtains and had never bought any pictures, wall hangings, flowerpots or decorations of any kind. He didn't even have any refrigerator magnets. Every horizontal space was covered with empty take-out boxes or the transcript pages of Michele's interview with Katherine about Dr. Zeus.

At the airport, she recognized his car and had already maneuvered her bag through one line of waiting cars and up to his by the time he came to a stop. She threw open the back door, tossed in her bag, and jumped into the front seat before he knew what was happening. She turned to him and they kissed until the honking behind got too loud. He drove with his left hand while she held the other. "I missed you I missed you I missed you."

He tried to be gentlemanly when they first got to his apartment, but the place was so empty there was nothing really interesting in it but the bed. She was every bit as eager as he was. He loved her long, strong legs, her breasts a little too small for her rangy frame but gorgeously tipped in brown and perkily awaiting his touch. Afterwards, he lay on his back and she rested her head on his chest. He traced her skin with his fingertips. He didn't feel any of that tension in her body he had felt in their college days. She was happier now. He wondered what had caused that change, if it was his doing or ....

"I heard that men do that. That they fall asleep," she said as she threw a leg across his body to wake him up.

"Sorry."

"It's okay. I read somewhere it's just hormones."

"I'm so content now. I feel like right now I have everything I ever wanted."

The next morning they awoke to a brilliant fall day and walked through a nearby city farmers' market, and she made a simple salad out of the lettuce and cucumbers and beets and cauliflower they bought while he cooked two steaks in the broiler in his tiny kitchen. She giggled every time they bumped into each other. They'd bought some wine, too – Malbec, she suggested. He'd never heard her ask for a specific wine before.

They both admitted they were surprised the meal was actually so good.

"I'm going to help you clean up," she insisted.

"No, you're not. There's not room for two people in there."

She stood in the doorway, gently bouncing a shoulder against the doorframe while she watched him clean up the broiler pan. Neither one of them wanted to talk about food or broiler pans or garbage disposals. She left him alone and disappeared from his sight as she wandered around the apartment.

"Hey. *What is this?*"

He poked his head out. "Oh, you can't read that! It's a transcript of an investigative interview. It's confidential. I had to promise I wouldn't let anybody see it if I took it home."

"Is it you asking the questions?"

"No, it's Michele, this woman I work with. She's another investigator."

She put the transcript down, but she had obviously read pretty far. "This doctor raped this woman? Did he go to jail?"

"No. And the Board closed the case too. No corroborating evidence." He smirked at the legalistic term.

"Wow. It sounds like the interviewer – what's her name, Michele? – really believed her."

"She does. But she's not the one who decides whether to charge or not." He came out to sit next to her on the sofa. "Michele's taught me a lot about, you know, how the world actually works, as opposed to how it's supposed to work. Sometimes you find out a horrible thing happened, like Zeus raping Katherine, but you just can't do anything about it. But Michele's not bitter at all. She's really funny. Really cool. I wish you could meet her."

"Do you work with her a lot?"

"Oh yeah. All the time."

"So you and Michele are fighting against rapists while I'm sitting in class listening to everybody's stupid opinions about how *Hadley v. Baxendale* should have been decided in the nineteenth century."

"You make it sound like I'm having fun. It's not fun most of the time. It's really frustrating."

"Except when you and super cool Michele are laughing about it?"

"You make it sound like ...."

She touched him. "I'm sorry. I'm really worried about us living in two different worlds. Can't we figure out a way to be together? Why don't you come to law school with me next year? You were already accepted two years ago. I still don't understand why you didn't go. You could have gotten loans, and while you were in law school you could have deferred the interest on your college student loans."

"You don't realize how much in debt I already am. If I added law school tuition on top of it, I'd hardly be able to pay the interest."

"Well!" She took his hand in both of hers and held it until he looked into her eyes. "I think I know a way you could swing law school."

"I know what you're thinking. But I couldn't take your father's money for law school tuition."

"Listen, I know a way you would have to accept his money. I know something that would make it a horrible insult if you didn't accept it … *if it was our wedding present.*"

He took her in his arms. "Oh my God, Sarah. You really want to marry me? I guess I should get down on one knee."

"I'm the one who's asking. I should do it." And she did. He couldn't believe he deserved this woman.

"Yes, of course, I will marry you," he said, pulling her up awkwardly into his arms. They celebrated their engagement right there and then.

But later that evening, doubts woke him from sleep. Should he take the money for law school tuition from her father? Dave had reason to resent the way the very wealthy class rode roughshod over the lives of ordinary people like him. If he took her father's money, wouldn't he be expected sooner or later to work for her father, or one of his businesses, or for some wealthy person like him, or for one of their corporations? Wouldn't he be expected to spend his life using all of his energy and brainpower and education to make the rich even richer at the expense of everybody else?

··· ···

"So you'll marry me but, like, some day far in the future?"

The rest of the weekend hadn't been so happy. He told her he wouldn't take her father's money. And he couldn't explain it to her without revealing the bitterness against the very rich that overcame him at times. He didn't want to make her feel like she was one of the exploiters he held a permanent grudge against.

"Right now I'm paying 40% of my salary to the bank to pay off my college loans. If I up it to 60, I'll have it all paid off in four years."

"By then I'll be two years out of law school. We'll still be in different worlds."

Sunday was lazily sexy and relaxing, but their undeniable contentment with each other was tinged with melancholy because she was leaving and because there was no viable plan for the future.

"I want to be with you," he mumbled on the way to the airport. "It's just ... I don't want to be beholden to your father ... " – how could he say it without calling her father an exploiter? – "I mean, I would feel like I was *his* lawyer, really, for the rest of my life."

"I think you're being silly. You don't even know my Dad. He's great. You and he are a lot alike, you know."

"Oh, sure."

While he was waiting with her at the airport before she left, he told her that another complaint had come in against the doctor who raped Katherine, the woman she read about in the transcript. The same doctor was apparently messing with a sixteen-year-old female patient.

"He's still doing it?"

"Nobody's sure. But they wouldn't even let me open a case. I went out on my own and talked to this girl anyway. There wasn't even a case open, so it might have been technically illegal."

"Why did you do that?"

"The situation seemed really fishy. He was seeing her every week, which was exactly like what was happening to that woman Katherine in the transcript. Frank said to close the case, but I kept imagining Zeus turning this sixteen-year-old girl into an addict while we just ignored the problem."

"They wouldn't open the case?"

"No, they wouldn't. When I talked to the girl, she said she'd had a baby when she was about fourteen. She had no complaints about Zeus."

"Of course she's not going to complain if she's an addict and he's giving her all the drugs she wants."

"Exactly. I think maybe she is. That's the problem. How far do I go to prove my hunch is right?"

"You're talking to a law student. I think you've gone too far already."

Chapter 18

Diane

I don't know what being really addicted would be like, but I must have had some kind of addiction to Dr. Zeus because he was all I could think about. He wrote me a note to get out of school, and we went to his condo at the ocean again, driving 100 again, this time getting a ticket while the cop eyed me and asked if I was his daughter. He took me to get a new bathing suit, and not to one of those flip-flop-and-beach-chair stores. It was one of those expensive designer stores that Mom or Dad would never even let me go into. He told me to get whatever I wanted, but out of habit I picked the cheapest one even though it was pretty slutty and the orange color would clash with my hair.

"You're buying by price tag," he noticed. "I don't want you to do that. Get what you want."

I picked up a green and white striped bikini with a white faux leather belt and matching top and bottom jeweled silver clasps that would probably tarnish in a minute if you ever actually wore them in the salt water. He came over while I was looking at it.

"That's a nice one."

"How much does it cost?" I turned it over, looking for the price tag.

He put his hand on mine, pushing it away so I couldn't read the price tag. "Diane, I don't want you to ever mention price in my presence again."

It cost $699. He flipped his credit card down on the counter in front of the cashier. Then we went to his condo ten floors above the beach that was better than anything my family would ever be able to buy. In that condo, this handsome doctor who was risking his marriage for me took off my clothes and made love to me. Then he watched me put on my new bathing suit and we went out to the beach, where we lay on towels on the burning sand. I was lying face down, and he kissed me between the shoulders and began running his hand up and down my spine. I could feel him unclasping my top and I said no.

"There's hardly anybody else out here on the beach," he coaxed. "We're in a special world with each other, aren't we? That's the beauty of it. No rules apply – don't you think?"

I let him unclasp it. I don't think anybody noticed. I let him stroke my back. Then he quickly rubbed his hand over the bottom of my bathing suit before I squirmed away. I don't think he was even horny then. He just liked to break all the rules. I could understand that. Doesn't everybody deserve a special time when they can just reach out and grab whatever they want? I was getting a whole day like that. Zeus was getting his. I knew he was hoping someone on the beach would see him touching me. Then he tried to slide his hand under my suit, and I said no for real.

I meant what I said when I told Woody I wouldn't take any more drugs from Zeus, but I broke my word on the way down to the condo that day. I was feeling just a little bit bad, and Zeus kept saying the pill would help, and I thought maybe he was right, maybe one pill would be just enough to get me up to even. But the feeling I got was much better than even, and Zeus confessed when we got to the condo that he had given me a pill twice as strong. That was probably the reason the shopping and the condo and the beach had been so much fun.

But I don't like to be tricked, and giving me that double without telling me pissed me off. And I didn't like him trying to put his hand inside my bathing suit on the beach. It wasn't like he needed it. I remembered Carl coming back again, so hungry, like every forty-five minutes, but Zeus never made love to me more than once or twice a day. He didn't really need me then on the beach. It was just for his ego.

I felt horrible the next day in school. My head ached and my nose was running. I thought I knew the cause – and the cure. I took another route to the cafeteria so I wouldn't run into Woody. I saw Kate sitting there alone. Her thick blonde hair was bobbed straight now, her face was a little thinner, and she had a more sophisticated look than when we were hanging together in middle school. But she smiled at me with those same green eyes when I sat down across from her.

We had been friends since we were seven years old. I taught her how to drink when we were fourteen. I introduced her to Lucky then. And I was the only one she told about Lucky's creepy family background, the only one who knew she almost gave up on him because of that. But she didn't, and they'd been together ever since. They both had tried to be nice to me when I was pregnant, and I still felt shame that I let Sue shoo them away.

"You don't look too good."

"I think I'll be okay in a day or two. Can you do me one favor? Don't tell Woody I'm sick."

"Did something happen between you two?"

"It's got nothing to do with Woody. But it's worse than you think." That was so true. I chickened out and pushed back my chair to leave. Kate had never looked down on me for getting pregnant, but she had no idea what I was doing with Zeus.

She came around the table and hugged me hard. "I missed you. I want you back. All the way back. I thought it would happen real fast once you were back in school, but it didn't. What's wrong?"

I lost it then, couldn't hold back the tears. She took me in the girls' bathroom and we went into one of the smoky stalls and she dried my tears, ignoring the flushing and traffic and gossip on the other side of the grey steel door. I stopped crying, but that stall was no place to talk, so we went outside towards Lucky's car, which was in the parking lot. Once my tears were over and we were out there together under the blue sky, I felt giddy for a minute, almost like I was fourteen and free again.

"Remember the first time Lucky ever drove us in a car?" It was just a silly memory that popped back into my head. "When we were fourteen? Remember he thought he could drive a car – because he had operated a backhoe? And he thought driving a car would be the same? And he jerked us all the way across Glenwood in the dark without turning the lights on?"

Kate smiled. We got in the front seat of the car. Of course, it was a no-brainer that Kate would have a set of keys to Lucky's car.

"I can't tell anyone else, not even Woody," I started. "Kate, I'm in love with a guy."

"Oh. Cool."

"He's my doctor, Dr. Zeus." She didn't scream out, so I kept going. "He's married, but he and his wife never sleep in the same bed. They don't even talk. He's lonely for somebody to talk to."

"A doctor? How old is he?"

"Forty-three, I think. You don't believe a doctor could be in love with me?"

"Any guy could fall in love with you."

… …

The next day I couldn't make it to school. It felt like I had the flu. I stayed in bed all day. My back and legs ached. I lay in bed, looking at my tablet when I could. Nothing on the internet seemed very funny; but then my mother came in after work and said maybe she should call the doctor, and I broke out with a laugh so loud I think it scared her. Then Lisa came in and brought me a glass of water I hadn't asked for. She stayed a little while, and I tried to pay attention to what she was saying. I did hear one thing.

"Mom says I should have a regular doctor. She wants me to go to the same one you go to."

I bolted upright and clawed at her hands. I must have looked like the devil staring out from the pale husk of a half-dead girl's face. Her eyes grew so big I was sure she was listening.

"DO NOT GO TO DR. ZEUS!"

She heard what I said. I held her hands more softly. Her fingers were longer than mine, and I knew she thought her hands were too big. They seemed so beautiful to me I started crying, crying into those innocent hands rather than my own.

I was a little better the next day, and I went to Woody's garage house after soccer practice. He was lying on his bed typing on a tablet when I walked in. He sat right up and looked around like there was something I wasn't supposed to see, but I think it was just that he hadn't cleaned up the place. Or maybe he didn't want me to see that he was looking up recipes.

"I'm cooking for Ms. Nesbitt and me tomorrow night."

"That's cool. What are you making?"

"She likes that Oriental stuff. You know, tofu, bean curd, raw tuna, soy sauce. We never had that kind of stuff in my house when I was a kid."

"What was your mother like?" Nobody ever said I was shy or afraid to jump right in. Woody's eyes looked shocked for a second, then he looked back at his tablet. "I mean," I went on, "when you were little."

He started typing, poking slowly on the tablet. "She was nice." Then he went back to his slow poking.

I jumped next to him and took the tablet out of his hands. Everything just came pouring out. "I broke my promise to you and took oxy from Dr. Zeus again, right from his hand. He gave me an extra strong one without telling me. It made me feel really great for a few minutes."

"Why are you telling me all this, Diane?" He ran his hands up and down his arms and started fingering his tattoos.

"I was sick, really sick for almost a week after I stopped."

He stood up and paced back and forth. The place was so small he could only go about three steps in each direction. Then he opened the door to go out.

"Don't go. Please."

"I just gotta … I'll be back in a minute." I went to the door. He ran across Ms. Nesbitt's tiny back yard and through her leafy tunnel of a driveway to the street. I didn't know what else to do, so I turned back inside and started straightening his place up.

When he came back he was still jittery, drumming his fingers on everything in sight. He sat far away from me on the bed.

"My mother died from that stuff. I don't like to see you on it."

"He gave me another prescription." I pulled it out of my pocket. "I can't tell if it's the super-strong kind or not." I tried to show it to him, but he wouldn't take it. I let it float down on the bed between us. I knew it really didn't matter if it was double-strength or not. I felt like some kind of holy martyr for not getting it filled yet. But I hadn't been able to just tear it up. Just getting it out of my pocket was all I could do right then.

"I'm sorry about your mother," I said. "I can't believe what I did. One time I licked those pills right from his hand, like a dog. We played like it was a joke."

He looked over at me, his hands for once not twitching or fiddling with anything. "The way I see it, everybody fucks up. You just got into the real messy shit kind of early. Because you're not scared of anything."

"I wish I could be like you, Woody. You've got your head on so straight. Ms. Nesbitt's so lucky to have you here."

"Ms. Nesbitt?"

"I was trying to think of somebody …." I stopped. *Somebody who gives a shit about you*, I was going to say – but it hit me then how sad that was. So I just said something else. "I mean, I'm lucky to have you here."

He didn't do the thing I most wanted him to do right then. I had been hoping he would tear up that prescription. I hadn't been able to tear it up myself. He completely ignored it, like it was my problem I'd have to solve on my own. I still couldn't tear it up, but I left it there on his bed when I walked out.

Chapter 19

David

Ms. Porter: You went back to Dr. Zeus after he raped you?

Ms. Bolt: Yes.

Q: How did that happen?

A: I was so humiliated. And I felt so stupid. I couldn't tell my husband. I couldn't tell anyone. I went home and I felt so awful I got right in bed about 7:00 o'clock. Anyway I started feeling worse so I took a double dose of those pills. That was okay, but in the middle of the night I took more. I was in kind of a daze for days. I didn't care if I lived or died. I used up 30 days of those pills in one week.

A: What happened then?

Q: Then I felt even worse, worse than I had ever felt in my life. I just wanted to kill myself. So I called him and told him that, and he said don't, but come in to his office.

A: And you went in?

Q: Yes, but he didn't even see me. As soon as I got in, his receptionist handed me a prescription and said the doctor said to fill it right away.

Q: So you didn't even see him then?

A: Right. But the next time I called when the pills were gone, about two weeks later, he said I had to see him in his office, after hours. I knew what I'd have to do to get that prescription.

Michele tapped him on the shoulder. "Kendall wants to see you."

"The cat lady?" He mouthed the words.

Michele nodded. "Yeah. She's on intake today. Anonymous caller. It sounds like it may be that guy who called about Zeus a couple weeks ago."

Dave shot out of his seat and bounded down four cubicles to Kendall's office. Kendall sat behind the desk, her blonde hair roughly pushed back and a phone to her ear, her eyes glued to a screen that Dave couldn't see. All three chairs were stacked with files and Kendall's personal junk. All the walls were covered with pictures of her cats, each titled with the cat's name. Kendall held up a finger to signal him not to interrupt her now. Dave edged around her desk so he could see what she was looking at on the screen. He was glad to see that it wasn't a cat video. It looked like Kendall had progressed from cat videos to some type of vacation site, which she was watching intently as the anonymous complainant bent her ear.

The caller apparently wasn't allowing Kendall to get a word in edgewise. She just kept holding the phone to her ear. David looked at the screen. It was a pretty racy photo for a vacation site. He wondered if Kendall was into soft core beach porn. Then he noticed the purple hair, and he recognized the girl being fondled in the sand.

Dave frantically motioned for Kendall to put the phone on speaker. She sighed dramatically but finally did what he asked.

"I remember your voice," he interrupted the anonymous caller. "You called last week and talked to me. Where did you get this picture?"

"I took it myself. There are lots more."

"How do we know it's Doctor Zeus?"

"Press play. You'll see him real close up."

Dave started to ask how he knew the girl with the purple hair was a patient, but he stopped himself. He couldn't risk anyone finding out that he had already interviewed Diane Morrell. He couldn't take a chance that the anonymous caller would know this and blurt it out over the speaker phone.

"We're going to put you on hold for just a second." Dave desperately wanted to get Kendall out of the room for the rest of the conversation.

"No, we're not," Kendall butted in. "Tell us how you know the girl in the video is a patient of Dr. Zeus's."

Dave held his breath.

"I know her. Her name is Diane Morrell. She told me Dr. Zeus is her doctor. I found out she's seen him five times in the last few weeks. I have proof of that from financial records. Copays."

"How old is this girl?" Kendall asked.

"Sixteen."

They never did get the caller's name, but when they told Michele and Frank about the call and the video, they both agreed to open an investigation. Then Frank saw the video and said to pull out all the stops. "We know he's done it to two patients," Frank fumed. "He's probably done it to twenty, if not a hundred. We're going to find every one of them if we have to close down all our other investigations and put everybody on his case." He gave Dave a list of everything that should be included in the subpoena:

- New Town Partners' complete patient log for the last year;
- the name and complete medical record for each patient seen during that time;
- the complete personnel file of every partner and every employee;
- the time sheets of every partner and employee for the last year;
- the complete paper and electronic billing records

for every patient for the past year;
- all of Dr. Zeus's bank records for the past year;
- Zeus's 401(k) and IRA records;
- his tax forms for the past three years;
- the title to every car he owned, together with his car repair and gas receipts and automated toll records for the last three months.

"Is all this really necessary? Shouldn't we just focus on this girl? Maybe send Michele out to interview her first?"

"You're telling me how to investigate a case?" Frank was not amused.

"Of course not. I just wondered if we should focus on just her records, and of course any information we can get about their day at the beach."

"Newbie, we know for sure now there's at least two, Katherine and this Diane girl. Where there's two, there's probably a lot more. We need to talk to all of them. Remember, half of the patients who are molested chicken out, and half of the rest are crazy. We need six or eight because half of them won't show up at trial. We're not going to trial with just Katherine and Diane. This guy's super slick, and a super sicko. We need to take him down big."

· · · · · ·

"Michele, there might be a problem. What if this girl Diane doesn't want to talk about it?" The two of them were in Michele's office. Frank had unceremoniously taken the case from Kendall and given it to Michele, with his permission to involve Dave in the investigation.

"What do you mean?"

"What if this teenager, Diane, doesn't want to be involved in the investigation?"

"Oh, that happens all the time. I'll talk to her. It usually takes a lot of hand-holding to get women to open up about what happened." He looked at her like he didn't understand what hand-holding had to do with the job of being an investigator. Michele smirked at his naiveté but went on. "That's why it's such an insidious crime, Dave. The more the woman is abused, the more ashamed she is, and the less she wants to talk about it. That's why we would never send a man out on the first interview. So, you're out of luck if you thought you would be in on that. I'll do it by myself."

He left her cubicle and went back to his own, where he put his head in his hands and tried to figure out how bad a mess he had made. He was sure if Michele interviewed Diane, Diane would mention that he had interviewed her earlier. He would be in real trouble with Frank. Dave reminded himself that he had always considered this as just a short-term, stop-gap job. Maybe it would be a narrower gap and a shorter term than he had planned on.

But more important was the possibility that he had ruined the case against Zeus. When he had visited her at her school, Diane said she had no problems with Zeus. In fact, she seemed perfectly happy with her treatment by Zeus. Would she really change her story when she talked to Michele? Maybe she was having a completely illegal and unethical but nevertheless hot and happy affair with Zeus. She looked like the kind of woman who could pull that off. But the most worrisome fact was that she had denied it once, and if she changed her story now the Board might never believe anything she said.

"What's wrong, Dave?" He had come back to Michele's office to confess. He could not control the pitch of his voice standing up, so he tried sitting down.

"I never meant to stay in this job for too long," he started. He had her attention. Her dark eyes were sharply focused on his.

"Are you quitting?"

"No. Not unless I have to."

He confessed the whole incident to her. Michele's face fell. She stared down at her desk for a long time before turning those eyes back to him.

"I thought you had more respect for us."

That really hurt. Michele wasn't going to get lost in the trivia of figuring out what to do now or how this would affect the case. She had hit on the real issue.

"I know." He didn't even try to keep his voice from shaking, or his hands trembling. "*You* work hard, and *you* play by the rules every day. And I come in, an arrogant short-timer, and .... I don't know what I was thinking."

"You were thinking you were better than this job."

He had never admitted this to himself. For an instant it seemed like she had exposed his soul right there in that room, and the two of them were sitting there examining it, and finding out right then and there how small it was.

... ...

Was it another weakness, this compulsion to make his life sound interesting to Sarah, even if he had to confess what an ass he'd made of himself? He told her the anonymous caller had contacted them again, this time sending them a video of Dr. Zeus fondling a young girl on the beach.

"Is it ...?"

"Yes, the same girl I interviewed."

"So she was lying to you."

"Well, when I interviewed her, she said she was happy with the services he was providing. Maybe she is."

"Hmph. It doesn't matter if she's very happy. She's a minor. So are they finally going to open an investigation?"

"Yeah. But the thing is, I had to tell Michele I had already interviewed her. When Frank finds out I'll be fired."

"Oh, no! Something like that could affect your getting into

law school, too."

He hadn't thought of that. A wave of dread passed through his body. Why had he done this, anyway? Was it all really just because of his zeal to bring about justice? Or was part of it so he could brag to Sarah about how bold he was?

She went on. "This lady Michele hasn't told this Frank guy yet? Is she holding it over your head or something?"

"No. No, she's just very disappointed in me. And she thinks that, because of me, we may not be able to use this teenage girl in the case – even though we have a video."

"I hadn't thought of that. If she lied once, nobody will believe her when she changes her story. But the part about Michele being very disappointed in you. Is that the main reason you're upset?"

"It's a big part of it."

"I'd better come up there."

"You don't have to come up here to try to save me."

"Oh, like you wouldn't come down here to save me if I was in a mess like this."

Chapter 20

Diane

Woody invited me to the home-cooked oriental dinner he was making in Ms. Nesbitt's house. I called my mother to let her know where I'd be. It was really fun to be able to call my mother and tell her the actual truth about where I was going. Inviting somebody to your house for a cooked dinner seemed so old fashioned, but I think the old fashioned stuff was Woody's doing. Ms. Nesbitt wasn't that old, maybe 35. And she had always been more out there, on the edge.

She used to be Kate's and my English teacher in middle school. She was fired once for holding an outdoor class that turned into a parade making fun of the principal's schemes, but they had to hire her back when it turned out she was right.

"Diane, the last time I saw you, you were about eight months pregnant and carrying it well. You look marvelously healthy now." Ms. Nesbitt always tried to be nice, but she didn't always understand there were things people might not want to talk about. "You had the baby and gave it up for adoption, right? Was it a boy or a girl?"

"A girl." Just those words brought back that picture of her little squished-up face to my mind. I couldn't talk. I looked desperately at Woody for help.

"A girl?" he said. "I didn't know that. What was her name?"

That made everything worse. I started sobbing and couldn't stop. Not giving her a name seemed like a horrible crime. I collapsed into a chair next to the kitchen table and cried and cried. Ms. Nesbitt put her hand on my shoulder. Woody got a glass of water and put in in front of me. "Cry all you want," Ms. Nesbitt said. For some reason that struck me as funny, and I laughed in the middle of all that crying. They sat there with me without saying anything at all until I had cried and laughed myself all out. I put my head up, blew my nose, took a drink of that water. "Thanks, guys."

"You did what was best for her," Woody said.

Later, when we were back in his garage, I asked Woody about his life again. He had grumbled and walked out the first time I asked, but I figured he wouldn't have invited me to this dinner if he wasn't okay with me now.

"Tell me, really. You owe me one for making me cry in front of Ms. Nesbitt."

He said he was twelve when his mother died, long before he became the teenage procurer of alcohol and master of the reveries in the woods. He started this career in the woods just by taking booze from his father's stash. Later he paid older guys to buy it for him. His father eventually lost the house from the drug debts his mother had racked up, and then he disappeared. I asked Woody if he had ever looked for his father and he said no.

"Why not?"

"Because if I look, I might find him."

He really had nobody. It hit me that he had no reason to be nice, but he was nice to everybody. Besides going to high school classes, he now had two jobs, one using his old beat-up car to pick up plans and deliver small things for a construction company and another one on Saturdays, working the counter at a dry cleaners. I could imagine him working with all kinds of people, getting to know them, getting them whatever they needed, whatever would make them happy. The same kinds of things he had been doing two years ago in the woods.

We had to let loose about Ms. Nesbitt.

"Can't she do something about that hair?" Woody laughed. "It looks like she has a thousand red Slinkys bouncing around on her head."

"Don't be cruel. She can't. I was in her class a whole school year. If she sprays those curls to tame them down, they all stick out sideways like springs."

He lit up a joint and we shared it.

"She's cool in her own way," I said. "You know the way she kind of tilts her head sideways when she talks, and you can't quite tell if she's talking to you or not? She can't help it. But after a while you start to think it's ... I don't know, *charming*?" I took another hit. "Or it would be a charming look, on a dog." I thought I was so funny.

He laughed. "She's a good lady. I'm going to find her a guy."

It was getting dark. I had to get home and do some homework before Zeus called after eleven. "Thanks for the dinner and all. I didn't really mind you all talking about my baby."

"That baby is lucky. She's in a good place, I'm sure."

I was halfway out the door when he called me back. "Is that guy still giving you oxycodone?"

"More prescriptions. Here." I pulled all three of them out of my backpack and handed them to him. He threw them on his desk, right on top of the old one which was still sitting there from a few weeks back. "I never fill them. But he still hands pills to me. I took one more from his hand. I wasn't going to tell you."

He grabbed me by the shoulders and shook me hard. "You promised you stopped."

"I did. Get off me!"

He dropped his hands, but we both stood there, both breathing hard.

"I think I can keep off them now."

"I don't see why you go out with him at all."

"We help each other. It's not just the pills like you think."

... ...

162

Of course, telling Kate something is the same as telling Lucky, so when I was in his car with her and Woody a few days later it was like a meeting of all the people in the world who knew I was hanging out with Dr. Zeus.

"We missed hanging with you last year." Lucky sounded like he meant it.

Kate arranged this ride. She sat in the back with me when Woody got in so it wouldn't seem like a double date.

We drove around to a bunch of construction sites. Lucky's father was a small-time contractor, and so Lucky was interested in what was going on at the construction sites where Woody worked. Lucky had always worked with his father and now was doing some jobs on his own. He and Woody knew all the contractors in the area.

"You know, Lucky and Woody are working on our own school now," Kate announced. "On the new annex. Can you believe it?'"

"Just a little subcontract," Lucky explained. "Off the books, you know. Just a little drywall work. You know, taping and spackling."

Woody laughed. "We have to do it at night so nobody will recognize us, you know, as students." He laughed again. "It's so hard to see at night. We can't use too many lights either. So the first couple walls looked pretty crappy."

"Yeah, Fli-Bi-Nite contractors had a pretty rough start."

Lucky took out a joint and passed it around. We passed a huge brick complex set back far from the road.

"That's the Academy Church, where I went to school last year. See, there's the school building. And there's the gymnasium building behind it."

"And Dr. Zeus's office is in there? In the gymnasium? That huge building behind the church?" Kate asked.

"Yeah."

"Oh!" Woody was excited. "I remember something now. I

know the guy who built that medical office inside that complex. It's like inside the gym, right? Man, he told me that thing violates every building code that's ever been written."

"I guess Jesus gave them a pass on that."

"Do you and this guy Zeus actually go out on dates, or what?" Lucky asked.

"We do, but we can't go any place where people will recognize us." There was like this total silence in the car then. "I know. Sometimes I wonder if he's too old. But nobody my age has even talked to me in the last two years."

··· ···

Robert was always trying to call or text me. Usually I totally ignored him. I don't know why I picked up the phone that night – maybe because I was feeling good after riding around with Kate and Lucky and Woody, feeling strong enough to get Robert to leave me alone once and for all.

"I saw you on the beach at the ocean with Doctor Zeus."

"Shut up, Robert. You don't know what you're talking about."

"Do you want me to forward you the video? Or should I just put it on YouTube?"

"Quit stalking me! I'll call the police, I swear."

"Oh ...." His voice came out very low, then it was like he gave up talking. Then he started sniffling and crying. "Why? Why?" he cried. "You are so beautiful, in body and soul." He sniffled a little more. "But you defile yourself, over and over." More sniffling, deep breathing. "I want you to know that I have dedicated myself to Jesus."

"That's nice, Robert, I guess."

"My mission from Jesus is to save you, to wash away your sins in the sacred river of my pure love."

"I don't believe in that kind of Jesus."

"No! No, you must. You have to."

"Jesus wouldn't want you putting pictures of me on the internet." The phone went so quiet I thought he had hung up. "Robert?"

"I would never do that, Diane. I would never do anything to harm you."

Chapter 21

Hartwicke

Hartwicke felt like a huge lion whose lifeblood was being sucked away by a million tiny fleas. First, he had drained $15,000 from their joint bank account for the bribe to Concord Mews for Kyra's freshman year. This was on top of the $28,000 tuition. The various repairs done to the Jag while it was under Marcie's control totaled almost $10,000. He paid that from the joint account also. But the Kia was a different matter. The credit card company would pay for the damage to the Kia if he filed a report explaining how the accident happened. But he couldn't file a written report without risking Elena finding out exactly how it did happen. So he paid that bill, almost $2,300, from his secret account.

He still couldn't use his own garage. He had to park the Jag across the street to hide from Elena the broken headlight and the damage to the passenger side door from the collision with the Kia on Marcie's front lawn. On top of that, he had gotten an inspection ticket while he was driving the Jag to the beach with Diane, and he had 30 days to get the headlight fixed. That would have to be another cash deal. If the Kia damage cost $2,300, he figured the equivalent damage to the Jag would probably be over $8,000. And then there was Marcie, who was nagging him for $3,000 to get her own car fixed.

Then Grunk called him up and told him the Board had expanded its investigation and subpoenaed just about every record New Town Partners had ever created. The Board wouldn't say what they were after, but it looked like they were interested in his female patients. They had never closed the case about Katherine, and now it looked like they might have had another complaint from another woman.

"Who?"

"The Board won't say. They won't tell us anything."

"Tell *us*? Who is *us*?"

"Yes, *us*. New Town Partners has hired me to represent them in the investigation," Grunk told him. "I'm calling to see if you want me to represent you personally also."

"Yes, of course. I already paid you $10,000."

"That was a retainer. From when the case appeared much simpler. As it is, you have used up most of that already. I would require another $15,000 retainer for the kind of complex advocacy that's now going to be required. At my rate, which is $300 an hour, $450 an hour for any trial work, I'd be surprised if in the end it won't cost you twice as much."

Zeus was still fuming from that call when he got another one. It was from his manager at PeakResults Labs. Referrals for tests had fallen drastically. Zeus's partners at New Town were not sending any samples at all to PeakResults for testing. A few private doctors who knew about their services were still sending some in, but that wasn't enough to pay expenses. They wouldn't be able to meet payroll the next month unless Zeus pumped in cash.

"Give me a number."

"To keep running, we're going to need $55,000 a month more than what's coming in now. I'll need it in cash from you, unless your partners start referring samples here, or unless you can get a big chunk of Freeland Hospital's referrals."

"Can't you lay people off?"

"I've laid off everyone we possibly could and still legally call ourselves a lab. It'll cost that much just to keep this skeleton operation going and meet our payments on the lab equipment."

"What if we just shut down?"

"We will still owe over $350,000 for the lab equipment. For which, you might remember, you are personally liable. The lenders aren't going to forget that."

At $55,000 a month, his secret cash hoard of about $150,000 wouldn't last long. And Grunk's bill would eat up most of what was left of his and Elena's joint money. But he had an idea.

••• •••

"I need those referrals now, John. I can't wait until after I'm on the Board."

"We've worked well with each other before, Hartwicke," Billings replied. "When conditions are right, I'm sure it will happen."

"Let me ask you if you think these conditions are right. There's this nurse friend of mine. Hottest piece of ass east of the Mississippi. Very good nurse. Husband left her. Desperate for money. There's a job opening in the hospital now for chief pediatric nurse. She'd be great at that. She really needs the money. I could get her to apply. She's really desperate, if you know what I mean."

Billings squirmed around in his chair, as he often did when the topic under discussion was women. Zeus looked at Billings's large, lumpy body, bullet head, receding hairline, thick black-framed glasses, sallow skin, bad clothes, and appreciated why the only women Billings ever got were the desperate kind.

"Oh, you must mean Marcie Thompson! She already did apply. Lovely lady. Spunky. She and I already had an interview, a very private interview. I think she's already pretty much got the job sewn up."

Zeus was at a loss for words. He'd never been outmaneuvered by Billings before.

••• •••

"Diane? Where were you? It's after midnight. I've been

calling for hours."

"Just goofing around, driving around with some friends." He could hear her yawn as she said this. She didn't seem the least bit alarmed that she had missed his call. Was he wasting his time chasing a sixteen-year-old dingbat?

"I'm calling to apologize to you."

"For what?"

"For trying to grope you on the beach."

"You were pretty gross. Trying to be, anyway." Her voice was still sleepy. He didn't hear any indignation. Was that a good sign or a bad sign?

"There's something about you, something that makes me want to show you off to everybody."

"That was pretty gross." She was focusing on that one little thing, he noticed.

"I'm sorry. But I mean I wish we could be more public, in a regular way. I'm so proud of having you as my girl. I wish I could take you out in public. I'd be so proud to introduce you to my friends. It'll happen. We'll get there some day."

She seemed more alert now. "I don't see how that can happen, unless you got a divorce."

This call wasn't going as planned. The plan had been to make sure the little bitch kept performing on cue for her master.

"You're right, Diane. I know. A divorce."

"Could that ever happen? Really?"

"I'm saying please give me some time. My dream is you will be Mrs. Zeus within a year."

Chapter 22

David

Michele came into his cubicle with a look he could not decipher, then dropped onto his desk a printed document which was stapled to a large manila mailing envelope. Uncharacteristically, she left without saying anything. It was obviously a court document. The caption indicated it was a "Temporary Restraining Order." He skipped to the last page.

> It is therefore ORDERED that the Defendant State Board of Medicine's subpoena issued to New Town Partners, LLC, in Investigation No. 4322 be, and it hereby is, QUASHED; and

> It is further ORDERED that the Board CEASE AND DESIST from pursuing Investigation No. 4322, and any and all other investigations of New Town Partners, LLC, or Hartwicke Zeus, M.D. unless and until permitted after further proceedings in this court.

Michele came back in. "That's our Zeus case. Does that suck or what?"

"We have to stop our investigation? Until when? What are these 'further proceedings?'"

"There's a meeting in Frank's office in fifteen minutes. We're both supposed to be there. Frank's already screamed at our own lawyer. She's on her way up to the Board now."

Dave and Michele arrived in Frank's office on time, but the prosecuting attorney, Nancy Hunt, had not yet arrived. Nancy was not actually an employee of the Board. She worked for the

Office of State Government Counsel and had been assigned to represent the Board. She didn't always arrive on time for Frank's meetings, and Frank usually made a point of not showing up himself until five minutes after she finally did arrive. But he was too upset to play those mind games today.

"I should have known to expect this load of shit from Grunk," Frank grumbled as he edged past their chairs to his seat behind his desk. But instead of sitting down, he kept standing, staring out the window. "That slimy bastard sneaked into court behind our backs, and now his slimy client can rape all the women he wants until we get this thing undone."

With the slightest movement of her eyes, Michele signaled Dave not to comment.

"Where's Nancy Hunt? How the hell did this happen?"

Nancy appeared in the doorway. She was thin, tall enough in high heels, with a curtain of straight brown hair held back with clips to reveal a severe, no-nonsense expression. Dave had worked with her once before, in her role as prosecutor in the Agazzi case. "Hello. Sorry I'm late. Grunk didn't inform me this was coming. That sleaseball slimed his way into court and got the judge to sign this without giving us any notice. He went behind our backs straight to the court."

Frank managed to sit down. "What do we do now, counselor?"

"Stop the investigation until I can file an opposition in court."

"How long will that take?" Frank looked suspicious.

"Depends." She asked for a copy of the subpoena Frank had made Dave send to New Town Partners. They waited while Nancy read this over too. "Oh. Oh. Oh. Um, this subpoena. I can see why they complained. It's way overbroad. It's oppressive, really. They'd have to turn the place upside down to comply with this. What are we actually investigating?"

"We have a video of him fondling a teenage female patient on the beach." Frank liked to keep the focus on the evil they were fighting.

"Oh Jesus! That one? And now Grunk's got the judge to stop the whole investigation. Talk about a bad start."

"What are these 'further proceedings' that the order talks about?" Dave was so upset himself he didn't mind sounding ignorant.

Nancy looked blandly at him. "'Further proceedings' means there will further action in court. It means there will be another court hearing where the judge will decide whether to permanently ban the Board from investigating Zeus."

"He can do that?"

"He can do anything. He's a judge. But that's not likely to happen. If you guys modify the subpoena, make it a little less oppressive, I think I can get him to lift the order entirely, but not until after I can get my day in court."

"We can't do anything at all until then?"

"No investigation can be done until I get the court to lift the restraining order. But you guys have to modify that subpoena first."

"We need everything listed in that subpoena," Frank challenged her.

"You're just not going to get everything listed in that subpoena. No way. Impossible. Modify that subpoena now, or I can promise you the judge is going to force you to permanently close the case."

"Forget it, Counsel!" Frank yelled.

Nancy stood up, clacked out of the room in her high heels and slammed the door.

Dave and Michele froze. Frank was breathing heavily. The muscles in his arms were visibly contracting. A whole minute went by. Dave started to get up, but Michele glanced at him and shook her head. There was a moment of complete silence.

"Okay, do what she says," Frank pushed himself back in his chair so forcefully Dave feared its springs would snap. "Withdraw the subpoena. Cooperate with Nancy. Call her, Michele, and make nice. But this really sucks."

"Do you think the court will let us start up again?" Dave braved to ask.

"Best case scenario, we get to reopen the case 30 or 60 days from now. But who knows what he might have done to that girl by then."

Dave followed Michele back to her office. "Is this what happens here? Nothing? Nothing happens to Zeus? Not for what he did to Katherine, not for what he's doing to Diane?"

Michele shrugged. "I asked Nancy. She guessed Zeus spent $10,000 on that motion alone. The doctors with money can put up an unbelievable fight. Sometimes it takes years."

Dave retreated back to his cubicle. The more he thought about the case, the angrier he got. Because of some smart-ass attorney trick, Zeus had just bought another 30 to 60 days before the case could even get started. Regular people couldn't do that. When they got a summons they showed up or paid the ticket. When they got a tax bill they paid it. If they molested a teenager on the beach they'd be immediately hauled off to jail. But people like Zeus could keep the Board from even starting to investigate.

He found himself at the door to Frank's office. "Frank, what are we diddling around for with Zeus? If we can't do shit with the case ourselves, why don't we just send that video to the police?"

"Come in, Newbie. Close the door." Frank smiled. He liked it when his employees talked tough. "I'd like to go out and just beat the shit out of Zeus myself." Frank was sufficiently politically correct not to say this so loud it could be heard through the door.

"Why don't we call the police?"

"Newbie," he started. He said Dave's nickname with a gentler ring than ever before. "I was a cop for seventeen years before I came here. The cops wouldn't touch this case with a ten-foot pole. All we've got is an anonymous video. The girl isn't complaining. It was obviously consensual. We don't have a victim. We don't have a crime. Even if she's underage, who's to say he wasn't just putting suntan lotion on her. That's exactly what she'll say, because her other choice is to be humiliated in a public courtroom. And that's assuming the cops can find her. And they're not going to spend a lot of time looking. In case you haven't noticed, there have been over two hundred murders so far this year in this metro area, over 50% of them unsolved."

"If we reported it, wouldn't it at least scare him?"

"Not him. The guy's a narcissist. He doesn't give a shit about anything. You punch him, he punches back. If this case was charged criminally, the only one who would be scared shitless would be Diane."

Dave went back to his office carrying the court papers. He stared at the judge's signature on the court order and wondered how much the judge had been influenced by Zeus's power and position. And money – anybody who could afford to hire Grunk had to be rich. At Grunk's request, the judge had gone out of his way to stop the entire investigation just because one subpoena was bad. And the judge did it without giving the Board a chance to respond. Dave couldn't help believing that the judges always listened more closely to the voices of those on top of the heap. The little people like Katherine and Diane theoretically had an equal right to be heard, but Dave was starting to understand that the judges couldn't really hear them above the constant racket make by Eli Grunk and all the other silver-tongued lawyers who spent their professional lives renting themselves out to the rich.

··· ···

Dave's mother had started as a bookkeeper for a department store chain in town. Then she went to school at night to become an accountant, leaving him in the care of one aunt or another after school and at nights. His father had died of cancer when Dave was two. For a few years, his aunts rotated shifts as his babysitter. Then his mother finally got her degree, and it was like getting to know her all over again. But gradually, as he approached high school age, she began to spend more and more time at work as the business expanded, and as she was asked to serve on committee after committee, write report after report. Then old man Herz, the CEO of the chain, had a stroke and was rendered virtually comatose; but he wouldn't quit. They couldn't make him quit because he and his relatives owned a huge stake in the stock of the company. For several years, they literally propped him up at board meetings while Dave's mother spoke for him. She ran the entire business during those years, acting as CEO in all but name.

His mother was working at another job now. He had just finished talking with her over the phone when Sarah called. Sarah got right to the point. "So, have you thought any more about my proposal?"

"What do you mean? Yes. The answer is yes. I want to marry you. I promise to marry you. We need a ring, though. You obviously don't have much experience proposing."

"I'm not usually that spontaneous. But now we need a plan too, don't we?"

"I'm all the time now trying to figure out how I can make it work."

"Without money from my family, you mean."

"Without your father financing our whole lives."

"Not our whole lives. Just your law school tuition. Just a great wedding present." He could hear her sigh. "You've never even met him. He's smart, and kind, and funny. You would love him."

The long silence on the phone meant they'd decided to let it go, again.

"We'll figure a way, I promise," he said finally. "That's all I think about when I'm not at work."

"At least you still have a job. We're lucky Michele didn't tell Frank what you did – I mean contacting that girl after he told you not to."

"Michele did give me hell, though. A big lecture on professionalism. It really made me think."

"Like what?"

"She said I let her down. She's such a good soul, and she's on my side. What she said really made me feel awful. To tell the truth, it's still bothering me."

"No woman ever told you that before, I bet."

Chapter 23

Hartwicke

Marcie was leaning back lazily in the huge chair left in the office by the previous Director of Nursing. Her skirt had slid up. She started to snap her knees together when she heard someone coming, but when she saw it was Zeus she changed her mind.

"I see you're comfortable in your new position," he began.

She looked up with her usual sly smile. He wasn't really happy she was part of management now.

"Congratulations," he continued. "I hear you slept your way into the job."

"I found I could fulfill a pressing need the CEO had."

She was absolutely unrepentant in flaunting her slutty career move. If she only knew he would be on top soon. In every way. And when he was, he would never trade a job for a one-time fling with her like that pathetic loser Billings had.

Then she surprised him. "Thank you for paying my car repair bill."

It hadn't been that much. Only $700 for CV joints for the old clunker, much less than he had estimated. He could have paid to fix her car long ago and avoided all that drama about the Jaguar and the rented Kia and the collision between the two. But the whole mess was worth it if it taught Marcie he would always end up in control.

His day had gone as well as could be expected, considering the human dross he had to deal with. He had met with Donald Thomas, the managing partner of New Town Partners, late that afternoon. Zeus had blown his mind by showing him a check for $325,000, almost the full amount he still owed for his share of the medical partnership. And as soon as he assured himself that Thomas's eyes were practically bugging out of his head, Zeus pulled the check back.

"One thing, Donald. When I first came here, I thought we had an understanding that New Town Partners would refer all of its lab work to PeakResults Labs. It started to happen, then it mysteriously stopped."

"That probably wasn't an accident. I hear the other physicians talking. Nobody is impressed by the one-half of one percent interest in PeakResults you gave us."

"I can go one percent, but I need those referrals, now."

"Still, peanuts. But the main thing I hear is the other physicians don't like you. They don't like that you stalled on making your partnership payments to New Town. They don't like hearing the patients complain about your quickie examinations. They don't like that we can't always reach you when you're on call. They don't like you parking in their parking spaces."

"Do you want the money or not?"

"You legally owe it to us anyway."

Zeus held up the check. "You can have it right now. You're the managing partner. You can make them refer all their lab work to PeakResults, if you have the balls to use your own authority."

Thomas shifted in his chair and stared down at his desk. Zeus wasn't really sure Thomas could force all of the other doctors to use PeakResults. But he knew Thomas was practically salivating over that check – and didn't like being called a wimp. When Thomas hesitated for another second, Zeus thought he had won. Zeus felt like the ringmaster holding the whip, watching this little Thomas dog jump.

"I'll give you half, half the referrals."

Zeus was shocked. He couldn't believe Thomas had the guts to lowball him like that. What a piece of scum he was! "Half? Why not all the referrals?"

"You still haven't given us all the money you owe us. Even

after you give me that check, you'll still owe us $75,000."

Zeus quickly calculated that if PeakResults got half of the New Town referrals, the lab could probably limp along for a few months more without too much of a drain on his own personal account. And if he got together the remaining $75,000 soon and got the other half of the referrals, PeakResults could defnitely break even. Zeus didn't have the $75,000 right then, so he had no choice but to submit to Thomas's proposal. The surge of euphoria he had felt walking into the office dissolved into a sour taste in his stomach. He gave Thomas the $325,000 check in return for half the referrals, but he left feeling he had been cheated.

"I'm going to be on the Board of Trustees of this hospital soon," he now told Marcie. By then he had practically forgotten his anger at Thomas and was focusing on the big picture of the riches and power he would soon acquire because of his hard work, his intellect and, especially, his unmatched cunning.

Marcie leaned back, her tiny body almost lost in the giant tilting chair. He interpreted her legs-open pose as a gesture of submission. Of course it was submission. Once he got on the Board of Trustees, her job would be dependent on his good graces. Once he was on the Board of Trustees, he could make the hospital pour money into PeakResults. Marcie's submission would be total then, and he would even find a way to make Billings pay for stalling his appointment for so long. He could feel the power coursing through his veins even now, and he thought Marcie could sense it too.

Apparently, he was wrong about the Marcie part. As soon as he put his hand on her leg she slapped him so hard the sound of it echoed off the hallway wall across from her open office door.

"You bitch! You little cockteasing whore!"

"I love it when you talk sweet to me."

A woman walking down the hallway slowed down and

briefly glanced in but then kept going.

"Close the door," Marcie ordered.

He did as he was told. He knew there was only one reason for closing the door. Turning around, he was excited before he even saw the way she was sitting on the edge of her desk, her expression sassy and her legs open and waiting for him. While they were doing it, he wanted to feel that extra little bit of spice from having her under his total control. He commanded her to thank him for fixing her car.

"I already did that."

"Oh yeah." Marcie got him so hot he sometimes lost track. "Okay. Well, tell me how much you need me inside you."

"About once a month is plenty."

••• •••

"You emptied out my 401(k)!" Elena ran toward him like she was going to knock him down. "Jesus Christ, Hardy, you signed my name! That's fraud! I could put you in jail! I will put you in jail!"

Zeus put out his hands to keep her at arm's length. "Let me explain, honey." He spoke in a very calm voice. He knew the person who spoke in the calmest voice always appeared to be the one in the right. "It's an investment. I used that money to get PeakResults going again. It'll pay off in a few months, and I'll pay you back with interest."

"You know we now have to pay income tax on that whole amount. That's almost $150,000 tax. And the ten percent penalty for early withdrawal. That's another $32,500."

He hadn't known that. He just knew he had asked his receptionist to call the broker and request the forms to be sent to his office, and that he had been required to sign Elena's name because she was the sole owner. There had been some additional queries about the transaction from the brokerage, but he had ordered his receptionist to tell them in no uncertain terms that Elena wanted to withdraw all of it, period.

"It doesn't matter. You have to spend money to make money. PeakResults is going to get tons of referrals from New Town now. And once I'm on the hospital board, PeakResults will be raining money on us." Zeus was unhappy about revealing even this much about his plans to Elena. Small minds could pick away at any scheme, and he had long ago pegged Elena as the smallest of small minds.

"PeakResults? And how much of PeakResults do I own?" She put up her hands to box his ears, but he grabbed her wrists.

"Come on, Elena, honey. You know whatever is mine is yours." She was stronger than he thought.

"Zero. I have zero ownership in PeakResults. I have zero ownership of that secret money market account you've been hiding somewhere. And now I have zero retirement." She pushed him back hard against the wall, but he swung her around and pushed her back into it, pinning her wrists down at her sides. He leaned into her.

"Okay," he said. "Okay, Elena, I underestimated you. But the money, your 401(k) money, that was all needed to keep us from losing everything."

"God, you're an idiot. Throwing good money after bad. *My* money!" She struggled against him, and he pressed her closer.

"I did it for us. At least we're not bankrupt now." She squirmed against him, but he pushed her harder into the wall. "But to get real money, to get your 401(k) money back, I'm going to have to get on the board of Freeland Hospital. That's where you can help. You can get your father to support me. He has connections with most of the current members of the board at Freeland." He knew Elena understood connections. When she had moved from Freeland Hospital to Garden City Hospital years ago, her own career had taken a meteoric rise, probably because her father was then CEO of Garden City.

Her father was now retired but still had connections all over the state. "We can do this together. Together, we can come out of this hole. Get your 401(k) back."

He held her wrists tightly and pressed her close so she couldn't kick. He could feel her breathing heavily, her chest pushing out against his. She didn't say anything. Then he could feel her shoulders and arms relax. He wanted to take her then, badly; he thought she could tell. And he was sure she wanted him, as all women wanted him once they got close enough to have a chance.

"Let me go," she said. "Let me think. What you've done is awful."

"I've created a great opportunity for us to be rich."

He let her go. Although she was still breathing heavily, she didn't jump into his arms as he had expected. She just held herself stiff like she was fighting off her passion for him. He wanted to take her then, make her succumb to him once and for all. But she bumped him away and ran up the stairs.

Two mornings later, as he was crossing the street to get into his car – and still congratulating himself on neutralizing Elena – he suddenly found himself standing in the road, his key hand extended stupidly towards an empty parking space. Elena! He turned around and faced the house, that grand white house with the two-story portico and faux marble columns she was so proud of. She wasn't as fond of the real marble statues of Greek gods he'd installed along the walkway, but he didn't care if she didn't appreciate his finer ideas. He did care that she was now messing with his Jag. He stormed back into the house.

"I sold it to pay the first installment on Kyra's tuition," Elena informed him flatly.

"What!"

"We are out," Elena rubbed her thumb and fingers together, "of money. The deposit on the tuition is due in advance."

"Deposit? Those criminals. She doesn't start there for eleven months."

"You're the one who insisted she go there. You're the one who blew all our money, yours, mine and ours. Mine illegally. I'll make you'll regret this, Hardy."

So this is how it was going to be. He didn't really mind. But his curiosity about the car got the best of him. "Who'd you sell it to? How much did you get for it? That's a rare car, and you have to find the right buyer to get half what it's worth."

"I took it to the dealer. You didn't tell me the right front fender was smashed in. I should have realized you had some reason for parking it across the street."

"What did you get for it?"

"They said repairs on those old cars are really expensive."

"*Old*? They called it old? When they sell you one like that, they call it a *classic*."

"They said old. Anyway, after deducting for repairs and all, they gave me $12,000."

"What! Fixed up, it's worth 75!"

"That's the price they would give me for it. On the day I needed the money."

He didn't rage at her. If this was war, he would make it a cold war. He went down to the dealership immediately. They told him they gave her only $12,000 because they really didn't want that old car. Again, that word grated on him. It had been his father's car, the car he had driven since high school. He demanded it back, claiming it was a fraudulent transaction because his wife had signed his name to the title without his permission. They said they had already wholesaled it to a classic car dealer. He figured they'd gotten about $25,000 for it. He demanded it back anyway. The manager shrugged his broad shoulders. "What do you expect me to do? The car's gone. What I *can* do, Doctor, is sell you a new one."

· · · · · · ·

"I can't wait to see you." The eagerness in his voice was genuine.

He'd noticed a slight difference in Diane's responses to him lately. There was sometimes a half-second delay, as there was this time, and he wondered if he'd given her too many drugs. But he loved to feel his medicinal and sexual powers working on his sixteen-year-old love slave. He felt she was his greatest creation. If the drugs had made her a little slower, so much the better.

"I can't go to the condo, not this weekend," she said now. "Lisa's in a pre-season basketball tournament. It's kind of a big deal in my family. The whole family's going."

"My friends really want to meet you at the condo."

"I'm sorry. Basketball …. It's kind of a kid thing, I know. I want to try to grow up so quick you will be so proud of me."

"I really wanted to show you my new car."

"New? Really? What color?"

"I'll show you on our next trip."

Chapter 24

Diane

Zeus's new maroon car was smoother and quieter than his old one. Riding in it was like sitting on a soft leather sofa that was flying over the road without touching the ground.

"Do you like it?" He smiled that devilish smile. He could always make me feel like the whole wide world had been invented just for us. I didn't really care about cars, but I was trying to care about the things he liked.

"It's really nice." I couldn't think about the car. I was nervous about meeting his friends. "Who are your friends I'm going to meet?"

"A physician and his wife. I knew him in residency years ago. They just moved back to town. They don't know anybody."

"So I guess they have to like me, or they still won't have any friends."

He smiled. "They'll like you."

"You really think they'll believe I'm nineteen?"

He smiled over at me. "Diane, you could pass for twenty-one if you had to. You're smart and articulate. You look mature. Your body's mature. Tell them you graduated from high school last spring and you're starting community college in a nursing program."

I hadn't thought about how many lies I'd have to tell to be his girlfriend in public. That part was not going to be fun.

He pulled off the highway onto the parking lot of a strip mall. "You're nervous, aren't you?"

"Yeah."

"Have you taken your medication?"

"No. Not today."

He reached into the console and poured two pills out of a bottle he had stashed there. He held them up to my mouth. "No wonder you're feeling bad. Here, these are fast acting. Take them right now with your soda."

"I don't want to." I turned my head.

"Take them!" He put them up to my mouth again.

"No!" I hit his hand and knocked the pills on the floor.

I thought I saw a hard look flash into his eyes, but it disappeared so fast I decided I must have imagined it.

"I just thought you needed it," he said. He looked sad. I was really sorry I had been so mean.

"Thanks." I said. "I want to be honest with you about the drugs. They're nice, but I don't always need them."

"You've got to learn to live faster." Then he screeched the tires and pulled out on the highway and passed about ten cars in about a minute. He didn't have the radio on, and all you could hear was each of us breathing hard and the soft purr of the engine. I asked him to slow down and he did. It meant a lot to me that he listened. Why couldn't I do what he wanted sometimes? Why not be all happy and fuzzy for him just this once, like he wanted? I undid my seatbelt and scrabbled around on the floor for the two pills and took them with my soda.

"You didn't have to do that, Diane. I have a lot more right here. You can have whatever you want, as much as you want. Just ask."

Chapter 25

David

Ms. Porter: Katherine, do you know how many times you went back to his office to get your oxycodone prescriptions filled?

Ms. Bolt: I don't know. All through the spring and early summer.

Q: Do you know if he kept a medical record each time?

A: I don't know.

Q: Were these scheduled visits? I mean, do you think your name would be on the patient log for these visits?

A: I would call .... I mean he knew I needed those pills, and he'd tell me what day I was allowed to come in. It's not like I could plan ahead. I mean I couldn't control how many I was taking. I couldn't control what days he would let me come, either. Sometimes I think he made me suffer an extra day on purpose.

A: Why would he do that?

Q: Just to show me he was the boss, that he could make me do whatever he said.

Q: To get back to the records for a minute, I gather you don't know whether your name was written on the patient log or not.

A: No. I'm sorry I'm not much help. I wasn't noticing much. I ... was out of control.

Q: And did you and Dr. Zeus have sex on any of these occasions?

A: Yes.

Q: How many times?
A: Every time.
Q: In his examining room?
A: Sometimes there. And he had his own
little office behind. Wherever he wanted.
Q: I know this is embarrassing, but I have
to ask you these questions. What type of
sex did he have with you?
A: Every type. Whatever he wanted.

"Frank wants to see you later, before the Board meeting this morning." Michele spoke in a low voice as they stirred coffee together in the break room. "Come into my office right now and I'll tell you. It's a good news/bad news kind of thing."

He followed her into her cubicle.

"What's up?" He had learned to speak almost in a whisper if anything important had to be discussed in a cubicle.

"Frank's taking the Zeus case to the Board this morning. He's going to ask them to charge Zeus in Katherine's case."

"I thought the court ordered us to stop."

"The court told us to stop *investigating*. This isn't investigating. Frank's cutting short the investigation and going right to charges. If the Board agrees with him and issues charges against Zeus, we'll have to go to the administrative hearing with whatever evidence we already have."

Dave by now had some idea of how the system set up under the Medical Practice Act worked. The investigators received complaints and collected evidence. If they thought they had enough evidence – and if the offense was serious enough – they recommended charges. The Board then decided whether to issue charges. If the Board issued charges and the case didn't settle, it was then sent to an independent Administrative Law Judge who held a hearing. That hearing could be every bit as lengthy and convoluted and adversarial as any court case. The Administrative Law Judge would issue a decision about 120 days later, either revoking or suspending the doctor's license – or completely dismissing the charges. A doctor who was unhappy with the Administrative Law Judge's decision could then appeal to the regular state courts.

"Does it make any sense to charge now?" Dave asked Michele. "All we have now is Katherine's testimony."

"Right. And Zeus has her medical records – which he created – saying she was delusional. But, you know, I believed her, so maybe the Board and the Administrative Law Judge will believe her."

"So we're charging him with the Katherine stuff?"

"And I think you should stay away from the Board meeting this morning."

"What?" There was nothing Dave wanted to do more than watch the Board vote to charge Zeus for all the things he had done to Katherine.

"He's going to be talking about the Diane Morrell case, too – you know, that teenager. You can't be sitting there in front of the Board when Frank does that. You don't want to be there if the Board members start asking whether we've ever interviewed Diane."

"Can't I just tell them the truth – if they ask?"

"If you surprise Frank right there in front of the Board, you'll be fired. And if you're there, and you see Frank say we haven't interviewed Diane, you'll be letting him lie to the Board. Unintentionally on his part, but it will still be a lie, and he could get in trouble – in which case you will too."

> Q: I know this has been really hard for you, Katherine, but it was important that we know all the details, even the embarrassing sexual details. Thank you. I have just a few more questions. Is that the only place you had sex with Dr. Zeus? In his office?

A: Yes. Well ... no."

Q: What do you mean?

A: He took me down to his condo at the beach once.

Q: Okay. And did you do pretty much the same things you did in his office?

A: Um, no.

Q: Okay.

A: It was a beautiful place, nine or ten floors up, right on the beach. It had a balcony overlooking the ocean, and two bedrooms.

Q: Okay.

A: We were in the bedroom. I was ... *servicing* him. That's what it was. He had given me a little oxycodone, but he never gave me enough until he was completely spent.

Q: Okay.

A: And I was begging him then, but he said I had to do something else first. I was lying there thinking, what else could the man possibly want?

Q: And what was that?

A: I never thought I would ever do anything like that.

Chapter 26

Diane

If you're a girl and you want to feel like the queen of the world, have your gorgeous, rich doctor boyfriend glide you down to his condo at the beach in his new car smelling like leather and perfume while your oxycodone high tingles you all through inside. I was feeling great but at the same time thinking it was too good to be true. I knew it was an oxy high and not real. Zeus asked me if I wanted to hear some music. Then he asked me what I wanted to listen to. I said Nicki Minaj. I knew he would hate rap but he found her on Pandora and put her on anyway.

I started thinking of those oxy prescriptions Zeus had written for me that were piled up on Woody's desk in his garage house. Once I asked Woody why he didn't just throw them away. He said it wouldn't do any good if he was the one who threw them away. I had to do it myself. I thought that was silly then; I thought I'd never use oxy again. But I didn't ever throw the prescriptions away or rip them up. I guess I'm not as strong as I thought I was.

I started thinking about Woody. I knew Woody didn't really approve of me going with Zeus. But he would never say it right out. If I asked him, he would always say it was okay. "You gotta do what you gotta do." He said that every time.

I think he meant you have to do what you're fated to do, even if you'll suffer in the end. It was like he thought my love for Zeus was fated to drive me down. But I was more curious about Woody than worried about myself. I knew he had plans. He wanted to go to college, in business. He would probably have to start in community college. It seemed like he would be good in business. He always seemed to know how to get things done and keep people happy. But when I said anything like that to him he would just look down at the floor. One afternoon it hit me that I could just ask him where he was coming from.

"Where was your head at," I asked him. "I mean back then, when you used to hang around the woods bringing pot and booze for everybody."

"I don't know." He shook his head like he didn't want to think about it.

"I'm not complaining," I said. "I thought it was fun."

"I just don't like to think about that time in my life."

"Why not?" I kept at him.

He jumped up and started pacing back and forth, about four steps in either direction inside his garage house. "That's all I am to anybody. The guy who gets the stuff for them."

"That's not true."

He stopped and turned to me, looking all tall and sinewy but still a little skinny, and with his head bowed so he could meet my eyes. "Even you," he said. "The only reason you first talked to me in school was you wanted to get some pot."

"That's not true," I said, trying to remember exactly what was the first reason I talked to him. "I liked you. I knew you'd be nice to me. Come on. Calm down."

He sat down on the edge of the bed. "Okay. But tell the truth. Did you send Lisa to me so she could get pot?"

"Lisa? What? No! Never. Oh, that little bitch! When was this? What exactly happened?" I bounced up off the bed, practically knocking him off too.

"Yesterday. She's sitting with some girls in the cafeteria, not exactly talking with them but at the end of the table. I come in and she stands up and goes up to me. I already knew who she was. I thought maybe she wanted to give me a message from you or something. But she comes up to me and says she's your sister and right away asks if I can get some weed for her."

"You said no, right?"

"Right. I thought she'd get mad. I mean, that's what people want me for. But she just got all nervous and ran away. She didn't even go back to the table."

The thing that stuck in my head, besides my plan to slap Lisa silly, was Woody saying that's what people wanted him for.

"That's not what people want you for. They like you because you're a cool, independent guy." I could tell he liked that. But I didn't want him to think I was coming on to him. "And I think Ms. Nesbitt has the hots for you."

He laughed. I was getting ready to go, but he asked me to wait.

"Diane, people ask me a lot for special favors. I wasn't going to tell you about all of them."

"Lisa. I know she's really tall and all, but she's kind of young for her age. You know what I mean?"

"I don't mean just about Lisa." He met my stare. "People try to use me to do sketchy shit for them all the time. You know that guy with the black pants, the one who calls himself Deacon? He said he'd give me $500 if I got your cellphone and gave it to him for an hour."

After that I never once let my cell phone out of my sight day or night. The other one, the secret phone Zeus gave me, had some very personal texts on it, and I erased all of them as soon as I got back home from Woody's garage that afternoon. So much for all those text messages that said my breasts were works of art.

Now I reclined in my seat in Zeus's new maroon car, relaxed, and thanked God for sending him to me. The soft air from the vents in the leather dashboard ruffled his silky dark hair. We had just crossed a long, arched bridge with a view of the wide river below. The river was a pristine blue-green and kind of fringed with grey wooden piers that were slotted with dainty white sailboats. Past the bridge the road curved and sliced through a field of sparkling green marsh grass. I wanted to hold his hand and so I took it off the steering wheel and made him drive with his left. It was the pills that were giving me that extra dose of courage.

My thoughts wandered back to Woody again. I was glad I had remembered it was his nineteenth birthday the week before. I drove him and Kate and Lucky out to a McDonalds and we hid in a corner and I gave him a pathetic cake I had made at home. I was sure we could have had a huge party at Ms. Nesbitt's house, but Kate said she thought Ms. Nesbitt might actually be stuck on Woody and we shouldn't encourage her. Woody had never talked about having a girlfriend, but Kate and I decided he deserved to have somebody his own age. For his birthday, I gave him a sweatshirt that said "No Sale" in big letters on the front.

It felt strange to have to talk to Lisa about drugs, but it turned out I didn't have to say anything. The second I came into her room, she jumped up and closed the door behind me and burst into tears.

"I'm sorry! I'm such a dork. I was just trying to be ... I guess like you. He probably thinks I'm so weird to just walk up to him like that. Tell him I'm sorry. Please."

It looks like my work here is done, I thought to myself. I was tempted to walk out of the room right then, maintaining my superiority over my little sister in every way.

"It's okay, Lisa. He likes you. He was just embarrassed. He's always trying to forget about his past. Just don't ask him for drugs."

··· ···

We crossed a long bridge over the sound and cruised up Ocean Highway, first through the jumble of small motels and parking lots and old, white rental houses and hotels crowding to the very edge of the sidewalk, then through the land of bigger brick and concrete hotels and motels, then finally to condo land, where you could sometimes see from the road a speck of the ocean between the twenty- story condos. But Zeus drove right past his own condo building and kept going for maybe an hour. He finally pulled into another resort town, an older-looking one, and down a couple of side streets until he pulled to the curb right in front of a no parking sign and got out and motioned for me to come too.

It was a jewelry store he wanted me to see. I kind of rolled my eyes because I'm not big into jewelry at all, but I followed him in. Big windows on two sides lit the place up with sunlight. The owner, a short guy with black hair and a moustache, jumped to unlock any case Zeus wanted to see. Zeus held up bracelet after bracelet against my arm. Some were emeralds, some rubies, some garnets, some opals – they had to tell me what kind of jewels they were. They never said how much any of them cost. I grabbed one and looked at the tiny price tag hanging by the tiniest string: $4,995. The owner waved his hand and said ignore that tag. Still, I couldn't help but think of the two long Saturdays the whole soccer team spent washing cars behind the 7-11 to earn the $395 it cost to buy team jerseys. I told Zeus I thought jewelry was a waste, but he said it was for him, he liked to see it on me. I made the mistake of saying "ooh" at an emerald necklace and he immediately said he'd take it. I looked at the price: $6,995.

"No. This is really stupid."

Zeus held it up to my neck. The owner, who was acting all cool about the whole thing, said he could probably come down a few hundred dollars.

"This exquisite woman deserves this exquisite necklace. Cut the price $2,000 and I'll take it."

"Sir, I couldn't do that. I could lower the price maybe $500."

"You can do $2,000, I know. But I'm in a hurry. Let's stop

wasting each other's time. $1,000."

"As you wish, sir."

One swipe of his credit card and I was walking out wearing an emerald necklace that everybody would probably think was just colored glass because all I was wearing was shorts and a stretchy tank top. He took me to a fancy little restaurant in the little town for lunch, but I felt all out of place because of my clothes. He told me there was no hurry because his friends wouldn't arrive at the condo until the evening. By the time the lunch was over and we had driven back to his condo, my high had worn off and I was feeling kind of achy.

Chapter 27

Hartwicke

He had engineered his way out of all the traps set for him by the smug and sanctimonious people in his life. Elena, for one, had no hold on him. In fact, she was trapped herself. She couldn't even divorce him until he had enough money to pay her back. And so she had to be on his side.

Zeus's prospects of taking over Freeland Hospital were looking good. He had been working on Billings, dangling rewards in front of him, pandering to his weakness. Now, finally, he had him like a laboratory dog, ready to salivate on cue. With Billings' support, he was a shoo-in to be elected to the Board of Trustees of Freeland Hospital. Then everything would fall into place. He and Billings would insist that the hospital send all of its lab work to PeakResults Labs. Within a few months, with PeakResults really cranking, he'd be able to pay off the rest of his partnership fees to New Town Partners and get 100% of their referrals too. There might be a few lean months, and he might have to turn in the Jaguar that he was leasing and take back that emerald necklace to the jeweler. But only a small minded and short-term thinker would let things like that stop him.

But he wondered if his previous plans had been too small. The real money was in acquisitions. A hospital that bought a medical practice assured itself of a constant stream of paying patients. And once a doctor's practice was acquired by a hospital, every patient of that doctor would have to pay the hospital a substantial fee – even if the patient never set foot in the hospital. Knowing this, hospitals paid obscenely high prices to acquire medical practices. Why couldn't Freeland

Hospital buy out New Town Partners and capture all their patients? And in the process pay him, one of the partners in New Town, double or triple his investment? And grow the hospital at the same time?

Why not think even bigger? Elena worked at Garden City Hospital, one of the biggest competitors of Freeland Hospital. From her contacts in the Human Resources Department there, she had learned that Henry Dewberry, the CEO of Garden City Hospital, had terminal cancer. It was only a matter of time until he would have to resign. Once Zeus got control of Freeland Hospital, why shouldn't he go after Garden City while their leader was incapacitated? Compete with Garden City to capture the few remaining independent medical practices in town? Make things hard on Garden City and don't let up on them until they agree to send all of their lab tests to PeakResults, too? Or maybe even force Garden City to merge with Freeland Hospital? The path to glory seemed simple, but only for a man with vision, and guts enough to fight his way down that path.

On the trip back to the condo from the restaurant, Zeus looked over at Diane with a trained physician's eye. She was touching her temples like she had a headache. Probably the oxycodone he had given her at the beginning of the trip was wearing off. Poor girl. He didn't want to give her any more, not yet. It was sad that she had already run through last week's prescription before she even got in the car. He actually didn't like seeing her so weakened and dependent, but women were women, and she was one of them, and he guessed this was the way of the world. The first thing that was going to happen now that she knew her place was he was going to fuck her without a condom.

"I need some clothes," she said, suddenly looking up and shaking off her torpor. "Will you buy me some clothes?"

"Clothes? Why clothes?"

"Because I just realized, I need to look older, for your friends.

Can we buy a skirt or something? I'm sorry, I should have thought of that before I left."

She picked out a green sheath dress. She stood in front of the mirror and said oh God, I'm going to look like my mother some day. He noticed the roots of her hair were coming in light brown. He hoped she wasn't growing it out natural. He preferred the full-on, in-your-face purple look. If she needed more oxycodone, she certainly wasn't showing it then. When they got into the condo she started straightening everything up.

"Let it alone, Diane. The housekeeping service has been here. It's fine."

She dropped the vacuum cleaner wand she had in her hand. "I'm nervous. It's exciting, being your real girlfriend and all. I guess I'm acting stupid. I mean, I'm starting a new life with you, and the first thing I do is start channeling my mother."

"I can give you something for the nerves. But let's hold off for now."

"Thank you for the clothes. And the necklace. Thank you for everything. I mean it."

"Want to go for a walk on the beach? The sun's still awfully hot, but there's a cool breeze coming off the ocean."

Ignoring his question, she walked into the kitchen area and opened the refrigerator. "Do we have any food here? I mean what are we going to give these people?"

"Let's walk on the beach, Diane."

She kept moving around the condo straightening things, almost like she was stalling going out for a walk with him. If this was a symptom of withdrawal, it was a kind he'd never seen before. He wondered if she had her own stash of amphetamines she'd gotten from some of her teenage friends. Finally he cornered her, took her wrists in his hands, and forced her to look him in the eyes.

"Don't you want to go outside with me?"

She looked away and refused to meet his eyes for a minute.

"Okay. But can we just hold hands outside? Nothing else? You know what I mean."

The ocean reflected the orange tint in the sky from the late afternoon sun. The fine white sand was so hot it hurt their bare feet. Diane pulled him into the seething foam at the edge of the ocean as they walked along. She smiled the most beautiful smile at him then, and he felt a surge of real pride that he possessed this gorgeous creature.

She was pulling him along through the white froth that tickled their toes. "What should I talk about with your friends?"

"Just be yourself."

"A high school student? I don't think so. But how can I say I'm in nursing school? What if they start asking questions about that? I don't know anything about nursing."

"I'll handle anything like that if it comes up." He was starting to get annoyed with her questions, but he couldn't let her know this.

"Do your friends have any children?"

"No."

"Do you think they'll ask if I have any children?"

"Why would they ask that?"

"Don't doctors think like that? You know, regular girl, *primipara*, whatever else. If they ask, what should I say?"

Her eager questions kept coming. He'd thought she'd be more on one track by now. He thought she'd be begging for more pills. She hadn't even jumped at the wine he offered her before they left the condo. She stopped walking but kept holding his hand so he was forced to turn to her. Her face was suffused with the same pink hue that colored the white condos that followed the slow curve of the beach behind her. He ached to take her right there in the surf, but she had told him he couldn't. As of that moment, she still had that mysterious bit of control over him.

"If they ask about my baby, I'm going to just tell them the

truth," she said. "I have to tell the truth somewhere."

"Right." She had no idea how pointless was her worry.

Chapter 28

Diane

Robert was probably recording every minute of our walk on the beach. That's why I had to keep Zeus from kissing me there, even though I would've jumped his bones right there in the surf if no one was looking. I knew Robert could get Zeus and me in trouble with those pictures he already had, but I didn't think he would. He'd probably just watch that little video a thousand times all by himself. I suspected I could start talking about Jesus to him again and sort of string him along for another year or so until I turned eighteen, when Zeus and I could be all open and legal. But I knew Robert was one pathetic dude, and messing with his head like that would be cruel.

My baby girl was sixteen months old that day. Maybe that's why she was so much on my mind. Zeus seemed a little bitchy when I asked him what I should tell his friends about myself. Maybe he was just jealous that I had another life. I can't get over how my life has been changing again and again. I'm just not tied down to anything solid like most people. But that's what I wanted, not to be tied down. I guess that had something to do with why I gave away my baby.

I know when she's eighteen she'll be able to look me up and see what her real Mom is like. I wish I could tell her right now that she was a real love child, not just a screwing-around mistake child. And that's the truth.

I might as well face it. I'm a liar now. The lying started with the church. They had me saying things I really didn't believe. I said I believed in Jesus so he would take away the pain, but I didn't really believe. Now Zeus and I loved each other, but the whole thing only worked because of a bunch of lies, lies to my parents, the school, my soccer coach, and even to Lisa. So what I was thinking then as we walked on the beach was whether I'd have to lie to my daughter later.

"Is something wrong, Diane?"

"I just have a headache."

"You could use more pain medication. Maybe tonight."

I didn't have a headache. And I had been lying to him all along about filling those prescriptions and taking all those pills.

Back inside, just inside the closed door, he took me in his arms and we kissed. That brought back all the joy I had missed. I pushed myself into him. He ran his hands down my back and all the tension and all my crazy thoughts melted away.

"I love you, Diane."

"I love you too."

I got him to sit down on the sofa next to me. I kissed him and then pulled back, ran my hands over his chest, traced the features of his face with my fingertips. Kissed again. I couldn't believe he was all mine, and I wanted to enjoy every part of him slowly now that we were finally alone together. He looked pretty buff in the grey T-shirt he'd worn on the beach. The little sweat crescent under his armpits just made him seem like a real man to me. He put his hands in my hair, framed my face with his fingers, touched my lips. We were taking our time. I guess that's something you can do when you already know where things are going to end up. It was calm and exciting at the same time. I ran my fingers through his hair.

"Oh! You have a grey hair."

"More than one. I hope that doesn't disqualify me from being your boyfriend."

"No, I like it. I mean, you're a real man."

But I couldn't stop myself from calculating how old Zeus would be if my daughter wanted to see us when she turned eighteen. He would be 60. I'd be 33. Would my life be straightened out so I could stop lying by then? He poured us both a glass of wine, and we went out on the balcony to drink it. The outside air was really hot, but we were in the shade and there was a little breeze. The beach below was almost empty. I finished one glass of wine and asked for another. I wasn't really that into wine, but I'd told him no a couple of times and I was starting to feel like an old grouch. He was happy I drank the wine. He liked it when I was silly and playful. How could I complain about that? What if I had married Carl and gone to live with him and our baby girl in his father's tiny apartment in Florida? We wouldn't have been able to afford a place like this. Maybe one weekend every three years or so – and even then we would be spending all of our time watching to make sure she didn't toddle right off the balcony.

He poured me more wine. I let go of my paranoia about Robert filming everything and let Zeus fondle me through my clothes while we were still outside on the balcony. I curled my arm around his neck and kissed him. He pulled back a little, kissed my eyes, my ears, my neck. He talked to me in between kisses, his breath warm on my neck.

"Diane, do you understand? I don't just want to be your boyfriend."

"I do. I'll do it. I'll marry you as soon as we can. I want to."

"Wow, you've made me so happy." He hugged me really hard. We were still standing on the balcony, and then I almost hoped Robert was filming us. He let me go, put his hands on my shoulders, looked in my eyes. "Before I met you, Diane, I was just going through the motions. I had big plans, but I couldn't seem to get them started until you came along."

"I wish I had plans like that."

"*Our* plans. They're *our* plans now. And you can help me. I need you."

I wanted to make him happier than he'd ever been before in bed. He had my blouse completely unbuttoned before we even left the balcony. He loved that he could make me moan with his touch. He was really getting hot himself.

"What if your friends show up early?"

He said he'd lock our bedroom door and put a note on it just in case. Inside the bedroom, I smelled cologne mixed with the sweaty smell of his T-shirt. He kissed me gently.

"I wish I could make you forget every other woman you've ever known."

"You already have."

He undressed me standing up, very slowly, and then stared at me like he had never seen a naked girl before – which of course was totally ridiculous, with him being a doctor and all. Still, I had never felt so totally naked, with him looking at me so closely, and the cool air from the air conditioning pouring down to remind me every second how bare my skin was, and my body growing goose bumps right in front of his eyes. It was embarrassing, and my heart pounded, and then I could feel more heat inside, and that was embarrassing me even more.

Our life together could not be a normal life, I knew. And there would have to be more lying. I hoped my daughter would have a normal life and never have to lie. My life just wasn't working out that way. I'd have to miss out on being true to a lot of people. But Zeus loved me in a way that nobody else did. He said we would have a spectacular life together. He said we would teach everyone we met that all you really need is to be brave.

I stepped up to him and yanked his bathing suit down. He cried out in surprise, then pulled his shirt off. Then he stood close, pressed himself to my belly. His hands were on my waist and he was breathing really hard.

"Do you love me?" he said.

"Yes."

"Will we be partners forever?"

"Yes."

"Will you do anything I want?"

"Yes."

But I guess that wasn't completely true because I still made him use a condom. So then he did it rough and fast and I was like, okay, I turned you into this animal and now you're using me like one, so I hope one day I can learn to like it like that.

Right afterwards, there was a noise outside. It sounded like the outside door of the condo opening and closing. "Don't worry," he said. "They won't come in here."

We collapsed side by side, and I cradled his head into my chest and ran my fingers through his hair.

"You said you would do anything for me. But you wouldn't even let me love you without a condom."

"I'm sorry. Anything but that." Didn't he understand I would die if I got pregnant again? It was bad enough having one little girl haunting me for the rest of my life.

"If you got pregnant, I could take care of it."

Get rid of it, he meant. Our own baby. I pushed him away and sat up on the side of the bed. I did have a headache then, and I still felt achy.

"You're not feeling well?"

"No. Pretty bad, in fact."

"I have all the oxycodone you need in my briefcase. I'll get it right away."

Did he really think that was the cure for everything? Even for his pounding way of lovemaking? But he was trying to help, so I murmured thank you. It seemed like he'd been pushing the pills on me all day. I thought about taking more. But I just knew if I took any more oxy we'd be doing it without a condom. And what if I got pregnant, and he aborted our baby? It was already bad enough being a *primipara*. I had no idea what the word for me would be then.

He didn't bother to dress or even take the condom off on his way to the door. Then he turned back and stood over me, lifted my chin so I had to look at him. There was a hard look in his eyes I had never seen before.

"I'm getting you the medication you need. I know how bad you need it. You're going to feel great again. We're going to do great things together, Diane. But now you have to do something very special for me first." He went out without putting any clothes on and closed the door.

The whole condo was quiet. I wouldn't have felt this bad if I'd kept my promise to Woody not to take any more oxy. But I knew I could live without it, and I could still just say no when he came back with it. Zeus thought I was addicted because I lied to him all along about taking those prescriptions. I realized there was only one person in the world I was always totally honest with, and it wasn't him.

Then the door opened and Zeus came back into the room, still naked and still with the condom dangling. And then another man came in behind him. He was an old, half-bald white guy with huge glasses and a white, button-up short-sleeved shirt barely covering his humongous gut. I screamed and sat up, but he walked right up to the bed and kept staring at me. I tried to cover myself with the sheet, but he put his knee on it, and it wouldn't move. I tried to cover myself with just my hands instead. He kept staring at me. I got up and ran into a corner.

"What the hell?"

"Yeah, what the hell's going on?" Fat Guy echoed me. "You said she'd be on her knees, begging, like that other woman."

Chapter 29

Diane

Zeus disappeared out the door. I was still standing in the corner, hiding myself as best as I could with my hands. Fat Guy came toward me very slowly. He had a creepy smile on his face like he thought this might be some kind of game. I opened my mouth to scream but no sound came out. Then I was really in a panic. If he got any closer I'd never get out of that corner. I turned around to face him with my hands at my sides. He broke into a bigger smile. He pushed his glasses back up on his face. He was staring at my body and very slowly coming closer. My whole body was shaking, but at least my legs seemed to be able to hold me up.

"Don't you know the deal, honey?" he said. "He sold you to me. You take care of me all night, you get all the drugs you need." He lifted his eyes to my face like he expected me to be happy. Meeting his eyes was worse than having him stare at my body. His sloppy grin showed how sure he was he owned me. My mind went blank.

I forced myself to take a step towards him. My legs were still strong. He stopped and spread his arms out like I was supposed to run into them. I kicked him right in the crotch as hard as I could. He howled and bent over. I jumped past him and was just about to open the bedroom door when it opened itself and Zeus came back into the room carrying his black leather travel bag.

"Get her back in the corner," he said. "I'll take care of her."

"This wasn't the deal." Fat Guy's voice behind me was strained. "I'm no rapist."

"We're in this together now," Zeus yelled back. "Just keep

her in the corner." His hand went into his bag.

Fat Guy, still bent over, turned toward him, his voice strained with pain. "Give her something. A roofie or something so she won't remember this."

"Don't worry." Zeus was the only one in the room who seemed calm.

Fat Guy was still bent over. He couldn't keep me in the corner. Zeus's hand came out of his bag holding a little bottle of something and held it up to the light. I slipped past Fat Guy and kicked Zeus's arm. The bottle fell out of his hands. Zeus just stood there, his arms hanging down at his sides, with a look on his face so sad I thought maybe I had misunderstood.

"He said you sold me to him." I was stammering, I was trying so hard to get him to understand.

Zeus got a puzzled look on his face. "Diane," he explained in a suddenly hushed voice, "this is a patient of mine. He has psycho-sexual problems. He's gone off his medications. I was going to give him a shot to calm him down."

"Oh."

Fat Guy was finally standing up straight and kind of staggering towards us. The mental patient who had gone off his medications was the only one in the room who had clothes on. Zeus actually still looked great except for the limp condom dangling off his dick. He put out his hand for mine. "Let's get him out of here. I'm so sorry about this, my love."

I had about a quarter second to think, and it wasn't enough. Zeus grabbed my arm instead of my hand and pulled me hard and bent me backwards onto the bed. Then I panicked because it hit me that maybe that needle was really meant for me. I tried to wrestle Zeus's hands off my arm, but his grip was really strong. Fat Guy was loosening his belt. Zeus leaned back and reached for the needle, trying to hold me down with one hand on my chest.

I pulled my knee all the way up to my chest, and when

he turned around I kicked him with my heel right in the face. There was a crunching noise and he stumbled back away from the bed. I got off the bed, and they both backed away from me. I had to get out of that room right away.

I picked up the first thing I saw, the new sheath dress that was lying on the bureau, but my hands were shaking so much I realized it would take me forever to get it on. I had to get out of that room. Zeus was coming toward me again, taking his time now. He stopped to pull off the condom. In the two seconds it took him to do that I grabbed his bathing suit and his shirt from the bed and ran out the bedroom door.

I didn't have time to think because Zeus came out of the bedroom after me. My cell phone was on a little table near the outside door. I grabbed it and opened the door and ran outside into the condo hallway. He came after me. I was barefoot and naked, but at least I had clothes in my hands. He came after me naked, with one hand covering his bleeding nose. I prayed there would be somebody at the elevator so I could yell for help, but the hallway was empty and the elevator doors were closed. I pulled open the door to the fire stairs near the elevator and got behind it, but he must have seen me because he ran up and tried to pull it open from the other side. I was holding it closed with all my might. But he was stronger than me and was gradually getting the door open. I heard like a moan of despair come out of me and echo down the fire stairs.

Then the elevator dinged, and I could feel him let go of the doorknob. I waited a second, then let go myself and ran down two flights of stairs before stopping to put on his bathing suit and shirt. Then I ran down two more flights, then took the elevator the rest of the way down.

In case he had somehow gotten to the lobby, I took the elevator two stops below to the street level indoor parking garage. The light was dim, but there was no one around. I walked toward the doorway that led to the back parking lot. It was paved with sharp stones that were super-hot from baking in the sun all day, and I could only mince my way along in my bare feet. I had to get to the coastal highway.

There was a long driveway from the back parking lot to the coastal highway. I tried to force myself to walk on the hot tarred driveway, but the pain was so bad I had to keep swerving into the sand, looking for shady spots under the prickly weeds. Finally my feet hurt so much I had to stop and sit down on my butt in the burning sand on the edge of the driveway, trying not to cry, caressing my knees, too scared to look back to see if Zeus was following me.

But I had to. All the back windows of the condo looked out over this long driveway that stretched about two hundred yards through this weedy wasteland to the coastal highway. Anybody who looked out from the back windows of the condo could see me hunched down there like a wounded animal. I wished I had brought my shoes, but there hadn't been time.

Nobody came out of the back of the condo, so I just crouched there and tried to think. I was still gripping the cell phone I took on my way out. Before I left home, I had given my regular cell phone to Kate to keep at her house overnight, because I was supposed to be spending the night there, and my mother has an app that can track where it is. All I had now was the secret cell phone Zeus had given to me. He had told me never to call anybody but him on it, and I obeyed him, so it didn't have anybody else's number on it. I didn't know Woody's or Kate's or Lucky's or Lisa's numbers. So the only person I could call on that phone was Zeus. The only person who could call me besides Zeus was Lisa. I'd given her my secret number, but I had made her swear not to call me unless Mom or Dad had a heart attack or something. They'd have heart attacks anyway if they saw how I'd messed up.

I saw Zeus coming down the driveway toward me, now fully dressed and carrying his cloth bag. He was holding a washcloth or something over his nose. I stood up and tried to make it further down the driveway, but the pain was just frying my feet and I had to stop after about twenty steps. When I turned around, he just kept coming closer, smiling. I thought about calling 911, but I knew I would rather die than have the world find out what I had done.

When he got real close I jumped up and kicked at him, but I missed. That hurt both of my feet so bad I cried out and crumpled down as he came closer. He just laughed. I was sure he would now bring me back to the condo – and Fat Guy. All I could hope for was he'd give me such a powerful roofie I'd wake up not even remembering who I was.

Suddenly a huge black car screeched to a stop between us. The front-side passenger door popped open. A voice yelled "Get in!"

It was Robert. I crawled in and closed the door and curled up in a ball on the front seat. I could feel the car backing around and then shooting forward, but I wasn't looking where we were going. I was just trying to stop myself from shaking. Soon we were going all one way without stopping, so I knew we were on the coastal highway.

"Where are we going?" My usual voice was gone.

"Just getting away from him."

"Pull in one of these roads to the right. We can wait and see if he comes up the coastal highway. That's the only road going this way."

He did as I said. I uncurled myself and sat up. My feet were stinging and my legs were covered with scratches. Zeus's bathing suit was riding up my legs. His T-shirt was covered with sand and smelled of all kinds of sweat. We looked for Zeus's car following us, but we didn't see anything. Gradually I felt like I was coming to myself. I asked Robert to turn the air conditioning down. We sat there in silence until we could be sure he hadn't followed us, then we just sat there in more silence. I was almost as afraid of Robert as I was of Zeus, but I was trying not to think about that.

"Diane …."

"Buy me some shoes!"

I wouldn't even talk to him until he did what I said. He bought me flip-flops at a beachwear store. I also made him buy me a blouse and some cheap girl shorts with a pocket big enough to hold a cell phone. I left Zeus's stuff on the dressing room floor.

"Take me home. Please."

But he didn't. He drove back to the same spot where we had looked for Zeus's car to pass.

"I want to call Lisa, but I don't know her number," I said.

"I don't have her number either."

"Then can't you just drive me home?"

He didn't move to start the car, didn't say anything. The sun wasn't beating down as hot, but I still had only flip-flops, a cell phone with no numbers, no money, no pocketbook.

"Take me home."

"You are home."

"Seriously, Robert …."

"Deacon."

"Okay. *Deacon*. Okay. What do you want with me?'

"I want you to look at yourself."

What did I do to make Robert want to stalk me, to make Zeus want to drug me? Did Zeus really try to sell me to Fat Guy, or was that just some paranoid idea I got from the drugs I took? Why was I still taking drugs? Right then I couldn't think of a reason why Carl could have ever loved me. I wasn't proud of what I'd have to say to my daughter in the future. I hadn't been much of a sister to Lisa. I hadn't been much of a daughter to my parents. I was lying to everybody. But I knew pretending to be saved by Jesus wouldn't help. That would be just another lie.

"You don't have to convince me how bad I am. I already know it. Just take me home."

"You turned your back on Jesus. But we are all sinners. Jesus will take you back."

"Am I a worse sinner than you are?"

He paused, looking out at the setting sun across the coastal highway. "I don't know. You need to tell me what you've done. Everything you've done."

"You tell me. You've been spying on me for weeks. You were supposed to be hosting one of those retreats today, but I knew you'd probably be spying on me instead."

"I needed to know" – his voice was suddenly weak – "I needed to see … needed to study you to see …. I wanted to learn your spirit, through your flesh."

"What!"

He turned to me and put both elbows on the console between the seats, pushed his face close to mine. His eyes were scary and he was breathing hard. I pulled back.

"My soul is tortured every time I watch that video of that lecherous doctor touching you. Tortured! Why do you allow it, when your spirit is so pure? I can't understand it."

"Can you calm down? Come on, get back in your seat."

"I can't stop loving you, Diane. That feeling is so strong, I know it comes from God. He would not torture me like this if He did not mean for us to be together."

"I don't believe that. I'm sorry. I don't feel that way."

He pulled back a little, and his eyes softened. I guess even a demented church man can feel real pain when he can't have what his heart most wants. He was in pain, and all the bland churchy certainty had drained out of his expression. He went on, his voice now low and shaky.

"I'm sometimes afraid my love for you is mixed with foul desires." His weak voice now scared me more than his overbearing deacon's voice ever did. "Some days, Diane, all I think about is what you're doing with other men. I know I shouldn't do that. I know that means I am a sinner myself."

"Everybody is," I breathed into the silence of that giant car. I had never been more certain of anything.

"But Jesus said to embrace the sinner. Could you do that?"

"What?"

"Embrace me, please. I've suffered so much for you. Please, Diane. Please."

He leaned way over the console toward me, then reached out and grabbed my breast before I even realized what was happening. He was moaning and whining like an injured puppy as he clawed at me like some wilder animal.

Thank God for the high console. Trying to lunge over it, he got his legs caught under the steering wheel. I got out of that car before he could get on top of me, and I headed for the shoulder of the coastal highway as fast as I could in my flip-flops. But then he started the car and cut me off, screaming out the window.

"Why, Diane? Why is it such a sacred, holy commitment when other men love you, but when I feel the same way about you I'm just a disgusting thing?"

I walked around the car and kept going. I made it to the shoulder of the coastal highway. I kept looking back to see what he would do. He didn't move. His car was still at an angle and blocking half the road. The land next to the highway was desert-flat, and I could see back a long way, but the car just sat there until it was out of my sight.

I flip-flopped my way back as far as the beach shop where we bought the stuff. There weren't any benches, so I just leaned back against the outside wall. Two hours later my back was tired and my feet hurt and I was really thirsty, but I still hadn't come up with a plan. It was getting dark. I would die rather than call the police or my parents. I figured if I tried hard enough, I could probably get some guy to drive me back all the way home – but that might lead to a whole different bunch of lies. Anyway, I just couldn't do that. The manager of the store came out and asked me if anything was the matter. I said no and moved on down to the front of a closed surf shop.

My Zeus phone buzzed.

R U OK

It was Lisa! I called her back and we talked so fast I don't remember anything we said.

Before I was even finished, Woody's old car pulled up in front of the surf shop with Lisa sitting next to him in the front seat! Lisa jumped out and made me sit in front next to Woody. I guess they could see I was shaking. Lisa noticed that I was wearing new clothes.

"Zeus bought them for me." I wasn't ready to talk about running out of Zeus's condo without my clothes.

Woody steered the old car toward the coastal highway. I had my knees folded up against my chest, but I almost tipped off the seat when he put on the brakes.

"Stop. I'm so freaked. Can we all get out of the car just for a second?"

He turned the engine off. I got out. They must have been afraid I'd do something weird, because they both got out real fast. I ran up and jumped them, hugging them both at the same time. Then I was crying. They let me squeeze them until I stopped shaking. The traffic flew by on the coastal highway.

I let them go. Back in the car, Woody made me sit in the back with Lisa. He would never tell anybody to wear a seat-belt. All the time I'd been standing in front of that closed surf shop I hadn't given a second's thought to what had actually happened at the condo and whose fault it was. All I had been thinking about was how to get home. Now that I was with my two friends the whole deal came, like, pouring into my soul and it was too much and I blanked out and kept holding Lisa's hand tighter and tighter. I couldn't tell them the whole story just then.

"Someday I'm going to ask you guys how you did this." This was probably a half hour after we started for home. It was the first thing any of us said.

"You can ask Lisa right now." I heard a smile in Woody's voice. "She masterminded the whole thing." Lisa wouldn't meet my eyes. Woody went on. "She found out Robert didn't show up for church services today. She figured out he was stalking you. We've been driving around down here for hours, looking for his big, black car."

"I finally freaked out and texted you," Lisa mumbled, trying not to be the hero.

I had a sudden flash that maybe Woody was into her. I could understand why they could like each other. But I still felt like something had been jerked out from under me. In the back of my mind I had been thinking of Woody as a special friend, but I knew all I had done as his friend was take from him. It had been all one-sided. I could see now he could probably use a new friend who was not such a burden. Of course, he was way too old for her. But who was I to complain about that?

Chapter 30

David

"Come in, Newbie, Michele." Frank was hunched behind his desk in a defensive position, while Nancy Hunt, the Board's prosecutor, sat in the only upholstered visitor's chair, her arms tightly crossed. Dave and Michele pulled up bare wooden chairs next to hers to form a semicircle in front of Frank's desk.

"Explain to us what happened. Nancy." Frank liked to act like he was Nancy's boss.

"Okay. Long story short, the court dissolved the Temporary Restraining Order and we can continue investigating Zeus. But only Zeus, not the rest of New Town Partners."

"And we had to file affidavits spilling the beans on what evidence we already had on Zeus," Frank interrupted. "Now he knows everything we have on him. He's probably already covered his tracks, changed all the medical records of all the women he did this to."

"Come on, Frank. We all know Zeus has long since covered his tracks." Nancy, as the state's lawyer, not Frank's employee, could talk to him like that. "There won't be any smoking guns in any of these records. But now that the Temporary Restraining Order is lifted, you can do the one thing that might help the case. You can interview that teenager, Diane Morrell. If it's not too late."

"But now," Frank grumped, "he knows everything we know about Diane Morrell too."

"Can he stop her from talking?"

··· ···

Eli Grunk had found out from the court hearing that the Board investigators had not interviewed Diane yet. Making a move virtually unheard of in defense practice, he pushed for a quick hearing before the Administrative Law Judge who would hear the Board's charges against Zeus. The only charges filed so far were about Zeus's rape and drugging of Katherine. Grunk obviously wanted to move Katherine's case along before the Board interviewed Diane or added her to the case.

Frank subpoenaed every document possibly related to Dr. Zeus and his medical practice, including all of his employment and partnership agreements with New Town Partners and with Freeland Hospital. He asked that the documents be supplied within five days instead of the legally permitted ten.

He got them all in three. The pile of documents from Freeland Hospital had a yellow stickie note protruding from it. The note was stuck to Dr. Zeus's application to renew his privileges there. There was a very faint penciled check mark next to question 18.

··· ···

Michele said she couldn't invite Dave along to her interview with Diane.

He nodded. "It's because I screwed up by talking to her before, right? When I went out to her school?"

"When there was no case open. Right. Frank still doesn't know that. Let's hope he never finds out."

"Again, I'm sorry."

Her smile seemed genuine. "Don't beat yourself up, Dave. Everybody makes mistakes. I'd rather have someone who's over-enthusiastic than someone who doesn't give a damn. You're a real asset to this unit."

It surprised Dave how much this little compliment meant to him. He wondered if Michele had made mistakes as bad

219

as his when she first started. He wished he could emulate her perfect balance of enthusiasm, hard work and humor. And she seemed at the same time to have a very busy home life. She had told him a lot of funny stories about her two little girls. But these were just standard stories shared with the workers in the whole long row of cubicles near her. He really didn't know much about her personally.

Sarah had ambushed him the last weekend he was down at Duke. The weekend started great with her fierce hug at the airport arrival lounge. Then they went to a movie by themselves, then met another couple for a drink. Andrea was in her torts class. Her boyfriend didn't like to talk. Sarah was nervous, and so Dave realized it was up to him and Andrea to keep the conversation alive. They did it, and he thought the evening went well.

"You and Andrea," she said when they woke up in her bed the next morning. "Are you attracted to each other? Or do you both just have this, like, skill at talking with people you just met?"

"It's a skill," Dave said quickly, smiling at her insecurity. "I've watched my mother do it her whole life. Last night, the more I saw you getting nervous, the more I knew what to do. The more I knew what to do, the more I calmed down."

"So, does that mean we're, like, the opposite of compatible?"

"It means I can take care of you."

She put her hand on his chest. "Oh, you like that, don't you?"

That night, she told him she had made reservations at a restaurant called The Collective, but he chafed at the requirement that he wear a sport coat and tie.

"I don't like any place with a dress code. Is this one of those places where the waiter stands behind you the whole meal and re-folds your napkin every time you go to the men's room?"

She laughed. "I never thought about that. I guess so."

"Why are we going to a place like that?"

"Because ...." She hesitated. "Because, Dave, we're going there to meet my father."

Her father had grey hair, straight, close-cut but combed, an open, somewhat ruddy face, and the same hazel eyes as Sarah. Clifford had an easy smile Dave found hard to resist. The team of unctuous waiters laughed at Clifford's every comment, pretended to tell him secrets about the various appetizers and entrees, acted as if his every choice of food was a stroke of genius. Clifford seemed to accept the self-abasement of these sycophants as his due, without even thinking about it.

Dave knew waiters sometimes had to act this way to make a living, but the main waiter in particular was so unctuous that Dave suspected he was overdoing it on purpose, deliberately making himself into a caricature of a servile flunky. He wondered if he spit in the food on its way out of the kitchen.

"This was a trick," Dave said to Sarah the minute Clifford left for the men's room. "You didn't tell me until too late that we were meeting your father."

She waited to answer until she had stared off a hovering waiter. "You thought *I* was going to pay for The Collective?"

"I had no idea what The Collective was. I had no idea a dinner for three could cost a week's salary. What a waste!"

"I wanted so badly for you to meet him. I was hoping you would see what a great guy he is." When Dave didn't respond, she went on. "When my mother died about two years ago I thought we were both going off the tracks. But we helped each other. A lot. I was just coming out of that when I met you." She took a breath. "Just wait, Dave, you'll see. You'll like him."

Clifford came back from the men's room without noticing that his seat had been repositioned, his napkin re-folded, the crumbs from the pre-dinner bread smoothly scraped off the white tablecloth, the butter tub of ornate porcelain replaced with a new one, his wine glass refilled. The waiter asked him if he needed anything else right away. Clifford responded with an absentminded flick of his hand.

Clifford was entranced by his daughter. He glanced at his food and met Dave's eyes when they talked, but his default gaze was always at Sarah, and it didn't matter whether she was talking to him, or arguing with Dave, or looking down at her plate, or staring out the window. Sarah complained a little about the drudgery of law school, but everyone at the table knew she would finish with honors and manage to stamp her own personality on any project she undertook with her law degree.

"Did you notice," she said, "they don't give you any salt here?" She had just bitten into her plank of wild-caught salmon, and her eyes were darting all around the restaurant.

"Some restaurant people," her father murmured, "think it's an insult to the chef to ask for more salt."

"Fuck that. Oh, excuse me, Dad. Hey! Over here! Can I get some salt?"

Sarah's lurching out of the genteel role was no surprise to her father. Clifford smiled. Admiration for this girl was something he and Dave definitely had in common. And Sarah didn't make any secret of her admiration for Dave. This was the whole point of the dinner. Clifford got the message, and between light talk about politics and pop culture, he engaged Dave gently throughout the dinner in conversation about his job, his family, his career plans, what he did for fun. And no matter how ordinary Dave's life story was, Clifford seemed fascinated. He seemed envious of Dave's youth and energy and passion.

"What do your parents do for a living?" Clifford seemed aware that he wasn't supposed to give Dave the third degree about his family's financial situation. He acted only mildly curious.

"My father died when I was two. My mother is an accountant. She's done pretty well. For a few years she was acting CEO of a medium-sized department store chain."

"Oh yeah?" The old man's eyes perked up. "What chain?"

"The Herz chain. They had 22 stores. I'm sure that's not very big by your standards."

"I might know something about that chain. Wasn't it sold about five or six years ago? I think the people running Black Star – wonderful people – arranged a sale of the majority share of the stock from the family that owned it. I remember a story that was going around about that."

"A story?"

"Yeah. The word was old man Herz had a stroke. He couldn't walk. He couldn't talk. They had to prop him up at the meetings. Somebody had to sit next to him and pick up his hand every time there was a vote."

Clifford laughed. Sarah didn't.

"Is that what you do? You buy companies?" Dave looked really interested.

"M&A. Mergers and acquisitions. We help companies that want to merge." He chuckled. "That sounds nice. But more often, we help companies to buy out companies that don't want to be bought out."

"I suppose a lot of employees of those companies get hurt."

Clifford put his fork, laden with salmon, back on his plate. "It does happen. Companies get moribund, too comfortable. They sometimes keep workers they don't really need just out of inertia. When two companies merge, inertia goes out the window. They have to re-think every job. It's a matter of efficiency."

"So you think these acquisitions make for a more efficient system?"

Clifford shrugged. "It's supposed to work that way. Honestly, we aren't involved in that part, the aftermath."

"Who benefits from a more efficient system?" Dave persisted. He could see Sarah's eyes widen with alarm as Dave's conversation slowly morphed into cross-examination.

Clifford had forgotten about eating. "In theory, everybody benefits. In practice, the shareholders probably get the most substantial benefit. People like me are probably second – only we get our benefits up front." He picked up his wine glass. He still looked comfortable with himself and with this conversation, but he eyed Dave carefully. He sipped from his glass before putting it down. "Some people do get hurt."

Dave excused himself to go to the men's room. When he came back, he said he wasn't feeling well and was going to walk home. Then he ran out of the restaurant. He was too upset to enjoy the mellow ambience of this college town. He ran aimlessly at first, then back toward Sarah's place, though he suspected that might not be the right place for him now. He jogged slowly along the two-mile stretch of road that led to her apartment. He looked only at his own path, deliberately ignoring the cloying, tawny twilight filtering through the high trees.

He heard the car stop behind him, heard the door slam. He kept running, but she caught up to him. She took his hand, and he could not bring himself to pull free. The car pulled up next to them but she waved it off.

"Dave, what's wrong? Are you sick?"

"Not physically."

"What's wrong?"

"What's wrong is I can't really be friends with him."

"Why not? It seemed to me that you really liked him."

"He has, like, all the money in the world, doesn't he?"

"He has more than he'll ever need." She pulled him to a stop, faced him. "But you already knew he was rich."

"At my work, the rich doctors get away with everything, including rape."

"What's that got to do with my father?"

He broke her hold on his hand but then reflexively put his

hands on her waist. She looked worried, her eyes searching his.

"Old Man Herz was in a nursing home the whole time Black Star was trying to make a deal for the company. So my mother worked sixteen hours a day for six months to make that deal happen."

"You told me she was like, the CEO in all but name, right? So, she did it? She made it happen, right?"

"Yeah. When the deal finally went through, old man Herz was paid $8,000,000 for his 'extraordinary services' in bringing about the sale. And my mother was laid off."

Chapter 31

Diane

I told Lisa and my friends that Zeus had started acting so stupid in the condo I had just run out without thinking. Kate knew I hadn't told her the whole story, but I wouldn't talk about it. After a while she stopped asking, but then there was this little dead spot in our conversations. The fun slowly drained out of being with her, and with Woody and Lucky too. I stayed in my bedroom by myself during the afternoons.

Lisa would come in even if my door was closed. She knew I owed her something since she and Woody saved me. What she wanted was more attention. She would come in with the excuse of wanting my opinion on what she was wearing. Lisa was the kind of girl who would read a lot into your personality by the clothes you wore, but she was just learning how to wear clothes herself. Now she was on the basketball team and had some friends, but I could tell she didn't have a best friend because she wasn't hanging on the phone or texting with any special person all the time.

She kept bringing up Zeus. I did tell her a little bit. I told her we made love on the boat and in the condo at the beach. She just stared at me when I said that, and I knew what she wanted to know.

"It was good. He was so nice, mostly. One time at the end he was kind of rough. I don't think I'm into that." Her eyes widened, but I didn't tell her any details. "He's just too old for me. I guess. That's all there is to it."

The next time she came in I could tell she was nervous. She sat backwards on my little desk chair with her long arms and legs all hooked and folded around it, looking like she might tip it over any minute.

"What's up?" I asked.

She mumbled something. The only word I heard was "Zeus."

"What about Zeus?" I was getting tired of her questions on the subject.

"Your story of what happened at the ocean that day with Zeus. It isn't true." Lisa was so self-conscious she was embarrassed to catch me in a lie.

"Why do you say that?"

"Because of the clothes you were wearing when we picked you up."

"I told you Zeus bought them for me."

"I thought about that. He would never buy you such a cheap rayon top."

She was right. And I didn't have the heart to make up another lie.

"I had to run out of Zeus's condo fast that day. I didn't have time to put on my clothes."

"What!"

I told her the whole story. She didn't throw up, or back out of the room, so I guessed we were still friends.

"I'm not even sure what was happening at the end. Zeus said Fat Guy was a mental patient who was stalking him. Zeus said he was getting ready to give him a sedative when I ran out."

"Is that true?"

"I don't know. The whole scene just freaked me out. I mean really freaked me out. Maybe I was paranoid from the drugs. I can't think straight about that day."

I told Kate, too. "I'm afraid to be alone with him now. But maybe he needs me, and maybe I'm letting him down."

"Maybe think about this part, Diane: he almost got you addicted."

... ...

227

I quit the soccer team before the season was over. The games didn't seem important any more, and the fun gradually drained out. I let a perfect set-up pass go right by one day, and the coach yelled at me, and I realized my mind was somewhere else.

To my surprise, the person who really got upset over my quitting the soccer team was Mom. I was up in my room a lot more then, and one day she came home early from work and came up to talk to me.

"You seemed so happy when you were playing, or even talking about the games. And the coach told me you have the most potential of any girl on the team."

"You were hoping I'd get a college scholarship so you wouldn't have to pay, right?"

"Oh!"

She was hurt. I looked at her closely for the first time in ages. She had always been pretty, with the same brown eyes and light brown hair as mine, but that was the first time I noticed she had those creases at the corners of her eyes like middle-aged women get. She had turned forty the year before, so I guess I should have expected it, but it was a weird feeling that my own mother was getting old. It didn't seem fair for my mother to get old before I could get to know her.

"Sorry, Mom. All I ever hear you and Dad talking about is how much college costs. But I didn't mean it. I didn't really think you came up here to talk to me just to save money."

I hadn't felt when I was pregnant that she cared about anything but the disgrace I had put on the family. Back then, I just felt these, like, rays of disappointment shooting out from her whenever we made eye contact. That's part of the reason I latched onto Sue and the church. Out of range of my mother's stare and in the company of the church people, I turned from being a disgusting embarrassment to a chosen vessel of holy life.

Sitting next to her up in my room now, I had this sudden urge to ask her something I'd never had the nerve to ask before.

If I had wanted to keep the baby, would she have helped me raise it here, in her house? I was just about ready to ask this, but then it hit me how sad it would be if I found out now the answer was yes.

"I know, honey. It's okay. You get your sharp tongue from your Dad. He says you'd be a great lawyer. But, honey, I miss the old you. You used to be so funny at the dinner table. You haven't seemed the same lately."

"You miss the way I was?"

"I know I always complained about you teasing Lisa in front of us, but to tell the truth, I sort of liked it. I mean, it meant you were both there, both with us, like all four of us mattered."

I was living such a sketchy life I had no right to tease Lisa any more. But I couldn't tell my mother that. And it just didn't feel right to trash-talk with Dad after all that happened. We weren't talking that much, and most of the family seemed a little down. But the funny thing was, Mom was the family member who had changed the least. She never had made fun of people or tried to be funny. Even though Mom usually laughed along with the rest of us, I could tell she didn't really think the whole world was such a joke.

"You liked it when we used to trash-talk each other?"

"Of course. It meant you cared. But now you're acting so depressed. Is it something you can tell me?"

I didn't think my Mom had ever been in any kind of trouble like mine, so it must have been hard for her when I was pregnant to pretend like it was the most normal thing in the world. I told myself back then I was glad she was acting so casual about it, but I guess that actually hurt me a little inside. It felt was like she was saying: yeah, yeah, you screwed up, so let's get on with it and do either Plan A or Plan B. When I tried to talk about Carl she listened, but I could tell her mind was always somewhere else. She never talked about how I'd feel when the baby would come. Maybe she was afraid herself.

She had always followed the rules, and I guess she just didn't know what to do when her daughter blew them all up in front of her face.

I hugged her then and held on, but then I pushed her back because the least I could do was look her in the eyes when I told her the truth.

Chapter 32

David

This was Dave's first hearing. He knew they had nothing to support the rape charge but Katherine's testimony. They had discovered nothing at all useful in the records subpoenaed from Dr. Zeus. If you just looked at his medical records, it looked like a routine case of knee pain. Sprinkled throughout the records were occasional statements that Zeus had counseled Katherine to cut back on the massive amounts of narcotics she was taking. Of course there was no mention of any sexual contact between Zeus and Katherine. And Zeus had recorded in his notes from every visit after the third that Katherine appeared to suffer from delusions and fantasies of a sexual nature.

Nancy Hunt was prosecuting the case for the Board. The courtroom looked like a real courtroom, only there were no sheriffs or bailiffs standing around. The Administrative Law Judge was not quite a real judge, but she had special authority to hear this type of case. Her name was Vivian Cliquot, but when Dave asked Nancy to pronounce the name again she said the only name they would use that day was "Judge."

Nancy put Michele on the stand to testify first. Nancy asked her simple questions about when she received the complaint, how she had interviewed Katherine, and how she had subpoenaed her medical and prescription records. Michele came across as straight-faced, clear-eyed, restrained but not intimidated, just the kind of witness who could get across the main points without going into so much detail the judge would lose interest. Watching Michele now, Dave thought this testifying didn't seem too hard.

"Ms. Porter, you testified you received this complaint over

two years ago?" Grunk was beginning his cross-examination of Michele.

"A little more than that. Almost two and a half years ago."

"And you interviewed Katherine Bolt soon after that?"

"The same week she filed the complaint."

"And you subpoenaed her medical records from Dr. Zeus, and all the pharmacy records. When did you do that?"

"Probably within a month of the interview."

"And that's all the evidence the Board has in this case?"

"I can't say that. I'm not in charge of prosecuting this case."

"But you heard the opening statements made here today, did you not? Ms. Hunt here, the prosecutor, didn't mention any evidence other than Katherine's statements, the medical records and the pharmacy records, did she?"

"That's correct."

"So the Board had, over two years ago, all of the evidence it has now. But it did not charge the case then, did it?"

"For a time we were trying to get additional evidence."

"But did you actually obtain any additional evidence?"

"No."

"Okay, how long did this search for additional evidence, this fruitless search for additional evidence, go on?"

"Maybe about three months."

"So after that three-month period, after the Board stopped even looking for additional evidence, the case just sat at the Board without anything happening for at least 21 months, did it not?"

"Correct."

"Ms. Porter, isn't it true that New Town Partners later sued the Board and obtained a court order stopping the Board from its outrageously abusive investigative practices?"

"I don't agree with 'outrageously abusive investigative practices.' It's true that Dr. Zeus and New Town Partners sued the Board."

"And isn't it true that the Board charged Dr. Zeus within the next two weeks?"

"Correct."

"Without any more evidence than it had 21 months before?"

"Correct."

"So the Board ignored this case for 21 months, and during those 21 months it wasn't looking for and didn't find any additional evidence." Grunk's voice suddenly boomed. "Then the Board suddenly brought charges against Dr. Zeus *just two weeks after* Dr. Zeus brought the Board to its knees in court! Come on! There are no coincidences, Ms. Porter. This was retaliation for filing the suit against the Board in court. Why else would the Board act when it did?"

Michele smiled sweetly. "We had just received a video of Dr. Zeus fingering a teenage female patient on the beach. That was why we decided we had to act."

Grunk bent over like he had been punched in the stomach. He had accidently let in evidence that Zeus was molesting another patient. But he recovered quickly and asked that Michele's answer be stricken because it was not in response to his question. Nancy Hunt said it was, and after a few minutes of arguing, and a re-reading of the question by the court reporter, she won that point. Then Grunk argued that what he said wasn't really a question at all but just a "rhetorical flourish." The Administrative Law Judge did not seem pleased to be told that her time was being wasted on rhetorical flourishes, and she ruled that Grunk had indeed asked a question and that Michele had been entitled to answer it. Her statement that there was a video of Zeus fingering a teenage female patient was now an official part of the record.

"Grunk blew it," Nancy explained to Dave during a break in the proceedings that followed. "You're never supposed to ask a *why* question. And you're never supposed to ask a question you don't know the answer to. Those are the two basic rules of cross examination. If you break those rules, you risk being told exactly what you're most afraid of hearing."

... ...

They had told Katherine she didn't have to be there until 10 o'clock. This saved Katherine from having to be in the room with Zeus for the first hour of the hearing. At quarter of ten Dave was sent out to find her and sit with her. They told him to hold her hand, but he knew of course they didn't mean that literally.

Dave breathed a sigh of relief when he saw Katherine arriving outside the huge glass door of the building. She was dressed up probably as fashionably as she could manage. Up close, her eyes were red. He introduced himself and they sat down.

"I don't think I can do this." She wasn't even looking at him.

"Why not?" Immediately he regretted his sharp tone.

Katherine sat staring straight ahead, so he decided to try again. "It's normal to be a little wary of seeing him under these circumstances."

"You don't know how humiliating ...." She pulled a mirror out of her pocketbook and dabbed at her face. She looked much older than her 42 years. She made herself take a couple of deep breaths. "I suppose I have to do it to keep him from doing it to other women."

Dave wished he had thought of saying that himself. "That's really important," he managed to say.

"It can't be any worse than group counseling. They broke me down, made me tell everything there. It was supposed to make you stronger but, I don't know, I think I just felt more ... common."

The door to the hearing room opened and Zeus suddenly came out, all five feet ten of him in his tailored Italian suit. He started when he noticed Katherine, and she shrunk back from him. Then he swaggered right up to the bench she was sitting on. He stopped at a spot where she would have to look away to avoid looking right at his crotch. Dave stood up, eager to push him away, but he stood there frozen as he heard Katherine take a quick breath and saw her raise her eyes to meet Zeus's.

"How are you doing, Ms. Bolt?" Zeus's fake concern was nauseating to Dave. Katherine didn't answer but just gave him a red-eyed stare. "I hope your knee is feeling better."

Katherine nervously clasped and unclasped her hands. Zeus continued to stare down at her from two feet away. Dave watched for the slightest little movement that would give him an excuse to punch Zeus's lights out – and maybe bloody that beautiful Italian herringbone fabric. But Grunk, who had followed his client out into the hallway, saw what his client was doing and quickly pulled him by the arm and steered him away.

Katherine suddenly stood up.

"What are you doing?"

"It's never going to stop. It's never going to stop. I'm sorry." She took off down the hall.

Dave gave chase, walking fast by her side. "Think about those other women. Get it over with today. You'll never have to see him again." That was all he could think of to say. He reached out to take her hand and guide her back toward the hearing room, but at the last second he realized how frightening that would be to her, so he pulled back. They were approaching the security guard station anyway, and the female guard had turned around and was watching him closely. He had two seconds to try to convince her to change her mind, but words failed him. The security guard took one step sideways as if to block him, he stopped, and Katherine plodded out to the entrance, struggled to get the heavy glass doors open, then disappeared around the corner heading towards the parking lot. Dave turned around to see that the hallway was already empty. The hearing had reconvened.

Dave took a breath, opened the door to the hearing room, and went in. Michele was again testifying on the witness stand, facing him, but she stopped mid-sentence when he came in. The judge looked up. Nancy Hunt turned around to see who it was. Dave had no idea what to do. In the sudden silence, he walked down past the empty spectators' chairs and up to the table where Nancy Hunt was working next to a pile of legal pads. He didn't know what to do there either, so he just sat down next to Nancy.

Dave explained in a whisper that Katherine had fled.

"There goes our best chance of winning the case," Nancy sighed. "Oh well. Let's see if I can get the transcript into evidence."

But Grunk would have none of it. "Your Honor, didn't we hear, not more than an hour ago, that Katherine Bolt is present today and is going to testify to this alleged abuse by Dr. Zeus? Now she's apparently not coming, and so the prosecutor wants to put in the transcript of an interview with her. Dr. Zeus was not present at that interview, and he did not have the opportunity to cross-examine Katherine after she made these horrible allegations. Ms. Bolt clearly made a conscious decision not to testify. And so I'm asking you, in the interest of due process and basic fairness, not to allow the Board to put this transcript of something she said over two years ago into evidence."

The judge sat up in her chair with a puzzled look on her face.

"So is she going to testify in this case or not?"

"Apparently, Your Honor … apparently, as things stand now, at this point, no."

Zeus laughed out loud. Grunk shushed him but couldn't help smiling himself. Nancy asked for a short break and met Dave and Michele outside the hearing room.

Nancy used her typical blunt terms. "We got nothing now.

Case can't get any worse. All I can do now is stall and wait for a miracle to happen with Katherine." Nancy drummed her fingers on a spot on the table next to the tuna fish sandwich she had bought from the vending machine. "Here's an idea," she finally said. "We also charged Zeus with lying on his last application to Freeland Hospital. We weren't going to deal with that until tomorrow. Maybe one of you can make a quick call to Freeland Hospital and see if they can send somebody up here today instead. Maybe we can drag things out for one more day with that."

••• •••

An hour later Dave and Michele sat alone in the canteen. They had succeeded in getting two witnesses from Freeland Hospital to drop everything and come to testify against Zeus. Nancy was at that moment in the hearing room eliciting testimony from the two Freeland Hospital witnesses. She had told them to take their time in answering and not to leave out any detail or document they felt like throwing in. Her plan was to make their testimony last the rest of the day. She had sent word that the plan was working. But there was no plan for the next day.

"There is only one possible plan," Michele said. "I'll go to Katherine's house tonight and ask her to change her mind."

••• •••

Nancy came out two hours later.

"What happened?" They both jumped up.

Nancy's eyes looked tired but her posture was her usual ramrod straight. "Split the baby."

"What do you mean?" Dave said.

"Long story short, she will admit the transcript, but only if Katherine comes in and testifies that the transcript accurately represents what she said to Michele at the time of the interview and that it is completely truthful. She doesn't have to testify on the stand in front of all of us about the dirty deeds she did with Zeus."

"I've never heard of a ruling like that," Michele said.

"Me neither, but the rules are flexible in this type of hearing. The judge was leaning against us this morning. Something changed this afternoon. I think she sneaked a peek at the transcript during lunch."

"This still means we completely lose the case unless Katherine shows up tomorrow?" Michele knew the answer to her question was yes.

"Right. Unless Katherine shows up. But it doesn't have to be tomorrow now. The judge came back to the bench after a break this afternoon and said something had come up and she couldn't continue the case until next Thursday. So we have more time."

Chapter 33

Hartwicke

Zeus got back to town at 4:00 a.m. the morning after Diane ran out of the condo. He had been drinking heavily all night, including during the ride home, and when he arrived he crashed on the basement sofa so he wouldn't call attention to himself. His face felt like Diane had hit it with a baseball bat. His legs were still leaden and his mind was still groggy the next day when he made his way up the stairs to the kitchen around noon. Elena came and stood in the doorway.

"You disgusting fucker!" She spat it out vehemently – but quietly, so he guessed Kyra was in the house. Her hair was tied back in a bun and she was wearing an old blouse with the sleeves rolled up.

"It looks like you've been cleaning."

"Trying to get rid of any trace of you." He'd never been the object of such a harsh, steely stare. "I've found your secret bank account, and your secret 401(k). Don't even try to empty them. I put a freeze on all of them. By the way, P-A-S-S-W-O-R-D is not the best choice to use for a password."

"What is this all about?" It sounded like they were heading for a nasty divorce. He was too hung over to pretend he cared. But he was hoping she hadn't really found all of his accounts.

"By the way, what color hair does this Katherine have?"

"Who do you mean, *Katherine*?"

"The patient you raped."

"Oh. Is that what this is about? You read the charges. Why didn't you say so?" Sounding the proper tone was everything, and it came natural to Zeus. He slid into his patronizing doctor patter. "I had this patient named Katherine. No serious medical problem, and in the end I figured out all she wanted was drugs. A very unstable patient. I tried to help her. I went along with her complaints about pain. Maybe I went a little too far and gave her a little too many narcotics. Then, when I tried to taper off her dosages, she turned on me and made all these crazy, delusional accusations. As if I could be interested in such a pathetic addict."

"I asked you what color her hair was."

He searched her eyes but could not figure out exactly why this mattered. He didn't see any advantage in lying about this one, tiny, little thing. "Brown. Dark brown."

"So how's the purple-haired girl? Is she as good in bed?"

... ...

The charging document from the Board had come in the mail on Saturday while he was at the condo, and Elena had apparently opened it right away. Zeus was angry, but he was used to Elena opening his mail of late. He was much more worried about the other things that Elena had done while he was away at the condo. He found out she had gone to New Town Partners, where the office manager, who hated him, had let her see every file he kept there except for the patient files. She had let Elena search his desk, as well as every drawer and cubbyhole in every little cabinet in his examining room.

Elena even claimed to have gone to the clinic in the church gymnasium on Saturday. But he knew better.

"The clinic is locked on weekends," he smirked.

Elena was too proud of herself not to tell him. "Yeah, but the gym's open. And, you know, those clinic walls only go up so high. There were a couple of nice teenagers there shooting hoops. Tall guys. When they found out the poor doctor's wife had left her pocketbook inside, darn if they couldn't figure out a way to get over that wall and unlock the door from inside for me."

"You'll go to jail for that," he said.

"So, you want to involve the police? I'm sure they'll be interested in those long purple hairs I found when I was cleaning out the passenger side of your Jag before I sold it. And the condoms in your glove compartment that match the condoms I found in your desk at the church clinic. I know that clinic is only for teenage church girls. So I guess you're fucking one of them too."

Zeus knew better than to act upset. He gave her a frozen stare. "Elena, you are acting erratically. You appear to me to be suffering from some type of psychotic breakdown. If I can get the hospital psychiatrist to agree with me, I can have you put away for observation for 72 hours."

"Don't you dare threaten me."

"I'll make sure Dr. Kendall is aware of all your recent paranoid thoughts and uncharacteristic illegal activities. I'm sure he'll agree it's highly doubtful you could be trusted with having custody of Kyra."

Elena was too smart to believe he could do that to her so easily, but it was good to remind her how rough things could get.

· · · · · ·

Grunk charged extra to meet him on a Sunday, but Zeus hadn't been able to wait. They met at Grunk's office to talk about the Board's charges. Grunk searched Zeus's eyes and asked if he had read the charges carefully.

"I'm asking this because when the hearing starts up again you have to decide whether to testify."

Zeus met his stare and assured him he had.

"One important thing to get out of the way first. These charges are only relevant to your medical license," Grunk began. "By this I mean the Board can do nothing to you except take away your medical license. These aren't criminal charges."

"I got that." Zeus's voice showed impatience.

"But the facts alleged in that charging document, you know, having intercourse with the woman without her consent and while she was under the influence of drugs that you prescribed – that's a crime, that's rape."

"It didn't happen. I never had any sexual involvement with her whatsoever." Zeus made good eye contact and spoke without any hint of evasion when he said this. Grunk noted this with both skepticism and some satisfaction.

"But anything you say at the Board hearing can be used against you later in criminal court. So what I'm saying is you don't have to testify. I don't have to put you on the stand. And if that prosecutor Nancy Hunt calls you as a witness, you can take the Fifth Amendment and refuse to testify. So, do you think that's the way you want to go?"

"No, I am going to testify." Zeus saw Grunk look up sharply. "The whole thing is just her word against mine. I have to testify. I have to tell the real story."

"Very well." Grunk seemed to shift gears. "Understand you are in a kind of box. If you don't testify, the Administrative Law Judge will probably find you guilty, and maybe revoke your license. If you do testify, anything you say before the Administrative Law Judge can be used against you in criminal court. But I think your decision might be the right one. The police aren't interested in this kind of case. The Administrative Law Judge and the Board are your big problems."

Grunk then told him they would have to explain in detail his treatment of Katherine.

"What's that got to do with whether I had sex with her or not?"

"You need something to say on the stand, Hartwicke. We need to present you as the competent, efficient, caring doctor that you are. You can't sit up there and just keep repeating: 'I did not have sex with that woman.'"

"Okay."

"Let's take the first visit." Grunk had made an extra copy of Zeus's records which he now handed to Zeus.

"Okay."

"I see you noted her presenting complaint as right knee pain. I see you took her age, her height, weight, blood pressure, current medications, current complaint, medical history, *etc.* I see you noted that she had normal menses. You noted that she had broken her collarbone in a fall from a horse when she was a teenager. Is a broken collarbone an important fact? I mean if a woman comes in with knee pain twenty years later, would that change the way you diagnose or treat her knee problem?"

"I wouldn't think so."

"So why did you make a special note of it?"

"I don't know. I don't recall seeing that."

"You wrote it, didn't you?"

"No. I don't write this stuff. The office girls fill out all this stuff before I even see the patient."

"So you don't recall seeing that?"

"No."

"Still, a previous broken bone could have an effect on a current joint problem, couldn't it?"

"I guess. Possibly."

"So, as part of a thorough physical examination and medical history, you took into consideration her previous fracture, even though it took place twenty years before? Right?"

"Okay. Right. We took everything into consideration and did a very thorough evaluation." Zeus's answer, and his almost imperceptible nod, indicated he was catching the drift. But Grunk still didn't seem satisfied with Zeus's degree of professional concern.

"And I guess each and every part of this record is just a

small reflection of the degree of professional attention you paid to her problem?"

"Of course."

"And the part you wrote? That's just this one line here? *35-y-o WF c/o r knee pain 6 mo. worse sit/stand.* Is that all you wrote yourself?"

"Yeah. Plus the disposition."

"That's just: *aspirin*?"

"Yeah. And I also sent her for an MRI of her knee, and comprehensive blood testing, but it's not written down here."

"Oh. So you did do a very thorough investigation." Grunk perked up and actually smiled at Zeus. "But I didn't see anywhere in these records where you wrote down the results of the MRI or the blood tests."

"They're probably in the MRI or the lab reports, in the back of the file somewhere."

"But the MRI and the blood tests were never mentioned again in your own reports. Was that because nothing significant was found on the MRI?"

"I guess so.

"You guess so?" Grunk took a breath. "Hartwicke, that is not the kind of testimony that is going to make you sound like the consummate professional that you are. I suggest you look right now and tell me if there is any significant injury or disease shown on that MRI or the blood tests that you ordered."

Zeus skimmed through the file and peered at the MRI report. He looked at Grunk glumly. He knew it was in his own interest to yield to Grunk on this one thing – and to give the performance required. Grunk sat up expectantly.

"The blood testing shows everything to be within normal limits. The MRI shows minor chondromalacia of the patella but no other injury or disease process of any kind." He looked at Grunk significantly before he went on. "It is very possible that a patient can still suffer significant pain even in the absence of a significant injury. So, after I carefully reviewed the results of the MRI, and the blood tests, I began Katherine on a regimen of symptomatic relief, starting with aspirin, then switching her to Celebrex, a non-steroidal anti-inflammatory drug. Unfortunately, neither of these had any significant effect on her symptoms. After carefully monitoring her progress, or lack of progress, for three months, I began her on a trial of oxycodone, a powerful opiod pain reliever. I want to stress that I gave her the choice of using this drug or not, after explaining carefully to her the side effects, including possible addiction."

Grunk smiled again. "Now we're getting somewhere. We'll have to meet again before the trial, and we'll have to go over the records of each visit, one by one. I want you to be able to explain your thinking for each and every notation you made. This next meeting is going to take a couple of hours, at least. And when you testify, your explanation of your professional treatment is going to take up three hours at least."

"Why three hours? That's way more time than I ever spent treating her."

"I know, Hartwicke. But after those three long hours of your calm, competent testimony about your professional, caring and medically sound treatment of Katherine, people will hardly be able to remember she said she was just fucking you silly for drugs."

··· ···

Zeus was capable of forgetting any insult or injury as long as the perpetrator was not obstructing his current plans. Back at the condo, when he first tried to get back in the door after unsuccessfully chasing Diane down in the hallway, Billings had closed and locked it against him, leaving him standing naked outside the door. Billings was standing right on the other side of the door but wouldn't open it. Zeus instantly boiled over, and he banged on the door with his fists, elbows and knees, so consumed by wrath that he temporarily lost sight of his goal, which was to get back inside the condo without anyone noticing him running around naked. He calmed down a little when Billings opened the door behind the chain lock.

"Let me in."

"You're not going to hurt me?"

"Of course not." And by then he was already sizing up Billings's weaknesses, making a plan so cold and calculating there was no room for anger. In a few seconds, Zeus was inside and the door was safely closed behind him.

"What the fuck!" Billings's complaint sounded like a pitiable yelp, nothing more. "Didn't you tell that bitch what the deal was?"

Zeus didn't respond until he had his pants on and belted and zipped up.

"I don't know what you're talking about." Zeus's voice was slow, precise, and cold. "Diane and I were having a nice romantic day until you barged in with your zipper down and tried to rape her."

"You know that's not true."

"That's what Diane thinks is true." Zeus looked very satisfied with himself. "We discussed what you did to her. She's still too upset to come back here now."

"You fucking, fucking liar!" Billings took a step towards him but Zeus stood up to face him. Billings had three inches and 175 pounds on Zeus, but he was intimidated when Zeus showed no fear. Zeus met his stare from six inches away and made his threat more explicit.

"I'll call the police right now," Zeus challenged him. "Diane's hobbling around this condo right now wearing a man's bathing suit and T-shirt, and no shoes. The police will find her, then they'll come here. Diane and I will both tell the same story. You won't even have a chance to go home. You'll never see anything but the inside of a jail cell for the rest of your life."

"Don't do that! What do you want?"

"Same thing as always. Board of Trustees. Make your phone calls right now. I want to hear your end."

"I'm not staying here like a sitting duck."

The only type of courage Billings exhibited that day was the courage to run. He had already zipped up his own pants, so all he had to do was grab his tiny overnight bag and run out the door.

But Zeus visited him in his office at the hospital the very next Monday.

"She's a juvenile," Billings shot back as soon as Zeus accosted him. "She has a nice rack, but you can tell she's a teenager. You've been fucking a teenager." This was supposed to be a threat, but the speech sounded too practiced. And there was a barely audible quiver in Billings's voice as he said it.

"So we had an affair. Shame on me. But you tried to rape a child," Zeus calmly raised the stakes. "Let's call the police together. Pick up the phone right now." Zeus was betting that Billings had already shot his entire wad of courage. Billings leaned back in his oversize chair, his eyes downcast, looking down remorsefully toward his crotch, as if all his troubles emanated from that area. Except Billings was so fat he couldn't even see his crotch.

"I need to be put on the Board of Trustees," Zeus commanded. "You will do this now."

Chapter 34

Diane

Half of the time I still wanted to be with Zeus. I missed him most late at night. But sometimes this tingling sensation would come into my arm and then it would turn into pain and then it would be like I was still feeling Zeus's fingers gripping my arm so tight in the condo.

I cried a lot at night about my baby. I was feeling sorry for Carl and hoping he was doing okay. But I couldn't cry just for Carl any more. I missed the little triangle of mommy, daddy and baby that could have been, but I didn't miss the single guy who was now in Florida and living in a room with his father and washing his car every minute he wasn't working. And now I didn't feel guilty about not missing him. I started thinking Carl wasn't like me at all. I started thinking that's why I dumped him. It wasn't because we were too young. It was because we were too different. Marrying Carl wouldn't have made any sense. And now the idea of going back with Zeus was too scary. Why do people always tell you to follow your heart?

This medical board lady named Michele called and said she wanted to come see me. She said the medical board might charge Zeus for what we did together, and he might lose his license. She wanted me to help them and maybe testify in court against him. I put her off. I wanted the chance to talk to Woody first. When I found him, he was sitting on his bed right across from his desk, fiddling with an electric heater he was trying to get going. He put it aside when I came in.

"What did you tell her?" he asked.

"I told her to leave me alone."

"Why?"

"I don't know. Whatever he did, I did it too. He didn't force me to do anything."

"You said he tried to hand you over to that guy, that fat guy, in the condo."

My voice went fast, panicky, just at the memory of that moment in the condo. "Maybe I imagined some of that. I don't know."

He reached over to his desk, picked up a little box and dumped it on the bed. All the oxy prescriptions Zeus had written for me flew out and scattered over his ragged bedspread. "You didn't imagine *these*." I'd never heard that tone in his voice before. "He was trying to get you addicted." I didn't challenge that, and he went on. And it got worse. "And you were lying to him all the time about taking those pills. What kind of shit relationship was that?"

"So now you're saying the whole thing with Zeus was sicko!" Heat rose up in my chest. "You never said that before." It seemed like Woody was changing on me. We'd been together on this, talking about this Zeus thing all the time it was happening.

"You made it seem like it was okay for me to lie to Zeus about taking those pills." I spat out the words.

He threw his leg across from the bed to his desk, blocking my way out. I was really pissed.

"You bastard!" The words just came out.

His face pinched like he was in pain, and he started to move his leg out of the way. But then he stopped and said real quietly, "I'm not a bastard. I had a regular family. For a long time."

A stab of regret for what I had just said hit me hard and brought me to my knees right on the floor of his garage. I didn't mean literally he was a bastard. I knew he had nothing, nobody. You'd think, with that story, Woody would be a criminal or at least a druggie by now. But he wasn't. He was a great, straight guy, the kind of person I was hoping to be.

Still kneeling on the floor, I hid my face, pressing it into the mattress. "I didn't mean that. I'm so sorry, Woody. I want to be your friend. Always. But you've been telling me one thing all along, and now you're changing it."

"Not changing it. I never liked you going with Zeus."

"Because I had to lie?"

"I never liked any of it."

"So all this time you thought I was a dolt, but you pretended to be my friend so at least you could keep me away from drugs."

He moved his leg so I could go or stay. "I didn't pretend anything." He sat up, hands on the mattress. "It's never been any of my business who you fell in love with."

So we argued, but then we made up. Woody was too good a friend to give up. He saved my life by helping me stay off those drugs. He made me do it, but somehow he made me do it *myself*. What an amazing guy!

••• •••

I knew the woman from the medical board wanted a complete confession from me about what I did with Zeus. And she wanted to record me telling it on tape. And she wanted me to get up in some kind of court or something and tell it all in front of a whole bunch of people, including Zeus.

The woman said Zeus appeared to have followed a "typical pattern" in our affair. She said it wasn't uncommon for physician predators to get women in the position of trading sex for drugs.

"That's not what he did with me."

"What did he do with you?"

"I don't want to talk about that."

"There is a type of physician who learns women's weaknesses from treating them medically, then preys on those weaknesses." She was hinting maybe Zeus was this type, that he was preying on me.

Or was she trying to tell me that Zeus had other lovers? But I figured she would tell me if she knew something like that. Maybe she was just that kind of bitchy woman who is unhappy whenever any other woman is happy with a man. But I got a little shaky from all her talk about *patterns*, and I asked her point blank if she was saying he'd had sex with other women patients. When the phone went silent for a minute I hung up.

··· ···

Mom invited that lady from the medical board to our house so she could interview me in our living room.

"Why are you doing this to me, Mom? Because you hate me, right?"

"They can subpoena you and make you come in. I'm just trying to make it easier on you." She said she didn't know exactly what it was about, but I think she had an idea.

"Honey, I know your life hasn't been easy the last few years. And I know I haven't made it any easier. Everything was all so new and shocking to me. I didn't know what to do."

"You didn't do anything to hurt me."

Her smile was sad. "I'm going to try to actually help. But I could do it better if I knew what you were thinking."

But that would be hard – to figure out myself what I was thinking.

Michele had told Mom a parent had to be at the interview.

"I knew you didn't want it to be Dad," she told me while we waited for Michele to arrive. Then it got quiet between us. I was afraid she was going to ask for a preview in my own words. When neither of us said anything, I figured she was just as much afraid of hearing the story as I was of telling it. With both of us silently squirming there, it hit me that maybe I wished Dad were there instead. Dad was a litigator, and nothing seemed

251

to faze him. I knew he would forgive me, and then he would take fact after fact and pile it up into something and then shoot it out of his litigation machine and somehow make Zeus pay. But maybe that's why Mom was trying to keep him out of it.

Mom compulsively smoothed her light brown hair back over her ears. We always teased her that she went off every morning to her public relations job with such smooth and pretty hair, then came back in the evening with what Dad called "the rat's nest of worry." She always laughed, lowered her eyes, then smiled at all of us, her torturers.

It hit me just then that I'd had my family all wrong all along. We always ate dinner together, and Dad would be the main entertainer. He was funny, and he could get a reaction out of any of us, and we tried to give him back as good as we got. He always played the role of the outsider, pretending to be the poor lonely guy surrounded by all these women. But that wasn't true at all. It was Mom who was really the different one. She laughed at all of our stories, but she never told one herself. Nobody made much fun of her, probably because she didn't have the heart to retaliate. Mom was just a spectator, the quiet smiling audience to all our teasing of each other. She was actually the outsider. I had never thought about that.

Michele arrived then and started to drag me through the whole story, starting with the first time I saw Zeus. I was terrified I would have to talk about things I did that maybe even Mom had never done. But Michele went over it all once real fast, and I was so relieved we didn't have to go into all the gross details. It was all just dates, places, and "did you have sexual relations with Dr. Zeus on that occasion?" Mom acted so good with it I started to think she wasn't such a prude after all. The only times she bit her lip during the interview was every time I admitted to another lie I had told her.

"Now, I know this may be a little embarrassing, but now we have to go a little more into the details." Michele suddenly announced.

"What kind of details?" This was Mom.

"For each time and date, any actual medical treatment that took place, drugs prescribed, pills handed out in the office. Details of the sexual experiences."

"Details?"

"A lot of times we find out the victim knows something ... saw some detail that can help prove her case."

"You want Diane to go into detail about the sex too?"

Michele sat up straighter. "Sometimes the details are critically important. They can prove the victim knows something that only a sex partner would know."

All the talk stopped for a second. I could hear Mom gulp. Then she looked at me. "Honey, I know I have the right to be here during this whole interview. And I will stay here with you now if that's what you want. But I'm going to give you the choice right now if you want me to stay and hear all the details or not."

Michele turned toward us, a sharp look in her eyes. "This is procedure. A parent must be there when we interview a juvenile."

"Is there an actual law that says that?" Mom hadn't been married to a litigator for twenty years for nothing.

"It's Board procedure."

"So there's no law, and Diane's statement will still count, even if I'm not here."

"I'm asking you to follow the procedure, Ma'am."

I didn't care what the procedure was. I couldn't imagine Mom listening while I told every sketchy detail of all the private things Zeus and I had done.

"I love you, Mom. Get out."

Chapter 35

David

Michele persuaded Katherine to come to the hearing – but only by telling her that all she had to do was verify that the transcript of her statement given two years before was accurate. Katherine appeared on the next hearing day outside the huge glass doors to the hearing building, looking lost, and Dave had to go out and steer her inside. She would not look Zeus in the eye when she entered the hearing room. It took her a long time to walk the seven or eight steps to the witness stand. Prosecutor Nancy Hunt acted strong and supportive as long as Katherine was in her line of sight, but then she turned and rolled her eyes at Dave when it took her almost a full minute to climb into the witness chair.

Nancy asked her a few simple questions in an attempt to calm her down. Her voice was steadier by the time she finished reciting her name and address, the general time period when she had been seeing Zeus, that she had filed a complaint, that she had talked to Michele and given a recorded interview on such and such a date. Nancy asked her if she wanted to take a drink of water and she said yes, grabbing the glass with both hands.

Nancy then began an elaborate description of the transcript of Michele's interview with Katherine. She held it up in the air, slowly and ostentatiously handed it to Grunk for his inspection, asked Katherine to read the title page, including the transcribing company's certification that it was a true and accurate copy of the taped interview of Katherine Bolt. Nancy had Katherine leaf through page after page and verify that yes, this is what she had really said.

Nancy had two purposes for this, she had confided to Dave.

First, to make it seem like a hefty piece of evidence in itself, worthy of consideration by any Administrative Law Judge. Second, and more importantly, to give Katherine time to calm down, get used to the hearing room and its procedures, get used to answering questions from the witness stand, and – Nancy hoped – finally get up the courage to tell her story in person in front of the judge.

It didn't work. After Nancy's elaborate presentation, and Grunk's florid objections to admission of the transcript, the judge turned to Katherine with an almost sisterly look.

"I don't understand, Ms. Bolt. You are already here on the witness stand. You say the story you told in this transcript is true, and I agree it's a horrific story. All you have to do is tell your story here, right now, in front of us, and give Dr. Zeus the chance to ask you questions about it. Then I'll be able to hear your story live, right here in the courtroom, and I'll be much better able to decide if it's true."

Katherine turned her head away from the judge and looked down into her lap. "I can't." She seemed even more intimidated now that the judge was questioning her. She was trembling. "I've done all I promised I would do. That's all I can do. Goodbye." Then she stood up quickly and walked out of the room without making eye contact with anyone. The massive wooden courtroom door clicked closed in the dead silence that followed.

The judge sighed and looked at Nancy Hunt, eyebrows raised, palms up. "If she doesn't have the guts …?"

Nancy interrupted her. "Your Honor, we did produce Katherine. And, as you requested previously, she did testify that the transcript was true and correct."

"I know what I ruled, counselor. I will admit the transcript. Now I will have to decide whether I believe it or not. Frankly, so far, I'm not leaning towards believing it."

"Your Honor, we have an additional witness who can

provide testimony on the validity of that transcript."

"Please!" Grunk pretended to sigh in exasperation. "Not yet another Board staff person! Let's face it. Nobody knows if Katherine's story in that transcript is true except her and Zeus. There's no other witness who can say."

The judge seemed exasperated herself. But Nancy Hunt was not about to be brushed off.

"But no, Your Honor, this is not a Board staff witness. This is a fact witness who will corroborate a critical fact that is in Katherine's transcript."

"What is this?" Grunk interrupted. "There's nobody who can verify anything that she said. It's just her word against his. We've seen all the medical records, all the pharmacy records. All the records support my client's innocence. Not a scrap of it supports the story Katherine told in that transcript, a story that she was *not* willing to repeat under oath today in front of Dr. Zeus."

"Your Honor, if you'll bear with me for just a few minutes, I think I can establish by this new witness's testimony that Katherine's statements in the transcript must be true."

The judge held up her hand, tired of the argument. "We have a half hour until we normally break for lunch. If you think you can be done in ten minutes, with 20 minutes left for cross-examination, I'll allow it."

"Thank you. I call Marcie Thompson to the stand."

··· ···

> **Ms. Hunt**: Could you state your name for the record, please?
> **Ms. Thompson**: Marcie Lila Thompson.
> **Q**: About that "Marcie." Is that short for something?
> **A**: No. Just Marcie.

Q: Are you familiar with the Respondent here, Dr. Zeus?

A: Very familiar.

Q: How do you know him?

A: I'm a nurse. We met when he was a resident at my hospital years ago. We kept in touch even when we were married to different people.

Q: This keeping in touch. What did it amount to?

A: Sex. We met and had sex three or four times a year.

Mr. Grunk: Your Honor, I object. Dr. Zeus is not on trial here for being a bad husband, or for having affairs. We will concede that Ms. Thompson has willingly consented to having sexual intercourse with my client on occasion over the years. In every case they were consenting adults. This had nothing to do with his medical license or with the Medical Practice Act at all. It's just an attempt to smear his character so as to prejudice the court against him.

Ms. Hunt: This is all just background. I haven't gotten to my point yet, a point which will show that Katherine's transcript is reliable and should be admitted.

Administrative Law Judge: Overruled. I'll allow it. But you'd better have a point, Ms. Hunt.

Ms. Hunt: Okay. Now, we've established, Ms. Thompson, that you've had intercourse many times with Dr. Zeus.

Ms. Thompson: Many times, in many ways.

Q: So you are very familiar with Dr. Zeus's anatomy?

A: Very.

Q: Good. Please describe for us in detail his penis.

Chapter 36

Hartwicke

"Is it true?" Grunk and Zeus were meeting back in Grunk's office that same afternoon. "Does your penis when erect take a sharp turn to the left?"

"That's true of a lot of penises."

"I'll take that as a yes. Do a lot of penises have a purple birthmark the shape of, I think Marcie said Paraguay, on the inside of that curve?"

"That bitch. I'll kill her. Anyway, Marcie said Paraguay, but Katherine didn't say Paraguay in her transcript. Katherine said Madagascar."

"So you think we should compare maps of Paraguay and Madagascar as part of our defense?" Grunk's sarcasm was obvious, but Zeus decided to let it go. He needed Grunk, at least for now.

"I know who's behind this. It's Billings. He's got Marcie on his side somehow and he's getting his revenge on me through her."

"Revenge? For what?" Grunk was used to representing bad characters. It paid very well. The guiltier his client, the more he charged for setting up his elaborate evidentiary smokescreens. But he seemed tired now.

"Nothing. Just hospital stuff. Some people there are jealous of me."

"Okay. Let's get back to our business. Paraguay or not, I still think we have a 50-50 chance the judge will disregard Katherine's transcript. She definitely didn't like Katherine walking out of her court."

"Then we'd be home free?"

"From that charge, yes. But I'm worried about this video they say they have showing you fingering a female patient on the beach. A teenager."

"That's false! That's totally false! I was not *fingering* anybody. We were just lying innocently on the beach. I was just putting suntan lotion on her back. I wish you could see that video."

"Doc. Doc. Can't you see? They have us in a bind. The only thing the judge heard was Ms. Porter's description of the video. And Porter said it was a teenager, and a patient, and she used the word *fingering*. We could get the video and put it into evidence to refute the fingering allegation, but it's still going to put you in a bad light. The judge would then see the whole video. I assume the girl is very young like they said and, God forbid, one of your patients."

"Let's forget about the video."

"Okay then." Grunk sighed. "The video is technically irrelevant to our case. The judge hasn't seen it, and she probably never will unless we bring it up again."

Grunk's phone rang then, and he swiveled his chair sideways to get a modicum of privacy. Zeus couldn't hear all of the mumbled conversation. Grunk swung back toward Zeus. "New development. The prosecutor has just informed me that they are amending the charges to include a new patient, a teenager named Diane Morrell. They just told me she is the girl in the beach video."

··· ···

They hadn't broken the news about their divorce to Kyra yet. Zeus knew Kyra wouldn't side totally with Elena. It was against female nature to turn against the father just because the mother had. All young females sensed the strength and suckled at the sustenance that the father figure provided. No matter what evil deeds he had done, Kyra would just as likely blame her mother as him. But Kyra's sympathy wouldn't be enough. Elena would probably get custody, plus the house; and even though she had stolen all his money, she still held the moral high ground thanks to the feminist logic that dominated the society they lived in. He knew he needed to think up a way to stab her in the heart.

Grunk had refused to act as his divorce lawyer, saying it was too rough a business for him. Zeus hadn't had time to call his business lawyer, Bill Ferris, but he had the feeling he'd get the same answer from Ferris anyway. Elena had found both his secret money market account and his secret 401(k), forged his signature, and cleaned them both out. They totaled over $400,000, and he had no idea where she'd hidden the money. She had put a freeze on all three of his credit cards, claiming they'd been stolen, and when the new ones came in the mail she took them and hid them before he even saw them. She'd missed one secret bank account, but it had only $17,000 in it. There was not a credit card attached, and so when the car leasing company notified him that his credit card company had declined to pay his $799 monthly lease payment on the Jag, he had to drive over there and write a check for that amount, plus the late fee. He earned over $13,000 a month from New Town Partners, but they refused to give him an advance now, and over half of that sum would ordinarily go to his mortgage payments on the house, the house Elena would probably take away from him anyway.

He stopped eating any meals at home. He ate out at restaurants, using cash from his remaining bank account and from the petty cash account at New Town Partners. He signed up for every credit card solicitation he got at the office. Within a few days he had two new credit cards with a $25,000 limit on each. Grunk had already told him his fee would double now that there were two women accusing him, and Grunk wanted his money up front. He paid Grunk $25,000, taking one of his credit cards to the limit in one swipe.

When the amended charges were sent to his house, Elena read them first and lay in wait. She slapped him hard across the face as soon as he came in the door. "I knew it! You sick soul, you pervert! A teenage girl at the church! She's the one whose purple hair I found in the Jaguar, right?" She tried to slap him again but he grabbed her wrists. She wouldn't shut up. "Who else have you been sticking your stupid crooked penis in? What am I supposed to tell Kyra?"

He steered her by the back of her neck to the living room. "You fucking whore!" he said in a harsh whisper. "If you mention this to Kyra I'll have you committed."

"It's not that easy to commit someone."

"I'm a prominent physician. My wife has been breaking and entering into offices, looking at other people's medical records, forging signatures, stealing 401(k)s. Most problematic of all" – he reached for something on the side table – "she's been tearing up" – he demonstrated – "things she cherished, like the only picture she had of her grandparents' wedding."

She grabbed at his hands, but the picture was already torn. She looked around frantically for her other pictures, but Zeus was gone from the room by the time she collected the rest. Zeus was determined she would not get away with separating him from Kyra. Kyra belonged to him as much as to her. If she told Kyra her father was a danger to her, Kyra would automatically be damaged goods, for the rest of her life. And he would not stand for being the father of damaged goods.

··· ···

When they left for the mandatory family orientation at the Concord Mews School two nights later, Elena was still stewing. They did agree it was critical to convince that snotty school that they were an intact family that could be counted on to continue to donate over the years.

"Why are you two so unhappy about this school?" Kyra was now noticing things that she would have been oblivious to a year before. "You both said it was a good school. And it seems like an okay place to me."

"We're not unhappy, dear." Elena looked straight ahead through the windshield.

"Oh, come on. You guys look like you're going to a firing squad." This was a first, coming from Kyra, who only rarely had ever had a conversation with both of her parents at the same time, and who had never challenged them. But Kyra let it drop after that, and they rode the rest of the half-hour drive in silence.

The main purpose of the meeting was to dun the family for more donations, but the school also put on a presentation from each of the academic departments. Zeus was glad to see Kyra step up and engage in conversation with one faculty member, though he was disappointed it was the head of the art department. Zeus's stony silence drained the life out of any conversations Elena tried to start with the teachers, or with the other parents. Zeus was angry that he still had to attend this function even though he had already made sufficient cash gifts to cover all the donations due for the first year. But he enjoyed watching Elena squirm as each of her attempted conversations died out. She didn't have the nerve to tell anyone there they were splitting up. She was more embarrassed than he was by the medical board's charges against him. She was under his control.

He stood mostly apart at the non-alcoholic school reception that followed the formal presentations, focusing on the humiliation he might suffer in the divorce proceedings. He finally noticed a blonde woman who was trying to engage in conversation with him. He was totally bored by now with all the middle-aged women who wanted to flirt with him, but he always paid a hint of attention just in case there was something special involved. In this case, the mother's teenage daughter was involved. She had light brown hair, which was probably the real color of her mother's hair but was much thicker and longer, and she was a little taller than her mother. She hung at her mother's side, a little shy but not afraid of poking in a word or two. Zeus caught Elena's glare and couldn't help yanking her chain. He stood facing mother and daughter, opened his eyes wide and spoke with false animation, touching each of them frequently on the arm to emphasize his points. He raised his eyebrows and smiled at the teenager's every comment, and he was pleased to see both mother and daughter follow the ancient submissive female pattern and smile in return. All the while Elena's eyes smoldered. Life didn't get much better than this.

Except when he remembered Elena would get at least half of everything. As she glared at him, he slid his hand down to the small of the teenager's back. Elena took a step forward as if to smack him, but then she quickly turned back and headed toward a door on the other side of the room.

It was fun to feel the initial involuntary quiver in the teenager's back, then her body's acceptance of the calming force of his touch. But he had no interest in her once Elena had gone, and he took his hand off. The mother hadn't dared protest his touching her daughter, but she looked relieved when he stopped. The whole thing was more fun than he had ever expected to have at this reception.

He went through the door Elena had exited by. It opened onto a short hallway with a hardwood floor covered in an Oriental runner. He heard Elena's voice in the first office to his left, and he looked in. Elena sat in a chair with her mouth set tight, a desperate look in her eyes. Across from her, relaxed in his cozy swivel chair, his leather elbow patches prominently on display, sat Kiley Fontaine, the so-called dean of the school. He could tell by the smirk on Fontaine's face that Elena had already started confessing something to him. Was the bitch now going to tell everybody? He had a sudden premonition of driving to pick Kyra up one day and being told by some anonymous security guard, or by that snotty Fontaine himself, that he wasn't on the list. Men were often banished from the very lives they created, thanks to the female-centered society they lived in.

Elena seemed to be preparing the groundwork with Fontaine to set the father-exclusion in motion. But Zeus wasn't immediately alarmed. It would take a court order, and she would need a lawyer, before she could exclude him from Kyra's life. And there was a reason Elena didn't have a lawyer yet, he knew. Elena most likely had one or two more dirty tricks up her sleeve, and she wouldn't go to a lawyer until she had finished breaking the law herself.

He wondered what she had found when she went through the records in his medical clinic in the church auditorium. Of course, he never wrote anything incriminating in the records themselves. And there had been only one other teenage girl besides Diane. He hadn't taken her out anywhere. He hadn't written down her narcotic prescriptions. But the records would show an unusually high number of appointments, one every two weeks post-partum until Diane came into his life and totally took over his sexual imagination.

"We're going now," he commanded.

"Oh, you have to go so soon?" Kiley Fontaine affected a simulated upper-class condescension toward the working doctor, that mere mechanic of the human body. "I was hoping you and Elena would have time to learn more about the Concord Mews philosophy of education."

"We have to shove off. I'm on call at the hospital tonight," he lied.

"Maybe Elena and Kyra could stay a little longer. I'd be glad to give them a lift home, if it's all right with the three of you."

Elena stood up. "No thank you. I guess we should go."

"Does Kyra want to go?" Elena asked him as she walked back to the reception room with him, taking his arm, daring him to throw her arm off.

"I have no idea. I want to go."

"Are you determined to make this hard on her too, Hardy?"

"I might."

He dragged Kyra away from the art teacher and they marched out of the room, arms linked, until they had to disengage to get through the door. He started the Jag and revved it high so the *blat-blat-blat* of the exhaust note reverberated off the walls of Concord Mews. The sound matched his rage.

"Why are you guys acting so weird?" Kyra now sounded more worried than brave.

Elena said something, but it couldn't be heard over the deep growl of the engine.

"Are you two getting a divorce?" She whimpered out the last two words like her courage had failed her.

He let off the gas for a second. *Blat-blat-blat*, then just a very low rumble.

"Yeah, we're getting a divorce."

"Why?"

"All this ... *crap*." He motioned toward Concord Mews. "It's putting too much of a strain on us."

"That's bullshit, Hardy." Elena made her voice heard. "Kyra, the medical board has charged your father with doing some very bad things, things that may mean that our marriage can't go forward."

"But what will happen to me?"

"Your mother's divorcing me because of you."

"Don't twist my words, Hardy!"

"I mean, Mom and Dad, no, it's not what I want." The high, plaintive note in Kyra's voice cut through the low rumbling of the engine.

"It's what your mother wants. That's what counts. When there's a divorce, men have no say in what happens."

"Why can't Dad stay, Mom?"

Zeus popped the clutch and they sped away, suspending all talk for a second as their heads were slammed against the headrests. They all stopped talking, caught their breath as parked cars and streetlights flashed by on both sides.

"He can't stay ...." Elena voice was shaky. "Your father can't stay because he has betrayed me, and because they have charged him with doing some awful, disgraceful things – and its best that we part ways."

"Why don't you say what you mean, Elena? Kyra is turning into a woman, and every time she's around me you think she's trying to tempt me sexually. You're splitting the family up because you don't trust Kyra to be around her father."

Chapter 37

David

"I'll catch you up in six words, Newbie: our case is going to shit." Frank folded his arms, then let his elbows bump on his desktop. He nodded toward Michele. "Tell him what happened."

Michele got to the point right away. "Diane's backed down."

"Now she's saying it's not true?"

"No," Michele shook her head. "Her mother just called and said she wouldn't testify."

"Can't we make her come and testify. We could subpoena her, right?"

"Newbie, Newbie, Newbie," – Frank assumed a look of fatherly patience – "you never subpoena your own witnesses against their will. You never know what they're going to say. Usually they're so pissed at you they deliberately won't remember anything."

Dave turned to the prosecutor. "Can't we go forward just on her transcript, just like we're doing in Katherine's case?"

"Don't forget," Nancy Hunt responded, in a somewhat less patronizing voice than Frank's, "the judge hasn't decided yet whether to believe the story in Katherine's transcript. If it weren't for that Paraguay testimony from Marcie, I think the judge would have already discounted it."

"But didn't Diane talk about all kinds of prescriptions for narcotics. I mean like, 480 pills in six weeks? Can't we find those prescription records? Wouldn't that corroborate her transcript?"

"They would, Newbie, if we could find them." Frank's voice was gruff, like he was in a hurry now that Newbie had been brought up to speed.

"Zeus wrote nothing in his records about oxycodone," Michele explained. "And Diane said she never actually filled the prescriptions. So there will be no pharmacy records. These prescriptions look like they don't exist, as far as the case is concerned. And Diane's whole story comes off sounding like some kind of fantasy."

"There's nothing we can do except keep going forward." Nancy Hunt's reaction was true to form. "Go with what evidence we have. There's always a chance the judge will believe what's written in the transcripts."

"There's one thing," Michele said. "Diane said she gave those prescriptions to some guy named Woody. She said he put them ... I think she said in a garage or something. It didn't make any sense to me at the time, so I didn't get any details."

"Nobody's going to believe a story like that," Frank interjected.

"But why would anybody make up a story like that?" Michele came back at him.

"If it's true, it'll help. Okay, find this guy, Newbie. Find the prescriptions, if they exist," Frank summed up. "And do it today."

Sarah had arrived in town that morning without warning because, she said, they needed to talk. Sarah was generally not big on heart-to-heart talks, so he knew it was serious. But he had to call her and tell her he would be late because he had to find this guy.

··· ···

There was an evening chill in the air by the time he found the garage. A single electric heater, the only source of heat, buzzed as they talked. The large window in the back cast a weak shaft of sunlight across the bed. Dave expected hostility because Woody was a friend of Diane and she was no longer cooperating with the investigation.

Woody was a little taller than Dave and awfully skinny. Dave was wearing a suit, something Michele recommended for interviews, but he felt immediately uncomfortable and took the coat off. Woody, who was wearing jeans and a long-sleeved pullover shirt with tattoos still visible at the neckline, just laughed.

"We are investigating this doctor, Dr. Zeus, who may have taken advantage of a friend of yours, Diane Morrell."

"Diane and Dr. Zeus? Yeah, they've been going out. She's always going back and forth about whether he loves her. I think the whole thing stinks."

"Because she's underage, you mean?"

"No. I don't care about that."

"How do you know Diane?"

"We go way back, from when before she had the baby. We used to hang out in the woods together sometimes. With her friends Lucky and Kate. We're all still friends."

"Just friends? I mean you and Diane. Are you two more than friends? I have to ask questions like this."

"Big detective job, huh? Yeah, Diane and I are just friends."

Dave smiled to himself. This was the first person who had ever thought he had a "big" job.

"I'm just an investigator."

"You have to go to college for that?"

"Yeah. But it's not a big deal. Just something to pay off my student loans while I'm waiting to go to law school." Dave immediately chastised himself for downplaying the importance of his job. If his job wasn't important, this interview wasn't important. And if the interview wasn't important, why should Woody cooperate? "But I found out the Board does some really critical work," he added. "I mean, there's some really bad doctors out there."

"Zeus was always trying to get Diane to take that oxyco-done," Woody said. "Did she tell you anything about going to a condo, and there being a third person there?"

"She told us about that incident. Just the bare facts. She isn't entirely sure what was going on there. She agreed to come and testify about the bare facts, but now she's backed out and won't testify at all." Dave looked at Woody. "Do you know of any reason why she would back down? Do you think her parents told her to keep quiet, or do you think maybe somebody is threatening her?"

"Nah." Woody seemed certain. "She would have told me if it was any of that stuff. I think she's just still halfway in love with him."

"I don't get women," Dave admitted. "Not any of them."

Woody laughed. "Who does?"

"My girlfriend ...." Dave began. He realized this interview was going a little off track. He had been taught it was okay to reveal a little about yourself to an interviewee so as to break the ice and find common ground, but he knew he didn't really have to do this with Woody. He just wanted to talk to Woody right then, maybe because Woody was a guy – and maybe because, right at that moment, there were two women, a woman at work whom he admired and a woman in his apartment whom he loved, and neither of them was hesitating to tell him he wasn't quite making the grade. "My fiancée, I should say. Her father runs a Wall Street company that screws over poor people. Now she wants me to be his best friend. I mean, what's that all about?"

"I think you're asking the wrong guy." Dave looked up to see if Woody was just brushing him off, but Woody's tone was closer to apologetic. "I haven't got a girlfriend, or a father."

"It's not your fault if you don't have a father." Dave knew he was getting further off track, but the conversation between them seemed to be flowing easily and he didn't want it to stop.

Woody nodded in agreement. Dave could feel that he was gaining Woody's trust and congratulated himself for following his intuition. He let Woody talk.

"No, he was a drunk, in and out of the house all my life. My mother died when I was twelve and he disappeared for good a little after."

"So who did you live with after that?"

"Lived on my own. Until they took the house away. Stayed at friends' places in the winter. Had a part time job off the books. Sold some weed."

Dave started to tell him that he didn't have a father either but realized then that the two stories didn't compare. But then he told his story anyway.

"I guess there's a lot of that going around," Woody shrugged. "Looks like it didn't slow you down. You said you graduated from Rutgers? Not bad."

"Not bad. What about you? You don't have any criminal record, do you? I have to ask that."

"No. Every cop in town knows who I am, but no, no criminal record."

"You seem to be doing okay yourself. What's your relationship with this Ms. Nesbitt?"

"She was my English teacher in middle school. She's let me live here ever since I turned eighteen. I can use her bathroom. We cook together sometimes."

"She's like, your unofficial foster mother or something?"

"Ha!" Woody laughed. "I don't see her as a foster mother. No."

"Um, if it ever came to you testifying, your relationship with Ms. Nesbitt might become an issue."

"Relationship?" Woody laughed even louder. "I got tattoos on my body no teacher should ever have to see. Anyway, I like to stay within the same generation."

"I guess Zeus doesn't believe in that."

"He's scum, Dave. Tell me what I can do to make him pay for fucking with Diane."

··· ···

When he finally got back to his apartment, Sarah was energetically clinking pots and plates around in the kitchen. She had no experience cooking, he knew. She had been a member of the oldest eating club at Princeton and had never expressed the slightest interest in cooking any food herself. But she had gone to the grocery store and decided while she was there she would make shrimp croquettes for dinner based on a recipe a woman in the checkout line told her about. There was burnt seafood smell in the air. He took a bite and tried to be polite about it. Then she took her first bite, ran to the sink and spit it out.

"Oh my God! That is disgusting!" she cried out from the kitchen. "Why didn't you tell me?"

Dave started laughing so hard he couldn't stop. "It is awful," he said between spasms. His eyes teared up with laughter.

Later they held each other on the sofa. She quickly got over her humiliation about the shrimp. Cooking wasn't important to her, he already knew. Of course, there was no reason she should ever have to worry about cooking when the waiters at The Collective or some similar fancy restaurant would always serve her up whatever dish she wanted and compliment her on her excellent choice of food at the same time. But he decided not to mention The Collective tonight – or anything else that had to do with her wealth or her father.

But she brought it up. "It seemed to me you really liked my Dad before you found out what he does for a living."

"I did."

"But you don't like him now."

"I don't."

"I don't see why."

"Let me tell you the rest of my Wall Street story. My mother couldn't pay my college tuition after she was laid off. That's why I have $145,000 in student loans to pay off. Tell your Dad and his friends on Wall Street thanks a lot."

Chapter 38

Hartwicke

Kyra pushed her way out of the back seat of the Jaguar and ran into the house the instant the car stopped. Elena was in the front seat and was bent over and squished against the dashboard, and she stayed collapsed in that position with her hands to her face even after Kyra was gone.

"You are ... utterly despicable," she finally muttered. "To say that to your own child .... She's only twelve! She idolizes you. She thinks everything you say is true."

"I know." Zeus was disappointed Elena wasn't looking at him and couldn't see the quiet smile on his face.

"How much you must hate me! You're willing to damage your own daughter to get an advantage over me!" She pushed the seat back and stared at him like he was an alien creature she'd have to try to understand now with some faculty other than her heart.

"Why don't you calm yourself down before we go back in the house."

"In the house! Over my dead body, Zeus. You're never setting foot in that house again."

"I suggest you calm yourself down, Elena. And think about this. If you don't let me back in the house, it will prove to Kyra that you don't trust her to be around me."

He could hear Elena trying to control her breathing. He smiled as he watched her pathetic, desperate, female efforts to think her way out of his trap.

"And then Kyra will always believe," he twisted the knife further, "that she broke up our family because of her perverted desires for her father."

"*Despicable* isn't a strong enough word, Hardy."

"What's it going to be, honey?"

...   ...

He knocked on the door of the vinyl-clad house in the suburbs. A woman opened the door a crack and stared at him, then shut it in his face. "Honey," he heard her yell up the stairs, "there's this guy here asking for you. I don't know him. Take a look yourself."

Zeus stuck his foot in the door as soon as Billings opened it. "You have a finished basement? A couple of days will be all I'll need." He brushed past both Billingses with a suitcase in one hand and a bag of clothes in the other. He had tried to register at an extended-stay hotel, but by this time he had maxed out both of his new credit cards. He kicked himself for not applying for more. Billings's basement would have to do for now.

But long-term, money would not be a problem. Billings might hate him, but he was running scared, complying with almost his every wish. Billings was still terrified that Diane would report him as a rapist. Zeus told him he had taken a picture of him standing in the condo with his fly open and Diane naked in the background. Zeus told him Diane could identify him and would report him to the police the instant she learned his name.

Billings got the message. At the very next meeting of the Board of Trustees of Freeland Hospital, he allowed Zeus's name to be put in nomination for a seat on the board. Zeus pushed him to move faster. Billings then called an emergency meeting of the Board of Trustees to be held by teleconference. The only emergency was Billings's frantic need to put Zeus on the board right away. There had been some quizzical looks on the faces of those few trustees whose faces could actually be seen on the teleconference screen, and a few questions from others who were driving in their cars at the time and could only be heard on the phone, but the board usually gave Billings credit for knowing what he was doing. They voted to approve Billings' suggestion, and within two weeks Zeus had been put on the Board of Trustees.

Zeus had planned to spend the next few months persuading the board to send the hospital's lab work to PeakResults Labs, his company, but he sped up the plan once he realized how frightened Billings was. Billings obeyed his command and immediately, without board approval, ordered all of the hospital's outside lab work to be sent to PeakResults. Billings would mention it later to the Board of Directors as an administrative matter, a small detail that might save the hospital money and that they shouldn't worry about. Orders had already been given to send the lab work out, and PeakResults would be producing a stream of money in a few weeks. Zeus set up a new business checking account for that money to make sure Elena couldn't get her hands on any of it.

After a week and a half, Billings's wife had had enough. She kicked Zeus out. Zeus then drove directly over to Marcie's. She met him at the door. But just as on his first visit to the Billings home, the door didn't open all the way.

"No way," she said as soon as he asked. "I have kids, Hartwicke." Her red hair was styled and she was wearing a skirt and blouse, on a Saturday. He wondered who her new love interest was. He didn't mention what she had said about his penis at the hearing. He knew she had enjoyed ridiculing his genitals and helping the prosecutor to crash his career at the same time. They were always going to be slapping at each other like that. He loved it. But she wouldn't let him in the house that day. He checked into a cheap motel.

So then he tried to get her fired. It didn't work because Marcie was already a favorite of the rest of the Board of

Trustees. And that pathetic Billings seemed to think he owed Marcie a lifelong debt just for the one little boink she'd given him. Billings wouldn't move against her, and Zeus was way too busy to spend a whole lot of time thinking up ways to get revenge on her. In any case, he appreciated that she had even worse morals than he did, and he knew the day would come when she would be in heat for him again. He couldn't resist a woman who liked to be taken fast and hard. And so in the next few days he surprised himself by admitting he still liked having Marcie around the hospital – even though, occasionally, he thought he heard a voice softly paging "Doctor Paraguay" over the PA system.

••• •••

"Your original retainer will no longer suffice." Grunk broke the bad news the minute Zeus arrived in the office. "I've already spent over 60 hours on your case, not including the court case about the temporary restraining order, and even at the discounted rate of $333 an hour, the retainer's been used up."

"How much more?"

"With this new complainant, Diane Morrell, this is now a new case. This is not the case you engaged me for originally. Check the terms of our agreement. I need an additional $25,000 retainer to defend you against this new charge."

There was no use yelling at Grunk. There was no use bargaining with him. The $25,000 would soak up the credit limit on the new credit card he had just gotten that day in the mail. But he had no choice but to hand it over. Zeus could only hope that one day he'd be on call when Grunk was brought to the emergency room.

"I've already gone over all of Diane's medical records," Grunk began. "That was free. I did it as matter of my own curiosity. It looks like you saw her for quite a while after the baby was born. But I couldn't figure out why."

"Counseling, mostly. Doesn't it say that? This girl gave birth at the age of fourteen. She was very upset that her body had changed. Needed a lot of reassurance that everything was normal. I remember she was very worried. I might have given her a prescription for Xanax once."

Grunk stared at him. "The charging document says you wrote her prescriptions for a total of 480 twenty-milligram oxycodone pills."

"That many? She kept complaining about pain. There was nothing physically wrong. I hadn't realized it was that many."

"But you didn't write any of that down?"

"I didn't? You know, she always asked for those on the way out the door, or sometimes she would come on a day when she didn't have an appointment. I guess I should have written it all down. I didn't realize she was manipulating me. She has a very manipulative personality."

It seemed like it was a real effort for Grunk to raise his eyes from the yellow legal pad he was writing on to meet Zeus's. "So, are you telling me that you never touched this girl inappropriately, never had vaginal sex, oral sex, or anal sex with this girl, never kissed her, never told her you loved her."

"No."

"Never took her on your boat? Never took her to your condo? Never bought her presents?"

"She was on my boat once. We didn't touch. She wore long white pants. She was trying to decide whether to leave her church. She felt a lot of guilt. I was just trying to counsel her."

Grunk looked at him like he was gauging whether he dared put him on the stand. He started to crack a smile, but then stifled it as if he were disgusted with himself. "The condo?"

"I did take her there once. She seemed so anxious I thought a day at the beach might help her cope with her difficult situation. That's where that beach video came from. Oh! You know I guess I did touch her once. Not inappropriately. I was putting suntan lotion on her, nothing more. Nothing beneath the swimsuit line. I swear to God. Please look at that video."

"Just putting suntan lotion on. The one incident captured on video just happens to be the one and only occasion when you touched her." Grunk sighed. "Okay, if that is your defense, I'll put it on."

Grunk, however, looked like he might have a better idea. "But another option is to surrender your license. Then you would have nothing on your record but that you surrendered your license for personal reasons. None of the rest of this would be public. You could go to most other states, and you can always go to D.C., and just start over. And you could still own your lab here. You might even be able to stay on the Board of Trustees of Freeland Hospital. I could offer your surrender to the prosecutor, and if she accepts it you can go on your merry way. Plus, I'd then be able to give you back possibly as much as half of your new retainer."

"I'm innocent, and I want it proven on the record."

"What about that six-thousand-dollar necklace you bought her?"

"Jesus, what a manipulator she is! We ate some lunch next door to a jewelry store. She had one of those things girls have, you know, a charm bracelet or something like that. I gave her my credit card and told her to go in and buy another charm, just to cheer her up. I know jewelry can change any woman's mood. I was thinking she'd get a charm for about 10 to 20 dollars and get a giggle out of it. It wasn't until I got the bill two weeks later that I realized the little bitch had soaked me for $6,000."

Chapter 39

Diane

I was sitting at the very top of the stands watching the first soccer game of the playoffs. I missed soccer but felt like I needed to hide from my old teammates. I had quit the team to hide out at home, but everybody from Lisa to my mother to Zeus to the lady from the medical board had found me there. I knew I was disappointing all of them except Zeus by deciding not to testify against him. It was a bright, sunny day with air so clear and still you could see all the way across the school fields. We were winning 5-2 even after missing two easy goals. I was sure I would have made at least one of them. The day was so beautiful I was in a kind of a peaceful trance until Woody showed up and sat down beside me.

"Hi." I tried to sound happy to see him. I guessed I owed him that. Then I said what I meant. "What are you doing here?"

"Talk to you," he said, leveling those grey eyes on mine. "Can we take a walk when the game's over?"

"Yeah. Let's go right now. We can't lose this game."

There was a path that ran past the soccer field, through a tiny woods on the grounds. As we walked along that path, Woody took my arm above the elbow and softly gripped his hand there like he needed to guide me along. It was the exact same thing my soccer coach used to do when she was walking with me along the sidelines and trying to tell me something. Coaches weren't supposed to touch anybody, but I liked to be touched like that. It helped me concentrate on what she was saying.

"What is it?" I said.

He walked me a few more steps before he answered, guiding

me in the middle of the path even though he sometimes had to walk in the weeds himself. "I found out something you need to know."

Everyone else had thrown in their opinions about me and Zeus. Mom was pretty nice about it. She called the medical board for me and told that Michele lady I wouldn't testify.

But even Lisa had an opinion.

"Mom told me," she said one day, "you changed your mind and you're not going to testify against Zeus. She told me not to bug you about it. But what gives?"

"I think maybe I was wrong. That guy in the condo acted kind of psycho. I think Zeus was just trying to save me from him."

"That's not what you said before."

"I thought Mom told you not to ask me about this?"

"I don't care what Mom said. I don't care what you told Mom. I can't believe you just changed your mind." Her new habit was to just walk into my room whenever she wanted and flop down on my bed. She took up a lot of room everywhere she went. And she was a lot more bitchy these days.

"What's wrong with you, Lisa?"

"I don't know. I just get used to one idea about you, and then you change."

Now Woody walked me down the path away from the soccer field. He stopped just where the path came out of the woods and curved around on top of a small hill overlooking the football field.

"Can we sit down?" He smoothed a layer of leaves near the top of the hill so we could watch the tiny players below running around and banging into each other as they practiced. Every once in a while a faint laugh or shout of joy made it up the hill to us. The sun was already setting behind us.

"Why are you here?"

"You must be still in love with Zeus or else you would

testify against him."

"I think I might be wrong about what happened at the condo."

"I don't get it. Why did you change your mind about what happened there?"

I still had the sensation of his soft coach-touch on my arm. I was still waiting for him to steer me straight. It was so different from the flashback of pain I got whenever I remembered Zeus's hard grip on me that day in the condo.

"I still have that phone Zeus gave me a long time ago. He texts me every night."

"Oh." He adjusted his long legs which were stretched out over the crinkly leaves.

"I don't text back. Do you think I should?"

He opened his mouth like he was going to say something, but stopped.

"Don't you think if two people really love each other they can make their own rules?" I asked.

He adjusted his legs again, sat up straighter. "I don't care about rules. Sometimes one person takes advantage of another. That's what I care about."

"Even if Zeus isn't as good as I thought, I don't want to hurt him."

Woody stared down at the field for so long I thought he might have forgotten what we were talking about. But no. "I talked to a woman yesterday. She was a patient of Dr. Zeus's a couple years ago. He gave her drugs until she was addicted, then he made her have sex with him to get more."

"You're making this up!"

He took a quick breath. "Then he took her to his condo and this strange guy showed up and he rented her out to him for the night."

"You're lying!"

"The woman told me herself. Her name is Katherine. I'll

take you to meet her now."

"You're lying! How do you know this woman?"

"I can't tell you. It would get somebody in trouble if I told you."

I remembered a little plaque Woody had posted on a wall inside his garage, the only decoration in the whole place: *To live outside the law you must be honest.* That was the best description of Woody I'd ever seen. If I couldn't believe Woody, I couldn't believe anyone.

Down on the field, the players were now all gathered together standing in a circular crowd in a post-practice meeting. I really missed being on a team, working together. I wasn't on anybody's side now.

I thought I had gotten away with something by loving Zeus without becoming an addict. But everything he told me was a lie. I should have known he'd never invite his friends to the condo to meet his sixteen-year-old girlfriend. I should have known he bought me that stupid emerald necklace because he thought he owned me. I should have known he was rough in bed with me because he was angry I still made him use a condom. I should have believed what that pain in my arm was telling me.

And it was too much. I started crying and couldn't stop. We were there in the woods for a long time. Woody was not the kind of guy who would tell you to suck it up and move along. He seemed nervous about what to do, and so I had to stop crying. He coach-walked me all the way back up the path to the parking lot. Then he put me in his car and drove me to Katherine's house. Afterwards, he drove me home.

"Look, Diane, I didn't want to be the one to tell you this stuff. But it had to be me. I was the only one who could."

"I know. I know."

"A bunch of people at the medical board know about Zeus, but they can't legally say anything."

"I get it. I get it. You live outside the law. You can be honest."

Chapter 40

David

They were cleaning up in the kitchen after dinner. They still hadn't talked about why she had come. Sarah would think he was putting her off again, but he just had to tell her something else first.

"This guy Woody is amazing. He's got nothing, he's got nobody, he lives in a garage, but he kept Diane off drugs, he saved the evidence against Zeus, and now he's somehow got her to agree to testify."

"You did it too. You're the one who found him."

"He always knew Zeus was taking advantage of Diane, but he couldn't say it to her."

"Until you convinced him."

He let the pot he was washing slide under the soapy water of the sink and turned to her. He waited until she looked up. "You believe I'm making a difference, don't you?"

"I believe in you."

Her simple declaration filled him with joy. She was a strong-willed, strong-bodied, brilliant and decisive person. She believed in him and she needed him and she was not afraid to say it. He couldn't imagine life without her. He held out his arms. "Come here?"

She had a pile of dishes in her hands. "Why?"

She still hadn't mentioned why she had come, but suddenly he knew. He understood her. She didn't mix easily with other people, but when she loved somebody she loved somebody. Those things, the important things, were black and white to her. As she had told him many times, she couldn't live in a nuanced relationship.

"You still want me to be friends with your Dad, right?

"Yep."

"Can't you see what he and his Wall Street friends did to me, and to my mother?"

"Dave, if companies couldn't lay people off, they'd go under, and then everybody would lose their jobs. That's just … *economics*, I guess."

"It's my life, and my mother's life, fucked up. The last few years, you and your father have been hopping around the world to Rio and Paris and Sidney and Madrid while my mother went back to being an entry-level accountant for $700 a week. It's unfair, and it was your father and his good friends who did it to her."

"I'm sorry." Her voice broke. "I wish it didn't happen. I really wish it didn't happen." She regained her composure, then caught his eye with a look that embodied both sympathy and incipient panic. "I never realized you were jealous of me being rich."

"Jealous?" But he couldn't lie to this woman. "Okay, I am jealous. It eats away at me every time I think about your father." He tried to decipher her reaction to his confession, but her eyes were simply narrowed and her mouth frozen half open. "I'm sorry. Maybe I am like that. Maybe I am that small."

··· ···

When he had first come into the office that morning, Michele had rushed up to him in the hallway, obviously excited. She waved him into her cubicle.

"Diane called. She said she changed her mind. Now she will testify! You did it somehow." But Michele immediately lowered her voice, and her tone was suspicious. "But there's something funny about this. Diane told me she knew all about what Zeus did to Katherine. She knew her name, Katherine.

How did she know her name, and all the *confidential* details of our Katherine investigation, Dave?"

"I know what you're thinking. It wasn't me who told her, I promise. I promise on our friendship it wasn't me."

"How could she have found out, then?"

"I only talked to her friend Woody, the one who lives in a garage. He had all the oxycodone scripts Zeus wrote for Diane. And he gave them to me."

"Great! But what did you tell him about Katherine?"

"Nothing, but the guy won't take no for an answer. He was on the internet before I was out the door, looking up court records for the name Zeus."

"He has internet in his garage?"

"He has this really long ethernet cable that runs through a window into his landlady's house."

"He hacked into …? Does his landlady know about it?"

"She knows about it."

Dave now knew how to go right to the edge of the rules without breaking them. He had mentioned to Woody that *sometimes* predators like Zeus had multiple victims. Sometimes there were civil suits, sometimes divorces. Dave hadn't even known you could look up lawsuits just by the name of the defendant, but Woody was well on his way to figuring out the whole of Katherine's story before Dave had even left the garage.

··· ···

He made Sarah sit down on the tiny balcony of his apartment and have a glass of wine. They were polite to each other, but they weren't really talking. They were both equally upset. The trees across the parking lot were glowing in their fall colors. The sky was a pale blue with trailing streamers of gold. The days were getting shorter and this would probably be the last time they could sit out like this.

"I can't do it, Dave. I can't marry you and have you secretly hating him."

"You have no idea about the real world, Sarah. Let me tell you about this guy, Woody. His mother died of an overdose and his father abandoned him. He has no place to live but in a garage. He's nineteen, going to high school and working part time at two jobs. He's a talented guy, and a kind one. He helped this teenage girl from becoming an addict, and now he's convinced her to testify against this perverted doctor. But what does he say about himself? 'I'm a zero.'"

"Nobody should say that about himself."

"You have no idea what it's like to be at the bottom of the barrel. His choice was between foster care and living secretly in friends' basements. Now he's moved up in the world and lives in a garage. When you're that poor, you can't even make the best financial choices. You can't afford the 'economy' size box of cereal. You eat your too-expensive cereal with water instead of milk. If you do have an old car and you get a parking ticket, it costs you a week's groceries. It's not your fault, Sarah, but you have no idea how many good people are being put down like that, down to zero."

"Why did he say he thought he was a zero?"

"He didn't say, but it's obvious, isn't it?"

She reached over and took his glass and took a slow sip. "Maybe you're right. I mean, that I could never understand his situation. But in one way I really can. Because I had a mother who died, too. And I know that's the worst thing that can happen to you."

Her words threw him off track. Without his wine glass, he didn't even have a prop to play with to hide his confusion.

She finished the rest of the wine as if she were getting up courage. "I'm just going to say this. I see how you live. I see what you care about. What you care about is justice. I don't think you care all that much about money. You are jealous, but you're not jealous of my money."

"Why else would I be jealous?"

"You don't see it, do you?"

"No, I don't see it. Why else would I be jealous?"

"Because, Dave, you never had a father. And I have one of the best around."

He was stunned, speechless. It felt like she had hit him with the lowest of low blows.

Never ask a *why* question. Never ask a question you don't know the answer to.

Chapter 41

Diane

Lisa played her first official school league basketball game, and she was pretty good for a beginner, but some guy yelled out "hey, skinnybones" and she heard it and she was crying in my room afterwards. "How come every guy in the world is in love with you, but I'm just a freak." She had dried her tears but still had a sour look on her face.

"Guys are not as dumb as they act. They like you. One day one of them will get up the nerve to talk to you."

She left my room, but I called her back.

"Zeus was just using me," I confessed right off. "He does it all the time – gives his women patients drugs, makes them have sex with him. I am the dumbest dupe in the world."

"Oh."

"He still sends me texts. Everything he says is a lie. Don't ever go near that man."

She wanted to see the phone. I kept it in my top bureau drawer.

"He doesn't actually call any more. He's scared now that the medical board is after him."

She picked up the phone. "Look. There's a text right now. *Call me.*"

"Let me have that."

"No, look, here's another one. *Call me urgent.*"

"Lisa, just take the phone and throw it away."

She tossed it back into the drawer. "You throw it away."

I told her about going with Woody to see Katherine.

"It was so pathetic, Lisa. When she heard what happened to me, she cried so much she could hardly talk. She practically begged me to show up at the hearing."

Mom softened Dad up and then told me I had to talk to him. Something about him always makes me want to hold my head up high no matter how much of a stupid idiot I've been. He likes me with my head held up high, fighting back like he does every day at his job.

"A gynecological exam every two weeks? I should have guessed something strange was going on," he started.

"I kept everything hidden with all those lies I told."

He was my father and he didn't want to talk about my lies. "Diane, when you fall in love, you apparently go all-in."

"Dad, what's wrong with me? Really."

He laughed. "Wrong? That's not a fair question to ask a father. You just have to learn some things. A guy can be nice to you in some ways, maybe in a lot of ways, but if he's not nice to you in all ways, something's wrong."

"Did you think Carl was nice to me in all ways?"

He froze for a second, surprised. "I did."

"But ...?"

He hesitated. "Okay. I thought he was really nice to you, but I also thought he was dumb as a box of rocks."

Carl forgive me, I laughed. Dad had a way of getting to the point. I guessed his main point was to let me know that he knew all about Zeus. He asked me if I wanted him to come to the hearing.

"I'm afraid you'll hit him."

"I'm not going to make this worse. I want like hell to sue him, but Mom made me promise not to do that either."

"You and Mom work together, don't you?"

"We're pretty much all-in."

... ...

I hadn't looked at the Zeus phone since the day I showed it

to Lisa, but I picked it up out of the bureau drawer the night before the trial. I was going to count how many times he had left *call me* on there before he gave up. Zeus did to Katherine everything he did to me, plus more. He never even bothered to send her on an ego trip like he did me. He just got her addicted. He didn't buy her a bathing suit or a $6,000 emerald necklace. Her husband was pissed at her, and they were poor now, and she had to go to crappy free group counseling meetings every week. She said she wanted to go to real counseling but couldn't afford it. I guess she never had friends or a smartass sister to call her out every time she started to go off the deep end.

I counted his texts from the past few days: *Call me* or *Call me urgent*, 27 times. Then the last one was different. I read it again. Then I read it a hundred times.

I know where your baby is.

Chapter 42

David, Diane

David

"Where's our witness?" Nancy Hunt looked accusingly at Dave and Michele when she came out of a closed meeting in the judge's office. "The judge is getting antsy."

"Zeus's not here either," Dave observed, a little irritated that Nancy was looking at him like it was his fault their star witness had failed to show. "Maybe they ran off together." He didn't mean it seriously, but the humor was too black for the moment. Both women looked daggers at him.

"The judge said she will probably give no weight to Katherine's statements in the transcript. She will not admit Diane's transcript at all," the prosecutor continued, a note of despair creeping into her normally matter-of-fact voice. "If Diane doesn't show up soon I'm sure the judge will dismiss the case entirely."

They were all sitting there, Nancy tapping her foot, Michele studying the patterns of the floor tile, Dave straining to see through the far-off entranceway into the parking lot, when Grunk came out of the hearing room and approached the group.

"Looks like a dismissal," he smiled.

"It's not over until it's over," Nancy replied.

"Zeus got held up at the hospital," he explained. "But I just got a call that he's on his way."

"Good for you." Nancy's harsh tone was just a smidge more hostile than her normal tone.

"So we would like to offer you a deal." Grunk ignored Nancy's snippy comment. "You have no witnesses, no other evidence that the judge believes, absolutely nothing that shows that he ever touched anybody. We both realize the case will be totally dismissed as soon as we go back in there. So I'm proposing a settlement."

"Keep talking." Nancy's icy expression didn't change.

"For purposes of settlement discussion only, and only if we reach a settlement right here and now, before we go back into the hearing room, Dr. Zeus will admit he wrote those scripts for oxycodone for Diane Morrell. And he will admit they don't match his office medical records. So if the Board will drop all the sex charges right now, he will admit that he created inadequate office medical records, and he will accept a reprimand for that."

"Even though" – Dave couldn't help interrupting – "Zeus prescribed criminal amounts of narcotics to this teenager who didn't have any illness. Not even knee pain."

"We won't admit to that. We will admit only that his office records were inadequate. Believe me, that's more than you'll get from this judge once she comes back on the bench. Think about it." Grunk turned and slowly walked away.

Michele broke the long silence with a sigh. "I guess it's better than nothing. Zeus will at least have some kind of mark on his record. But I know he's going to keep doing it."

"I don't think I could make this deal without the Board's approval," Nancy said. "That would require us to make a lot of quick phone calls right now." But she didn't whip out her phone, nor did anyone else.

"If we made this deal, we would be part of the problem." Dave pronounced, then dragged himself off the bench and walked away toward the entrance to the building.

··· ···

Diane

Your daughter in hospital alone critical condition.

The word *daughter* didn't even click right away. Then everything clicked and hit me at the same time – my baby ... dying? ... what hospital?... what is her name even? ... how does Zeus know? ... he's such a liar, he knows this text will turn me inside out ... but what if he isn't lying? ... do I need to call Carl? Why won't Zeus just text me where she is, and her name? He wants me to call him, that's why. That's all it is. But he is a doctor. Maybe they called him for some genetic information about the real mother or something. Maybe her adoptive parents abandoned her. Maybe she's dying all alone. All these ideas hit me at the same time like slaps from different directions and left me flat on my bed with my mind spinning.

I had to get my head straight. I forced myself off the bed and crept across the hall to Lisa's room. She was asleep. I just crawled into bed with her. But she jumped up and clocked me in the eye with her elbow.

"Ow!"

"What are you doing here?" Her loud reaction freaked me out even more.

"Shh. I have to talk to you." She went quiet, keeping her head on the pillow. I told her what Zeus's text said. "I don't know what's real any more, Lisa."

"Should we tell Dad?"

"I can't. I'm so mortified I kept that phone. Without telling Mom or Dad. I got to do this on my own."

"Do what?"

My mind started spinning again. I didn't know where to start. I wondered what Woody would do in my situation. He would figure out the simplest step forward and just take it. "First, I have to call Zeus back. I have to. In case the story's true. Because I can't go see her by myself. I don't even know her name. Let me stay in bed here with you when I call."

I called, but he didn't answer his private number.

"Call his hospital?" Lisa suggested.

I called the hospital. They acted annoyed that I actually wanted to talk to a doctor. They said he would pick up his messages at 6:00 a.m. I said it was an emergency. I said it again and they finally paged him or something.

"What happened to my baby? Where is she?" I couldn't scream it at him because I didn't want to wake my parents.

He waited half a minute before he answered. I could hear him talking to a nurse about some sheets.

"I'm not treating her, but I know where she is. She's very critical."

"Where is she?"

"Apparently, the adoptive parents are not available."

"Where is she?"

"I'll take you to see her as soon as I get off here."

"You're lying, or you'd just tell me where she is."

"It would be illegal for me to tell you even her name. But I'll drive you there and sneak you into pediatric intensive care as soon as I get off duty here. I'm risking my license just by doing that. But we've already broken a lot of rules for love, haven't we?"

He told me to meet him in the hospital parking lot at 6 o'clock that morning and he'd drive me to the other hospital where she was. Lisa listened to the whole conversation.

"You know I'm supposed to testify against him at 9 o'clock today, right?" I reminded her.

"Oh. I forgot this was the day."

"Zeus is probably lying," I said.

"Then don't go with him."

"But what if he's not?"

··· ···

Zeus drove for maybe a half hour. I didn't tell him Woody was following us in Lucky's blue Camaro. Zeus drove fast. It seemed like he didn't know where he was going. He wouldn't let me put the hospital's name in the GPS. He wouldn't even tell me the name of the hospital. He looked tired, and he kept using that as an excuse not to tell me anything. It seemed like a bullshit excuse to me. He wouldn't talk to me. Then, when I tried to tap the icon for the GPS to look for nearby hospitals, he grabbed me so hard my arm felt that same sharp pain as when he grabbed it in the condo. It was like my arm was reminding me how mean he was to me in the condo. But I would never need any reminding again after talking to Katherine. Zeus wasn't even pretending to be nice to me now. If he knew something about my baby, he wasn't telling me, and that was the cruelest thing anybody could do.

"There's no hospital, is there? There's no baby," I challenged him.

He didn't even bother to answer. Then I knew for sure his story about my baby was pure bullshit. I couldn't believe somebody could be so mean.

"Pull over! I want to get out!"

He still had his grip on my arm, and I had this flash that he might try to inject me with something. We were going about 95 miles an hour. I jerked my arm free and screamed at him. I unlocked my door and he locked it with his button and I unlocked it again and we played that game until the car started lurching from side to side. I wasn't going to jump out, but I thought opening the door might slow him down.

"My friend is following us in that blue car," I told him. "Slow down and let me out."

He checked the mirror, then jerked us onto an exit ramp. We raced down a smaller road, then he made a sudden U-turn. The blue car followed. Zeus stepped on the gas, got back to the highway and merged back on the entrance ramp so fast we slid back and forth and onto the shoulder before he got it under control again. The blue car was right behind. We swerved through the traffic on the highway, passing every other car on the road like it was standing still. It wasn't scary as long as we were on the big highway, but he turned off again onto a smaller road and screeched around corners so fast I held my breath. I was thinking about Woody, hoping he wouldn't hurt himself trying to help me.

It got worse on the smaller roads. Zeus didn't stop for stop signs or lights, and he drove on the shoulder, or whatever side of the road had less cars. I thought this would be the stupidest way to die anybody could think of. Woody fell behind, but I could still see the car, way back. Then there was a red light where traffic was backed up on both sides and there were no shoulders, and we really had to stop. I looked for Woody to catch up, but he had stopped for a different light a little ways back. Then our light turned green. Zeus looked over at me and smiled. Then the car suddenly died.

The motor wasn't running, the lights on the dashboard were off, the radio was off, and none of the buzzers that had been going off all through the chase were going off now. Nothing happened when Zeus turned the key, the motor wouldn't start again and there wasn't the slightest noise – except for Zeus's cursing, which really made me laugh once I figured out what was happening.

"Goddam, goddam Jaguar! Goddam piece of junk!" The car behind us started honking. Zeus pounded on the wheel until I thought he'd break his hand. I was so high on the idea that I wasn't going to die that I didn't think of jumping out at first. He wasn't looking at me when I undid my seat belt, and he barely looked up when I opened the door and stepped out onto the road.

I couldn't help it. I leaned my head in the window. "Thanks for the ride." I started back toward the blue car, which was quickly catching up. I couldn't help it. I went back to Zeus's window again. "Hey, maybe I'll see you in court."

Chapter 43

David

She had an angry bruise under her eye, her purple hair was pinned up haphazardly so it showed its brown roots, and she was wearing jeans and a wrinkled long sleeved top. But Dave couldn't have been happier to see her.

He had walked out of the hearing offices in utter despair, without an idea of where he was going – right then or with the rest of his life. He had stood motionless out on the sidewalk in front of the building for a long time, not willing yet to just find his own car and close this sorry chapter of his life. Zeus was getting away with it because the whole system was rigged in favor of the rich and powerful, because a teenage girl couldn't tell the difference between rape and love – and because Dave had put too much faith in that girl's best friend.

Barely admitting to himself that he still held out any hope at all, he scanned the lot one last time for Woody's old Toyota. It wasn't there, but then he saw a whole group of teenagers burst out of a blue Camaro. He saw Diane and Woody rush toward the door of the hearing building ahead of the others. The other guy and two girls followed them. Dave raced to catch up. He heard more car doors slamming behind him.

Inside, Nancy Hunt forgot her stoic stance and rushed up and hugged Diane. "You were with Zeus, weren't you? Did he try to get you not to come? What the hell happened to your eye?"

····· ·····

Nancy Hunt led Diane through the whole story, day by day, drug by drug, sex act by sex act. The judge seemed immobilized, paying rapt attention throughout her testimony, waving off with one hand the first few technical objections raised by Grunk until he got the message and sat down. Near the end of her direct testimony, Nancy tried to have Diane go through the story of what had happened that morning, but Grunk objected that it had nothing to do with the case, and the judge agreed. Still, as Diane completed her testimony, the judge looked angry. She stared at Diane's face and reflexively put her hand to her eye.

"The judge thinks Zeus did that," Dave whispered to Nancy. "Don't you think you ought to clear that up, let her know that she just got accidentally clocked by Lisa's elbow?"

"Yeah. Hmm. Maybe." Nancy stared past him as if she were taking guidance from afar. "On second thought, no. She didn't say who hit her. Let's have some fun. Let's see if Grunk has enough nerve to ask that question."

He didn't.

He did his job, though.

> **Mr. Grunk**: You claim you didn't realize what Dr. Zeus was up to at first, but you were actually quite sexually experienced at the time, weren't you?
>
> **Ms. Morrell**: Well, I had a boyfriend a long time ago. We were in love.
>
> **Q**: That's not my question. My question is whether you were sexually experienced before you even met Dr. Zeus.
>
> **A**: My boyfriend and I had sex. I got pregnant. I had a baby. I gave it up for adoption. I guess you could say I was experienced.
>
> **Q**: You had a baby before this time?
>
> **A**: Yes, when I was fourteen. My mother's doctor took care of me then. But when Dr. Zeus started at the church clinic, everything he did was different.

Q: Didn't you expect things to be different,
feel different, after you'd given birth?
A: Yeah, that's what everybody said. But
he said it in a different way. He said it like
I was better, more of a woman, you know.

··· ···

Mr. Grunk: You and Woody forged those
prescriptions so you could sell them, right?
Ms. Morrell: No.
Q: Isn't it true that Woody is a known
drug dealer.
A: He did that a long time ago, in middle
school.
Q: But he has sold illegal drugs for money,
right?
A: I guess so.
Q: I'm not asking you to guess. You know
that he has sold illegal drugs for money,
don't you?
A: Yes.
Q: Would there be any reason for Dr. Zeus
to write all of those prescriptions for you
if you weren't taking any of the drugs.
A: He thought he was making me happy, I
guess.
Q: So your testimony is he thought you
were taking the drugs.
A: He thought I was taking the drugs.
Q: So you were lying to him about taking
the drugs?
A: Yes.
Q: You were lying then, but you want us
to believe that you're telling us the truth
now?
A: I was just trying to make him happy.

Q: Who are you trying to make happy
now?

••• •••

Mr. Grunk: So, your testimony is that
Dr. Zeus, who is 43, had sexual relations
with you, a sixteen-year-old girl who was
also his patient, took you to his condo,
tried to inject you with some drug against
your will, then tried to give you to a total
stranger to have sex with, then chased you
naked down the hall – all this, and you
never called the police?
Ms. Morrell: I didn't. I couldn't. I mean,
my parents thought I was a decent girl. I
thought I'd rather die than have them find
out.

••• •••

Grunk gave up questioning her, turned around and made his
way back to his chair with a resigned but not really unhappy
look on his face.

"She was great. That was a bravura performance," Nancy
whispered to Dave. "The only question is, is there anything
at all I need to ask on redirect? Do you think Grunk scored
any points at all?"

Nancy cocked her head as Dave breathed a suggestion.

Ms. Hunt: Have you by now told all of
this to your parents?
Ms. Morrell: Yes.
Q: Did they make you feel, like you feared,
that you were not a decent girl?
A: No. they were great. Just great. And ….
Q: Take a minute to compose yourself. Do
you need a drink of water?

A: No. No, I'm okay. And my sister too,
she's been great. And I've been so much
trouble to them all.
Q: I didn't see your parents in the building
today.
A: They're waiting out in the parking lot.
Q: Why in the parking lot.
A: I wouldn't let them come in.
Q: Because you're still embarrassed about
what happened?
A: Because I don't want my Dad to run
into Dr. Zeus. I'm afraid of what he might
do to him.

Zeus testified. He went on at such length about the ana-
tomical differences between a *primipara* and a woman who
had never given birth that even Grunk could not pretend to
stay interested. He denied that he ever touched Diane except
as required by his medical treatment – except for the one time
he put suntan lotion on her at the beach at her request. He
said he had taken her on the boat only once and that he had
not touched her there but instead counseled her because she
was feeling guilty about leaving the church. He said they had
been at the condo only once, and he denied that any other man
had been at the condo with them at any time. He explained
her gynecological condition in minute detail as it had changed
from week to week, though he admitted he hadn't written
anything about this in her medical record. He denied writing
any of the oxycodone prescriptions that Dave had retrieved
from Woody's garage. He explained that at the time Diane
was being stalked by a deacon at her church, and he expressed
his medical opinion that she might have been taking so many
illegal drugs that she confused her doctor with her stalker. He
said he bore no ill will toward Diane and sincerely hoped she
would get off drugs and straighten out her life.

Grunk asked Zeus if he harbored any feelings for Diane other than the feelings any physician would naturally have for any young person going through such a difficult life transition.

The answer obviously was supposed to be no, but Zeus wanted to keep talking. "Yes. Yes I do." Then, even though Gunk quickly held up his hand as a signal for him to stop talking, Zeus went on. "I feel like I have to be more than fair to this troubled young girl. She called me this morning to confess that her whole story is a lie. I met with her to try to find a way to end these proceedings and spare her any further embarrassment." Zeus smiled. Grunk didn't. Nancy laughed out loud. Grunk rushed him through to the end of the story. Zeus managed to get in that a very loud hot-rod type car started tailgating them on the interstate, and he had taken evasive maneuvers to try to get away. Then his car stalled, and Diane had run out into traffic, and he never saw her again until he came into this courtroom an hour ago.

Nancy wrote Dave a note this time. "He's such an idiot. Just wait."

"What if I told you that the marina records show that you took the boat out three times during this period? Would that change your testimony?" Nancy began her cross examination.

"I might have taken it out again. Not with her, though."

"What if I told you the security cameras at the marina show that Diane was with you all three times?"

Dave had done his homework during the past weeks while they had been otherwise just waiting around for Diane to change her mind.

"Then the security cameras are wrong, or the scene was faked by your overanxious investigators."

"Okay, let's take a look at the footage." Nancy started digging deep in her briefcase.

Zeus shifted his weight in the witness chair. "Okay, maybe I was wrong, maybe it was three times," he admitted.

"Three separate times with Diane?"

"Okay."

Nancy had even more fun with the emerald necklace Zeus had bought for Diane at the beach. By showing him the receipt, she got him to admit he'd bought it, but he said he bought it for his wife.

Nancy turned and reached into her briefcase again. "What if I told you that the security camera for the jewelry store shows you buying that necklace and putting it on Diane's neck yourself? Would that change your testimony?"

"No. Diane was just helping me. She was modeling it for me. I bought it for my wife."

"I have an affidavit here from your wife that says you have never given her an emerald necklace and in fact have not given her any jewelry in the last two years. Does that change your testimony?"

"No. I bought it for her, but I ended up not giving it to her."

"Why was that?"

Dave's ears pricked up to hear Nancy use the forbidden cross-examination question: *why*.

"I'll tell you why," Zeus responded sourly. "I didn't give her the emeralds because she filed for divorce. As soon as she read these reprehensible charges the Board lodged against me, she filed for divorce. My family is going to be split up. I'm the only one who has suffered any real harm here, and it's entirely the Board's fault."

Nancy had to regret asking that question, but she covered up her mistake well and soldiered on as if nothing had happened.

"And did you buy Diane a bathing suit, a green and white bikini to be exact, at La Mode beachwear shop down at the beach?"

"I don't remember."

"For $699, on your American Express card?"

"If you have the receipt, I guess I did."

"So you did?"

Zeus shrugged. "I did."

"But that was two weeks earlier, wasn't it? Look at that receipt. You bought that bikini for her two weeks before you bought the emerald necklace."

"Yeah."

"And Diane's on the video camera in both stores."

"If you say so."

"Do you want to stop and look at the tapes."

"No. Okay, if she's on both tapes, she must have been down to the beach with me twice, not once."

"So you're changing your testimony on that point too."

"Yes."

Over the course of a long afternoon, it turned out that there were many, many points at which Dr. Zeus had to change his testimony. Dave and Michele had discovered a mountain of evidence, much of it seemingly inconsequential when first collected, that contradicted his statements, one after another. Zeus was an excellent liar, but his method was like that of a counterpuncher, a boxer who waits to be hit and then hits back harder. He could make up a quick and outrageous lie to get around every bit of truth that was thrown at him, but he couldn't be bothered with the more difficult task of creating a complete fake story that held together under hard questioning. And so Nancy punched hole after hole in his testimony.

"Now let's talk about your meeting with Diane just this morning."

"Objection, Your Honor," Grunk stood up. "You have already ruled that Ms. Morrell's activities this morning are irrelevant."

"Overruled," the judge intoned immediately. "Your client brought this issue up in his direct testimony. Ms. Hunt has the right to cross-examine on this issue."

In response to Nancy Hunt's questions, Zeus made up a

story about why he had met Diane that morning. Nancy let him talk. "Look, I know it's not in my best interest to be talking to a witness right before the hearing, but she was so regretful I just couldn't pass up the opportunity to let this young girl confess and get this off her chest – and to forgive her. That's what I thought was going to happen. But once we were driving and her drug dealer boyfriend started to chase us and try to run us off the road, I realized she had set a trap for me."

> **Ms. Hunt**: How was this meeting arranged?
> **Dr. Zeus**: By phone.
> Q: Who made the call?
> A: Diane did.
> Q: She initiated the contact with you this morning?
> A: Yes.
> Q: Did she use the phone you gave her?
> A: Yes.
> Q: Didn't you send her numerous text messages on that phone in the previous 48 hours? Don't look at your lawyer. Answer the question.
> A: It's possible. I don't remember.
> Q: Is it also possible that twelve of those messages said "Call me. Urgent."
> A: That's possible.
> Q: Isn't it true that the last message, a message sent early this morning, was actually about her baby, the baby she gave up for adoption? Don't look at your lawyer. Answer the question.
> A: I don't remember.

Because Zeus didn't remember, the judge allowed Nancy to bring the cell phone to the witness stand and read the displayed text message into the record. At that point, the judge sat up.

> **Judge:** Wait a minute. Dr. Zeus, is this
> true? Is her baby in critical condition right
> now?
> **Dr. Zeus:** No.
> **Q:** Oh. Has she passed away?
> **A:** No.
> **Q:** Is she in the hospital?
> **A:** I have no idea where she is.
> **Q:** You made this all up?
> **A:** [No response.]

The judge looked like she was about to be sick. Nancy glanced at Dave, who gave her a hidden thumbs-up behind the counsel table. Nancy took a relieved breath like it was all over. Then she suppressed a smile and jumped to her feet again for one last question.

"Dr. Zeus, did you hit Diane, hit her in the face, while she was in your car this morning?"

It didn't matter what Zeus answered. No one believed anything he said by this time.

But Grunk wasn't done. "I call David Green to the stand."

Grunk typically named all of the Board investigators as potential witnesses, just in case something came up. But he rarely actually called them to the stand.

> **Mr. Grunk:** Isn't it true, Mr. Green, that
> you had inappropriate contact with Diane
> Morrell before the Board even opened an
> investigation about her?

A shot of adrenaline flooded Dave's body, sped up his heart, threw off his train of thought. He looked out over the hearing room. Michele's dramatic eyes caught his. He had to make a decision. Nobody at the Board but Michele knew that he had broken all the rules by interviewing Diane. Diane had already been excused after her testimony and had left the building. He could deny that it happened now, and no one could contradict him. And it had hardly been an interview; Diane had pretty much refused to talk. Nothing important to the case had come out of the interview – but now it just might be the irregularity that would get the case thrown out of court. As he watched, Michele raised her hand, elbow bent, as if she were taking an oath herself. He was supposed to tell the truth. He nodded at Michele. He wouldn't mind losing his job so much as he would mind screwing up the case and letting Zeus off scot free. But losing Michele's respect would be worse.

> **Mr. Green**: Yes, I interviewed her very briefly once at her school.
> **Mr. Grunk**: When there was no case open?
> A: Correct.
> Q: And where did you get her name?
> A: We had received a complaint about her treatment by Dr. Zeus.
> Q: So you got her name from the Board's files?
> A: Yes, I guess you could say that.
> Q: The Board's files are confidential, aren't they?
> A: Yes.
> Q: There are civil and criminal penalties for misuse of the Board's confidential files, are there not?
> A: Yes.
> Q: So you broke both the civil and the criminal law by using the Board's confidential files to set up a rendezvous with Ms. Morrell, didn't you?
> A: It wasn't a rendezvous. It was about her case.
> Q: But there wasn't a case open, was there?

A: Technically, no. But we had a complaint.

Q: So let me repeat my question. You committed a crime by misusing the Board's confidential information, didn't you?

A: I don't think I was misusing the information. So, no, I don't think I committed a crime.

Q: We'll let the judge decide that. Your witness, Ms. Hunt.

Ms. Hunt: No questions.

"Why didn't you ask me to explain?" Dave complained to Nancy as soon as he got back to his chair. "Nothing happened. Diane didn't want to talk about Dr. Zeus at the time, and I just left."

"I can't ask questions I don't know the answer to." Nancy spat out. "You never told me anything about this. For all I knew, you would have answered that you two had sex on the counter in the school counselor's office."

Chapter 44

Diane

"Your friends seem really nice," Mom said. She meant Lucky and Kate and Woody. They had waited in the parking lot all morning, along with Lisa and my parents, for me to come out from testifying. I knew they would be there, but I still lost it when they closed in around me in the parking lot.

Dad apologized and said he should have come in with me.

"That's okay. They said it was better that way. So it wouldn't look like some kind of crusade against Zeus."

"But that's what it is, isn't it? A crusade against Zeus. That's what it should be, anyway."

"Right, Dad. But they don't talk like that in there. I guess you've never been in a courtroom or you'd understand."

My friends said goodbye, and Dad drove Lisa, Mom, and I back home. Mom said it was interesting, talking with my friends. "But I have to admit, it took me a while to get over those tattoos."

"Oh, you mean Woody? He had, like, a previous life. It wasn't ... so nice." And then suddenly it hit me how nice my life was. I had done a lot of dumb things in the past two years, but Mom and Dad acted like they were just ordinary mistakes that all girls make. So I had made a lot of mistakes, but I was still good enough for them. And I remembered I had always been good enough for them. I had never needed to buy people's love with pot or carve swear words into my arm.

"Lisa, you wouldn't believe it. That black eye you gave me – everybody in there thought Zeus did that to me."

"Perfect!" Dad laughed and pounded the steering wheel. "Perfect."

And that was all we ever said about it. Except on the way back I confessed about the Zeus phone I had kept, and Lisa and I told them about the text from Zeus last night and the car chase early that morning. I didn't talk about the hearing. I figured Dad already knew what it was like to be in a courtroom and Mom didn't want to picture me being torn to shreds by lawyers, which never happened anyway because – I could tell – Zeus's lawyer knew I was telling the truth.

... ...

I tried to get back on the soccer team, but they wouldn't let me because the regular season was over and they were already into the playoffs. I watched a couple of the playoff games from the stands and hung around with Kate and Lucky some.

I liked going to Woody's garage, but that would be coming to an end soon when he finally graduated at the end of the semester. Sometimes Lucky and Kate came too, and I took Lisa once. When Lisa was there I wouldn't let anyone smoke pot. I knew that was hypocritical, but I couldn't help it. She got pretty good at basketball and, with the help of her big sister, started to learn how to wear her clothes right. She still came in my room a lot, but after it being fun for a long time I was starting to get tired of it. How do you tell your lonely little sister to go get her own friends?

When it got to November, and the weeks toward the end of the semester were winding down, I started to feel this dull ache inside. It wasn't in any particular place; it was more like a spirit ache. It was worse every time I left Woody's garage. I knew what it was. I went through a couple of weeks telling him I owed him everything and promising him if he ever needed anything I would be good for it. He finally shut me up: "Okay. Okay. Diane, I got it." Like he was angry. That was embarrassing.

"Here's my problem," I said to him one cold November afternoon as we huddled near each other on his bed close to the heater. "I jump into everything too quick. Everybody says that, and it's true. Everybody says talk to your friends and listen to them before you make a big decision."

"Sounds like a good idea."

"You are the friend I trust the most. You're the one who I trust to tell me whether to jump or not."

"Okay."

"But that's a problem now."

"What?"

He wasn't getting it, even though my hand was on top of his. What was I doing anyway? Asking his advice about whether I should fall into his arms? For all I knew, he was meeting some hot woman in her love nest every night after work. Jumping in is my problem. Everyone says that.

I jumped up instead. "I'm leaving now. I don't think I can come back."

Chapter 45

Hartwicke

He arrived with his own locksmith because he was sure Elena had already changed the locks. No one was home, so he moved his clothes into the guest bedroom. He'd gotten one piece of free legal advice from Grunk about his divorce: don't move out of the house. Once you leave, Grunk had explained, the house basically becomes hers until you prove you are entitled to get it back. Zeus didn't tell Grunk he had already moved out, but he knew he could fix that. He just moved back in. Kyra arrived home an hour later and ran up into her own bedroom and locked her door.

Elena was enraged when she got home an hour later and saw he had come back. "Get out! I can't believe what you've turned into, Hardy. You're a pervert, and a sex offender, and a drug pusher."

"Don't be ridiculous, Elena. The girl broke down on the stand. She's deranged. She admitted she and her drug dealer friend were forging prescriptions."

"Sex with a sixteen year old. The purple hair, the condom. Do you think I'm stupid?"

"She's a fully developed female." Zeus restrained himself from explaining to her all of his theories about young females in the prime of their sexual lives. But he couldn't stop himself entirely. "She's as tall as you."

Elena looked at him. "So is Kyra."

Elena had threatened to have her lawyer file papers to get him out of the house, but he doubted she'd go through with it. The only way she could get him out of the house would be to say that he was an accused pedophile who posed a threat to

Kyra. But that would screw up Kyra's mind even more.

Early the next morning he made his way down to the kitchen. He was surprised that Kyra was already there, sitting at the table eating a bowl of cereal. She turned her head away when he came in, giving him time to look her over in secret. She was as tall as Elena and Diane, but it was mostly long legs. Nothing on top, she just looked like a tall twelve year old. She had washed her long hair and combed it straight, but it still looked wet. He hoped she was going to dry it and look pretty before she left for school. Kyra had an oval face with very dark eyes that looked a little lost in a sea of pale skin. She didn't answer his greeting. He wasn't going to beg. He took his time scrambling eggs and brewing coffee. As he turned to sit down across from her, she stood up, hands shaking, left the table and took her cereal bowl to the counter, where she kept eating.

"You know, Kyra," he said, "it's okay for you to look at me."

Kyra put down her spoon but turned only halfway toward him. He said her name again and she finally turned her head just a little. Her mouth was half open and her face pale. A strand of her hair fell across her face and she brushed it back with a sigh of relief like this was one thing she could do that no one could claim was a come-on to her father.

The harm he had done to Kyra was an unfortunate side effect of his need to defeat Elena. But he still hoped that she was salvageable. He decided to focus the blame on Elena. "Your mother thinks you have sexual designs on me. She's just sick, Kyra, sick in the head."

"Why... why does she think that?" Just mentioning *that* brought a deep flush to her face.

"Some women's minds get twisted when they get to middle age. Their hormones get out of whack and it affects their thinking. They see all younger women as sexual rivals. They can't help it."

Kyra turned all the way toward him, her eyes still not quite on his, her face now ghost white. "But don't you see? I mean, now, *everything I say*, *everything I do* is going to be wrong."

He waited as despair remolded her face, froze her body, made her vulnerable to his soft, commanding voice.

"Honey, *I* know you did nothing wrong. *You* know you did nothing wrong. It's your mother who has the problem."

"Dad, I'm so ... stupid. I don't even really know what sex is about. Me and my friends don't even look at it on the internet." She finally raised her eyes to his. He had won. She would talk to him. It would be a long time before she trusted Elena again. Her voice was tentative now, but almost normal. "Dad, I hope I didn't ever, I mean accidentally, you know ...." She turned and ran out of the room.

••• •••

Grunk was not optimistic. "The judge clearly believed that girl Diane. Her story that you gave her those prescriptions made a lot of sense. The handwriting looked just like yours."

"It's all phony."

"Why'd you hit her?"

"For God's sake, I didn't hit her!" Zeus found it really annoying that nobody believed the one true statement he had made on the witness stand.

"She came off like a good girl who just fell in love."

"And what, really, is wrong with that?" Zeus challenged him.

"Doc. Doc. Zeus. You can't talk like that, not in this century, not in this country. I'm not saying there's not any hope. That male investigator clearly went off the reservation when he interviewed her when there was no case open. He violated the law. It's a technicality, but I've won worse cases on technicalities."

"When will the judge decide. It's been a week already."

Grunk looked up. "Oh, I should have told you. The average time for a decision is four months."

"Four months? To decide which one of us was telling the truth?"

Grunk shrugged. "Think of it as a time to make some more money. Pay off those credit card bills. Hire a good divorce lawyer."

··· ···

Zeus had underestimated the strength of the bond between Elena and Kyra. For the whole of his married life he had blocked out all their constant nonsensical female chatter about clothes and decorating and who among her friends was currently mad at whom. And of course Elena was there in the house every evening, or else driving Kyra everywhere while he was working days and nights making the money that enabled them to live such a frivolous lifestyle. But he hadn't expected all of this to have so strong an effect that Kyra would start talking to Elena again even after he had so cleverly poisoned her mind.

"I'm taking her to therapy," Elena announced once when they ran into each other in the house. These encounters only happened about once a week, their schedules were so different.

"There's nothing wrong with her."

"There *wasn't* anything wrong with her, until you started making her think she had come on to you. Now she's not sure about anything. And you did it just to get back at me. I underestimated how low you can go, Hardy."

Zeus didn't respond. It wasn't a question. He didn't feel the need to say anything back.

"I told her it's normal for children to have counseling when their parents are undergoing a divorce. I go sometimes too. But it's taking me forever to convince her she didn't do anything wrong. But I think I'm finally making progress."

"Good for you."

"She has to decide whether it's she or her father who is a

319

pervert. That's almost an impossible choice for a twelve-year-old girl."

Chapter 46

David

Nancy Hunt ignored Dave completely when the investigators gathered together in the hallway after the hearing was over. He heard Nancy say that the hearing went extremely well. She thought the judge believed Diane was telling the truth. The one problem was the surprise glitch at the end, when it came out that "an investigator" had talked to Diane before the investigation was even opened. That possibly screwed everything up, Nancy told them. She didn't make eye contact with Dave when she said this. It didn't get any better in the following week. When she came to the Board offices, Nancy would talk to everyone except Dave.

"This is your punishment," Michele explained. "This is how Nancy is. She hates to be surprised at a hearing. She is still angry you didn't tell her ahead of time."

"I didn't want to tell anybody but you."

"What's really scary is, the judge might make a big deal out of it and throw out the whole case."

••• •••

Sarah was packing up, making more noise than was necessary. He tried to stop her, but she put her hands up to keep him away. Her face was frozen with determination. Her eyes teared up.

"Don't go," he pleaded as she turned back and zipped up her suitcase.

"Oh," she said, not turning around. "I know it's wrong. You're not supposed to give ultimatums to people you love." She turned to face him. "But I can't help it. As long as he's around, I've got to have my father in my life. I'm so sorry, Dave. I love you so much."

She did look really sorry, which is why he couldn't understand what was happening. He loved a lot of things about her, but he loved especially her passion. He knew she loved her father, but he didn't completely understand how she felt.

"All my life I got along fine without a father," he insisted. "If we got married, I'm sure I could be civil to him."

"*Civil?*" She stood right in front of him, breathing hard. He would give anything to crush her into his arms, absorb her sobs. But her sorrow wasn't anything you could cure with a hug – or with a logical syllogism. She was who she was. And he loved her that way.

"I understand, Sarah. You and your father come as a package deal. I'll take it. I'll take the whole package."

"That's not what I mean. I couldn't stand it if you just … just *tolerated* him. I know maybe I'm weird, but I need you to be, to be at least … *open* to, you know, the idea of …."

"You think I'm not open? You think I'm some kind of damaged goods because I didn't have a father?"

"No," she shouted. "I love you. That's why this hurts so much."

Chapter 47

David

Michele was waiting for him as soon as he got off the elevator outside of the Board's offices.

"It's here." She was almost whispering. "The decision in the Zeus case is here."

"You said it would be months before the decision came out." Dave had been counting on this.

"Everybody's surprised. It usually takes three or four months. Frank's waiting in his office for you."

Michele noticed his sudden look of panic. "No, it's got nothing to do with you personally. Frank always makes sure he gets the decisions first. No one's allowed to read them until he reads them himself, out loud. And everybody who's worked on the case has to be there."

"Oh shit. Michele, what if the judge throws out the whole case because of what I did? Frank would fire me in front of everybody."

"You took that risk, Dave, when you told the truth at the hearing." She put her hand out and lifted his chin up a fraction of an inch. "You told the truth. You should be proud of that at least."

"But what if the judge doesn't throw out the case but just mentions that I did it?"

"Frank wouldn't like that. He probably wouldn't invite you to his crab feast next summer. But I don't think he'd fire you if it didn't hurt the case."

Frank sat behind the big desk in his small office. Michele, Dave and Nancy Hunt sat like grade school pupils in chairs backed against the wall and facing him. There was one thing

Dave didn't have to worry about. There was no chance that Nancy Hunt would tattle to Frank about his unauthorized interview. Nancy just wasn't the kind of person who would do that, Michele had told him. The only person who might spill the beans was the judge.

"All right, let's start." Frank pulled out the decision, a stack of papers almost a half-inch thick. Dave knew he should be worried most about whether that sociopath Zeus would go free to prey upon women patients again, but his mind kept coming back to his own little slip-up and how much he would be blamed if the case fell through.

"Finding of fact #1. This case arose out of complaints made to the State Board of Medicine. The Board of Medicine has jurisdiction over complaints about physicians under Section 1-222 of the Health Occupations Code. The Board's procedures are further set out in regulations at 3.45.832.009 of the Regulatory Code. Physicians in the State are required to comply with the provisions of the Health Occupations Code. If the Board receives a legitimate complaint that a physician has violated the Health Occupations Code, and if after a hearing that complaint is sustained by a preponderance of the evidence, the Board may sanction that physician according to that statute and the regulations promulgated thereunder.

"Finding of fact #2. I am an independent administrative law judge appointed pursuant to Section 45-788 of the State Government Article. I am not employed by the Board, and my decision is made independently.

"Finding of fact #3. The original complaint in this case was filed over three years ago by a patient who will be called Patient KB. A complaint may be filed in writing or on an internet form found on the Board's website. Patient KB filed a written complaint, which was denoted as Complaint # 13-76220 by the Board. The investigator who originally received the case was one Allison Ivy. The record does not show whether Investigator Ivy is a male or a female, nor does it show when or why Investigator Ivy was removed from the case, if indeed, Mr. or Ms. Ivy was ever actually assigned the case."

Frank had just made it through the first page of the decision. Holding the decision flat on his desk by the stapled corner, he flipped the next page over with the index finger of his other hand, and sighed. "You know," Frank looked up at his captive audience, "the Gettysburg Address was only 272 words long.

"Finding of fact #4. The respondent, Hartwicke Zeus, M.D., was represented by Eli Grunk, Esq. Mr. Grunk filed a motion for dismissal, arguing that the statutory time limit for bringing charges had elapsed because there was a two-year gap between the filing of the complaint and the filing of the charges. The Board, represented by Nancy Hunt, Esq., argued that the one-year time limit in the statute was directory, not mandatory ...."

Frank started flipping faster and paraphrasing rather than reading every word. "More motions were filed. More responses to motions were filed. The judge made various rulings for various reasons, *yada yada yada*. Okay, let's see. Here we go. Katherine was interviewed. Oh Jeez, now she quotes the transcript of Michele's interview with Katherine, word for word." Frank flipped faster. "Okay, here we go. Finding of fact # 112. Patient KB came to the hearing , but she but refused to repeat her story on the witness stand or to be cross-examined .... Yes, and what? What?" Frank flipped the next page forward, then back. "I guess we have to wait until later to see what the judge makes of that."

Dave was now sure that his little slip-up would be discussed in detail somewhere in the judge's 175-page document. But he did feel a little stab of hope Frank would pass it by in one of his *yada yada yadas*. Frank was flipping the pages pretty fast.

"Here we go. Finding of fact #178. If Patient KB had not testified at all, the undersigned might well have credited the transcript of her testimony because it was supported by the medical records of her drug use and by the inordinate number of appointments wherein this woman saw Dr. Zeus for knee pain. However, the undersigned was very impressed that Patient KB, after coming to the hearing and swearing under oath that the entire transcript was true, then contemptuously refused to allow the defense counsel to cross examine her. Dr. Zeus, on the other hand, took the stand and patiently explained the complications that caused him to prescribe so many narcotics for this case of intractable pain. Admittedly, Dr. Zeus recorded none of these complications in the medical record. If Dr. Zeus had been charged with failing to create an adequate medical record, perhaps an affirmative finding could have been made on that charge. The charges in this case, however, deal only with alleged rape and deliberate prescribing of an addictive substance for an immoral purpose. In the circumstances of this case, I cannot make a finding of guilt based solely on the transcript of Patient KB's interview, and for that reason I will find that the charges with regard to Patient KB are not proven, and those charges will be dismissed."

"Jesus!" Nancy Hunt exploded. "She fell for Zeus, that lying piece of shit. We are so fucking screwed."

"Thank you for your astute comment, counselor." Frank continued flipping pages. "Okay, here's Diane."

Dave held his breath.

"Finding of fact #264. Complaint Number 16-43928 was filed by an anonymous caller who provided a video of Dr. Zeus apparently molesting a young girl on the beach, a girl who was later identified as Patient DM. After engaging at first in some unorthodox methods – footnote 86 – the Board eventually received a written complaint signed by Patient DM's mother. That complaint ...."

Could it be that easy? Frank was not going to take the trouble to read footnote 86? Yes, it was! Yes, he wasn't! Frank read on, in excruciating detail, about the contents of the complaint, the person who first investigated the complaint (Michele) every phone call she made or received about the case, every letter she sent, every interview. Frank was looking really bored as he kept flipping. The judge repeated almost every word of Diane's interview and testimony and of Zeus's testimony in response. Finally, she seemed to realize that her job was to make a decision.

"Finding of fact #376. I found Patient DM's testimony hard to believe. Admittedly, the handwriting on the prescriptions closely resembles that of Dr. Zeus. But if, as she testified, Patient DM was not interested in taking narcotics, there is no rational reason why she would accept so many written prescriptions for narcotics from Dr. Zeus. At the time, she was associating with an admitted drug dealer, and Patient DM and the drug dealer may have forged those prescriptions for some unlawful purpose. Patient DM's testimony was more detailed and specific than that of Dr. Zeus, who on cross examination was forced to change his testimony in many instances. Patient DM's tale of Dr. Zeus's attempted prostitution of her with the man she called Fat Guy in the condo was almost beyond belief."

Frank stopped but did not look up, leaving his employees to look at each other. Michele's sigh filled the room.

"Finding of fact #377. But perhaps *almost* is the important word here. It would take an extraordinarily devious and conscienceless physician to attempt to prostitute a sixteen-year-old girl who was his patient. One factor in this case, however, leads the undersigned to believe that Dr. Zeus may be such a physician. On the morning of the hearing, he admittedly called patient DM and falsely told her that her daughter was in critical condition in the hospital, alone, and that the adoptive parents were nowhere to be found. Based on this false story, he drove Patient DM out of town at a high rate of speed, apparently for the purposes of making her unavailable for the hearing. Whatever his motivation, he showed a willingness on that occasion to exacerbate the suffering of a mother already torn from her child – and thus to violate one of the most basic tenets of human decency. I believe that Dr. Zeus actually has no grasp of the concept of human decency. Therefore, I believe he could, and did, do each and every one of the manipulative and perverted and corrupt things to which Patient DM testified."

"Yes!" Nancy shouted. Michele's eyes were teary.

"Wait a minute," Frank warned them. "We haven't seen the punishment. You never know what these nutcase judges will do." He flipped to the end in the silence that followed his words. He stared at the last page for way too long.

"He has to take a course on proper CPT coding." Frank's voice was weak. The silence in the room grew even deeper. But then he smiled. "Nah. Just kidding. Revoked. Permanently. He'll never practice in this state again."

Chapter 48

David

After he finished his reading of the judge's decision, Frank congratulated Michele and Dave on doing a good job on the investigation. In what was a magnanimous gesture for him, he even congratulated Nancy Hunt. Nancy nodded but still didn't make eye contact with Dave, whom she still blamed for almost ruining the case. But Nancy's anger wouldn't last more than a few more days, Michele told him later when they were discussing the decision in her office

"But what happens when Frank gets around to reading footnote 86? It says right in there that I broke the rules by interviewing Diane after he refused to open the case."

Michele waved her hand dismissively. "Frank's never going to read footnote 86. He's never going to read any more than what he's already read. Nobody will read through that whole thing. It's unreadable."

Dave was learning that the world was a more whimsical and complicated place than he had ever imagined. Michele put her palms down in front of her on her desk as if she was keeping that surprising and tricky world on a level plane, and under their control. "Why do you still look unhappy? We won. The good guys do win sometimes."

"I lost Sarah."

He didn't say anything else, giving her a choice whether to get involved in his personal life.

"I thought you were engaged? How did this happen?"

He told her Sarah had given him an ultimatum. "I asked her for time. I said four months because I thought it would take that much time for the Zeus case to be decided. She blew up and left. If I had only known it would be over in two weeks."

"If you don't mind my asking, what was the ultimatum?"

Michele had two qualities that made him willing to explain. She was as kind as his mother, and she was not his mother. He told her about Sarah's father's Wall Street firm and how some of her father's friends at another Wall Street firm had ruined his family's finances. He told her about the dinner with Sarah's father. He admitted Sarah's father seemed very nice. "But he doesn't even realize the human damage his firm causes. The rich are pounding on us all the time, aren't they? Look at how Zeus got away with it for so long just because he's rich."

Michele narrowed her eyes like one of her children had just said something stupid. "Zeus didn't get away with it because he's rich. He got away with it because he has no conscience. He's a clever, narcissistic sociopath. It's got nothing to do with his money."

"He wouldn't have gotten away with it for so long if it weren't for his money."

"He got away with it for so long because he's a doctor, and everybody expects your doctor to be on your side."

··· ···

When he arrived at her apartment complex Sarah met him on the outside stairway landing and patted him on both shoulders like a grandmother might do. Her high energy level had been transformed to a jittery nervousness. He hated seeing her like this.

"I know I look a mess," she started. "I'm going through withdrawal. From you. Are you here to torture me more?"

"Can I meet your father one more time?"

"Are you going to be *civil* to him?" She spat out the word.

"I guess not. Not necessarily civil. I want to tell him about the damage his friends did to my mother's company, and to my mother, and to me."

"It won't change his mind about his mergers and acquisitions firm. He really believes it all works out in the end for the greater economic good."

"That's okay. I just want to tell him these facts. Stuff that actually happened. If he won't talk about that, then I'll know we can never talk about anything."

"You mean it?"

"At least we'll have an answer. I tell him what really happened, and what I really think. He can live with having a son-in-law who thinks what he does for a living is sometimes really cruel, or he can reject me. If he rejects me, I'll get out of your life for good."

"Dave, if he rejects you because you talk to him up front like that, he's not the man I always thought he was." She came close and offered a hug, but he stood with his arms at his sides.

"Maybe he's not the man you always thought he was."

"Then ..." she said, straightening up until she was almost at eye level with him, "then I'll know who's the better man."

"What good does that do me?"

She searched his eyes like she was surprised he didn't understand. "I'm a simple person, Dave. I'm going with the better man."

Chapter 49

Hartwicke

The decision on the Board's case took him by surprise. The judge took that little slut's word against his. And no matter what little rules he might have broken with Diane, she should have been grateful. He took care of her, body and soul. He helped her get over her stupid little teenage obsessions with the church and with her baby. He showed her the wider world outside – and a wilder world inside. He bought her clothes, and a $6,000 emerald necklace. Fortunately, she left the necklace in the condo when she fled. After a lot of bargaining, and after he threatened to file a lawsuit, the jeweler took it back, charging him only a $500 restocking fee.

Grunk said he could file an appeal, but that would take a year and a half and cost him another $25,000, and Grunk didn't seem optimistic about winning. And Grunk said the $25,000 would seem like chicken feed compared to what his divorce lawyer would charge if he decided to fight Elena to the death. Fortunately, PeakResults Labs was starting to get a steady stream of income from all the testing Freeland Hospital was ordering. Before he was kicked off the Board of Trustees, Zeus forced Billings to sign an exclusive three-year contract between PeakResults and the hospital. But Zeus's influence over Billings was quickly fading. Billings had figured out that Diane was probably not going to call the police on him, and Zeus was now on record stating that the fat man in the condo was somebody else, a deranged patient.

Zeus took a job with an insurance company as a private review agent, reviewing medical claims and deciding if the company would pay for procedures and drugs ordered by doctors. You didn't need a medical license to do that job. Grunk encouraged him also to apply for a medical license in Washington, D. C., the only jurisdiction, he said, where he had a 50-50 chance of getting a license.

Elena seemed surprised that he had enough money to hire his own divorce lawyer and fight back, motion for motion, against every move she made to get him out of the house or move the proceedings along. He got a court order requiring her to reveal the location of the money she had taken out of his accounts, but she was stalling on that. He was stalling on revealing his PeakResults assets to her. Because he could no longer practice medicine, he was disqualified from membership in New Town Partners. He had to hire his regular attorney Ferris to try to get his partnership money back from them. As soon as Ferris approached New Town Partners about this, they stopped sending their lab tests to PeakResults.

Elena started inviting her parents over often, and they would stay late into the night. The idea, he knew, was to make it as uncomfortable as possible for him to stay there. Her father wouldn't even speak to him now. None of this bothered Zeus in the least. And Zeus knew that her father's influence with the Board of Trustees of Garden City Hospital was waning. As soon as her old man was completely out of the picture, he'd start working to get Garden City to send its lab work to PeakResults too. Marcie had a special friend at Garden City, a friend who might want more of her special favors – or who could be blackmailed. Time seemed to be on his side.

The car dealer was having trouble fixing the electrical system in his leased Jaguar. Zeus drove there in his replacement Nissan Versa and demanded that his lease payments be cut in half until he got the original car back. The manager showed him the clause in the contract that said it couldn't be done, but Zeus made such a nuisance of himself they gave him 25% off anyway.

··· ···

Once word of his revocation hit the news, Elena received a call from Kiley Fontaine informing her that Concord Mews no longer felt that the educational experience available there was a correct fit for Kyra.

Elena confronted Zeus in the kitchen. "This is your fault."

"If we double our donation to $30,000 a year, I'm sure they'll let her in."

"We don't have that kind of money any more. Besides, I wouldn't want to send her to a school where money can so easily override their moral judgments."

"So, what's the problem, then?"

Elena smacked him hard.

"The problem is your daughter is dying inside. She's walking around like a zombie. She won't talk in therapy. She won't talk to her best friend, who's going to Concord Mews next fall. Some girls made fun of her when the story about you came out. She's looking up creepy things on the internet."

Zeus didn't back down. "She'll toughen up. It's time she learned about the real world."

"I can't understand why I married you."

"I'll tell you why you married me. You married me because you liked my looks, my money, my prestige. You wanted the big house, the big bank account, the big lifestyle. And you wanted to have it all without getting your hands dirty, so you could feel oh so virtuous at the same time. You're just a standard-issue cunt."

"Hardy, I know I'm not a saint. What I am is a standard-issue human. I'm going to teach Kyra that she is too. Then she'll have to learn to live with the knowledge that her father is not."

Chapter 50

Diane

Lisa would talk at the dinner table now. "There's a bunch of guys who sit together in the cafeteria. Every time I walk by they all start squeaking 'freak, freak, freak.'"

"Don't take that off them!" Dad jolted straight up in his chair.

"I don't. I always stop and look them in the eyes and ask who said that, but they always just look away. Then when I turn around they start again."

Mom sat staring with her mouth hanging open like she regretted ever wanting her daughters to talk about their problems. "Oh, honey, that's awful."

"Maybe you are a freak," I suggested.

Lisa looked at me. She could have said a lot of evil things back. She could have pointed out that I was just one of the whole pile of dumb women mortified by that sicko Dr. Zeus. But she knew I was just kidding her. She still came in my room sometimes, and when she did she no longer acted like I was some kind of sarcastic supergirl slut nobody could relate to.

I told her I was tired of being the third wheel with Kate and Lucky. Woody had moved into an apartment soon after the last time I saw him in the garage. I told her I couldn't get interested in anybody else after Woody kicked me to the curb.

"What did he say?"

I hadn't seen him since the day I walked out of his garage. I had been over to his new apartment once with Kate and Lucky, but Woody wasn't even there when we showed up. I took him a little plant as a house warming present. Lucky said it was way too girlie a present for Woody. They said his roommate, Helen, would probably end up taking care of it. I hadn't known about Helen. They said she worked at one of the construction companies he ran errands for. It was a tiny apartment with a view of just the back end of a warehouse, but it had two bedrooms.

"What did he say?" Lisa repeated.

"What does it matter? He's not into me."

"When we were down at the ocean trying to find you that day, all he talked about was you. For hours. I know he's into you," Lisa insisted. "What *exactly* did he say to you?"

....

Dad was working himself up over the boys insulting Lisa. "Lisa, the boys are interested in you, I know, but they're intimidated. Because you are so startlingly beautiful."

She looked at me and rolled her eyes. I said I agreed with the *startling* part. That shut Dad up. Even Mom snickered.

But who was going to make fun of *me*? "Dad, maybe the boys make fun of her because her sister is such a famous slut."

Nobody laughed. Mom looked down at her plate. I had thought it was great at first that nobody in my family wanted to talk about what had happened to me, but after a while it seemed like they were just too ashamed. I thought well, okay, let's find out right now, are we too ashamed to talk about me or not? But then Lisa changed the subject.

"Did you first meet Dad in school, Mom?" she asked quickly. She was trying to help, I knew. She was embarrassed for me.

"No, dear. I met him ... at work, I guess you might say."

"I was her lawyer," Dad added. "Your Mom was my first client."

"What? Really? What was it about, Mom? Were you sued, or arrested or something?" Lisa and I were both talking at the same time.

Mom had been the newest employee in the personnel department, and after a year she applied for a promotion. The guy who interviewed her blocked the doorway when she tried to leave and said she was a very attractive candidate – then groped her until she screamed for help. My mother's face turned red when Dad got to that part of the story.

"You went to court? Who won?"

"I was afraid to take it to court," Dad explained. "No witnesses. It was a *he said/she said* case."

"You? Afraid? Really, Dad?" I said.

"It was my first case. I was so blown away by your mom it was hard for me to think straight. My boss said settle it."

"And I didn't want to go to court," Mom added. "They never admitted anybody did anything wrong. But they gave me the promotion, and they fired the man who did it, and they gave me a couple thousand dollars, most of which went to my lawyer."

Dad smirked. "I guess it turned out all right for everybody."

Everybody was quiet then. Dad seemed full of himself about the whole deal. So I couldn't let him off so easy. "So you got a wife and two daughters out of the deal, and you got paid for it too."

He smirked again. "Yep."

"So, what do you think I'm going to get out of Carl and Zeus?"

The mood in the room changed as if someone had switched on a red warning light.

"Honey, you don't have to talk about it if you don't want to." Mom's voice was kind.

"I do want to talk about it. Zeus Zeus Zeus Zeus Zeus Carl Carl Carl Carl Carl baby baby baby baby baby! There. I talked about it. I'll never see my baby again. Zeus mortified me in front of the whole world. I wouldn't let Carl use a condom that one time just so I could see what it felt like. Now I owe him something I can never repay. It all hurts, but don't you understand? It hurts worse if I can't say it around you guys."

... ...

I had to go to Woody's apartment late at night because he was working or going to school all the rest of the time. His roommate let me in. The kitchen and dining room and living room was all one room. It had a plate glass window but it didn't open, and there was no balcony. I was afraid to ask Helen if she was his girlfriend. She looked a little older than him.

"He just got home," she said. "He's taking a shower." That was kind of annoying because he'd known what time I was coming. But he came out in just a few minutes, his hair wet and grey eyes shining.

"How've you been?" he said. I said something bland, waiting to see if Helen would leave the room.

I looked around. "I don't know anything about your life now." Just then Helen excused herself and went back to her bedroom. That answered the main question I had about his life. "I miss you," I said. "I feel like I've lost my guardian angel. I miss talking to you. Don't you like me any more?"

He sat with his elbows on his knees and stared down toward his clasped hands. I thought he was looking at his *Fuck You* tattoo. He did that sometimes. I wondered if he thought that tattoo disqualified him from normal life or something. So I took his arm and I kissed it, slowly, seven times, once on each letter.

"I swear," he said, his voice deep, thrilling. "I will find a way."

"A way ...?"

"... to change it to *Diane*."

CPSIA information can be obtained
at www.ICGtesting.com
Printed in the USA
LVOW08*0834040917

547254LV00005BA/91/P

9 780998 380506